Imagine:
It's Millennium Eve.
The clock strikes midnight.
The ATM goes haywire.
And suddenly
you have $1 million dollars
in your bank account.
Now everything
you ever wanted—
and more than you ever
dreamed of—
is about to come true....

A COWBOY WITH LAZY BLUE EYES HAD ONE CALLUSED HAND WRAPPED AROUND HER THIGH.

And one of her stockings was gone.

She shot upright. "What do you think you're doing?"

"Trying to take off your other stocking."

"Do it and you'll regret it."

The cowboy's eyes narrowed. "I think we've got a communication problem here."

His face was burned dark by the sun. Tess remembered him now. He was the sheriff her brother had said would protect her. *Not with his hand on her thigh, he wouldn't.*

"Get your hand off me."

A vein pumped at his clenched jaw. "Don't go jumping fences until you get to them, Ma'am."

"If you really are the sheriff, then you'd better explain why you had your hand up my skirt."

Something glinted in his eye. "Doctor's orders. Too many clothes, he said."

Tess wasn't sure what a sheriff should look like, but it certainly wasn't *this*. She smiled icily as she pointed at his chest. "If you're the sheriff, where's your badge?"

He stalked across the room, yanked open his desk drawer, and shoved a tarnished, weather-beaten tin star into place on his shirt pocket. "Feel safer now?"

"Not much," Tess admitted.

2 0 0 0
KISSES

Christina
Skye

Island
BOOKS

ISLAND BOOKS
Published by
Dell Publishing
a division of
Random House, Inc.
1540 Broadway
New York, New York 10036

Dell® is a registered trademark of Random House, Inc., and the
colophon is a trademark of Random House, Inc.

ISBN: 0-440-23571-5

Printed in the United States of America

Published simultaneously in Canada

December 1999

10 9 8 7 6 5 4 3 2 1

OPM

To my mother,
who always has a host
of wonderful stories

And to my grandmother,
who came to the Oklahoma Territory
in a covered wagon when she was six

With warmest thanks to Connie Rinehold, Connie Flynn, Darleen Speers, Norm and Ruth Johnson, Susan Yarina, Jessica Wulf, Tony Rettig, Liz Wolfe, Heather Hagan, and Terri Hamilton

1

Some things were *almost* as good as sex.

Tess O'Mara took a deep breath. Excitement bubbled through her as she looked around the quiet room, thinking about the night to come. Chandeliers cast a soft glow over the elegant two-tiered observation lounge. Waterford crystal gleamed on white damask tablecloths. A dozen chocolate dessert courses waited to be whisked out at the first stroke of midnight, accompanied by champagne from five different vineyards.

Best of all, three more reporters had already called, pleading for exclusive interviews.

Yes, success felt *incredibly* good.

She checked her watch. In two hours the orchestra would tune up, ready to usher in the new millennium with a shipboard party for two thousand people. Tess had arranged every detail, right down to the 360-degree fireworks that would be set off at the stroke of midnight. Two years of planning.

Two years of dreaming.

The champagne would be vintage and the flowers would be rare Indonesian orchids of her own selection. She prayed that the evening would be a wild success.

Outside the ship's wraparound windows, snowflakes drifted down over the harbor. Tess danced from foot to foot, her pulse racing.

"Get a grip," she muttered to herself. "Remember your training. You've got a degree in marketing and eight years of experience, and that makes you a consummate professional."

She glanced at her reflection in the window and grinned. Good hair, but nothing fancy. Face too pale, mouth too wide. It was a face that radiated energy but would never be called beautiful. Long ago Tess had stopped seeing that as a limitation. She knew how to make people laugh, how to make them listen, and how to put them at ease.

And right now, professional or not, she was riding a wave of pure, heart-slamming adrenaline.

A phone rang outside in the staff area, and the double doors swung open in a rush. A woman with sleek red hair and a chic black pantsuit breezed into view. "Hold on to your seat. That was the Golden Wind Cruise Lines."

"The people who hung up on us twice last year?"

Tess's assistant smiled smugly. "That's right, only now they're seriously groveling. They want to talk to you first thing Monday morning about planning a charity event for them next year. Red carpet all the way."

Tess felt her grin growing wider. Even the competition was calling. She let out a jerky breath. "Tell them I'll get back to them, Annie."

"Will do." Her assistant chuckled. "By the way, a reporter has phoned five times, pleading for tickets to the party tonight. I told him the cruise had been sold out for months, and he offered me four figures if I'd slip him a ticket anyway.''

''Four figures?'' Tess braced one hand on the wall.

''That's what he said.'' Annie named a preeminent daily paper sold across the nation. ''I *still* turned him down.''

Tess felt her chest squeeze. She looked down and saw that her hands were shaking. *Calm,* she told herself. *Professional.* ''Did you tell him that only those signed on for the whole six-month cruise are eligible to attend tonight?''

''Oh, he knew. He just didn't like it. After he finally finished fuming, he said to congratulate you on an inspired marketing campaign. He wants to interview you next week, then maybe fly you down to Ft. Lauderdale and take some shots aboard the ship. He was considering an ongoing story, with installments at every port of call. Especially the Hemingway night in Key West.''

''I'll have to call him back.''

''Good idea. Make him suffer.'' Annie's eyes narrowed. ''Are you all right, Tess? You look shaky.''

Tess *was* shaky, but she was also walking on air. News coverage of the cruise was snowballing, just the way she'd hoped it would. ''Shock, that's all.''

''Get used to it. Something tells me this is just the beginning,'' Annie called as she retreated to a corner to answer her cell phone.

Tess stood absolutely still, watching twilight fall over the churning waves in the harbor. She heard Annie laugh in the corner, her voice slipping low in an intimate conversation on her cell phone.

Her boyfriend, no doubt.

Tess thought about her own nonexistent love life. Maybe she would meet someone special tonight. Her boss, Richard Mainwaring, the mercurial guru of Boston public relations, had hinted he had a friend he wanted her to meet. If Tess hadn't had a thousand other details on her mind, she might have been more intrigued at the thought.

But how could she think about anything but work? For months, her whole focus had been her carefully planned millennium cruise, docking in a dozen ports between Boston and Bora-Bora. In every port, festivities were tied in with local charities.

Tess's favorite was the Hemingway look-alike party in Key West, complete with two actors in a rhinoceros costume, ready to be felled by would-be Papas. Proceeds would go to a wildlife preserve in Kenya. For those of a literary bent, there would be shipboard writing classes and a series of lectures on Hemingway's novels, led by a Harvard professor who had known the great man personally.

To Tess, this was the real theme of the millennium: celebrating life by staying young at heart and young of mind in an age of unpredictable change.

And tonight Tess was going to celebrate, too. She told herself she was entitled to some fun after the two-year war she had waged on this campaign.

Annie waved to Tess. "The chef needs to know when you want him to take the cake out of the refrigerator."

As Tess dug through a pile of silk roses to get to her meticulously prepared timeline of the evening's events, she couldn't help but visualize the magnificent millennium cake. Baked in the shape of an oversize silver ice bucket, its frosting rose in streamers of red and silver, forming a giant champagne bottle complete with cascading waves of confetti.

It had taken the decorator two weeks to complete and had cost a fortune, but the finished effect was worth it.

"Let's see," Tess said, flipping a page of her schedule, "the cake exits the refrigerator at 11:34 PM and enters the observation lounge at 12:01 AM."

"Great! I'll go tell the chef. Oh! The champagne's just arrived," her assistant called as she headed for the kitchen. "Thank heavens, nothing looks broken."

Tess muttered a few choice words, brushing her hair from her face. "At the price we paid, those bottles should come packed in platinum." She pulled a master list from her briefcase and started checking the cases of champagne against the list, to see if anything was missing. Just as she was finishing her inventory her assistant returned. Tess let her shoulders sag dramatically. "I still wish you were coming tonight, Annie, even though the cruise staff has been wonderful."

"It was a hard choice." Her assistant smiled slowly. "I finally had to draw the line between business and pleasure. After all, the millennium will only come once in my lifetime." She pressed her hand to her heart in a solemn gesture. "And if Stan asks me tonight, the answer is yes."

Tess straightened a row of foil-covered chocolate boxes on the table. "If he asks you what?"

"Anything." Annie grinned. "Whenever and wherever. With or without props, I'm his."

Tess felt a pang of envy for the long kisses and husky breathing, the feverish looks and searching fingers. How long since she'd felt that swift, hot descent into sensual oblivion?

She swallowed hard, unable to remember.

"Hey, you look pale." Annie shoved a cup into her

hand. "Drink this double espresso. You look like you need it more than I do."

Tess gulped the strong coffee gratefully. Had it actually been two years? Had her personal life been stalled that long?

She took another drink of coffee, refusing to think about it.

The caffeine was giving her a nice edge of energy when the statuesque cruise director emerged from the kitchens, clipboard in hand.

"Everything looks fabulous, including those chocolate raspberry soufflés." She studied Tess. "How do you feel?"

Giddy. Sick. Wonderful.

"Excited," Tess said levelly. "Are you coming tonight?"

The blond woman shook her head. Her chocolate-brown skirt and beige silk blouse fit her like wind around a flagpole, and Tess had to admire her style—all six feet of it. "I'm afraid not. My husband and I have a date for a candlelit dinner. *Very* private," she said, smiling mischievously. "It's our first anniversary, and we want to be alone at midnight." She grinned. "If you know what I mean."

Tess felt another tiny pang, which she resolutely ignored. "Sounds like fun."

The blonde smiled. "Well, congratulations are definitely in order for you. From what I hear, people are already lined up outside, trying to crash the party."

Tess was glad she'd hired a team of discreet security guards. She made a mental note to call ahead and check security as she held out a box of the premium chocolates. "Happy anniversary."

The cruise director gave a silent whistle as she studied the name on the box. "This is serious decadence you're handing me." Her head tilted. "Any chance you might save a bottle of Krug champagne in exchange for one cabin upgrade?"

Cabin upgrades could be *very* useful in soothing a passenger's ruffled feathers if something went wrong. "Throw in a private tour of the boat with the captain, and I'll give it a shot."

"Done. By the way, did you know that according to the Mayan calendar this isn't a new millennium at all. Actually the new year will be 5119?"

"Oh, go ahead and confuse me. Let's see, that leaves eight hundred and eighty-one years until I have to do this again." Tess glanced at her watch and gave a low moan. "I've got to dress and do something about my hair."

Outside the snow was picking up, great fluffy flakes of white that drifted down in exquisite silence.

"Our fearless leader just phoned," Annie called out. "He says to remind you to wear something sexy. He's got someone he wants you to meet."

Richard Mainwaring, Tess's boss and mentor, was a Harvard graduate who was blue blood by birth and New Age by choice. The fact that he was rolling in trust funds and blue chip stocks gave him the dangerous ability to indulge in every new fad that took his fancy. Last year it was an ashram in India. This year it was buying a solar energy–equipped yacht to cruise French Polynesia.

"What makes him think I need any help in the dating department?" Tess raised a hand as Annie started to speak. "Don't answer that."

"Richard has a lot of interesting friends. Maybe he's set you up with an inscrutable stranger in a turban."

"Sounds like the taxi driver I had last night." Tess

glanced at her watch and groaned. "Gotta go. If Mel Gibson calls, tell him his ticket's at the door."

"Break a leg," Annie said with a jaunty smile.

Tess grabbed her small suitcase and garment bag and headed for the stateroom she'd been assigned to use as an on-site office and, tonight, a place to change clothes. "By the way, if anyone calls to tell me I won the lottery you have my permission to transfer the call to my stateroom *immediately*."

"What, give up the good life?"

"You mean the long hours, the demanding clients, the millions of details to keep track of, and the excruciating phone calls? If I had a million dollars, I'd be sitting perfectly coiffed behind a polished Louis XV desk while I calmly issued orders to about a hundred workers."

Annie just smiled.

"What are you smiling at?"

"You. Millions or not, you'd still be out in the trenches. You love the thrill of a good product placement. But Richard's right," Annie added, shaking her finger at Tess, "you need to find a personal life. Remember the clock is ticking—and not just for the new millennium."

■

At twenty minutes to eight, Tess stood beneath the great chandelier in the observation lounge. She smoothed her hair and checked her watch anxiously.

Twenty-five bottles of vintage 1995 Perrier-Jouet champagne stood cork-free, breathing beside a similar number of Belle Epoque Rosé. She had verified that calla lilies decorated every guest's stateroom, along with a personalized box of designer chocolates hand-dipped and wrapped for the cruise. An elegant assortment of designer spa items had also been delivered to soothe the inevitable morning-after hangovers.

The cruise staff had undertaken all the serving arrangements, and now there was nothing left for her to do but sit back and relax.

Red silk clung to her body from bodice to ankle, brightened by simple rhinestone straps. The gown was Tess's only recent indulgence, and it made her feel like a million dollars. Garnets glittered at her neck and wrist, and not a hair was out of place. Her nerves were frazzled, but that was only to be expected.

She fixed a radiant smile on her face as the first guests arrived to the accompaniment of a string quartet. Soon she was elbow deep in Versace gowns and Armani tuxedos, sharing smiles, compliments, and congratulations. A multimillionaire software designer asked her to share his cabin on the cruise, then offered to fly her to Paris in his private jet, with the clear assumption that she would be sharing the sheets with him. Her flat refusal didn't deter his pursuit.

Considering the giddy excitement of the occasion, Tess took no offense. Tonight was all magic and merriment.

Champagne corks popped and diamonds glittered. By the time Tess had fielded a third not-quite-sober marriage proposal, she was starting to enjoy herself. The trick, she decided, was to keep the whole thing in perspective.

She was surveying the exuberant scene with quiet pride when an attractive man with a hint of gray at his temples beckoned to a waiter to refill her glass. ''May I? I'd consider it repayment.''

He had nice eyes, Tess thought. In spite of herself, she felt a stirring of interest. "Repayment for what?"

"Because looking at you in that amazing red dress makes me feel very young, my dear."

French, she thought. Very romantic. Also very experienced. "Now, that has to be the smoothest line I've ever heard."

"It's not a line at all. I speak with all sincerity. Right now you're exuding energy from every pore."

"I thought that was my perfume."

He chuckled softly. "You're very edgy. Things are happening fast."

"What things?" Why was he staring at her as if he could part invisible layers and see what was beneath?

His eyes narrowed as he drew her palm into his. "Fascinating," he murmured. "I see extremely bright colors swirling around you."

"I take it back—this is the smoothest and most inventive line I've ever heard."

He didn't seem to hear. "You have something exciting in your future."

"Tell me it's a million dollars and I'll go to sleep happy."

He looked toward her but not quite at her, his eyes slightly unfocused. "There's a great deal of green around your shoulders. Yes, I'm sensing abundance, great abundance. Of course, it might have nothing to do with money."

He was about to say more when a woman in a jeweled Vera Wang slip dress threw her arms around him. "Damien! How am I ever going to thank you?"

His eyes held a steady satisfaction. "Was I right?"

"Everything worked out just the way you said it would." She fluttered her perfectly mascaraed lashes.

"And I do mean *everything*. He was exactly as you described him." She flashed a platinum-set diamond that had to be at least ten carats. "The wedding will be in Martinique in May. You simply *must* come. Call me next week and I'll tell you everything."

Tess watched her walk away, accompanied by a man whose watch could have paid Tess's rent for about five years. She wasn't sure whether to be amused or bewildered. "You predicted that?"

The Frenchman gave a self-effacing shrug. "Some men build software. I see auras. I'm glad you turned down the private jet to Paris. He was definitely not your type."

Tess couldn't help smiling. "If he keeps offering me trips like that, he could become my type."

"I doubt it. It will take more than money to reach your heart."

"You don't look like a psychic."

"Actually, I'm clairvoyant and somewhat telepathic. I'm also a banker, which makes my skills very useful." He studied her carefully. "I'm Damien Passard. Richard is an old friend of mine."

Now Tess understood. This was the man that her boss had picked out for her. "I see. So *you're* the sacrificial lamb."

"It wasn't a sacrifice. He told me he knew a fascinating woman I should meet, and he was right."

Tess felt herself blushing.

"Your aura is particularly strong tonight. You've worked hard at your career in the last year. Unfortunately, that's left no time for your own interests."

Anyone could guess that, Tess thought. The description applied to most of the women under the age of thirty in this room. It didn't mean a thing.

"I see you have a degree in journalism. It might prove useful in ways you have yet to imagine."

Another lucky guess, Tess thought darkly.

"There are other currents swirling around you. One of them will be a wonderful adventure in a place that may seem somehow familiar."

Tess pulled her hand away. She was starting to be spooked by these calm pronouncements about her future. "Well, that was fascinating. Not that I believe any of it."

A frown edged across his forehead. "I see someone moving into your life very soon. He will touch you deeply."

"Is he someone here on the boat?" Not that she really *believed* in all this nonsense.

The Frenchman released her hand. "I'm afraid I can't say."

"Why not?"

"The energy is still unformed." He turned as Richard Mainwaring clapped a hand on his shoulder.

"I see you two have met. Damien is an old friend, Tess. He helped me handle my first agency contract."

Tess gave her boss a look that screamed *traitor*. "He's very nice for a sacrificial lamb."

Her boss gave her the boyish smile that concealed a razor-sharp business mind. "She's wonderful, isn't she, Damien? This whole millennium cruise was her idea. The cruise bigwigs are thrilled because their high-end bookings have doubled." He lowered his voice. "They want us as their permanent PR agency. At the figure they've promised, I'd be unforgivably stupid to say no." He smiled, raising his glass. "I almost regret that I can't take the cruise myself. I think I'd make a rather good Hemingway."

Damien chuckled. "You've got the moveable feast part right, anyway."

"We've had media people burning down the phone," Richard said smugly. "You've got an enormous bonus coming, Tess."

"That's wonderful." Tess tried to rein in her curiosity and failed. "Exactly how happy should I be?"

"*Very* happy. Head-for-a-week-in-Kauai happy."

Her curiosity zoomed into overdrive. "That could be expensive."

"You can afford it. Your cruise bonus will be in your account tomorrow, along with a matching figure as a gift from me. No, don't ask for details. Just go out and enjoy it." He smiled benevolently. "As your concerned, solicitous boss I'm requesting that you take a week off. That live Internet auction you held for charity last month was brilliant. It brought us at least a dozen new clients."

"So that was your idea, Tess?" Damien raised his champagne glass in a salute. "Now I know who to blame. I dropped an unforgivable amount on a Château Margaux 1900."

"You got off too easy," Richard said dryly. "Remember that island in French Polynesia?"

Tess definitely remembered. She'd drooled over the auction description for a week. "The one with the pristine white beaches and the drop-dead sunsets?"

"That's the one." Richard gave a smile, caught between diffidence and triumph. "Well, I bought it."

"You bought it?" Tess remembered the string of zeroes in the price. "You never mentioned that to me."

"I think I needed time for it to sink in. I'm heading off tomorrow morning, actually. Things will be dead here with the cruise finally on its way." Richard crooked his finger at a waiter hovering silently nearby. "I thought we'd share a special treat for the occasion."

Damien's brow rose. "Not the Château d'Yquem 1825?"

Tess watched the men as if they were speaking Swahili. Behind them, the waiter poured three glasses and offered each with a flourish, along with a napkin of antique Belgian linen.

"To us," Richard said solemnly. "To working hard and playing hard. May this gift from an old century ring in a new era of joy and abundance."

Tess took a careful sip and was instantly seduced by a concentrated sweetness that blended intense fruit and mellow acidity. "It's wonderful."

"Beyond wonderful." Richard closed his eyes, a look of reverence on his face. He took another sip and sighed audibly. "Paradise found." Then he looked at Tess. "As for you, I want you out of the office and out of Boston. Things will be very slow here after the holidays, and Annie and the staff can take care of anything that comes up until you return."

Tess crooked one brow. "Until I return from where?"

Richard raised his glass to a passing cruise bigwig. "Wherever you want. If not Kauai, how about Morocco?"

Damien shook his head. "Not suitable for her."

"Oh? Then what is suitable for me?" Tess asked, amused by the man's presumption.

"Someplace quiet with lots of color." Damien nodded slowly. "Someplace with history."

Tess refused to take their fussing seriously. She wasn't going to be maneuvered into a vacation that someone else chose for her.

"Why don't you try New Orleans?" Richard tapped his jaw. "You'd love the food and the energy, and the weather is fabulous this time of year. What do you think, Damien?"

"I think mystery and ancient secrets would appeal to her more, but that is just a feeling. New Orleans is certainly exotic. You could fly down tomorrow, my dear. Indulge in beignets, shrimp étouffée, and some marvelous jazz."

"You might as well have a fling while you're there," Richard added helpfully.

"A fling?"

Richard's gray eyes were gentle. "That thing two people do. It involves heavy breathing and general insanity for about three days before reason returns. You'll be a new woman when you come back."

"Maybe I don't want to be a new woman." For some reason the suggestion irritated her, and she swirled the wine in her glass, frowning. "But I'll consider it," she lied. She wasn't going to have her love life arranged for her, and a fling was definitely *not* on her agenda.

Not that she planned to dwindle away into middle age, successful, driven, and unhappy. Something would come up. The Frenchman might even be right in his predictions.

A yacht cut through the channel, adrift in lights that sparkled and broke in the churning waves.

"Twenty minutes until midnight." A waiter made the grand announcement as the first chocolate dessert course was brought in with full fanfare.

Damien raised his glass, then went very still. "Heat. I definitely see heat. Walls of stone the color of the sunset, and a city that rises to meet the sky."

"Are you picking up something, Damien?" Richard

asked gravely. "I can always use a good stock tip. Something to do with urban utilities would be nice."

The man's voice was low. "Heat and color. I heard a sound clearly, almost like drums."

"You mean oil drums?" Richard looked confused.

Tess frowned. "It has to do with me, not the stock market."

"Then you'd better believe him. Damien's never wrong." Richard reached out to shake hands with a prominent senator with white hair and a ruddy face. Soon the two were deep in conversation.

Damien stared at Tess. "His eyes are cool, the blue of the rain that comes at dawn."

"*Whose* eyes?"

"The one I see for you. The one you will meet in a place you have walked before. The connection is old for you, and you will feel its shadows where the stones rise warm in the sun."

"You're saying I'm going to meet a man, but he's someone I already know?"

The Frenchman took a slow breath. "You have walked through shadows together before. Your blood will know him, even if your eyes do not."

This was getting way too weird, Tess thought. "That's all very interesting, but I don't see any travel or adventure in my future. I planned to be chained to my phone devising a new chocolate campaign for the next six months."

He touched her hand. "The images were very clear, my dear. But I'm not used to this kind of intensity." His smile was wistful. "I must be older than I thought."

Tess didn't really *believe* any of his predictions, of course. She wasn't born yesterday.

But she couldn't ignore the exciting feeling of anticipation that came over her as she watched travelers surge toward the windows, where dozens of boats rocked at anchor, ready to release a barrage of fireworks. Could there possibly be someone waiting for her?

She had a sudden vision of bright colors beneath a turquoise sky. Maybe she'd head for Barbados and float in frothy water beside a pink sand beach. Or maybe she'd try Kauai.

The overhead lights flickered and went out, to a chorus of sharp gasps.

"Don't be alarmed, please." The captain moved past them in the darkened lounge lit only by candles. "Occasionally we experience a brief lapse in harbor power as we prepare to put out to sea. It's perfectly normal." As he spoke, the lights returned.

"So much for Nostradamus." A woman in black silk and too many diamonds raised her empty champagne glass. "And so much for all that Y2K gloom and doom."

A slender man with a receding hairline and gold-wire-rimmed glasses contemplated his champagne glass with morose satisfaction. "A lot of people won't have lights and phone service tomorrow. Food might even be scarce if transport systems break down."

The woman in black frowned. "How do you know that?"

"Because I've been working for two years to fix the bugs, but there are too many programs and too many codes, some of them written by companies that went belly-up years ago."

"So what do you predict?"

The man frowned at his empty glass. "Two or three local utility grids will go. So will most of the ATM machines in America."

The woman glared over her glass as her husband

walked up beside her. Tess recognized him as a former secretary of state. "Are you telling me that people have spent millions of dollars bringing their businesses into Y2K compliance for *nothing?*"

"Ma'am, the only things you can count on are death and taxes," the computer expert said morosely. "Even *those* might be postponed unless God has full-scale Y2K compliance." He snagged another glass of champagne from a passing waiter.

"I can't agree." A slender man in a perfectly cut Armani tuxedo contemplated his wedge of Brie on toast points. "As a banker, I'm fully prepared to state that all our corporate systems are in place. We've been checking scenarios for twelve months now with no problems."

"Is that a fact?" The programmer raised his glass, sloshing champagne over his wrist. "The Fed clears more than two trillion dollars in payments and securities every day, and you're making guarantees?"

A faint frown marred the banker's tanned face. "Every local bank has its own cushion of funds to cover problems."

His opponent smiled thinly. "What happens when that's used up?"

"*If* conditions warrant, we may borrow from other banks."

The programmer swayed slightly. "And if hundreds of banks are suffering the same problem, then good-bye liquidity."

The banker smoothed his tie. "It will never happen."

Outside in the harbor a boat horn thundered.

The crowd silenced for the space of a breath, maybe two, as if they were waiting for something to happen. Disaster? Writing in the sky?

But the spell was broken as colored lights cut back and forth over the harbor.

People cheered.

Confetti flew.

Party horns blasted.

Complete strangers threw their arms around each other, caught in wordless emotion. Thousands of white rose petals dropped from behind hidden alcoves in the ceiling, creating a sense of romance and enchantment as the crowd cheered as one.

Someone planted a drunken kiss on Tess's cheek. She dodged another kiss by leaning to the side, though she was smiling, caught in the sudden atmosphere of jubilation, as if the new millennium had somehow given them all a second chance.

Even Tess began to laugh as the banker shook her hand exuberantly and the computer expert leaned forward awkwardly for a kiss and missed. She lifted her head and felt her heart pound as great flowers of light spiraled into the sky and burst into glorious streams of color.

The end of a century, a millennium.

The grand beginning of a grand new era.

In the middle of the noise, one of her wealthy pursuers ambled back, giving her a drunken leer. "How about we forget Paris and go up to my cabin instead?" He swayed closer, winking. "My wife and I have an understanding about these things."

Tess controlled an urge to dump the last of her champagne over his balding head. "Well, I don't, and I happen to have other plans."

Damien Passard moved in front of her, looking angry and protective. "I think you'd better go before I do something physical."

The businessman frowned. "I didn't know you were coming tonight, Passard. No need to be nasty. I didn't know she was taken." The man staggered off toward the crowd gathered along the windows.

Tess felt oddly childlike, caught in wonder at the sight of fireworks trailing through the night sky. She felt her driving professional edge begin to soften at the sight of such beauty.

She was ready for the new millennium, ready for something wild and crazy to sweep into her life. Clutching her champagne, she was rocked by a yearning that left her dizzy.

"Do you think he's really out there, Damien?" she whispered. "That we'll run into each other on a crowded street or waiting in line for coffee? Do you think he'll know me and somehow I'll recognize him?"

The Frenchman gave a very Gallic smile. "Miracles can begin in the most insignificant way. For you, it will begin with color. Great soaring colors that touch your heart." The Frenchman stared out at the hundreds of boats rocking in the harbor. "For you, there is no question. He waits. He walks where the ladder rises to a city in the sky. He is remembering, too, in his way."

Ladders and cities in the sky? "Can't you just give me a name and a concrete time?"

The Frenchman chuckled. "It doesn't work that way." He brushed a strand of hair from her cheek. "A good adventure comes when you least expect it. At any time you may look up to find your man of mystery." His eyes held a secret knowledge as he raised his glass to hers. "Now make your millennium wishes, my dear. Close your eyes and dig very deep."

Wishes.

Where could she even begin?

Tess took a deep breath, searching through all the hopes she'd never dared to admit and all the dreams she'd never had time to pursue because of her hectic career. "I wish for something I've never done before."

The Frenchman rolled his eyes. "You wound me. What kind of resolution is this? To succeed, you must make your dreams very grand," he urged. "Try again."

She gave a wistful smile. "Then I wish to be spontaneous. Completely, absolutely spontaneous."

"You can do better than this. More," he commanded.

"If you knew me, you'd understand what a big change that will be," Tess said. She caught a handful of confetti and threw it up in the air, laughing. "Okay, I wish for adventure. I wish for a baby-blue Mercedes. I wish for—for red cowboy boots and a man who makes me see my life in a whole new light."

"Good, good. Put your whole heart into the wish."

"I want to ride a horse beneath the stars and tell stories all night before a roaring fire. I want to fall in love, *really* fall in love—so deeply that there are no questions and no limits."

"Excellent."

Tess's heart pounded as she was swept up in a dozen rich fantasies. Already waiters were bringing in trays of chocolate desserts and the chef himself ushered in the gleaming millennium cake on a wheeled cart. "But how will I know him? How will he—"

Sirens blared. More fireworks thundered over the last strains of "Auld Lang Sync."

Would her millennium wishes come true?

Was she ready for such a change if it came?

Tess pressed a kiss on Damien's cheek, dreaming about hot colors and wild adventures as lights exploded over the harbor. Amid screams and laughter and tears, clock hands slid forward, marking the progression into a grand new era.

And for a few minutes, caught in the cheers and the noisy laughter, Tess found herself believing that her wishes would all come true.

2

Tess awoke with a start.

Drums boomed. Echoes danced inside her head.

She opened one eye and winced. Bad idea. Movement plus hangover equals pain. *Major pain.*

It had been almost four o'clock when a taxi deposited Tess back at her apartment. The onboard cruise festivities had continued for hours, with flowing champagne and noisy dancing.

Before her departure, Tess had received two proposals of marriage, an offer to spend a week on a shipping magnate's private island in the Caribbean, and another invitation to experience carnal delight in the stateroom of a drunken millionaire.

But she hadn't met Mr. Right.

She might have dreamed about him though. She remembered a wild mixture of colors and heat, with cities of stone rising hot beneath turquoise skies.

Groaning, she pulled a pillow over her head, but the drumming grew louder. Tess tugged away the pillow and stared at the room, trying to place the sound. Several lifetimes later she realized the thunder was coming from her foyer, most likely from her front door. And it was definitely getting louder.

Outside, snowflakes were drifting down in the darkness. The clock beside her bed said 10:20 AM.

"Okay, okay," Tess croaked to the person pounding at her door. She sat up slowly and pulled on a long cotton robe, then padded to the door and stared through the peephole. "Agatha?" She unlocked the door, frowning. Agatha Spinelli, her fragile eighty-two-year-old neighbor, was leaning on a walker in the hall. "Is something wrong? You're not sick, are you?"

"I'm fine, my dear, just fine. I was worried about you when the power went out briefly. You must have been asleep."

Deeply asleep.

Blissfully asleep.

Dreaming of turquoise skies and hot wind, Tess thought. Thinking about a closet full of cashmere sweaters and a sleek blue Mercedes that could cruise to sixty in seven seconds flat. "No problem. Why don't you come in for a cup of tea?" Tess prayed she had some left.

"No, I really shouldn't stay. I'm expecting a call from my son. The cable's broken again, I'm afraid."

Not broken, Tess knew. Agatha had had to pull the plug on her favorite channels when the rates had increased. Tess had already sent a check to the cable company, arranging to have the service restored anonymously. She knew how much Agatha loved her nature shows.

She watched the white-haired woman wince as she gripped her walker. "Are you sure you won't come in?"

"No, I've got water boiling on the stove. I just wanted to check on you."

"You ankle's bothering you again." Tess saw the

lines of strain at her eyes. "When are you going to have that tendon operation?"

"My son's working on it. He's been saving for quite a while now."

"You'll outlive us all, Mrs. Spinelli." But Tess made a mental note to phone her son in Arizona and see about arranging for her to visit. The warm, dry weather would be good for Agatha's arthritis. "So what has been happening in the outside world? Did civilization topple and the world economy crumble while I was sleeping?"

"Aside from losing the electricity for a short time, things don't seem too bad. The phones seem to be working, but I've heard there were some minor problems out in California. Several stores have run out of milk. Stockpiling." The elderly lady shook her head in distaste.

"Any news about the banks?"

"I heard there were problems with some of the ATM machines."

Tess decided she'd better drop by her neighborhood ATM and withdraw some extra cash, just in case some kind of Y2K disaster did occur.

But first she had to present a gift to her elderly neighbor, who had a mean sweet tooth. "Breakfast is served." She held up a foil-covered box with a wicked grin. "We have dark chocolate raspberry cream, espresso chocolate-covered strawberries, and white chocolate truffles. I hope you're in the mood for decadence."

"Dear me." The woman stared in delight. "But those are very expensive, aren't they?"

"Cost is no object," Tess announced, opening the box with a flourish. "After all, it's a new era and we'd be churlish not to celebrate." Especially since Richard had hinted at what a nice bonus Tess would be receiving.

Tess froze. Her bonus! Recalling that Richard had

told her it would be in her account today, she was suddenly seized by curiosity about how much he'd given her. What was a lot of money to her was peanuts to a millionaire like Richard. She couldn't even begin to guess what he'd meant by "a week-in-Kauai happy" though she knew how much Richard would drop during a week in paradise.

"Is something wrong, my dear? You look pale."

"No, I'm fine." Tess restrained a frantic urge to run to the bank to check her account balance that instant. She held out the box to Agatha. "You first."

"You're certain?"

"Today chocolate. Tomorrow the moon."

In a blue Mercedes and red boots.

The elderly woman patted Tess's hand. "In that case, a white truffle would be lovely, my dear. On account of the new millennium."

After insisting that Agatha take the rest of the chocolate, Tess escorted her neighbor to her door and saw her settled comfortably. By then her stomach was growling, so she padded off to do a quick inventory of her refrigerator.

She found two cans of brandied cantaloupe balls.

A wedge of Gouda.

Peppered wasabi in a tube and cocktail marshmallows.

Tess stared at the bizarre ingredients and shook her head, trying to remember the last time she'd cooked a complete meal.

Twenty minutes later, tightly bundled in a long wool coat and a bright scarf, she made her way through the snow. After she stopped at the ATM, grocery shopping was at the top of her list. After that she'd rent some movies and read a good book.

There was a giddy feeling in the air, and every store seemed to be open with huge signs announcing special millennium sales in progress. Couples were walking hand in hand, and even strangers seemed to have a smile today. Perhaps the millennium had begun to work its magic after all.

People were already lined up inside the bank's ATM vestibule, and Tess got in line for one of the machines. She saw a woman in a fur coat sigh in relief when the machine disgorged her requested cash. A balding man in a Led Zeppelin T-shirt and a black leather jacket was next. He leaned over the machine, punched in a set of numbers, then studied his receipt in fury.

Tess immediately panicked, hit by a nightmare vision of cascading computer failures and global bank insolvency. "Is there a problem with the ATM?"

"It's working fine." The man crumpled his receipt. "It's just my account that's whipped."

Tess watched him take a step back. "What are you doing?"

"A complex programming maneuver that I learned my last year at Cal Tech." He cracked his knuckles. "Don't try this one at home, boys and girls." With a nasty grin he shoved up his sleeves and took a furious kick at the base of the machine. "That certainly made me feel a hell of a lot better," he growled. "Machines are like horses. Don't ever let them think they're in control or you'll live to regret it."

After he shuffled out, Tess inserted her card and keyed in her access code, praying the machine hadn't been damaged. At the next prompt, she chose the option of one hundred dollars cash back.

More gears whirred.

A metal door opened, depositing five crisp twenty-dollar bills in the tray, along with her transaction receipt.

"So much for Armageddon," Tess muttered.

Two young women stood behind her in line, waiting in obvious impatience. Clutching her receipt, Tess turned up her collar and headed outside. As the wind whipped up the street, she stopped to look at her account balance.

Her throat went dry at the string of numbers.

The very *long* string of numbers.

She stood frozen in shock. According to the receipt in her hands, her balance totaled $1,005,560.37.

Tess stared into the blowing snow, speechless with shock. A million dollars had been deposited in her account.

One million.

Which is how much Richard had dropped on his last vacation.

Snowflakes drifted down as she clutched her receipt. Richard had said she'd brought in a huge amount of business and her cruise project had been wildly successful.

A generous bonus, he'd said.

A *huge* bonus.

Sweet heaven, she'd never have to work again—except that she loved her job and she didn't want to do anything else.

But she could relax.

Take a trip.

Buy some new clothes—no, buy a whole new *wardrobe*.

She took fast, gulping breaths as giddy excitement bubbled through her.

One dream had come true. She was a success! All of her hard work had paid off.

Adrenaline pumped heady excitement through her

body. She felt as if she were soaring. Plunging her hands into her pocket, she stared at the giant sales signs around her, struggling to take in the sheer immensity of this moment.

Spontaneous, she told herself.

Remember the resolution.

It appeared she wasn't the only person scanning the shop windows. Men and women alike were staggering out of stores, laden with bulging shopping bags. The prices must be good.

Tess stopped in the snow and danced from foot to foot.

A *million* dollars.

She, Tess O'Mara, had nine figures separated by a decimal point and a whole day with nothing to do.

She was going to be spontaneous, all right. She gave a husky laugh and tossed her scarf over her shoulder, determined for the first time in her life to act on sheer impulse.

She had never been on a shopping spree, never bought anything that she didn't particularly need or that wasn't on sale.

She shoved her hands in her pockets, studying the signs that blazed in every shop window, announcing millennium sales. Everyone seemed to be open with an eye toward cashing in on the day that came only once every thousand years, and a party mentality prevailed everywhere.

Even at her trendy corner hair salon.

Tess frowned, studying her face in a window. She fingered her straight, shoulder-length brown hair.

Her gaze flickered back to the bustling salon.

Spontaneous, remember.

She took a breath, forgot all about her grocery shopping, then sprinted across the street.

■

"You're lucky I had an opening at the last minute."

Vincenzo Amalfi, better known by his professional name of Vido, was forty-one and looked ten years younger in black spandex biker shorts and a neon Hawaiian shirt. He rocked back on his heels, frowning as he fingered Tess's hair. "Three months since your last cut?"

"Give or take."

"I see highlights. Something that will really punch up your profile." He pursed pursed his lips. "I see energy. I see intelligence."

I see big bucks, Tess thought. But she was wise enough to keep her comments to herself. "Fine, you're the expert. I just want a change—but please, nothing outrageous."

"A change," he repeated. "Okay, what have we got?" He scrunched, tugged, draped. "Good texture. Nice volume. We'll go for the max. I'm seeing a texturizing cut here. We'll lay in a crisscross part, then maybe some copper highlights."

"Subtle," Tess repeated firmly.

"Subtle *plus* shine." Vido gave her bangs a tweak. "Into the chair."

Ninety-one carefully positioned foil rectangles later, Tess stared into a broad mirror, regretting the impulse that had put her into the hands of the volatile Vido. She'd probably end up looking like Madonna on a bad day. Or maybe like Dennis Rodman on a very good day, which was even worse.

A chrome hairdryer hummed around her head, making the tiny foil slips vibrate furiously. If there was any more ambient wind, she might reach flight velocity.

The high-tech clock chimed twice. Tess closed her eyes, afraid to watch as Vido eased the foil squares free and snipped quickly along her neck.

Damp strands fell. "Not too short," she murmured.

"Not to worry. You're going to turn heads with this hair."

Tess opened her eyes and gasped. Veins of gold, amber, and copper exploded through her hair, vibrating with primal color. She would turn heads, all right. She was going to bring traffic to a dead halt because people thought her head was on fire.

"But you said—I told you—"

"Fabulous! Very now! The highlights are perfect," he said firmly. "Now we go for a razor undercut. Something very 2000." Vido plunged his hands into her hair with savage energy, shaping and scrunching. "It's very fresh."

Tess swallowed hard at the sight of the stranger in the mirror. It was so different. It was so—*out there*.

Fifteen minutes later Vido was done, and Tess was paying the bill, studying her reflection in one of the salon's floor-to-ceiling mirrors. Soft curls kissed her face and the wild color lent radiance to her cheeks. She managed a small smile.

Wasn't it time she truly went for something different? She was a success, and that meant she had to start thinking like a success. From now on, she would think big and reward herself for reaching her goals. It was also time that she conquered her fear of shopping. No woman should reach the ripe age of twenty-eight without developing solid skills at handling salespeople, mastering their subtle forms of intimidation. Tess decided to view it as a professional challenge.

Where should she go first?

When Tess walked out into the snowy street, her gaze was drawn to a store window filled with bright streamers decorating hand-tooled cowboy boots in a dozen colors. An exquisite concha belt slanted across a matching fringed suede jacket and a creamy cashmere sweater set.

Now, *this* was shopping.

Tess refused to be intimidated by the indecipherable, handwritten price tags and the saleswoman who appeared to have stepped right out of *Town and Country*.

No backing down. This was business. This was a life experience.

Imagine Katharine Hepburn in *The Philadelphia Story*, she thought. Think of Grace Kelly in *To Catch a Thief*.

"Shop or die," Tess muttered as she clutched her purse, straightened her shoulders, and marched inside.

The boots were wildly beautiful. So were the silver concha belts and the fringed suede jackets. But the lingerie stopped Tess cold. She stared at it wistfully.

The saleswoman, who Tess had immediately dubbed Madame X, hovered superciliously. "May we be of assistance?"

There was only one person in sight. Probably she enjoyed the royal *we*, Tess thought. "I'm just looking right now."

Tess felt the chill radiate as the saleswoman dismissed her as someone who was far out of her league in this store. Irritation blended with embarrassment, and Tess was poised to leave when her tattered dignity resurfaced.

She studied the display of boots, then tilted her head, staring down her nose in a perfect rendition of Grace Kelly dismissing Cary Grant. "Don't you have anything of higher quality?" Her voice was arctic.

"We have some custom boots behind the counter." The woman's green eyes flickered, reassessing Tess. "But you will find that they are considerably more costly."

Tess gave a negligent wave of the hand. "I'd like to see the red ones." She gave a slow grin. "And the blue ones and the gray ones and the brown ones."

Ten minutes passed in an orgy of perfect hedonism. Tess tried on boots, belts, jackets, and sweaters, instantly transported by the drape of the butter-soft leathers and cashmeres. She turned one of the price tags, gave it a casual glance, and shrugged.

Madame X suddenly grew more responsive. "Something to go with the jacket, perhaps? We have a lovely silk jersey shirt with matching skirt. And of course, our cashmeres are exceptional."

Tess tried on everything in every color available, then turned to scrutinize the exquisite display of lace lingerie. Unable to resist, she slid on an old-fashioned pleated tulle camisole with matching silk crepe tap pants. The lavender silk fabric kissed her skin and left her feeling elegantly sensual.

"I'll take it," Tess said calmly even though her heart was pounding. "And the charmeuse nightgown and the suede jacket."

Madame X's lacquered smile nearly cracked as she calculated her commission. "And the boots?"

"Absolutely. The red ones with the silver studs." Tess ran a finger along a corselet of Alençon lace and threw caution to the winds. "This one too, I think."

As the saleswoman nearly sprinted from the room to begin ringing up the purchases, Tess called her back. "Oh, yes, I'll take that cashmere sweater set in the window, too." She did a quick mental calculation and smiled. "Actually, I'll take one in every color."

"Yes, madam. Of course. *Immediately*. And would you care for a cup of cappuccino while you're waiting?"

Tess nodded. She would indeed.

Two hours after she'd entered the boutique, Tess floated out into the street, foil bags draped over both arms. So far, so good. She wasn't prostrate from guilt yet.

She passed a travel agency and hovered over a rack of bright brochures, finally scooping up all of them. A specialty cooking store was next, netting her a gleaming silver cappuccino machine, an indulgence she had always craved.

Wind whipped at her cheeks as she swayed out into the street. She was clutching her packages, calculating how she would possibly get everything home, and then she spotted two huge sale signs emblazoned across the street, where cars glittered beneath a light dusting of snow.

Blue cars, red cars, silver cars.

Tess had always planned to get a car, but had never made the commitment. Now that she had some vacation time coming, maybe a grand road trip was the answer. She could go somewhere hot and colorful with lots of history. She thought about Damien Passard's cryptic comments and smiled.

She started toward the filled lot. Not that she actually meant to *buy* one of those sleek, gorgeous convertibles. Even though she'd always wanted one. No, she would simply window shop and ask lots of questions. Then she'd head for someplace that sold nice, sensible cars with good gas mileage.

Two hours later, Tess sat behind the leather console of a gleaming Mercedes CLK320 in metallic baby blue with oyster-leather interior. Normally, there was a two-year wait on this particular model, but the buyer had had to leave the country on short notice (translation: the IRS was hot on his heels) and his dream car was up for bid.

Tess stared at the blinking instrument panel, then at her bags and boxes stowed on the leather seat. Maybe she was getting a little *too* good at this shopping stuff. Not that she couldn't afford the car. It had been priced low as a 1999 model already custom designed for someone else. But Tess could live with a custom sound system, and there were all those safety features like four full air bags, emergency roadside assistance, and automatic rain-sensor wipers.

If she did happen to have an accident, the onboard global positioning system would automatically dial 911. How safe could you be!

Her checkbook was still burning a hole in her pocket after she'd parked, maneuvered her packages up the stairs, and unlocked her door, laden with shopping bags and the memory of the most excitement she could remember having in her adult life.

Dumping the bags in her foyer, she walked over to her elderly neighbor's apartment and slipped an envelope under the door.

She'd taken a great deal of pleasure in writing this particular check, which she was certain would cover the cost of Agatha Spinelli's long-postponed operation. What good was money if you couldn't make someone else happy with it?

She was certainly happy.

Now Agatha would be, too—as soon as she had that operation.

Once she was inside her apartment, she kicked off her shoes and flipped on the TV news. So far the new millennium was relatively calm. There had been limited power failures, and a few cases of food hoarding in the Northeast. Some graphic footage showed grim survivalists digging in across Idaho and the Southwest. Meanwhile, the Hong Kong stock market was extremely volatile, and a host of European businesses had discovered their Y2K compliance programs were too little too late.

Tess sat up straighter as a reporter described problems closer to home. A few small banks had experienced liquidity problems, and ATMs across the country were producing flawed information or failing outright. Tess made her first cappuccino, watching the reports stream in and feeling a trace of uneasiness.

As she sipped her cappuccino, she stared at her bank receipt.

Had Richard made an error in the amount? Or was this not her bonus at all?

She saw the bank's twenty-four-hour information number on the receipt and dialed impatiently, only to be told by a recorded message that full customer service would resume on Monday morning, after the holiday.

Tess paced the room and considered trying to track down Richard's accountants, then realized that would also be impossible until Monday.

With growing uneasiness, she flipped to another TV channel in time to see a report on survivalist groups. Two bearded men in camouflage jackets demonstrated how to kill a snake, skin it, and then toast the remains over a log fire made by rubbing two sticks together.

Shaking her head, she put Andrea Bocelli on the stereo and wrote checks to two charities. After that came another check to her old college friend whose husband had recently absconded with the contents of their joint bank account, leaving her flat broke. Finished with her spending, Tess dragged out the travel brochures and started making vacation plans.

MONDAY
JANUARY 2, 2000

A night of tossing and turning had left Tess feeling edgy and restless. She put in a call to the office, only to reach the answering machine. A call to Richard's home was equally useless.

Tess studied the table strewn with bags and boxes in growing uneasiness. What if the deposit amount wasn't a simple mistake by Richard? What if it wasn't from Richard at all?

She tried to stay calm as she dialed the bank and listed her account information. A customer service agent answered, asked for Tess's social security number and her banking code, then waited while Tess explained the situation.

A pause followed. Tess heard the click of a keyboard and a muted hum of voices.

"Yes, Ms. O'Mara, I have your account on the screen now." The agent clicked more keys. "I see two recent deposits to your account. One is a check from Mainwaring Services, which appears to be your usual salary deposit. The second . . ." More keys clicked. "Here it is. One million dollars." Papers rustled. "That's odd."

"What?"

The agent cleared his throat. "Usually we have an internal code for every transaction, listing the source. In this case the code seems to be missing."

"What does that mean?"

The voice grew guarded. "I'm not at liberty to go into detail at this particular moment. I'm going to transfer you to my supervisor."

Tess's hands closed around the telephone as a new voice came on the line.

"We have checked your account, and there seems to be a missing code, Ms. O'Mara. But rest assured, we will be investigating the deposit to your account thoroughly."

Tess glared at the phone. "Is this some kind of Y2K thing?"

"I'm not at liberty to answer that. We will make every effort to find the source of those funds, but it may take some time." The supervisor was firm, entirely controlled. She had no doubt been well schooled for just this sort of procedure.

Tess rubbed her arms, feeling like some kind of criminal. But that was ridiculous; *she* wasn't the one who had made the mistake. "How long before you have some answers?"

"That might be difficult to say. A week. Possibly longer."

"*A week?*"

"Excuse me, where can you be reached today?"

"At this number, but—"

"All day?"

Tess took a quick breath. "Yes, of course, but how—"

"Very good. We will contact you when our inquiry is complete. Have a good day, Ms. O'Mara."

Tess stared at the receiver in shock. *Have a good*

day? With a million dollars that she couldn't account for?

After some teeth grinding and angry muttering, she put down the phone and stood staring out the window. White flakes swirled in little eddies around skeletal trees. Another cold front was expected that night, bringing at least six more inches of snow.

Tess looked down and realized there were goose bumps all over her arms. Despite her heavy cotton sweatshirt, she was shivering.

The whole thing was absolutely ridiculous. This wasn't the Middle Ages, and bankers didn't work with an abacus and knotted strings. If there was some kind of electronic glitch, they would track it down, and that would be that. Meanwhile?

Andrew.

Her competent, practical big brother would know what to do.

■

Andrew O'Mara was Harvard '82 and Wharton '86, top drawer all the way. Brilliant, witty, and successful, he was everything her parents had always hoped he'd be and they'd never bothered to hide the fact. Andrew had always been stable and cautious, while Tess had been the creative, offbeat one ever willing to take risks. Andrew's top-level job at the Treasury Department had reinforced all his innate conservatism. Now his frequent junkets took him to Indonesia and Berlin, and Tess seldom saw him anymore.

But a brother was a brother. Andrew would have answers—assuming that he wasn't off in the Middle East or South America battling economic crises.

Tess breathed a sigh of relief when a crisp-voiced secretary finally put her call through.

"Andrew O'Mara here."

"Andrew, it's Tess." By now her palms were sweaty.

"Are you in trouble, Tess? You sound upset."

"I'm fine." *At least I think I'm fine*. "It's about my bank account."

"You're overdrawn? I can wire you some money. How much do you need?"

"I don't need money," Tess said tightly. "As a matter of fact, that's the problem."

"I'm not following you here, Tess.

"Money has been transferred into my account and I'm not sure that it's mine. I figured that you could tell me what I should do about it." Tess outlined her conversation with the bank.

"Sounds simple enough. Give your bank another twenty-four hours to straighten things out."

"When I mentioned a possible Y2K problem, I thought they'd reach right through the phone and strangle me."

"It's a sensitive issue right now," he said guardedly. "Until the dust settles, everyone's worried about possible litigation."

"What am I supposed to do until the dust settles? I have a million dollars in my account that in all likelihood isn't mine."

"Say that again." Tess heard a chair squeak. "You've got how much in your account?"

"One million."

Andrew O'Mara gave a low whistle. "And the bank hasn't given you any information? They should have a timed transaction code."

"The first agent I spoke to said he couldn't find any code. He thought it was strange."

"You bet it's strange." Her brother's voice sounded serious now.

"I'm expecting a large bonus from work, but Richard took off for Polynesia, and I can't reach him. Now the bank won't give me any answers."

"Give me the number of your account, and I'll see what I can dig up at this end. Meanwhile, sit tight. And whatever you do, *don't* spend any of it."

Tess stared at the phone. "It's a little late for that, Andrew. I, uh, bought a few things this morning."

"How few?"

Tess did a quick mental calculation. The number was higher than she'd realized. "Not quite sixty-five."

"Hundred?"

Tess swallowed. "Thousand."

"What did you do, put a down payment on an apartment building?"

"I bought a car actually. A Mercedes convertible— and a few other things. I'm not a spendthrift," Tess said defensively. "I had a huge bonus coming. Richard told me that flat-out."

"But he didn't tell you the exact figure?"

"No. You know how he can be. He loves playing boss. It's a control thing they taught him at Wharton. Maximize output by decreasing worker complacency."

"Look, just sit tight." Andrew spoke tensely. "I'll call you right back. It's probably nothing, but with an amount that size it doesn't pay to take chances."

It doesn't pay to take chances.

Tess rubbed the knot in her neck, watching snow gust over the trees. What had her brother meant by that?

She paced anxiously until Andrew called back a half hour later.

"Tess." Her brother sounded tired. "I want you to listen *very* carefully." His voice hardened. "I've checked all the activity reports for your bank, and nothing has been entered for your account. That alone is suspicious. I also find it odd that no one else has reported that amount of money missing." He hesitated. "Of course it *could* be a simple electronic oversight, or a mistake in the general ledgers. On the other hand, it could be something else."

Tess stared at the phone. "What kind of something else?"

"These might be the kind of people who would find it unhealthy to have dealings with the authorities."

"You mean because they're criminals?"

"It's possible. If so, you could be in danger, Tess. Whatever you do, don't touch another penny of that money until I have some answers. I don't want to give these people any way to track you."

"*Track* me? You think they'd do that?" Uneasiness veered into panic.

Andrew O'Mara cursed softly. "Listen, I have a bad feeling about all this. I think you should go away for a few weeks while I run a check on the source."

"Go away where?"

"Someplace isolated. I want you to start packing. Meanwhile, don't tell *anyone* that you're leaving, not even your friends."

"I don't believe you're actually telling me to go somewhere and hide." Tess laughed tightly, but Andrew didn't laugh back. "Andrew?" Her voice was shaky. "You're joking, right?"

His silence was worse than any answer he could have

given her. Then he bit back an oath. "I'm not joking, Tess. We've had a few other reports like this, and there may be a pattern here. Until I'm sure, I want to know that you're safe."

"Andrew, don't be ridiculous! I can't go away for a few weeks. I have a new chocolate account I have to get started on . . ." Then Tess's legs started to shake. Her brother would never joke about her safety. He might be overcautious, but the work he did gave him good reason to be.

Tess sank down into a chair by the phone. "What kind of place did you have in mind?"

"Someplace quiet. I know a spot that's way off the beaten track. An old friend of mine happens to be sheriff there, so it will be perfect. And I want you to leave *now*," he added.

"Now, like tonight?"

"Now, like this minute," her brother growled.

Tess frowned. "I'll never be able to get a plane ticket on such short notice."

"Forget flying. I want you to get in that new car you just bought and drive."

"Andrew, you're starting to scare me."

"Good. I don't want you to stop being scared until you reach Almost."

"Where?"

"Almost. That's the name of the town in Arizona."
Arizona.

Something nagged at Tess's mind, and she glanced down at the scattered brochures from the travel agency. On the top of the pile was a picture of jagged granite cliffs beneath a blinding blue sky. Caught in shadows was a dark outline of ancient masonry walls and jagged wood roof beams.

Tess stood frozen. There was something familiar about the place. She could almost hear the wind whisper through the cottonwood and mesquite trees, as if she had walked that rocky path and touched those walls of burning stone before.

Tess shook her head, irritated. Of course the scene felt familiar. She had seen a thousand shots like that in the epic westerns she'd devoured since she was a brat in pigtails. She had cut her eyeteeth on *The Searchers, Fort Apache,* and *Broken Arrow.* She could recite all the good lines from *Santa Fe Trail* by heart. So what? That was no reason to get swept up in some ridiculous flight of fancy.

Swallowing hard, Tess shoved the brochure back into a pile with all the others.

"Tess, are you there?"

"I'm all ears, Andrew."

"Okay, I want you to pack up, then hit the road. And for once, *don't* argue with me."

Outside, snow played over the gleaming hood of the Mercedes. Tess was having trouble breathing. "Do you really believe I'm in danger, Andrew?"

"Let's just say I don't want to find out that you are. Now get your pen and I'll give you directions to Almost. I just heard there's a storm front rolling in from Canada, and it could dump two feet of snow before morning. I want you out of Boston before it hits."

Feeling an oppressive sense of danger, Tess grabbed a pencil and started writing.

∎

The temperature had dropped and snow was blowing harder by the time Tess finished packing the car. Suitcases and boxes filled the trunk. More boxes along with books and shopping bags full of her new purchases covered the seats. She held a flashlight and three boxes of batteries, compliments of Mrs. Spinelli, who swore that Tess would need them sooner or later.

As she finished stowing the last bag, Tess caught a glimpse of herself in the rearview mirror. In her western-style suede jacket, she could have been a complete stranger. But there was something about that stranger Tess liked—the gleam in her eye, the flash of color in her cheeks, and the glint of her hair. She straightened up, her cowboy boots crunching on the dry, new-fallen snow, and took a final look around her.

The wind rose, scattering a flurry of flakes. Tess was intensely aware of her life as she stood in the snow, aware of this street, this building, this small corner of the harried world where she had lived for seven years. She wondered suddenly why it had never felt like home, only a place to stay.

All of her memories of this street seemed to be centered on work—fighting deadlines, battling stress, juggling pressures. Without planning to, she had traded in a real life for success. She had worked hard, planned well, and played by all the rules. But suddenly she didn't like those rules.

You can't have it all, a college professor had once warned her.

Maybe not.

All Tess wanted was one small part for herself. Now she had to decide which part that was and how much she was willing to give up to claim it.

She slid behind the wheel and pulled out of the parking spot.

The road stretched before her, winding past wind-tossed pine trees and snow-streaked sidewalks. Somewhere a tree branch shifted, cracking in the wind. She shivered, already feeling the pull of hot blue skies and burning red stone.

The dark pavement stretched out against the white drifts, caught in uncertain sunlight, beckoning her to an adventure like nothing else she had ever known.

With Damien's strange words ringing in her ears, Tess cranked up Andrea Bocelli and headed west.

3

White clouds piled up on the jagged blue-gray spikes of the Chiricahuas. Dust whipped over the foothills to the east.

Wind picking up. Storm weather coming.

Just his luck.

T. J. McCall frowned at the electronic beep coming from somewhere in his dusty denim pocket.

Not the beeper. This time it was the cell phone.

He shifted the reins into one hand and soothed his bay gelding with the other, then dug for the phone. *"What?"* he snapped as wind whipped dust and twigs around his face.

"Is that all you've got to say to an old friend?"

The cowboy's mouth tightened, drawing lines into his deeply tanned face. "If this is a prank call, you're gonna be real sorry come sundown."

"Prank call? You wound me." Low laughter spilled over the line. "How soon they forget."

"O'Mara? Damn, is that you?" McCall guided his quarter horse around a stand of prickly pear cactus and smiled.

"None other. How's life at the little house on the prairie?"

"Wrong state. Wrong century." T. J. McCall shoved back his sweaty Stetson and eased past a dry wash bordered by treacherous slip rock. "Wrong ecosystem."

"Says you. What's a cowboy know about ecosystems?"

"Hell of a lot more than a T-man from Georgetown."

"You got a point there. What's all that noise?"

"That's not noise, it's cattle. Three hundred prime Brahman steers to be exact, not that you'd know the difference. It's time to move them down to pasture."

"You really did leave it all behind, didn't you?" Andrew O' Mara was silent for a moment. Then he snorted. "Can you still shoot a match out of a matchbook at two hundred feet?"

"Maybe. I gave up smoking so who knows?"

Andrew O'Mara hesitated. "Listen, I've got something for you, McCall. It's important."

T. J. McCall stared at the ragged line of the mountains shimmering like smoke above the vast green floor of the Sonoran Desert. "Forget it, O'Mara. I'm out of the business."

"No one as good as you were ever pulls out."

"Wrong."

"Anytime you want back in, I'll make the call. You could have a Capitol assignment inside of a week. Probably Presidential in six months."

The cowboy sat up straighter, the cell phone gripped in hard, work-worn fingers. "I said forget it, O'Mara."

"Okay, I will. For now." Andrew cursed softly. "Meanwhile, this is a favor, McCall. It's *personal*."

"Say again."

"You heard right." Wind hissed, shaking the green clusters of a dense palo verde. T. J. McCall wiped a dusty bandanna over his sunburned forehead and frowned.

The silence held. Both men knew that a line had been crossed, all the normal formalities broken. *Personal* meant someone near and dear was in trouble. *Personal* was something you never refused, because next time you might be on the asking end.

Damn, why did it have to be personal? T.J. thought in disgust.

"McCall? You still there?"

"Right here. I sure wish I wasn't."

O'Mara took a long, harsh breath. "I don't like asking favors, but it's my baby sister. I think she's in trouble."

"Drugs?"

"Tess? She gets high on two aspirins and a cold soda. No possible drug problems with her." O'Mara chuckled grimly. "Not unless Starbucks coffee and Belgian chocolate have been upgraded to the controlled substances category."

T.J. smiled, being the proud possessor of a fairly developed sweet tooth himself. "Alcohol abuse? Don't tell me it's some kind of man trouble."

"No way. Tess's idea of a hot date is curling up with the latest issue of *The Wall Street Journal*. Everything's business with her."

T.J.'s lips twitched. "Good to see someone in the O'Mara family has to work hard to make a living. All the same, I don't see how I can help you." T.J. grabbed his battered Stetson as wind whipped down from the high ridges. His eyes narrowed as he studied the line of thunderheads gathering in the west.

"Just hear me out, McCall."

The cowboy rocked back in his saddle to the squeak of well-oiled leather. "You'd better talk fast. I've got a storm system moving in and three hundred restless cows nudging my tail. Right now they don't look very happy. In a second this cell phone's going to fade out of range and you'll be stuck, since I'm not heading back to town until later in the day. Might be one or two days if this storm holds out."

"I'll talk fast." O'Mara's voice hardened. "I'm sending her to you, T.J. Take care of her. If things work out the way I think, she's going to need your help—along with a lot of luck."

"Listen, Andrew, I don't have time to—"

T.J. cursed softly as the answering voice broke into static. Wind whipped pebbles and dust, cutting off his vision just as a nasty-tempered steer named Diablo took a plunge toward a steep dry wash.

T.J. spurred his mount forward and tried to forget all about Andrew O'Mara and his irritating sister.

■

Tess looked up from her map and gave a long, silent whistle.

A rolling sea of green stretched before her beneath the blazing sun. Low trees and dense shrubs straddled rocky washes on both sides of the highway. To the north and south jagged mountains rose to a blinding turquoise sky. Silence clung to the high canyons and light shimmered on rugged, red rock cliffs.

Where she was sitting was a long way from Boston. Actually, it was a long way from *anywhere*.

She rolled down her window and gasped. Hot, dry air

filled her lungs, rich with an exotic blend of sage, juniper, and blooming rosemary. So now she knew what the desert smelled like—fragile, exotic, and full of life, a universe away from the carbon monoxide and sea tang of Boston.

Wind rushed down an arroyo, spinning eddies of sand that hissed around the wheels of her Mercedes. For a moment the road before her was hidden in a veil of pebbles and twigs of dried sagebrush. She slid from behind the wheel and stretched slowly. Her shoulders ached and her new boots were dirty, but she was enjoying the trip more than she'd thought she would. The bright sun and hot weather suited her. So did the sense of high adventure.

She fingered her jacket guiltily.

It hadn't been *all* that expensive. Besides, she'd bought it before she'd discovered that the money in her bank account might not be hers to spend.

But for four days now her brother's suspicions had gnawed at her. She wondered if someone was tracking her right now.

Impossible, she thought. No doubt Andrew was simply being overcautious. She expected that when she finally reached Almost, there would be a jovial message from him assuring her that everything was fine and she could turn around and head home.

Out of the corner of her eye she saw something flash behind her in the deserted line of asphalt snaking back into New Mexico. Tess looked back, frowning. Was it a chrome hood ornament? The shimmer of a rearview mirror?

The uneasiness that had plagued her over the long drive raced into full-fledged panic at the thought that she had been followed here. But how? There had been no other cars on the road since she'd left the interstate.

A black RV lumbered out of the whirling dust to the west and swung wide onto the highway. Tess jumped back into her car and locked the doors. She had just started the motor when the huge vehicle fishtailed to a noisy halt in front of her, blocking the road.

A man poked his head out of the driver's window and shoved back a pair of mirrored sun glasses. "Nice car."

Tess cautiously lowered the window a few inches. "Er—thank you."

"Mercedes Cabriolet. Pretty damned snappy. Must have cost a bundle."

Tess fingered the gear shift. She was ready to shoot into reverse when she realized a cactus stood right behind her. She nodded uneasily, painfully aware that she was alone in the middle of nowhere, and this man was a complete stranger.

"Three-point-two-liter V-6 engine. Leather seats, I bet." The driver poked his head out farther, studying Tess intently. "Not from around here, are you?"

"No."

"You headed for Tucson?"

"Er—no. Albuquerque," Tess lied.

"In that case, you're headed in the wrong direction. This road goes west."

Tess gave a noncommittal shrug. "I guess I missed a turn back there. I'd better get going. I've got people waiting for me," she lied. "Maybe you could just move your RV so I can—"

His eyes narrowed. "How long since you left L.A.?"

"A few days."

The driver shaded his eyes, staring at the tangle of lace underwear spilling out of the bag on the passenger seat.

Nervously, she shoved the lace camisoles down out of sight, then pulled her jacket across them.

"Did you hear about the food riots?" His eyes took on a bright, almost fanatical gleam. "We read all about it on the Internet last night. Stick around and watch technology flame right into oblivion."

Tess had occasionally listened to the radio on her drive, but she hadn't heard anything about food riots or power grid failures. "Everything was fine when I left."

The man scowled. "Like hell. We've heard reports from northern Canada up through Alaska. They've had RTU failures on the offshore oil rigs, and shipping was closed down tight."

Tess stared in amazement. "They must not have reported that on the radio."

"Hell, no. Got to keep people quiet. Got to make things seem safe." He made a sharp gesture with one hand. "Damned government says jump and the press can't move fast enough. The big cities are going next. Damned scavengers will be roaming the country like animals. You got a rifle with you?"

Tess swallowed hard. "Gee, I knew there was something I forgot to pack. I only took my pistol and ammo."

His eyes focused, probing Tess and the dusty car. "You sure you're not lost?"

"Not a chance. I know these roads like the back of my hand. But my friends are waiting, and I don't want to be late, so I'd appreciate it if you'd back out of my way."

He didn't move. "Real nice car," he drawled. "Pretty lonely place for a woman to be driving a sporty little thing like that."

Tess felt her heart slam against her chest. ''Heck, no. Me and my pistol, we're a team. Nobody's going to mess with us.''

He smiled as he opened his door.

Tess didn't wait any longer. Her hands were shaking as she whipped backward and made a ragged U-turn, taking off the edge of a cactus and a chunk of paint in the process, and then sped down a narrow dirt road with her gas pedal to the floor. The Mercedes banged along the lonely road, washboard grooves making her teeth rattle. She took a quick glimpse at her map, then made a hard right onto a single-lane paved road. She checked the mirror and gave a sigh of relief when she saw that the RV had disappeared. Only then did real panic kick in.

Her hands began to shake so hard that she careened off the road into the dirt, while gravel spun up in a cloud. Suddenly the rear tires hissed, then mired down tight.

Tess slammed into reverse, her back tires smoking as they spun up dry sand and slip rock. She shot the gear into low and gunned the motor, her foot to the floor.

No luck. The tires screamed, but the car didn't move.

Finally Tess shoved the car into park and got out, staring down at the front wheel buried up to the axle in powdery sand.

Stuck solid.

Just perfect.

She turned, glaring out at the horizon. She was miles from any major city, the victim of a map that was probably years out of date. Behind her a dirt road snaked over boulders and twisted hills, shimmering in a heat haze like one of the vintage movies she'd loved.

It would have been wonderful if she had been sitting in an air-conditioned theater enjoying the view, instead of breathing CO_2 fumes and sand particles. She stalked around to the back and kicked the dusty rear tire, wincing as she nearly broke her toe. What was she going to do now?

Wind shook the velvet leaves of a mesquite tree, and somewhere nearby a cactus sparrow twittered from a sage bush, mocking her misery.

Tess's shoulders slumped. The Mercedes couldn't move without help. Given the endless miles of desert around her, walking *definitely* wasn't an option.

Out of the corner of her eye, Tess saw a brown shape slide out of a tangle of bushes above the wash, ears erect and long tongue lagging. Every movement of the spare body was economical and wary.

A coyote.

An honest-to-heaven, in-the-flesh coyote. Now, that was something you didn't see in Harvard Square or Copley Place.

Tess clenched her fists. She was gritty and thirsty and hot, several hours from any sizable dot on the map, and whining wasn't going to help her get out of the wash. She had a cell phone in the car, but it hadn't worked since St. Louis, and Tess hadn't had a chance to stop to have it repaired.

She drummed her fingers on the hood of the car, watching the coyote.

The animal stood frozen, thirty feet away, face to the wind and ears erect. Its keen eyes tracked her, then the coyote turned abruptly to the mountains, jumping across the arroyo. His paws dug briefly into the sand before finding traction in a narrow strip of scrub and wildflowers.

Tess stood up sharply. *Traction.* That's what she needed.

She scanned the backseat and saw her new suede

jacket. Even one tire track would mark the fine leather, but she had no choice. Tess drew a long breath. Never mind that it had cost her a month's salary. She could buy another one—assuming she managed to get out of the wash alive.

She spread the coat over the sand behind her rear tire, backed up slowly, then jolted forward with her wheels spinning. Sand and gravel scattered, but the car didn't pull free.

Too much weight.

Tess inspected the packed seats and hurled two heavy suitcases out the window. Sweaters, overcoats, and tailored business suits spilled out on impact, scattering over the sandy earth.

Whispering a prayer, she hit the gas again and sat frozen while the engine whined. She tried not to envision her bleached bones littering the lonely wash, discovered by some backpacker from Tucson a year or two later.

The back wheel rocked, then bit into her coat. The car shook and leapt up the sandy grade. Tess gave a shriek of joy and climbed entirely back onto the road before coasting to a halt.

Silence lay heavy over the wash. Her hands shook as she picked up her jacket and suitcases, then checked her battered map. Her next major turn should take her to Almost. If she was very lucky, she might arrive in time for lunch.

Tess slid behind the wheel and looked south, where a paved road crested the rise. Far in the distance she saw a dark outline.

Masonry walls.

Ruined roof beams.

She sat up straighter. Her heart did a jerky dance as she was struck by a sense of blinding familiarity.

Impossible.

Dust rose, blocking her view. When she looked back, the ruined walls were gone, lost in rippling waves of heat, as if they had been no more than a mirage.

∎

He watched, high on a jagged ridge.

His face was deeply lined, the color of the weathered sandstone where he crouched, his body insubstantial in the shimmer of midday's heat. He made no sound, staring south, where a retreating car sent plumes of dust across the road.

Somewhere a coyote howled from the chaparral. The old man did not move or raise his eyes from the car sliding behind a hill, not even when the first coyote's cry was met by another and another.

He smiled at the sound.

So the ''little wolves'' were still here, guarding these bare slopes. Perhaps it was just as well that they favored the higher ground where shadows raced beside ancient saguaros. Here there was no one to threaten or chase the wild creatures. Here there were only ghosts, shadows cast by ruined walls built by civilizations long vanished into dust.

He studied the clouds as wind brushed the mesquites. With a sigh he straightened his shoulders. She had come back, bringing darkness in her wake, just as she had long before. His fingers dug into the dirt as the coyotes raised their unearthly lament to echo off the high cliffs.

He turned away.

Veiled in the changing light, he began a chant older than the ruined walls above him, raising the sound to the sky until power rang through his chest. He could challenge or assist, control or deceive. A new millennium had come, but he knew that men's hearts did not change. Greed, envy, and fear walked just as they had centuries before.

Those who lived here spoke often of history and legend. Now they were about to learn that legends always had their cost.

■

"What do you mean the money isn't *there*? What kind of game are you playing?"

"It's not there. I'm looking at my account right now, dammit. Your last eight deposits are missing!"

"That's impossible." He had coded them himself.

"Tell that to the man who's flying in tonight from Seattle."

"That's not necessary," he replied in a deadly cold voice. "We'll find the problem and take care of it from our end. We always do."

"Damn straight, we'll find the problem. But if you'd like to stay alive, you'll find it for us first."

The phone clicked off.

He stared at the receiver.

He hadn't made a mistake. Had he?

4

Sheriff Jackson McCall was almost asleep.

His chair was cocked to forty-five degrees against a split-rail fence in front of the sheriff's office.

"T.J., you there?"

The tall cowboy, known as T.J. to his friends, scowled and shoved his Stetson lower on his head. He'd been up most of the prior twenty-four hours running down stray stock from a neighboring ranch and he wasn't overly pleased to be roused from a colorful dream involving palm trees, cool water, and a dozen nearly naked women in red sarongs.

His handset buzzed again. "T.J., I know you're there, and I know this blamed radio works, so you'd better answer me."

The sheriff of Almost, Arizona, didn't move a muscle beneath his battered Stetson. "What is it, Grady? Another hitchhiker with a sign warning us the world has ended?"

"Hell, no. That was last month. This is a whole lot better."

"I'm sleeping, Grady. You're on duty now. Call me when the mother ship enters final approach. Until then I've got a hot date with a lady in a red sarong."

Grady chuckled. "You're making a big mistake, boy."

"Mistake's my middle name." T.J. eased his broad shoulders back against the chair. His eyes were closed and he was already halfway back into what was becoming a very inventive fantasy.

Lately it seemed as if fantasies were all the sheriff had time for.

"Dammit, T.J., you git yourself off that chair right now. It's a woman I'm calling you about, hear?"

Sighing, McCall shoved back his hat and squinted down the quiet street. Then he rocked his chair flat and stood up slowly.

A powder-blue Mercedes convertible stood angled before the General Mercantile, one wheel hitched over the dusty curb. The other was flattening a crate that appeared to be filled with peaches. Or what had *been* peaches.

"You seeing that car, T.J.?"

"I see it."

Static crackled over the handset. "Bound to be a clear traffic violation in there somewhere. We can't let people go charging down Main Street in violation of town safety codes."

"Nothing violated that I can see. Except maybe those peaches." T.J. flipped off his handset as his grizzled deputy strode out of the café directly across the street and walked toward him. "You're just itchy because you always wanted a car like that."

Grady looked offended. "I am speaking as a man with honest town spirit. A man with a true concern for the welfare and livelihood of our respected citizens."

"And a man who's drowning in envy."

"You paint a sorry picture of a colleague and an old

friend, Sheriff. I am simply trying to see justice done. Can't have Main Street turned into an eyesore.''

"Give over, Grady. You're a deputy and no disturbance of the peace has taken place.''

The deputy ignored him, tugging a worn pencil stub from behind his ear. "Maybe we could go for property damage or a charge of reckless endangerment. I could get an interview for the paper." Grady started across the street, then turned impatiently. "Aren't you coming?''

"Looks like I don't have any choice, not with you chewing at my saddle."

T.J. shoved back his hat and stretched slowly, working the knotted muscles at his shoulder where a charging cow had snapped him sideways. He stared at the crushed peaches, which were already drying in the fierce desert sun.

Anything for news, T. J. McCall thought. In addition to serving as a deputy officer, Grady was also the editor of the *Almost Gazette*, and news had been scarce lately. It was downright pathetic how boredom could wear a man down.

"Relax, Grady. The Mercantile looks intact, and as far as I can see, no shots have been fired and there are no dead bodies littering Main Street."

They crossed the street, matching each other stride for stride.

Grady scratched his head. "Maybe the woman in the car is a spy for a foreign government." His eyes darkened. "Or maybe she's a key witness on the run from indictment in an organized-crime investigation."

"Maybe she's just lost."

"The trouble with you, McCall, is you don't have any imagination. Leastways go and git her name. There's still some space left in the next issue."

"There's *always* space left in the next issue."

Grady gave a low whistle. "Well, would you look at that."

T. J. McCall barely heard his deputy's comment. He was too busy staring at the vision emerging from behind the wheel of the Mercedes. She was a true apparition in soft denim and teal-blue suede, and her hair reminded T.J. of a sunrise he'd seen as a boy camping out in the Superstitions. He'd never seen that much red, gold, and silver in one head before, and it took his breath away.

Another tourist, he decided. He *hated* tourists. They brought nothing but trouble and complaints. Plagued with too much money and too little sense, in his general experience.

There was another possibility, of course. She could be that baby sister that Andrew O'Mara was sending to Almost.

T.J. scowled at the polished Mercedes and the even more polished female leaning against the hood. This sleek number wasn't *anyone's* baby sister. No woman who looked like that came to Almost except by mistake. There wasn't a sushi bar, day spa, or destination resort anywhere in sight.

The woman still hadn't noticed him, and for some reason that added to T.J.'s irritation. She was hunched over the hood, fiddling with her map, giving T.J. a clear view of her rounded backside.

He took a slow breath and let his gaze wander over the curves hidden beneath soft denim. A tooled leather belt circled her slim waist and a fringed suede jacket was slung over her shoulders.

Oddly enough, there were tire tracks running right down the back of it.

T.J. felt his throat go bone dry, the way it did when a dust devil cut over the mountains from Mexico, clogging his breath and whipping sand and grit in a dozen directions at once. Amazing how something so pretty could hurt so bad.

"You need any help interrogating her, Sheriff?"

"I think I can manage without backup, Grady. But thanks for the offer."

"You're the boss. But I reckon I'll stick around, just in case."

T.J. picked his way past the mutilated peaches. "Can I help you, Ma'am?"

She didn't seem to hear, bent over a wrinkled map she was awkwardly folding and refolding. Each time the folds came out wrong.

T.J. noticed that her hands were shaking.

"Ma'am?"

No answer.

He slanted a look inside the expensive car. The seats were loaded with bags, books, and some kind of fancy silver appliance. A pair of new red cowboy boots leaned against the passenger door. Excellent leather work, T.J. decided with an expert eye.

But there was no water anywhere in sight.

The woman swayed slightly. She ran her hand through that glorious mass of red-and-gold hair and turned.

McCall blinked. At that moment he remembered what it felt like for a mean horse to kick him hard in the backside.

The woman gave the word radiance new meaning. It wasn't just because of her fine skin or the moss-green eyes alive with amber glints. T.J. thought it might be the way freckles dotted her nose. Or maybe it was that full, stubborn mouth.

Suddenly he couldn't seem to breathe properly. He cleared his throat and shoved away an erotic vision of her mouth—on his body. "Ma'am?"

She was shaking and her face had gone sickly white.

"It just won't work." Her voice was painfully sexy, husky and low. Or maybe it was just dry.

"Forget the damn map," T.J. growled. "When was the last time you had anything to drink?"

"Drink?" She peered at him over the map, and T.J. felt something slam him hard in the chest. To his disgust, the sensation promptly moved lower, gathering just below the weight of his silver belt buckle. If this turned out to be Andrew O'Mara's baby sister, T.J. was going to be very, very sorry.

"That's right," he growled, "what have you been drinking?"

Her chin shot up. "Are you suggesting that I'm drunk?"

"I'm talking about liquid in general. Preferably water."

She frowned at something in the air over his head. "I had some wine last night with dinner. That was back in New Mexico. A zinfandel from Sonoma, nothing fancy. I had orange juice at breakfast. Unsweetened. Natural pulp. But I don't see why—" Suddenly her hand opened on the car hood. "I don't feel—" She took a sharp breath.

"Damn fool creature." If he hadn't been so gut-wrenched by that first sight of her, T.J. would have seen the signs immediately. As it was, he barely managed to lunge forward as she toppled onto his chest.

Out cold.

■

A crowd had gathered by the time Grady held open the door so that T.J. could carry the new arrival into his office. With no water in twenty-four hours, the blasted female was lucky she'd lasted this long.

T.J. settled his unconscious visitor on the cot beside his gunmetal-gray desk and spun his hat onto a peg by the door. "Somebody go get Doc Felton." He tugged off her suede jacket and unbuttoned the top three buttons of her white shirt to drizzle cool water over her skin. Just doing his job, he told himself. He damned well wasn't enjoying the sight, either.

Not her long, slim neck. Not the faint shadow below the edge of her shirt.

Grady cleared his throat. "Think she's someone important, T.J.? Someone on the run? Mafia witness? Government courier maybe?"

"We're never going to find out if you don't give her some air," T.J. growled. With quick movements he soaked a second washcloth in water from his cooler and laid it over her forehead. "The fool hasn't had any water all day."

"Yep," Grady said thoughtfully. "That'd put a body out sure enough." Grady stared at the cot in morbid fascination. "Maybe she's gonna die."

"Nobody's dying in my office," T.J. said tightly. "Now, everyone out. Floor show's over." But she still didn't move, and his anxiety grew. Heat stroke was never a pretty sight. She needed to drink, but he didn't dare force liquids while she was unconscious, in case she choked.

He was greatly relieved when the town doctor pushed through the door. Ernest Felton was sixty-something, with stooped shoulders and keen eyes that had seen just about every calamity and bodily trauma in forty years of general practice. "Got a patient for me, Mc-Call?"

"Hasn't moved an inch since I brought her in, Doc. She looks pretty beat."

The doctor slid a digital thermometer between her lips. "A hundred and one. That's a good sign."

"Sounds high to me," T.J. said.

"Not life-threatening." The doctor brushed her skin. "Cool to the touch. She's starting to sweat, and that's good, too. Any signs of nausea?"

"It happened too fast for that."

"Help me elevate her feet." Together, they slid a pillow in place, then raised her ankles. "First stage of heatstroke, I'd say, along with dehydration. She looks strong enough, but you'd better get her hydrated. Keep wet cloths in place. Do you have any ice packs?"

T.J. nodded.

"Use them. Armpits and wrists. Ankles and groin. Give her water as soon as she comes around, but keep it limited."

T.J. rubbed his jaw. As a law officer, he'd had his share of dehydrated tourists and lost hikers crazy from heat exhaustion. By now he knew the drill.

"I'll be back in an hour after I check on the Winslow sisters over at the nursing home." The doctor frowned. "Fool woman has too many clothes on. You might want to do something about that, Sheriff."

Like what—strip her naked? T.J. wondered grimly.

After Doc Felton left, McCall slipped ice packs under her arms and ankles, then drizzled cool water into her mouth. When she gagged, he stopped and tried again.

But she still didn't come around. Her arm swept out

and she muttered hoarsely, as if caught in a bad dream. She spoke again, but the sounds were choppy and made no sense to T.J. As he put another cold cloth on her head, she twisted sideways, breathing hard, her fingers stiff. Something had left her badly frightened.

T.J. only wished he knew what.

Five minutes later, as T.J. held a damp cloth to her cheek, her eyes opened. He looked into them and got lost in a green smoother than cottonwood leaves in spring. Wind seemed to whistle past his face, cool and sweet. *And you're a damned fool, McCall.*

She blinked and tried to sit up.

"Take it easy, Ma'am."

She closed her eyes, then took another long, hard look at him. "I loved you in *Braveheart*."

T.J. gave a long-suffering sigh. After a decade of being mistaken for Hollywood's azure-eyed superstar, he was resigned to the error. "How does your head feel?"

She tried to sit up, then sank back with a soft groan. "Like Apollo 13 just did a three-point turn on my frontal lobe." She rubbed her forehead, frowning. "Do I know you? You seem . . . familiar."

"If we'd met, Ma'am, I'd surely remember it. Probably just the aftereffects of the heat. Serves you right for traveling through the desert without water."

"What do you mean?"

T.J. shook his head in disgust. She really didn't have a clue. Then again, most visitors didn't. "Your body needs eight to ten glasses of liquid daily. In conditions of severe heat or exertion, the amount can double."

Her teeth chattered. "Is that why I keeled over?"

T.J. nodded.

She sighed. "You still seem familiar." She tried to

turn and then frowned. "Why are two bags of ice wedged under my arms?"

"I had to bring your temperature down." T.J. offered her a glass of water with a straw. "Sip as much as you can. The sooner you replace your fluids the better."

She didn't seem to be listening. "So you're really not Mel Gibson?" She sounded disappointed.

"No, Ma'am, I'm not." T.J. tried not to take it personally. "I'm the sheriff here."

She closed her eyes on a groan. "Don't tell me. You're McCall, the one Andrew told me about."

She didn't appear too happy at the idea. As it happened, T.J. shared her sentiments completely. "So you're Tess. Welcome to Almost."

"There weren't any signs that I could see."

"Last one fell down a few weeks ago. We haven't had a chance to replace it yet." T.J. frowned. The damned female was wearing way too many clothes, a heavy denim skirt and heaven knew what was beneath that. Probably silk and more silk. Doc Felton was right: something had to go.

Maybe his sanity, T.J. thought wryly. He placed another wet cloth on her head and fanned her face with a newspaper.

"I'm going to have to take off some of those clothes, Ma'am."

She didn't seem to hear. T.J. decided this was as good a time as any to correct her overdressed condition. Hell, what was he supposed to take off first?

He unbuttoned her shirt lower, pushed up the sleeves and waited. Still no response.

Didn't she realize this was afternoon in the *desert*? No one marched around in the afternoon sun without water. Muttering, T.J. went to work on her boots and belt.

Why did *he* have to be the one dealing with this crazy female? He hadn't tackled a woman's buttons in six months.

T.J. frowned. Or had it been longer?

Damn, that was unnatural.

He wiped her face again. She had a redhead's delicate complexion, but she hadn't worn sunscreen or a hat. He meant to give her hell for that, too.

"Ms. O'Mara?"

She was out cold.

T.J. decided that her clothes were going to have to wait.

■

Two people stood in the shaded bow window across the street, watching T.J. stride out of the sheriff's office. One was the owner of the General Mercantile and café.

"That's odd," Mae muttered.

"What's odd?" Doc Felton stood nursing one of Mae's famous butterscotch milk shakes.

"The sheriff. Man's fit to be tied. I haven't seen him that angry since that California promoter wanted to rent the town for an undertaker's convention."

Doc Felton elbowed in beside her and had a view of T.J.'s stiff gait as he strode toward his dusty Blazer. He was muttering as he swung open the door, then closed it again. He jammed his hat down hard, took a dozen angry steps, and kicked at the rear tire, then turned and stalked back up the steps to the sheriff's office.

The doctor rubbed his jaw. "Definitely looks angry. Must have something to do with that woman who passed out in the street today. Heatstroke, most likely."

"Who, T.J. or the woman?"

Doc Felton chuckled. "Maybe both of them."

"You don't say." Mae spread her hands on the spotless but worn Formica table beside the window. "She the one with all that red hair? Driving that fancy blue car?"

"That's the one."

Mae chewed on her lip. "You don't say."

The two stood at the window in companionable silence.

"Odd about T.J. being all stirred up like that," the doctor said slowly. "He doesn't stir up easily. Especially over a woman."

The two looked at each other.

"Then again, maybe not," Mae mused. "The sheriff doesn't get a lot of social opportunities here in Almost. Big, strong man like that must miss spending a few pleasant hours with a female."

More silence.

"Of course, if something went wrong with that fancy car, she wouldn't be leaving for a while," the doctor murmured. "They'd have to send for parts from California. Maybe even from the East Coast. Just hypothetically."

"Wouldn't want anything *terrible* to go wrong," Mae said. "Maybe a distributor cap or a fuel line." She stared out into the afternoon sun. "Might take a week to get a replacement part."

The doctor stared at the sheriff's office. "A week should be just about right. For a car problem, that is."

"And for two people to get to know each other." Mae watched little eddies of dirt spin around the spiny branches of an ocotillo cactus. "Our sheriff could use some company in that great big house of his."

"Does your brother still work at the Auto Palace?"

"Uh-huh."

"Seems to me," the doctor mused, "that he might know how to repair a fuel line. Or maybe even how to detach one. Just hypothetically, of course."

"Fuel lines happen to be his specialty." Mae smiled as she picked up the phone. "Just hypothetically, of course."

5

She was there again, amid narrow canyon walls filled with shadow, every rock familiar.

She stood on green ferns, the sun burning her shoulders. The wind carried the scent of silver sage and star flower as she slipped to the ground and drank from the still pool between the rocks, offering murmured thanks to those spirits who guard the precious water.

The sky curved in a vault of blinding turquoise from horizon to horizon, cut only by the glint of wings. Her heart moved, carried aloft like those swift, beating wings.

He would come for her.

She would wait.

She touched the painted figures on the nearby rock. The same patterns covered the fine clay bowls she built before the walls of her father's village. Always she worked with clean strokes, color balancing color, line matching line, lest her pictures bring shadows and disorder to those who looked upon them. Her pots were traded for turquoise and precious parrot feathers from the far south. Her father bargained carefully, swollen with pride at his daughter's work.

But if he knew she waited here for a man, he would drive her from his walls with his own hands and lay his curse on her blood.

Sunlight filtered between the canyon rocks, reflected off the small spring at her feet.

She shivered as a shadow fell across the ravine.

Raven and tortoise.

Swift sun and shining moon.

She whispered the old words for protection, her fingers tracing the stone figure worn knotted on a strip of leather at her neck.

His gift.

Bride token and totem.

Her fingers closed around the polished coyote worked by his own hands. She shivered at the touch, for the coyote is old and very clever, one who can trick as well as assist.

Why did her warrior not come?

She cradled his sun-warmed stone, wishing for his laugh, his hands loosening the feathers from her hair and the painted tunic from her shoulders.

Overhead the sun marched on, crossing rocks and ridge.

He would come as he had promised. Sometime before the rising of the moon he would stand before her, laughing as he drew off his bow.

But he did not come. And the fear grew in her chest like thorns.

Tess woke up feeling woozy.

She eased open one eye and winced at the light. Her throat burned, and she felt shaky when she tried to sit up.

She remembered trying to fold her blasted map, then standing up and—

And passing out cold. There had been a man somewhere nearby at the time. She tilted her head, still groggy, but not so groggy she didn't notice that someone had unbuttoned her shirt down to the lacy edge of her bra. And if that wasn't provocation enough, there was a cowboy with lazy blue eyes who had one callused hand wrapped around her thigh. And one of her stockings was *gone*.

Tess shot upright. "What do you think you're doing?"

"Trying to take off your other stocking."

"Do it and you'll regret it."

The cowboy's eyes narrowed. "I think we've got a communication problem here."

His face was burned dark by the sun. Tess remembered him now. He was the sheriff her brother had said would protect her. Not with his hand on her thigh, he wouldn't.

"Get your hand off me."

A vein pumped at his clenched jaw. "Don't go jumping fences until you get to them, Ma'am."

He had a slow, mellow voice and his eyes were even more startling than Tess remembered. He also looked exactly like a roguish actor whose face regularly appeared on magazine covers around the world.

"You're sure you're not Mel Gibson?"

"I'm sure."

"If you really are the sheriff, then you'd better explain why you had your hand up my skirt."

Something glinted in his eyes. "Doctor's orders."

"Oh, right."

"Too many clothes, he said."

Tess sniffed. She wasn't sure what a sheriff should look like, but it certainly wasn't *this*. She smiled icily as she pointed at his chest. "If you're the sheriff, where's your badge?" Even out here there had to be *some* dress codes.

He stalked across the room, yanked open his desk drawer, and shoved a tarnished, weather-beaten tin star into place on his shirt pocket. "Feel safer now?"

"Not much." Tess tried to sit up, but he held her still.

"Don't try to move. You're in no shape for it."

"I'm fine." She moved restlessly beneath his hand.

"Don't you *ever* relax, woman?"

"Not when I'm talking to a strange man who's had his hand under my skirt."

His lips twitched. "Point taken."

Tess gnawed at her sunburned lip. "Has Andrew phoned you today? My cell phone doesn't work, and I haven't spoken to him since last night."

"We talked about an hour ago. He said he was working on two leads."

So much for her hope that the problem would be solved by now. She started to rise, only to feel the room spin.

T. J. pushed her back onto the cot. "Tell me what you need, and I'll get it."

"What I need are some answers." Tess stared down at her waist, stirred by a sudden memory. "Did you take off my belt?"

"I surely did."

"And you unbuttoned my shirt?" she asked stiffly.

"It's a tough job, but a cowboy never sidesteps his duty."

"Very funny." She pushed away the cloth at her neck. "I want to phone my brother."

T.J. cupped her wrist, checking her pulse. "First you'd better drink some more water."

Tess took a sip from the glass he held to her mouth and then sat up slowly. "Andrew will probably be worrying. For some reason this whole business has him spooked."

"If he's spooked, there's a good reason." He handed her the phone, then turned away and started going through a pile of paperwork.

Tess still felt shaky, but she was getting more clear-headed by the minute and she was certain the arrangement wasn't going to work. Andrew would have to come up with something else.

She reached Andrew's crusty secretary, gave her name, then waited interminably to be put through.

The line clicked. "Thank heavens you called. I was about to send out my own search party."

"I can't imagine why. You had every state trooper between Massachusetts and Arizona watching out for me."

"Just keeping an eye on my baby sister. Since I couldn't go with you myself, my network of spies was the next best thing. I hear you did something to your hair."

"Just a few subtle highlights."

"Not exactly subtle, I'm told. Are you in Almost?"

Tess sighed. "I'm afraid so." Tess frowned at the mountains shimmering in the distance.

"So what do you think of Sheriff McCall?"

She was certain that the man in question was listening to every word she said. "Nice enough, I suppose—if you like that type."

"What type?"

"Oh, you know. Big." Slow. Arrogant. Irritating.

"Don't be fooled by that slow-as-molasses drawl. McCall is a good man, Tess. Otherwise, I wouldn't have sent you there."

Tess didn't want to discuss the sheriff. "What about your investigation? It's been four days now, Andrew. Someone should have reported that money missing."

"I'm working on it, Tess. We need more time."

"How much more time?" She hunched closer to the receiver. "How long am I going to be stuck here?"

"I can't say yet. So far there's nothing concrete."

"Of course there's not. You're letting this get all out of proportion."

"Until I verify the source of that million dollars, you aren't going anywhere. It's simply not safe."

"The deposit's probably from Richard's account. He can afford to give me that kind of bonus—or maybe he made a simple accounting error," she finished weakly with the feeling that she was grasping at straws.

"I need to be sure. So far I haven't been able to reach him, and his accountants won't release any financial information without his approval."

"You can forget about that. He just bought an island in French Polynesia and he'll be out of reach there for at least two weeks." Her voice fell. "Look, I can't stay here, Andrew. I haven't seen a single *Wall Street Journal* since I left St. Louis and I'm having serious news withdrawal. The last thing I want to do is stay boxed up in some dusty little town at the back of beyond."

"It's for your own good, Tess. When that money is traced and the coast is clear, you'll be the first to know. Until then, the subject is closed."

"No, I'm leaving tomorrow. Once I get to L.A. you can—"

Without warning the phone was tugged from her fingers.

"This is McCall. No, she's not going anywhere. Don't worry, I'll keep an eye on her. Yeah, I'll stay in touch." The sheriff put down the phone, his eyes glinting.

Tess scowled at him. "I wasn't finished talking to my brother."

"Too bad," he drawled. "The county budget is already stretched to a thread. We can't afford to pick up the tab for long-distance chatter."

"Chatter?" she snapped. "This is my *life* we're talking about."

"All the more reason to listen to your brother. Now, stop fuming and drink some more water. You're getting pale again."

Tess did neither. She stared out the window, where mountains rose like smoke against the green horizon. Maybe the landscape did have its own rugged beauty and maybe the light did fascinate her as it shimmered over the stark mountains. But Almost was still the back of beyond, and if she didn't find a real newspaper soon, she was going to lose her mind. After all, she had her career to consider. She had products to promote and a preliminary retail plan for the chocolate account to finish. How would she find market information in this isolated spot?

Absorbed in her problem, Tess pushed to her feet. Instantly, the floor seemed to pitch. She took a sharp breath and clutched at the wall, dimly aware of T.J.'s hands at her shoulders.

"I told you to sit down and rest."

"I don't want to sit down, and I'm not going to rest."

"I'll give you until the count of three." His voice was as dry as the wind hissing down off the mountains. "After that, I'm going to pick you up and toss you down onto that cot, whether you like it or not."

For one blazing moment, Tess resolved to face him down. She didn't have to take orders from a dusty, drawling stranger. "Forget it, Sheriff."

"Fine." McCall strode to the door and grabbed his hat from its peg. "Go on and work yourself into another stint of unconsciousness. You might have noticed that this is a small town with only one doctor, who is already doing the work of four men. Bringing him here will mean he can't see someone who's *really* sick, like young Jeremy up at the Bar D, who's recovering from pneumonia. Or the Winkler boy, who just had a bone marrow transplant and needs to be visited three times a week. But don't let any of that bother you, Ma'am. It's not your problem, after all."

Tess stood frozen. Heat filled her cheeks as she was struck by a wave of self-recrimination. "That was low," she spat out. "That was a truly low and unworthy thing to say."

T.J. shoved his hat down on his head. "The world is a low and unworthy place, I guess."

"I've been wondering exactly why I dislike you, Mr. McCall. It could be because you think you know what's best for everyone." Tess's chin jutted out. "Or maybe because you like snapping out orders to anyone close enough to listen."

T.J. glared at her, trying to keep control of his shredding temper.

The woman had the temperament of a Gila monster.

Once she got her teeth into a subject, you couldn't pry her free with a stick. "Let's get one thing straight here." He tilted back his head. "As a favor to your brother, I've agreed to keep an eye on you. The fact is, there are a few hundred things I'd rather do—like pull a hungry rattler out of its hole bare-handed."

"What a charming thought," Tess said icily. "Don't let me keep you."

"I'm not done yet. The people of Almost have their problems, but you're here as my guest. That means they'll take care of you and stand by you, but they don't need your whining or complaining when they've got problems enough of their own."

Tess's eyes flashed. "I never asked for—"

"And another thing: while you're here, you'll do what I say—not because you like it or because I enjoy giving orders, but because it's the *right* thing to do." He straightened his shoulders. "If you've got a problem with that, you'd better get your brother on the phone and tell him to send someone to chaperone you back to Boston because I haven't got time for bad-tempered heifers with more bellow than sense. Is that clear enough, Ma'am?"

If fury could have knocked a man down, he would have been prostrate. Tess stood rooted to the spot, frozen in anger. She opened her mouth, intent on telling him exactly what she thought of his loutish behavior, his arrogance, and his lamentable little town.

Then Tess looked outside and noticed a white-haired man crossing the street. He moved slowly in the shimmering afternoon heat, looking tired and favoring his left leg. He stopped twice to speak to women with children, then stood for a moment in the shade of the General Mercantile, rubbing his neck, black bag in hand.

The doctor, Tess realized.

And he looked every bit as tired as T.J. had described.

"Look, I'm sorry your town is small and I'm sorry about the doctor being overworked, but I can't stay here."

T.J. crossed his arms, staring at her. "Your brother thinks differently."

"He's being paranoid about this."

"Funny, he seemed perfectly sane when I knew him."

"This is different. I'm his little sister, and he's letting his imagination work overtime. This Y2K business has him all stirred up. Now he's seeing bogeymen behind every ATM machine."

"If he's worried, maybe you should be, too," T.J. said gravely. He slid on a pair of mirrored sunglasses.

"I'm still alive. Nothing bad has happened to me." She gave a sigh and eased a shoulder against the wall for support. "The worst thing facing me now is mental collapse from information withdrawal."

T.J. didn't move. "Information can be misleading."

"You have something against newspapers, Sheriff?"

"On occasion, yes."

Tess wished she could have read his eyes behind his mirrored glasses, but there was no sign of emotion in that tanned face.

She felt a burst of irritation. Maybe he had to stay in this forsaken outpost, but *she* certainly didn't. "Where I come from, newspapers spell civilization. That means a city, a place with more than three stores and four streets. I like civilization. I can get coffee whenever I want it and newspapers that run to more than four pages. I also like to be able to change channels on the radio and hear songs that don't have 'cheatin' or 'achy-breaky' in the first verse. Is that clear enough?'' she said acidly.

"Crystal clear.'' T.J. rocked back on his heels, his jaw hard. "You're a spoiled, pampered snob.''

"That does it.'' She turned toward the door, only to feel his hand close around her arm.

"You're going to stay put until your brother says the heat is off. Is *that* clear enough, City Girl?''

Tess wanted to scream. But first she wanted to plant a fist right in the middle of his face. "You insufferable, arrogant—*cowboy.*''

"That word's fine with me. I come from a long line of cowboys and down here it's a term of real respect.'' He tilted his hat slightly. "Now, as a cowboy *and* a sheriff, I'm giving you some orders. First, you'll stop fuming and rest. You'll also drink two more glasses of water. When I get back, I'll have made arrangements for where you'll stay.''

"I can hardly wait,'' Tess muttered.

"I've got work to do. Anything you need while I'm out?'' he asked dryly.

Had the man heard nothing she'd said? "Several back issues of the *Wall Street Journal* would be nice. Maybe a mochaccino latte with a double shot of espresso and some walnut biscotti.''

"The café's fresh out of biscotti.'' He drawled the last word out into three syllables, sparking her anger all over again. "How about homemade peanut butter bars with milk?''

Tess felt tears pressing behind her eyes, fueled by the headache that was driving nails into her forehead. She didn't like snapping at him but she couldn't seem to help it. "I believe I'll pass on the delicacies, thank you.''

"Your choice.'' His boots scuffed over the floor.

Tess ignored a wave of pain as she stalked to the cot. "Where is my handbag?"

"Out in the car, where you left it."

"You didn't bring it inside?"

"It will be fine," he said calmly.

"How do you know that? All my identification and credit cards are inside." Tess tried to control her panic. "Of course by now my wallet's probably been picked clean. Was the car locked?"

T.J. shrugged. "Didn't check."

"You didn't *check*? Oh, that's just perfect. Everything will be gone—my purse, my books, my clothes." She rubbed a knot at her neck. "My new coffeemaker," she whispered.

"Everything's there. Your tires needed filling, so someone took care of that for you."

"What?"

"The car was dirty, too, so someone washed it. After that a mechanic was going to go over your engine."

Tess went very still. "I don't believe it. Why would they do all that?"

"Because people take care of people here."

"Not me," Tess said stiffly. "I'm a stranger."

"Makes no difference."

"But I didn't ask them to—"

"Makes no difference," McCall repeated. "If a thing needs to be done, someone will do it. That's the way it is here." The phone rang. As he listened, McCall's face tightened with strain. He hung up, then went to a metal locker and drew out a long canvas duffel bag.

"Was that Andrew?"

"No," he said tightly. "It was for me." He slung the heavy bag over his shoulder.

   Tess felt an odd pressure at her chest. "I thought you said the world was a low and unworthy place, Sheriff."
   "Some parts of it are. Almost isn't one."
   Then he quietly closed the door behind him.

■

Tess finally did fall asleep, wrapped in her suede coat. Her dreams were filled with color and dust and voices that made no sense. She wasn't feeling notably refreshed when she woke an hour later.
   The room was empty. Almost's irritating sheriff was nowhere in sight.
   Tess sighed. She would have to apologize for some of the things she'd said to him, but the town *was* small, its choices painfully limited. It was also true that if Tess didn't get her hands on a major newspaper soon, she would become completely unhinged.
   A man with graying hair peered from the neighboring room as Tess stood up. "I'm Deputy Grady. Need any help?"
   Tess made a vain attempt to smooth down her hair. Her shirt was full of wrinkles, and she probably looked like the bride of Frankenstein. "I'm fine, I think. At least I'm better than I was a few hours ago." Delicious smells wafted from the table beside the door. Her stomach gave an audible growl as she made her way closer. "Food," she whispered reverently.
   "Mae figured you missed lunch so she brought a bite over from the café. Fresh biscuits and homemade gravy. After that, you've got your choice of fried chicken or cowboy chili." Grady rubbed his jaw. "You might want to go careful with the chili. Mae makes it mighty hot."
   Tess barely heard him over the growl of her stomach.

"It sounds wonderful." She found a plastic bowl and took a biscuit that was light as air. "Is the sheriff here?"

"He had to go up north. Official business."

"I hope it wasn't anything too bad."

Grady's eyes hardened. "Reckon it was. Hostage situation in a bank. Five people involved."

"Is the sheriff a negotiator?"

Grady seemed to find bleak humor in the question. "He doesn't negotiate. He's a trained marksman. If it looks like negotiation isn't going to work, that's when they call in T.J."

As Tess stared down at the biscuit, her appetite vanished. The cold reality of a law officer's job hit her, tying her stomach in knots. How did you prepare for trauma and death on a second's notice? And how did you forget the job later?

Grady's keen eyes probed her face. "Don't go fretting over T.J. The man's used to dealing with whatever comes up. Just you dig into that food. Mae will have my hide if you don't eat a healthy amount." He rubbed his jaw slowly. "So will T.J., come to think of it."

"Has he worked here long?"

"Five, six years, maybe. When I came along, he was already a legend. There's not an inch of this county he doesn't know firsthand or a person in town he can't call by his first name. He's done a good job for Almost, and everyone here knows it. He could get twice as much money up in Phoenix or Albuquerque, but he won't leave. He's a good man, Ma'am."

Tess felt the challenge in Grady's voice. "I'm not disagreeing with you."

His eyes narrowed. "Aren't you?"

Maybe she did resent T. J. McCall. Maybe she did suspect he was lacking in finesse. It wasn't her place to criticize the job he did here. But *staying* was something else.

"I'm not staying here." Tess paced angrily. "Not a *day* longer than I have to."

"You in some sort of danger?" Grady asked. "Must be, for the sheriff to act the way he did."

Tess shrugged, wary of saying too much to anyone, even this deputy. "Not exactly danger. I just don't want to be seen for a few days."

Grady studied her thoughtfully. "Man trouble?"

Tess started to deny it, then stopped. Why not? "Something like that. I was involved with someone. Then he started doing strange things like going out for a newspaper at three in the morning and meeting men in sunglasses on lonely street corners. One day he cleaned out the assets of his bank account and vanished for a vacation to the Caymans." Tess tapped her jaw, getting into the flow of her lie. "The police caught him at the airport as he was boarding the flight. He had several million dollars in crisp new U.S. currency wedged inside a hidden money belt."

"You don't say." Grady frowned. "That surely would make a fine news story."

Tess bent closer. "You can't mention any of this. There's a government investigation in progress, and indictments will be handed out. Political careers could be made and broken on this case."

Grady gave a low whistle. "That must be why the sheriff didn't mention any details. It's not like T.J. to be so secretive." His eyes narrowed. "You don't suppose that man will be following you here."

Tess gave a shrug. "Not unless he's invisible. I was pretty careful on the drive here."

Grady padded across the room for a drink of water

from the battered cooler. "So you and this Don Corleone fellow were close, were you?" Grady appeared to store the information away for future use. "Well, you're in good hands now. No one alive can protect you better than Sheriff Jackson McCall. Have some water."

Tess sipped from the paper cup, watching the mountains turn pink above the horizon in the late afternoon light. "When did the sheriff say he would be back?"

"No telling how long the situation will last. Have some more water. T.J. will skin me alive if you don't have some color when he gets back."

"I should check into my hotel." Tess dug in her pocket and consulted a sheet of paper. "The place I'm looking for is named Desert Vista."

"You can't stay there," Grady said flatly.

"Why not?"

"Because the Desert Vista burned down a month ago." Grady pointed through the window to a blackened pile of charred wood at the far end of Main Street.

Tess drummed her fingernails on T.J.'s metal desk. She couldn't bear to languish here, no matter what the irritating sheriff had ordered. She needed work, responsibility, newspapers. She also wanted to find out more about this odd town.

"Have you ever had a double mochaccino latte?"

"No, Ma'am, can't say that I have." Grady scratched his head. "I've seen them on TV though. I've heard all about that fancy coffee store called Starbreaks."

"Nothing better than Starbreaks," Tess said gravely. "Let's go for a walk, Grady. After that, we'll take my new cappuccino machine out for a test run."

6

Their first stop was Mae's café. The decor was pure 1950s, with spotless linoleum counters and rustic carved pine chairs. Deer and moose heads grimaced from polished wood walls that were tended with loving care by the sixty-something owner wearing a pristine white apron and solid brown hunting boots.

Mae patted her silver-white hair and studied Tess from head to foot before nodding in approval. "Sure do like that hair of yours. If I was even ten years younger, I'd try it myself. You showing our visitor around town, Grady?"

"Sure am, Mae. She wants to see everything."

"That should take about ten minutes." Mae squinted down the street. "Any idea where the sheriff went to in such a hurry?"

Grady rubbed his jaw. "Hostage situation up in Brinkley."

Mae sighed. "Well, you tell McCall to drop by the café when he gets back, no matter what time it is. I'll still be in the kitchen, laying in some pies. We just got in a shipment of peaches."

"I think I ran over a few this morning," Tess said guiltily.

"Not a problem," the older woman said, taking

Tess's arm. "Now, why don't you two have a seat here by the window and I'll see you get something to eat." She beckoned to a waitress with a sunburn and a big smile. "Sallyanne, bring the usual for Grady and a number two for our guest."

"Coming right up, Ma'am."

Mae slid into a chair beside Tess and poured three tall glasses of iced tea. "Wish we could offer the sheriff more than we do." She wiped her hands on her apron and dumped a hefty amount of sugar into her tea. "McCall hasn't had a raise in four years. The budget won't allow it. Darned shame, too." Mae patted Tess's arm. "So, Ms. O'Mara, what line of business are you in?"

"I'm in public relations."

Mae frowned. "I always wondered what that meant."

"I bring products to the public's attention using print medium, television, and special events." Tess stared in awe as the athletic waitress placed two plates filled with coleslaw and steaming fresh bread on the table.

"Rest of the food will take a while. We always cook to order here. None of that heating up. Grady, have yourself some more tea. You, too, Ms. O'Mara."

"Call me Tess, please."

"I'll be glad to. Only you're not one of those calorie counters, are you?"

"I doubt that anyone could count calories around your food. It's far too much temptation."

"I like this girl, Grady." Mae motioned to a waitress, who brought a huge portion of pork tenderloin with baked potatoes and a corn and red onion relish for Tess and a large bowl of chili for Grady.

"So you know about handling new products, do you?"

"It's one of the main things I do." Tess sighed as she bit into the relish. "Did you have something in particular you're working on?"

Mae moved her iced tea glass around on the table. "The fact is, I've been thinking about offering a line of chile products from my ranch." She grinned wickedly. "The hotter the better. That relish is my own recipe, in fact. You think maybe you could give me some advice on how I should start?" Mae frowned. "I'd pay you for your time, of course."

At this point, Tess would have paid Mae for something creative to relieve her boredom. "Let's don't worry about a fee. I'll find chiles a challenge, since I've never handled them before. The specialized food industry is one of the fastest-growing areas today. I'd have to do some targeted research and check out the brand penetration."

Mae grinned. "Sounds like that may be illegal."

A half hour later, after Tess had eaten as much of the delicious tenderloin and relish as she could manage, the waitress brought slices of cobbler. Mae dished a scoop of pale green ice cream onto Grady's cobbler, then gave one to Tess. "Try that and tell me what you think."

Tess took a taste, puzzling over the mix of flavors. "It's hard to say. There's pistachio and a hint of citrus." She pursed her lips and tasted a burst of intense spice. "What was *that*?"

"Pistachio jalapeño ice cream," Mae said proudly. "I make it myself. I've got salsa and barbecue products, too. Each of them comes in four different levels of heat. Grady here can take up to level two. The sheriff enjoys level three. Only Miguel can handle number four."

"Miguel?"

"Oh, you'll meet Miguel. Everyone does sooner or

later.'' Mae drummed her fingers on the spotless table-top. ''Think maybe you can help me design a label and make a catalogue?''

The more Tess tasted the ice cream, the more excited she became. ''I'd be happy to try. I don't know anything about chiles, but this ice cream of yours is wonderful. A sophisticated mix of sweetness and spices.'' Already Tess could think of a dozen restaurants that would give it a trial run.

Probably a few high-end resorts, too.

''Is that a fact? Well now, we'll definitely have to talk, my dear. Meanwhile, I won't keep you from your walk. Enjoy Almost.'' Mae smiled. ''Most of us do.'' As Tess got up, she touched her arm. ''By the way, are you married?''

''Er—no.''

''Are you close to getting married?''

Tess felt heat climb into her face. ''Not that I know of.''

Mae clucked her tongue. ''A pretty thing like you. Makes a body wonder about men today. T.J. isn't married either, you know.''

''How absolutely . . . fascinating,'' Tess murmured.

''Isn't it just. Well, you two better get going now. Don't forget to tell the sheriff what I said.''

■

Twenty minutes later, they had covered most of downtown Almost. Tess and Grady visited the feed store, the library, and the cluttered newspaper office. Everyone asked Tess if she was married, and everyone managed to inform her that T.J. was definitely unattached. When

Grady mentioned that Tess would be visiting for a few days, each person had offered her a place to stay in a tone of sincere welcome.

Tess realized T.J. was absolutely right. People did take care of each other here in Almost.

The walk had given Tess a dozen ideas for names for Mae's food products and the outline of an adventurous campaign to introduce her chile line via the Internet. From there, she could add specialty food stores and a few key restaurants. Tess had also been enlisted to judge a third-grade art competition and talk about women in business at an upcoming 4-H dinner.

When the mayor refused to hear of waiving payment, Tess graciously agreed on ten dollars per event.

Tess chuckled, wondering what Richard would say about that.

She was hot and happy, already sorting through plans for an auction to benefit the clinic that Almost desperately needed. Tess was fairly certain she could find a national magazine that would cover the story as a human interest piece. Then she could barter free medical equipment for the town because of the publicity.

She took Grady's arm, smiling broadly. "What do you say we go have some coffee, Deputy?"

■

Forty miles away, T.J. crawled across the roof in the shadow of the Dragoon mountains. He was careful to stay in the shade until he reached the edge of the balcony. He straightened his throat mike and activated his tactical headset. "Drake, are you there?"

"Right here. We have you in sight, McCall."

"You have someone covering the back?"

"Negative. The other teams were tied up on a major cost drug bust in Nogales. I'm afraid you're all we have, McCall."

T.J. breathed a silent curse. He was sweating beneath his black jumpsuit and tactical vest. It was hot on the roof, and he couldn't move once he was in position. His hands were starting to cramp, but he didn't allow that or any thought to disturb his concentration. He looked into the scope and framed the front window of the bank directly across the street. "Any activity inside?"

"The gunman just told us he wants to talk to the governor. We're trying to arrange it. He also wants a million dollars and a plane to Brazil."

T.J. sighted carefully.

The man had four hostages tied in chairs by the bank's front window. One other hostage was standing by the front desk. The perpetrator was holding a pistol to her head.

"He's picketed the bank for a month, swearing their computers are cheating people out of their money. He claims he lost twenty thousand dollars last month, but we checked and he's never had an account here."

"Any priors?" T.J. watched the gunman move restlessly before the window while he talked on the radio with the police.

"Assault and battery on his wife. He did three months of probation, then tried it again. The next day she left for Alaska."

"Emotional state?"

"Unclear. His landlady said he made four trips to Mexico in the last week, possibly for drugs."

"How are the hostages holding up?"

"As well as can be expected." Drake cursed softly. "One of them is my sister."

T.J.'s fingers tightened on the rifle. "Which one?"

"That's not a factor here, McCall."

T.J. knew what Drake was saying. His friend didn't expect special treatment for his relative. In fact, he wouldn't tolerate it. T.J. said one short, angry word. "Get those front windows open. I'll have only one shot, and I don't want to worry about glass deflection."

"He's not going to like it. Maybe we can turn off the exterior air-conditioning. It's going to be risky, though. It's your call."

T.J. knew the risks. The added stress might trigger the gunman, sending him on a rampage. But there was no other way to guarantee a clean shot if the situation deteriorated. "Do it."

Ten minutes later, the windows were open. T.J. adjusted his scope, measuring for wind and range. He had trained at two hundred yards, so the distance was good. It was the gunman's state of mind he was worried about now. He couldn't allow himself to think about Drake's sister being caught inside.

He looked through the scope and framed the front windows. He saw the man turn sharply and gesture, then throw something down on the floor. He shouted as he grabbed one of the women and jabbed his revolver under her neck. "Drake, are you seeing this?"

"Affirmative." Static crackled, then Drake's voice returned. "You are clear to fire," he said grimly. "Repeat, clear to fire."

T.J. tracked the man, waiting until the hostage was out of his line of fire. He focused, lining up for one shot in the back of the head, which would guarantee a clean takedown.

The gunman gestured wildly, slapping the woman and sending her to her knees.

T.J. squeezed out one shot.

■

T.J. slanted his forehead against the steering wheel as wind whipped through his open window.

The desert around him was silent. Only the wind whispered, stirring up sand and shaking the dry branches of ocotillo and smoky blue palobrea. The silence of the high desert could be unnerving to those unused to its secrets, but T.J. had always found pleasure in the silence. And he did so now.

Breathing.

Trying to block out images of shattered glass and a fallen body.

He stared down at two hundred miles of snaking canyons red in the fire of sunset. And he breathed. Letting the bright colors and the hot wind heal him, as they always did.

With each breath he restored another piece of his harmony. Violent death was part of the profession he had chosen, and T.J. was in no sense a cowardly man. He accepted the fact of death, even when the personal resonance of those deaths shook him awake at night, sweaty and shaking.

Grady said caring made him a better police officer.

T.J. hoped it was true.

By the time he pulled into Almost forty-five minutes later, the sun hung crimson above the horizon. The windows of the General Mercantile glowed hot and red with the sun's reflection. The distant mountains were hazed with pink. Next would come purple, gathering into the long velvet shadows of twilight, his favorite time of day. Already the moon hung low, a pale sickle in the darkening turquoise sky.

By sheer habit, T.J. swept his gaze along the street, looking for anything out of the ordinary that would require his professional attention. Three children were laughing, walking hand-in-hand as they crossed to the library. A truck was parked outside Mae's café, and Mae's nephew was unloading sacks of cornmeal. T.J. saw Grady's truck parked beside the bank. Near the heart of town, at least a dozen people were milling around outside Almost's historic jail, now a tourist attraction and museum.

T.J. stiffened. What in holy thunder was going on?

Music drifted through the Blazer's open window as T.J. pulled up beside Grady's truck. The high school principal waved to him as she drank from a white Styrofoam cup. Beside her, Doc Felton stood drinking from a similar cup.

As T.J. strode from the car, the music grew louder, its beat sharp and hot, flooded with a brooding bass. Fusion Spanish, he thought. Definitely *not* Grady's kind of music.

The door of the historic jail swung open again. People spilled outside in a wave of laughter. T.J. recognized two women from meetings of the town zoning committee. Three others were the wives of ranchers to the north, all with pre-school-age children.

"Evening, Sheriff," one called gaily. "Mighty nice sunset, isn't it?" T.J. noticed that she had a white cup, too.

He tipped his hat back in answer and managed a smile.

Where was Tess?

Where was Grady?

His grizzled friend emerged a moment later, balancing a tray with a dozen more neat white cups. "Anyone care for refills? Remember, drinks are on the house."

His words produced the nearest thing T.J. had ever seen to a human stampede. Whatever was in those cups had to be pretty amazing. T.J. hoped it wasn't a controlled substance.

He was striding toward Grady when Doc Felton cut in front of him and slapped him on the back. "This was a damned good idea you had, T.J."

"What idea?"

"We should do this more often. That young woman is right."

"Do *what*?"

"Socialize. Laugh. Present our complaints. It improves communication. As a man of medicine, I might even speculate that it lowers blood pressure and reduces systemic stress." The doctor thrust something into his hand. "Have a cup."

T.J. looked down.

Not a controlled substance, but the creamy brew in the cup didn't smell like Mae's usual concoction, which was generally strong enough to bend metal. Her late-night specialty at the café wasn't called the Yuri Geller Surprise for nothing.

He lowered his head and took a suspicious sniff. "Is this Mae's coffee?"

The doctor laughed. "Miss O'Mara made it. I believe you're holding a double latte. *Skoal*." He raised his own glass.

T.J. toasted back, took a sip. Definitely not Mae's coffee.

His eyes focused on Grady. "Can I see you for a minute?"

"In a second, Sheriff. Right now I've got to—"

"*Now.*" T.J. caught Grady's arm and pulled him away from the others. "Where's Tess?" he hissed.

"She was here a few minutes ago."

"Amazing as it may seem, that's not a hell of a lot of help." T.J. took another drink of coffee, his gaze sweeping the crowd. "What's going on here?"

"Nothing much. Tess and I took a walk around town. Then some of the boys from the Lazy Y came in, and the high school principal just happened to drop by when the coffee was nearly done."

"Just happened to drop by?"

"That's right. After that Mae's brother showed up. You know Bob. He works at the Auto Palace."

"I know Bob," T.J. said grimly. "What I want to know is where Tess has gone to."

"There was something wrong with her car. Doc Felton said it might need a new fuel line, so she went out to get something from the trunk. After that she was going to make a call from your office."

T.J. strode toward Tess's car. "You'd better pray she's there."

■

She wasn't at her car.

She wasn't browsing through the Wild West memorabilia in the visitors' room behind the old jail, nor was she admiring the views of the foothills from the garden behind the courthouse.

Where in heaven's name *was* the aggravating female?

T.J. strode into his office. Empty. She wasn't on the cot and she wasn't at his desk making calls.

Fear locked down hard. "Tess?"

He sprinted across the room and threw open the door to his private office, only to find it empty. "Dammit, where are you?"

Something rustled in the bathroom. The door was slightly ajar, and he pulled his Smith & Wesson from his holster. Silently, he inched toward the door, keeping his shoulder to the outside and his right arm free for a clear shot.

Focus.

Breathe.

He balanced on the balls of his feet, leveled his gun, hit the door in one smooth motion. "Police. Don't move," he growled.

The door snapped open.

Tess stared back at him, white-faced. She had a scrap of lace clutched to her chest and a skimpy pair of electric-blue underwear that clung like a dream to her backside.

And she wasn't wearing a hint of anything else.

7

Gut wrenched.

That was how T.J. felt as he took in Tess's mile-long legs. His head tilted slowly as he lingered over the sight of her slender waist and the thrust of high, full breasts.

Desire plugged him dead center at his chest.

He was an officer of the law, dammit. He was a friend of her brother's and he'd given his promise to protect her.

But he was a man first.

T.J. doubted any man this side of death could have looked away from the woman before him. His hand was still outstretched, gun level. It took an immense force of will to drag in a breath, force his hand back down to his side, and slide his gun into its holster.

"What was that for?" Tess asked hoarsely.

"I couldn't find you. I was worried." T.J. tried to ignore the filmy strip of lace stretched across her breasts. He wondered what would happen if that lace happened to slide down an inch or two.

Get a grip, McCall.

But he didn't turn away, and he couldn't stop wondering.

Gut wrenched and no mistake.

"I'm trying to dress here. I'd appreciate it if you

would leave," Tess said, two angry spots of color in her face.

"Sorry." He cleared his throat. "That is, I didn't mean—" T.J shook his head, fighting for sanity. He took a step backward a split second before the door slammed in his face.

Very smooth, McCall. Point a gun on her, why don't you?

He took a harsh breath. "You okay in there?"

He heard the sound of running water, followed by the rustle of clothing. "Oh, I'm just wonderful. I happen to love it when men bang open the door while I'm half-naked and stick a revolver in my face."

"It was a Smith and Wesson double-action automatic. No one in law enforcement uses revolvers anymore. Can't get enough rounds off fast enough for safety. They also have a dangerous tendency to jam."

"Oh, do forgive me. That makes this all *entirely* different." The door jerked open. Tess charged out, hands on her hips, fully dressed now.

Dear sweet heaven, how she was dressed. Her clingy little dress nudged the middle of her thighs and outlined every curve. At the moment it was definitely burning a path into his neural network. "Nice dress," he drawled.

"Forget the dress." Something whipped him across the face and drifted onto his shoulder. Blinking, he looked down and saw it was the lace she had been holding against her chest.

A garter belt. A white lace garter belt with tiny pink roses.

T.J. tried hard to swallow as the lace slid through his fingers. "I think," he said slowly, "that this is going to look a whole lot better on you than on me."

Her breath came out in a strangled puff of anger.

"This is *not* funny. What just happened was not funny. Not by any stretch of the imagination. You could have *shot* me."

T.J. shoved back his hat. "You might want to hold it right there. I'm a trained law officer with fifteen years of experience. Contrary to what you see on TV, we *don't* shoot first and ask questions later."

"You could have fooled me." Her eyes glittered. "I've seen baboons with more self-control."

"You'll want to consider your next words very carefully," T.J. said softly. "You can attack me, but not my work."

"You almost gave me a heart attack."

"Sorry."

"Sorry? And that makes everything okay?" Her face was pasty white and her hands were shaking hard. Delayed reaction, T.J. figured.

"I had my reasons," he said quietly. He had a sudden vision of Tess crumpled in a sandy wash, one arm thrown back at an unnatural angle and blood trickling down her forehead—all too possible, if her brother's concerns were accurate. And as long as T.J. had known Andrew O'Mara, the man's instincts had been unerring.

"I didn't open that door to harass or annoy you. I acted because there was a real possibility you were in danger. Grady had no business letting you out of his sight. It won't happen again, believe me," he snapped.

"What does *that* mean?"

"From now on, Grady, I, or one of the other deputies will have you in direct view at all times." He cut her off as she started to protest. "That's nonnegotiable."

"You can't—"

"I can. Your brother asked for my help and he got it. He's not going to be sorry." Dimly, T.J. realized his breath was coming hard and fast. "When these people come calling for their money—"

"—*if* they come calling," Tess snapped.

"*When* they come calling, they'll hit fast. They won't take time out for please and thank you. They also won't be overly concerned about who gets caught in the cross fire."

He wanted to see her suffer, just a little, for refusing to recognize the danger she was in. Only a fool ignored risks, and he didn't think she was a fool. He wanted to see her face go pale at his words.

Another man might have shrugged it off, only too glad to tell her that there was no real danger, and everything would be fine because they were the good guys and the good guys always won.

But T.J. wouldn't stoop to that.

He'd seen the good guys lose too many times to lie. He'd watched fine, decent officers cut down in the line of duty while the public turned a cold, uncaring eye. He'd seen criminals wave confidently, boarding planes to South America or the Middle East, where they could live like royalty beyond the reach of American law.

No, the good guys didn't always win. This wasn't some shoot-'em-up John Ford western, and the cavalry wouldn't be riding in at dawn. He was as close to cavalry as Tess was going to get.

But now, watching fear and uncertainty etch her cheeks and forehead, he felt an odd kind of pressure in his chest, compounded by a wave of protectiveness. "Look, maybe I was too hard on you."

She didn't move, her shoulders stiff. "No, you weren't." She gave a little shudder. "You were just doing your job, and I have to say that you are good at it. I see why Andrew said you were the best." She drew a jerky breath. "It's not your fault this happened. It's not your fault that one day I go out for a little cash and *boom*, suddenly I've got a million dollars in my bank account and my name posted on some master criminal's hit list. It's a little hard to take, that's all."

She was too pale, T.J. thought. Too edgy. "Maybe I should get you some water."

She didn't answer.

"Maybe I should get something stronger. I've got some single malt whisky in my desk. We could both do with a drink right now."

"Aren't you on duty?"

He glanced at the utilitarian wall clock. "Only for ten more minutes. You can get started while I finish out my shift."

"I hate it when you're nice. It makes me feel rotten." Tess ran a hand through her hair. "You probably think I'm acting like a horse's behind."

"I may have noticed a slight similarity on several occasions." His lips twitched.

Tess stared out at the street. "I don't know what's going to happen. I feel helpless and I don't like having my life jerked out from under me."

"Perfectly understandable."

"I don't want anyone to get hurt because of me."

"Why don't you let me worry about that?"

She studied him intently. "You do worry, don't you? I didn't see that about you at first."

T.J. rubbed his neck as a wave of exhaustion hit him. His shift was nearly over and he was anxious to get home. The last thing he wanted was a personal discussion about his emotional state, which wasn't in peak form after watching a man crumple under the force of his bullet. Criminal or not, every memory had a name.

"Look, why don't you gather up your things? Tom Martinez should be here any minute and then I'll get you settled up at Rancho Encantador. I've arranged for you to stay there for a few days."

"Maybe you should eat before we go."

"I'll be fine."

"Mae left you some chili in a thermos. A whole dinner, in fact. Let me get it for you."

"Don't bother about me."

Twilight was gathering in a veil of pink that edged into purple. The sky was deep lapis and the air was sweet and silent. In the half light, there were lines in T.J.'s face Tess hadn't seen before, and an air of weariness had settled about him.

Whatever he had witnessed that afternoon had to be bad. The least she could do was see he ate a proper meal before he left. Dimly, Tess realized it was her way of calling a truce.

Without a word, she turned and scooped chili into a bowl while T.J. stood with one foot braced on a box, staring out at the darkening mountains. Tess saw weariness in the hard set of his shoulders and resignation in his face.

She didn't like the sight of either.

She shoved the warm bowl into his hand. "Don't bother arguing. You've got to be ravenous, and there's no need to let Mae's amazing chili go to waste."

"Why do you care?"

The look he gave her was intent and measuring. Tess felt it roam over her skin and dig deeper. Suddenly her throat felt tight and achy. The room seemed too quiet, too small.

She didn't answer, uncertain herself of why she cared. In the awkward silence she covered one of Mae's

feather-light biscuits with butter, added some mashed potatoes and gravy, and shoved a second plate into the sheriff's hands.

His lips eased into a grin. "I'm getting a little loaded
up here."

"There's dessert, too. And the latte will be ready
shortly."

"Don't you ever relax?"

Tess measured out water for coffee. "I'm good at
hovering, not relaxing." She frowned. "They all like
you. Grady says you cast a long shadow."

T.J. made a noncommittal sound.

The silence felt intimate, making Tess more uneasy
than ever. "Maybe I shouldn't have told you. I didn't
mean—" She shoved another biscuit toward him. In the
process her high heel dug into his boot.

T.J. winced, but managed to hold his plates steady.

"Sorry. That was clumsy. I don't usually . . ." Her
voice trailed away as she stared up at his face, cast in
purple shadows. He had the most compelling eyes. And
there was a scar just above his eyebrow.

She stiffened. He was too close and too big. She
didn't want to be here alone with him, standing in this
beautiful, quiet twilight.

"There's no need to fuss."

"I'm *not* fussing." Tess blew out an irritated sigh.
"Maybe I am. I never have been much good at relaxing." Standing this close to him didn't help.

"There's nothing to it. All you do is find a soft chair,
kick off your boots, and let your mind drift. I'll have to
give you some lessons."

Tess looked up. "Lessons?" And then her heart
kicked.

His face was anything but relaxed. He was watching

her like a man who had all the time in the world. He was patient and implacable like the weathered boulders keeping silent watch over the endless red canyons.

Serve and protect, she thought.

The man could have been on a poster.

Like those rocks, T. J. McCall would be patient and abiding. Relentless in what he considered the performance of his duty.

"Isn't that chili too hot? I took a taste at Mae's and thought it burned the skin from my mouth."

"Nothing's too hot for me."

Tess swallowed. She absolutely wasn't going to read any double meaning into his words.

He finished his chili, his eyes never leaving her face. "By the way, Grady liked your garter belt."

Heat swooped into her face. "How did *he* find it?"

He came in while you were dressing. "It was over there, wedged behind a file."

"I looked all over. It must have landed there after I—"

"After you whipped me in the face with it?" he asked gravely.

Tess straightened her shoulders. "I simply tossed it."

"I've still got the marks on my cheek, Duchess. Those little hooks pack quite a wallop."

Tess made a strangled sound as a ball of white lace flew toward her. She caught it and stuffed it awkwardly in her pocket. How had they gotten into this conversation?

T.J.'s eyebrow rose. "If you're planning to take anything else off, just let me know."

There it was again, that damnable heat that shot up

her spine and burned across her face. "Don't worry, I *won't* be."

T.J. slanted his head back. Shadows brushed his jaw. "Might be downright interesting if you did."

"You've already seen—" She stopped with a strangled oath. There was no need to remind him what he'd seen when he'd burst into the bathroom with his gun leveled.

"That latte must be finished by now," she said stiffly. "I'll fill your cup."

T.J. slid his plate onto the nearby cabinet. Up close, Tess saw the telltale red marks he'd described, caused by the little hooks on her garter belt.

She shoved the steaming coffee into his hand. "Here. Be careful, it's hot."

But her aim was off.

The cup hit his wrist, toppled sideways, and spilled straight down into his lap.

8

T.J. shot to his feet with a muffled howl, his hand gripping his jeans.

"Oh, Lord, I'm sorry. I didn't mean to—well, that must feel terrible. There, at your waist. At your—"

His jaw locked. "I know exactly where the pain is," T.J. said hoarsely. "If I were a questioning man, I might think you did that on purpose."

"I *didn't*. Here, let me help." In a flurry of movement she caught a napkin and pressed against the hot coffee. Then she gulped, realizing exactly how her hands were spread—and over what part of his body. "Oh, I didn't mean—" She swallowed hard. "Sorry."

She could only stare, red-faced and mortified.

"I think I'll go change while I can still manage to walk," he muttered.

Tess stared at the closed door to the bathroom. What was wrong with her? She'd seen handsome men before. Not a single one had left her so jittery.

Muttering, she turned and began stacking dirty dishes for Mae. In the process, she managed to spill half a cup of chili down her arm. Fuming, she looked for the paper towels and saw them on the edge of T.J.'s desk.

Beneath them the drawer was ajar. A glint caught Tess's eye.

By the time she realized what she was staring at, it was too late to look away.

Photographs.

Neat Polaroids in a stack, each one capturing the flat finality of death. This must have been the man at the bank, Tess thought. But he wouldn't be taking any more hostages. Not ever again.

Tess gripped the desk. Her heart hammered painfully as the water in the bathroom hissed on.

As a sheriff, T. J. McCall had to see such things often, and probably far worse. Tess had seen the expression in his eyes as he'd stood at the window. Now she knew what had put it there.

She closed the desk drawer and then wrapped the leftover food in plastic that Mae had left that afternoon.

Behind her the door creaked. "Nothing major seems to be damaged, I'm glad to say."

Tess didn't turn. She was fighting to keep her emotions under control. At one glance, he would read her face, and she knew he wouldn't thank her for probing into his work or his personal response to it.

"Sun's almost down." Wind rattled at the window. "It will be dark soon."

Tess still didn't turn.

"Something's wrong."

She shook her head mutely, bending down to stack the leftovers in the picnic basket that Mae had provided.

T.J. crossed behind her. In the silence, Tess could hear leaves shift against the windows like strange, dry whispers.

"You saw the pictures, didn't you?"

Tess swallowed. "I didn't mean to. They were in your desk, and the drawer was open."

She drew a long breath. "How do you deal with things like that? How do you put the images out of your mind afterward?"

He was right behind her now, but made no move to touch her.

"We just do," he said after a long time. "It gets easier."

"I don't believe you."

"You'd do better worrying about yourself." Wind skittered up the street, tossing pebbles against the windows.

"Why? What do you mean?"

T.J.'s voice hardened. "I spoke to Andrew while I was out. He said that several people have been calling your office in Boston, trying to track you down."

Tess tried to ignore a flutter in her stomach. "You mean clients?"

"Afraid not. They never leave their names or any return number."

Tess felt fear sink in with sharp little claws. "You think it's them? Now that they've found out where I work, you think they'll be coming after me?"

"I think it's damned likely."

Tess spun around. "If these people can find out where I work, they can also find out where I live."

"It's likely."

She locked her fingers tightly. "My building is filled with elderly people. Most of them live alone. They wouldn't be able to protect themselves if someone came looking for me." Her breath caught at the awful image of sprawled bodies and fragile broken bones. "What if one of them were hurt because of me?"

"Now, hold on to your saddle. Your brother says

there have been no disturbances at your apartment so far.''

"So far?'' Tess shook her head. "One of those nice old people could be shoved down the stairs or pushed under the elevator. Maybe worse,'' she whispered.

"Stop looking for shadows,'' T.J. said grimly. "Your brother has someone watching your apartment right now, ready to report anything unusual.''

Tess stared at him, desperate to believe he was telling the truth. "You think so?''

He drew a hard breath. "Yeah, I think so.''

"Mrs. Spinelli is eighty-two. She has a bad ankle.'' Tess closed her eyes, trying to escape the terrible images. "Mr. McBride across the hall lives with two cats. He doesn't hear so well now. He probably wouldn't notice if someone crept up behind him and pulled him into the laundry room so he could—''

"Forget Mr. McBride and Mrs. Spinelli,'' T.J. said harshly. "It's you they want, not your elderly neighbors.''

"That's not very reassuring.''

"Chances are, no one has tracked you here yet. If they do, only a jackass would go up against me. And that's what it will take,'' McCall added grimly.

She let her hands fall, suddenly aware that he was mere inches from her, and of the faint hint of soap and sage that clung to his skin.

She cleared her throat as she looked across the street and saw at least five people staring avidly from the café. "I think we're making news.''

"Not surprised to hear it.'' He made no move to step away.

Tess cleared her throat. "This might just be giving people the wrong impression.''

Twilight shadowed his hard face, making his expression impossible to read.

Before Tess could answer, she heard footsteps on the stairs outside. "Sheriff, that you?"

"Right here, Martinez."

A tall man with ebony hair pushed open the door, wiping his face with a bandanna. "Sorry I'm late. A bunch of heifers got loose on the road over by Table Wash. I had to stay and help round them up."

"No problem." T.J. took a step away from Tess. "I finished the duty entries. If anyone calls about that hostage situation in Brinkley, put them through to me. No media contacts without my personal permission, is that understood?"

"Sure enough, Sheriff."

Tess saw the man grinning at her.

"Tom Martinez," he said, sticking out his hand.

"Tess O'Mara."

"Ms. O'Mara is visiting for a few days," T.J. explained. "She's doing research about the Southwest."

"You don't say. About time someone came out here and got the facts straight. We're not all dust and cacti." Martinez scratched his jaw. "Grady said to remind you to have a look at the old jail. Yesterday, those new hinges got stuck and some nervous tourist ended up locked inside all through lunch hour. The man swore he was going to sue when he got back to California."

T.J. sighed. "I'd better check it out." He looked outside as thunder rumbled in the distance. "We might have a blow tonight. Better check on that construction site behind the school. Sometimes the workers forget to put their equipment away. Wouldn't want everything to get washed away if there's a flood."

"I'll take care of it, Sheriff." The deputy's grin widened. "I guess you and Ms. O'Mara will be pretty busy tonight. Resting, that is."

"Not the way you're thinking. Ms. O'Mara wants to ask me some questions about local law enforcement here in Arizona. It's for her—research."

"Is that fact?" The tall deputy rocked back on his heels. "Sounds like a fascinating subject for a quiet night before the fire. Well, you two better git along before that storm breaks. Enjoy your research," he added with a chuckle.

"I'm sure we will." As T.J. held open the door, the wind spun, tossing twigs and fine gravel into the air.

Tess watched something trot past the next row of buildings. "Was that what I thought it was?"

"Probably," T.J. said calmly.

"But that was—"

"A coyote," T.J. finished as the creature ambled off into the shadows. "We get them every so often here in town."

Thunder rumbled in the distance.

"Let's move. It's going to rain like hell before too long." He set a brisk pace until they came to the old jail next to the courthouse. Through the windows Tess saw a single light burning from an old-fashioned dome fixture over the antique rolltop desk. While T.J. unlocked the door with a key on his ring, Tess looked in at the shadowed room. She had seen it that afternoon, full of sunlight and chattering people, but the mood was different at night. Now darkness filled the corners, heavy with history and something that might have been ghosts.

"Spooky, isn't it?" T.J. lit a small hurricane lamp on the old desk. "I've felt it ever since I was a boy staring up at those old wanted posters on the wall. My great-grandfather used to work here. He was a Texas Ranger before he wandered west. He shot a man down exactly where you're standing right now.''

Tess frowned. ''You're just trying to scare me.''

''No, Ma'am. That's God's own truth. It was my great-grandfather's last gunfight. He took two bullets in the lungs and just managed to crawl to the doorway for help.'' T.J.'s voice hardened. ''They tell me he was a long time dying.''

Lightning forked through the sky overhead. The globe light flickered, then came back on.

''That's terrible,'' Tess breathed.

''It happened often enough. Honest lawmen didn't usually last too long here in the Arizona Territory.''

Tess shivered, moving away from the shadows. ''What's wrong with the jail door?''

''It's one of these new hinges, I think. This whole frame is so old there's no way to repair it without a lot of restoration money, which we don't have.'' T.J. opened the door and examined it carefully. ''Grady is fanatic about keeping things historically accurate, so he's built a new hinge from scratch. Unfortunately, there aren't many descriptions to work from.''

Another bolt of lightning streaked through the sky. The dome light flickered and didn't come back on, and the old jail took on an orange glow from the dim light of the hurricane lamp.

''Probably knocked out the fuses.'' He cursed softly as the hinge grated to a halt. ''It shouldn't be too hard to fix.'' He dug in his jacket pocket and pulled out a small flashlight.

Tess followed T.J. into the cell and bent closer. She

could see the hinge now, newly polished iron that stood out against the worn metal frame.

T.J. ran his fingers along the outside of the hinge. "The spring is loose. I can see it sticking out." He pulled a Swiss Army knife out of his pocket and eased the blade along the metal fittings. "Here, hold the light."

Tess bent sideways to make a better angle for the light, at the same time glancing uneasily into the deep shadows. There was something creepy about the place as thunder cracked menacingly in the distance.

"Are you about finished there?"

"Does the storm make you uncomfortable?" Thunder boomed overhead, rattling all the windows.

"Thunder doesn't frighten me." But she inched closer to T.J.

"I'm glad to hear that, because the storm could go on for a while." He worked the broken hinge carefully. "Grady must have put one of the prongs on upside down. All I have to do is—" His words were lost as lightning forked directly above them and struck something nearby. The force of the impact made Tess lurch and drop the flashlight.

In the wake of the bluish flare, she twisted sideways, searching for the fallen light. The front of her dress snagged the star on T.J.'s chest.

"Hold on," he muttered. "You're caught against my shirt."

"I know exactly where I'm caught," Tess snapped. Her knee bumped his thigh and her stiletto heel rammed his ankle as she tried to pull free.

"Damn and blast."

"It's not my fault. If you'd just stop dancing around—"

The weight of his body swung her sideways, sending

her onto one heel. Tess hit the adobe cell wall, wincing as her elbow struck the old cell door, and T.J.'s long, muscled body followed her down, captured by the star that held her dress.

Then the heavy metal door clanged shut behind them.

9

"Are you all right?"

T.J. pushed to one arm on the floor, his elbow jammed against her ribs.

"I've been better." It took Tess a moment to catch her breath and squirm free. She peered through the near darkness. "Is this a bad dream or is that door really closed?"

"Nothing to worry about. Once I get this badge unhooked from your blasted dress, I'll take a look."

T.J. took a sharp breath, then twisted to his elbow. As he worked his badge from side to side, struggling to free the soft fabric without ripping it, her perfume teased his senses.

Forget the damned perfume, he thought in disgust. "Can't you stop moving?" he growled.

"I'm not moving. *You're* the one bobbing up and down like a motorized duck. And for your information, that's my rib you're stabbing with your elbow."

"It would help if I could find the flashlight. I can't see what I'm doing." T.J. wedged two fingers under the front of her dress. In the process he found himself palming the curve of her breast.

Being cross-eyed with lust wasn't going to help him get the job done, T.J. thought in disgust. But he couldn't think about anything else when she squirmed beneath him, one leg caught between his thighs and her breast wedged against his open palm. At this rate, a .357 cartridge to the forehead would be a mercy killing.

"Let me try," she muttered. "Twist sideways onto your back."

T.J. felt his eyes roll back in his head as she clambered closer and slid one leg over his. He tried not to feel those soft, restless hips grinding into his, every movement tormenting.

Sweat broke out on his brow. He was having serious trouble making his lungs work. "Maybe you can hurry."

"I've almost got it." Tess leaned sideways, rising astride him. "Just a little more."

T.J. tried to distract himself by thinking about the duty schedule for the next month. He would have to switch Tom Martinez, who was heading off for a two-week vacation in Cancún with his wife and children. Grady had asked for Tuesday evenings off so he could play bingo. And the other deputy—

All thoughts of the duty schedule fled as Tess rose, her hips sliding onto his aroused anatomy.

He had to find something that would distract him—something like a cerebral hemorrhage. Biting back an oath, he tried to twist sideways and break the contact.

"Stop moving, will you? I've almost got this stupid badge free."

"Duchess, if you do much more of what you're doing, I'm going to forget all about my damned badge," he said in a gravelly voice.

"What are you talking about? I'm not—"

He heard her breath catch, followed by a tiny gasp. She went very still atop him.

T.J. wasn't entirely surprised. He figured the engorged state of his body was something that would be hard to miss, even in the dark.

"This is probably a bad idea," she whispered.

"Not much doubt of that."

She tried to ease away, but her dress was caught even tighter now due to her movements.

T.J. closed his eyes, trying to ignore the soft friction of her hips against his savage erection. If the woman had it in her mind to kill him, she was doing a damned fine job. Much more of this and he'd be pleading for mercy.

Then her breast wedged against his forearm. Could a man actually die of lust, he wondered.

During another flare of lightning, T.J. saw the pale outline of her face. "I have a metal nail file in my bag," she muttered. "I think I can break off the back of the pin, but I need to get closer."

Her breath was a warm cloud in his ear. Her body was delicious, an X-rated fantasy of sliding hips and restless thighs. T.J. was fairly certain the top of his brain would lift off if she managed to get any closer.

"I think I've got it."

"Forget about the damned badge," he said hoarsely, tugging at the buttons on his shirt. Angrily he summoned all his control to keep from pulling her down and plunging his fingers into her wild hair.

Restraint, he thought dimly.

Logic.

He took a harsh breath. "Tess," he said roughly.

"Uhmmm."

He tried not to feel the curve of her stomach where it pillowed his erection. He tried not to want the naked friction of her body astride him, welcoming him inside her.

"Tess," he repeated harshly.

Her breath came in puffy jerks. "What?" Her voice was husky, as if she were dazed.

Her dress was still snagged on his badge, and that left only one option. Grimly, T.J. sheared off his remaining buttons, then peeled off his shirt, letting it fall against her.

In another jagged burst of lightning, he saw her staring at his chest. She pushed awkwardly to her feet, his shirt dangling from the front of her dress like a medieval banner of conquest.

T.J. frowned, finding the symbolism a little too obvious. The painful state of his hardened body made his voice harsh. "That's one problem solved. Now I'd better look at that blasted door."

She adjusted her dress awkwardly, then bent to the floor, searching for the flashlight.

T.J. closed his mind to the torture of her perfume. He heard the soft rustling of her hands on the adobe floor and winced as her knee brushed his. God grant him the ability to control his sanity a few minutes longer, he prayed. Just long enough to put a decent amount of space between them.

About half a continent should do it.

"Here's my nail file." She shoved a cold piece of metal into his hands.

At this point, T.J. was willing to do anything. He might even try sacrificing a goat or two.

He searched the ground in the dim light until he found the flashlight, then bent by the door. As he'd feared, it was locked tight. He could see the bent prongs of Grady's hinge gleaming in the flashlight beam. He brushed one end, only to feel the prong snap off in his fingers.

Tess leaned down beside him. "What do we do now?"

He glared at the hinge. "I could try to beat the thing senseless with your nail file." He gave a grunt of disgust. "I have training in all kinds of locks and electronic security bypass, but I never expected to get stopped by an antique door hinge."

"Give me the file," Tess said.

"Begging your pardon, but I'm not sure this is the right place or time for an amateur."

"One of my clients owns a high-tech security firm. One night we were talking about how all locks are designed on the same basic principle. After a few drinks, he showed me how a simple nail file or plastic credit card can bypass most of them."

"Is that a fact?" For some reason T.J. couldn't get past the part about a few drinks. "Just how many drinks did you two have?"

"A few."

"What happened after he gave you the crash course in breaking and entering?"

"Why do you want to know?"

Because he was irritated as hell at the thought of another man putting the moves on her and making her sigh with pleasure. "Beats me." He crossed his arms and stood back. "Be my guest, Duchess."

"So you're going to let the amateur have a shot after all?"

"Hell, if you can spring that hinge, I'll cook you dinner for a week. Make that a month."

She gave a soft laugh. "Get your apron ready, cowboy."

Lightning grumbled as she crouched beside the door.

T.J. knelt nearby, flashlight in hand, while she inserted the nail file down through the length of the hinge.

"There's usually a dead space somewhere near the middle. If so, I can—"

She twisted her hands, and metal squeaked.

"Well, I'll be damned." T.J. stared as the door swung open.

"Probably." Tess smiled broadly as she strode past him. "What are you grinning about?" she demanded.

"The sight of you with that nail file. I'm going to have to add a new item to my list of suspicious equipment. What other burglary devices do you have hidden in that bag of yours?"

T.J. saw her rummage through her backpack. "Two whole-grain energy bars. Ginseng tincture."

"What about these?" T.J. muttered, studying two squares of bright plastic. Were they protection for a sexual encounter? It was the right thing for any woman to do in this crazy age, but the thought left T.J. irritated.

"Perfumed bath salts from a cruise I just arranged. This one is raspberry leaf hair balm. Great fragrance." She dug deeper into the bag. "A half-eaten box of Godiva chocolates—hands off," she hissed. "And my trusty nail file, of course."

She held up a foil survival blanket. "I guess we won't be needing this tonight."

As they left the old jail, lightning skated over the mountains. Thunder boomed, echoing back and forth over the valley. T.J. saw Tess hug her arms to her chest, caught in awe. It was hard not to be overwhelmed by nature at its fiercest as another streaming bolt broke the sky, stabbing at the mountains. He had watched the magnificent light shows hundreds of times, and they never lost their power to amaze him.

Or their noise, he thought ruefully.

In another jagged flare he saw Tess's arms tighten. Her face was white in the split second of illumination. "Are you okay?"

She didn't answer.

"Tess?" T.J. gripped her shoulder, but she didn't seem to notice. Her eyes closed as she raised her face to the sky, murmuring words that were impossible to make out over the echoing thunder.

T.J. had seen a lot of things in his life. He'd walked through dusty fields in Tuscany and ancient châteaus in France. He'd rubbed tanning oil on pampered movie stars in Hollywood and walked in a human shield to protect high-voltage politicians who wielded their power like automatic weapons. But nothing came close to the sight of Tess in the stormy darkness, her face a pale oval raised to the night sky.

Electricity crackled in the supercharged air, making the hair on his neck stand on end. There was a dangerous magic in being close to such power when you knew it could slam you off your feet and whip the breath from your body.

Seeing Tess had the same effect, especially when she stood entranced, overwhelmed by the same dark magic.

Against every inclination, his fingers tightened on her shoulder. "Tess, we should go. It's not safe to be out in this."

Again there was no answer. But as the wind churned up the street, she opened her eyes. Her gaze locked on his neck, where a thin gold chain held a battered St. Christopher medal, a boyhood gift from his mother.

She reached out slowly, tracing the small oval as if it had deep meaning to her. Heat shot through T.J. at the brush of her fingers, and he ignored the instant hardening of his muscles. They needed to get moving and into real shelter. There was always a chance that a bolt would snap right over the ground and strike them where they stood beneath the jail's broad adobe porch.

T.J.'s hand circled her wrist. "Tess, what's wrong?"

She shook her head, as if trying to ward off unwanted thoughts. Then she raised the gold metal to her lips, whispering strange, husky words that reminded him of the Apache he'd heard spoken up on the White River reservation in the rugged rim country.

But that was impossible, he knew. So what in the hell was going on here?

The wind moaned, whipping up in circles and raking at T.J.'s hair and face. Even then Tess stood oblivious, shivering, caught in her private world.

"Tess, snap out of it." T.J. detached his shirt and badge from the front of her dress and worked his shirt around her shoulders.

Then without a word she sank to one knee and brought his hand to her forehead as if in some ancient ritual, all the while murmuring in that same husky voice.

T.J. pulled her to her feet, struck by a wave of uneasiness. Something was very wrong with her, almost as if the storm had triggered some primitive disorientation. Getting her inside was crucial, he thought.

He couldn't help feeling irritated. This was *supposed* to be his first weekend off in six months and he'd been planning a trip into Tucson. After some rowdy music, he'd been looking forward to a lingering night with an old and very companionable friend who'd just come through a nasty divorce.

Instead, he was fighting his way through gale winds with a woman who was acting more than odd.

He bit back an oath as lightning raked the air and

exploded against the weather vane on top of the old courthouse. A hail of sparks lit the air and the explosion knocked T.J. backward, with Tess still caught rigid in his arms.

T.J. felt his heart slam hard as he smelled scorched wood, melted metal, and ozone. He stood frozen, struck with the nearness of his escape. No one could have survived a direct hit from such a bolt. If he and Tess had been crossing the square, they would probably both be dead right now.

His hands weren't quite steady as he pulled Tess against his side and took an awkward step through the darkness.

Lightning arced high overhead from cloud to cloud. In its bluish light, T.J. saw a dark figure move across the deserted square in front of the courthouse. He moved neither slowly nor with fear, his steps absolutely silent and regular. If T.J. had been a superstitious man, he might have said the figure had walked right out of the lightning that had raked the courthouse.

But that was impossible, even though this strange storm seemed somehow to have distorted nature's normal rules.

T.J. fingered the edge of his holster, glad for the weight of his pistol. Then he caught the glow of silver. He recognized that outline, part of a belt buckle etched with an ancient figure of a humpbacked flute player.

T.J.'s breath hissed out in relief as recognition hit.

"Miguel, is that you?" He squinted, trying to make out the shape moving toward him in the darkness.

An old man moved onto the porch, his teeth the only brightness in his lined, shadowed face. "Of course. Who else would be crazy enough to walk in such a weather?" He wore black from head to foot, the only other color a heavy silver buckle at his waist. Even his hair seemed to hold the darkness where it hung straight to his stooped shoulders. But in spite of his age, an aura of power clung to the man, almost as if he had pulled down the sky, wrapping its ancient darkness around his body like a cloak.

Some called him a brujo, one of the wild shaman-magicians who walked the barren mountains of Mexico working feats of healing or evil with equal skill, according to their whim. Others said he was a deserter from the Mexican Army hiding out in the hills north of Nogales. T.J. dismissed both stories as pure fantasy. He had crossed paths often with the old man over the last ten years, and T.J. was convinced of the man's love for the land—if for nothing else.

"Even the song dogs have gone to ground in this storm," the old man said, squinting up at the lightning above the mountains. "The high canyons are already flooding."

Not will, but *are*. How would he know that, T.J. wondered.

"So much noise and force is pleasing, is it not?"

"Not if it strikes the courthouse and shorts out all the circuits," T.J. said grimly. "We can't afford another repair bill right now."

"It is difficult to have no money," the old man said gravely. "But there are worse things." He looked at Tess, and T.J. sensed his curiosity.

"My friend isn't feeling well. Something about this storm has upset her."

Miguel nodded slowly. "It is not unexpected. Such weather can pull the very soul from one who is unprepared."

"Don't tell me you're practicing magic without a license," T.J. said. "If so, I'd have to run you in."

The old man laughed, a husky sound as dry as scattered sand. "I enjoy the sight of her hair, bright with the colors of the sunrise."

"Now, how would you know about that?" T.J. asked. "You can't see anything now."

"I see what I see, Sheriff." Then he waved one hand sharply. "Take your woman and go before the hard rains come. It will be safer for her."

"Safer?"

"Go, Sheriff McCall." This time there was a flat tone of command to the words.

But T.J. didn't take orders easily and never had. "Just for the record, she isn't my woman," he said firmly.

The old shaman spoke in whispery tones. "She might be if you let her. This woman could be many things to you, I think." A faint smile brushed his lips. "Sometimes a path must lead far away before it brings one home. Now go."

T.J. was about to ask another question, when a sheet of rain swept down out of the west, carried by a slashing wind. The last thing he wanted was to get caught by flooding. "I'll remember that, Miguel."

"So you will."

Tess twisted against him, muttering. All T.J.'s uneasiness returned as he saw the whiteness of her face. "Tess, can you hear me?"

She murmured, her hands locked at her chest, still caught in whatever odd dream world possessed her.

T.J. sprinted along the porch toward his Jeep, guiding Tess beside him. Only at the far corner did he look back.

The old man was still standing, one hand locked on his heavy belt buckle. Now the silver seemed to glow, crackling with cold light.

■

He stood in the rain and wind, watching the two lonely figures run through the night. Just as they had run before, the old man thought. Once again past and present twisted close, though they had yet to remember.

But the woman had felt the brush of the lightning. Her dreams were stirring even now as she fought to hold the two times apart.

Miguel frowned over the words she had muttered. They were sounds he had not heard in decades, words that had long ceased to be spoken here.

They were the words of those who had walked the high canyons ten centuries ago, living in the cliff houses that had now crumbled away to ruin.

So she had begun to remember after all, he thought. A pity. It would make her danger even greater.

10

Lightning burned across her eyelids.

She smelled the smoke of piñon and juniper logs, fragrant in the night. Across the valley came the low throb of drums, offered as a prayer to the storm gods who walked the clouds.

The power of the night caught her, overwhelmed her. At the same time she sensed that everything about this night was distant and unreal. Yet which world was the dream and which world was true?

"Tess, can you hear me?"

Hard hands.

A voice she knew should be familiar. She opened her eyes to a stranger's face marked with lines carved by both laughter and sorrow. She ought to know that face, but the image fled, like a cunning mirage.

"How do you feel?"

She raised her hand and touched his brow. Again the memories, teasing and swift. "Feel?"

"Did the noise bother you?" He frowned. "It was the very devil when that bolt of lightning struck the courthouse."

"No," she whispered.

"No, the noise didn't bother you, or no, you didn't see?"

"I didn't—see." *Or hear or feel.*

Driven by some deep urgency, she touched his hair. Once, it had been longer. She saw it clearly, pulled back with a leather thong. Once, there had been pieces of silver at his ears and eagle feathers in his hair.

"You're shivering."

Was she?

"Dammit, you're freezing."

Dimly she felt strong fingers pull something around her cold shoulders. "It doesn't matter." Each word came stiffly, as if she struggled with a foreign tongue.

"Miguel said that a storm like this can steal your soul—not that I believe in his magic."

"Miguel?"

"The old man in the black clothes," T.J. explained slowly. "We met him outside the old jail. Don't you remember?"

"No." Tess closed her eyes. "I don't seem to remember anything."

"Not even me?"

His voice echoed hollowly, superimposed upon another's, low and husky and infinitely tender. Tess forced her mind away from its seduction. Something whispered that madness waited down that twisting path. "I remember enough."

Too much, she thought. She thought of a man who could track the smallest creature by scent alone. A man who walked in thunder, pounding on the sand to call down the great booming echoes from the sky. She thought of a man she had known once, centuries before.

Lifetimes before.

But that was impossible.

As his hand brushed her cheek, she shivered uncontrollably.

What was wrong with her?

"No," she panted. He couldn't touch her. She was forbidden to him by her tribe. If they knew, they would hunt him down and spill his bright blood over the sand as punishment. "Don't touch me," she whispered. But even as she spoke, she was gripped by a fierce longing. "They'll find out. They watch me always now."

"Find out? Who?"

Rain slammed against the roof. Tess barely noticed, caught in a flood of images like running water over sand. He had come from the north when snow blocked the high passes. He was not of her tribe, not of her people, who laughed at the soft skins he wore. A sky stone blazed at his neck, only a shade lighter than his piercing eyes, and his prayer stick held strange figures of animals she had never seen.

But his power was great. He had trusted in that power when he should have felt fear.

Tess locked her hands to her chest as her trembling grew. She closed her eyes, fighting the pain, only to see the images burn behind her eyelids.

The sweet brush of hands.

The dance of skin, frenzied in the darkness while drums beat out a fierce warning.

She said a word, low and hoarse. It was his name—the name he had once held, centuries before, when the mountains were young.

She was sitting out of the rain.

A car, she realized. Something brushed her shoulders. A blanket, but it was like no cloth she had ever seen. She stared at the fibers, marveling at their bright colors and precise stitches. How different the cloth looked. How different everything was in this place.

Strong fingers dug into her shoulders. "You haven't

said a rational word since we left the jail. I need to know what's going on here.''

Dear God, so did she.

"Dammit, Tess, talk to me."

"There's—nothing to say. I'm fine." She pulled away from his hands, fighting to clear her mind of the shadow images. "The storm must have made me dizzy, disoriented." She took a hard breath. "Can we just go?"

"You said things were different."

"I was confused."

"But—"

"Can we just *go*?" She felt her control breaking under his scrutiny and his questions. She needed to be calm, to be alone so she could sort out the feelings still churning through her. "I'm tired."

"So the hell am I," he muttered. "That doesn't make me forget how to speak English and worry that I'm being watched."

"It was just a mistake, all a mistake. Now can we go?"

"I'm going to have some answers, I warn you." Muttering, he started the Jeep and rammed the gearshift forward.

Tess watched the rain while the night blurred outside her window.

A few minutes later, T.J. said, "You're going to have to talk sometime."

She sighed, watching rain hiss at the windshield.

"Don't you want to know where you're going?"

"You already told me. It's a place you called Rancho Encantador."

"That's the one."

"Does it have a hot tub?" Right now that's what Tess wanted more than anything—something warm and soothing. Something so completely modern that she could not possibly forget where she was or *when* she was.

"Hand-assembled with saltillo tile. A waterfall runs through a little rock garden, right under the stars."

"It sounds like heaven." She sighed, hugging her body with her arms, fighting a wave of exhaustion. "I really appreciate your dropping me off on your way home."

T.J. fought back a grin. "No trouble at all, Ma'am."

There were many things that Tess had expected to see on the drive out of Almost. Ramshackle cabins with uneven roofs and no electricity. Grimy adobe homes slanting crazily against the hillside. But all she saw were saguaro cactuses that loomed up out of the darkness and cottonwood trees whispering in the wind.

Tess frowned. She didn't consider herself a snob. There was a great deal to admire about T. J. McCall and this town of his. He was a man of bravery and honesty, but they were from entirely different worlds. The gulf between them was beyond crossing.

"How long before we reach the resort?"

"No more than five minutes." T.J. pointed north to the foothills, where lightning raked the caps of rugged peaks.

She frowned. "It looks very isolated up there."

"The owner likes the isolation," T.J. said. "Now put on your seat belt. The drive can be a little rough."

Five minutes later, Tess decided bumpy wasn't the word for it. She'd been tossed up, down, and sideways as they hammered over a washboard dirt road until her bones screamed for mercy. Now she could see little in the darkness beyond scattered boulders.

She clutched at the window frame, trying to keep from pitching up and down. "Are we nearly there?"

"It's just beyond those mesquite trees."

As they rounded a bend, her breath fled.

The main building rose in curving lines and walls of windows. Lights bobbed from stenciled tin lanterns framing an oak door set into sinuous adobe walls.

"I don't understand." Tess pressed closer to the window. "There aren't any cars. No one else appears to be around."

T.J. pulled to a halt, got out of the Jeep, and swept open her door. He caught her arm as she stumbled, her vision focused on the undulating walls covered by lush crimson bougainvillea.

"Welcome to Rancho Encantador."

Thunder rumbled, closer than before. In the wavering flash of light, Tess made out the beamed roof and a row of mesquite trees that ran along the rounded adobe fence.

A house, she thought. An amazing house of adobe and wood with a whole wall of windows.

Not a resort at all.

"I'd offer you the hot tub, but with that lightning it wouldn't be safe. Instead, I'll show you to your room, so you can rest."

"You *lied*."

T.J. took her suitcase from the backseat. "Yeah, I did. Now, are you coming in or not? I'm soaked enough already."

"But—"

He was already gone, sprinting toward the open doors, where a woman in a bright red apron stood waiting, her hands on her hips.

Rain hissed across Tess's cheeks as she took another stumbling step, peering at the vision of light and wood and adobe before her. T.J. was waiting at the carved door, which was painted sky-blue.

"Tess O'Mara, meet Maria Lopez. Maria runs my house and everything inside it, me included. Don't be late for meals or criticize her cooking and you'll do just fine here."

"But—"

T.J. moved to the side and held open the heavy door. "Welcome to my ranch, Duchess."

Tess followed, aware of the housekeeper's narrowed gaze. She had every reason to be suspicious, given Tess's bedraggled appearance.

Tess brushed the beautifully carved antique door, then stared at the man beside her. "This is all *yours*?"

His housekeeper answered first, her shoulders stiff. "Of course it is. Señor McCall works hard to see that every beam and tile is perfect." She sniffed at the sight of T.J.'s shirt dangling over Tess's shoulders. "Now you both will go inside. A fire is made and you will have dinner, which I have been keeping for you."

Tess moved past, still in a daze. "It's all yours?"

"All four thousand square feet of it. A mite big, but I figure I'll grow into it." He led the way through a court-yard filled with blooming plants. Tess heard the sound of water running over large stones.

"I didn't expect anything like this."

At the front of the house, he pushed open a massive wooden door with a high lintel. She could feel that great care and attention had been lavished on the house— something she'd never expected of the rangy sheriff.

As T.J. flipped on the light, her breath caught. Pale adobe floors flowed through a room inset with stucco niches and bleached wood beams. Tess could imagine light flowing through the tall windows onto the row of pottery set on a shelf before the curving fireplace. Brightly striped rugs of red and green were the only other items in the room.

"Do you have something against furniture?"

T.J. shut the door with his boot. "I haven't had a lot of time for decorating. The walls were finished only last month. The beeswax took longer to rub in than we thought, but it definitely gives a nice, authentic shine."

Tess stopped dead. In the center of the room, light scattered in sparks from a cut tin chandelier over muted peach walls. She blinked, assuming she'd misunderstood him. "Excuse me?"

"It takes a while to build a house like this. Once it's done, a man wants to grow into it before he starts cluttering it up with things."

"You *built* this house by yourself?"

"Every beam and latilla," Maria said proudly. "Señor McCall is very good with his hands. He builds all kind of things."

T.J. rocked back on his heels. "Actually, I had a lot of help. I expect everyone in Almost left a mark somewhere." He ran a hand lovingly over a massive wood column. "Grady helped me peel most of the beams for the vigas in the ceiling. Mae helped me choose the layout of the windows, and Tom Martinez helped score the adobe floor. We tried to do as much as possible the old way. After all, if you're going to build a house, you may as well do it the right way."

Tess shook her head and tried to accept his casual explanation. This amazing house could have belonged to an industrialist or a real-estate executive.

It was certainly *not* what she'd expected of a laid-back, small-town sheriff.

She frowned, trying to work her mind around the

reality of it. There was definitely more to the man than she had imagined. She suspected there was also more to this odd town, whose eccentric residents seemed to conceal unusual talents.

"It's beautiful. Beyond beautiful."

He grinned, shoving back his hat. "Some of the stucco needs to be repainted, and there's one mural left to add in the courtyard. But I'm in no rush."

Tess eyed the clean, fluid lines of the room and caught back a yawn.

Maria opened a door across the hall. "It is good that the lights have come back on. Now you will both come and sit," she called. "The meal is prepared."

"But I'm not—"

"You will eat," the woman said firmly.

Tess looked at T.J., who shrugged as if this were an argument he'd given up trying to win.

"Why don't you change while I check on things in town? I want to be sure that lightning didn't set any fires."

"You will please hurry," Maria said calmly. "Señora O'Mara, you will like to sit down now."

"Actually, it's señorita," Tess said, summoning her very limited knowledge of Spanish.

"Hmmmph." The woman led the way into a room bordered by floor-to-ceiling windows. Bright woven textiles crowned a table of golden bleached pine. Tess sat down as Maria poured water and brought soup. "You will eat. The sheriff may be long at his calls." She clucked her tongue.

There was goat cheese with sun-dried tomatoes. Then Maria brought in squash soup with chiles and roasted corn, followed by a fragrant pork stew with fresh corn tortillas. Tess felt her appetite grow in a rush as T.J. returned.

"There are problems?" Maria asked.

"Nothing beyond the usual. The fire department lost their backup generator for a while, but not too long. There doesn't seem to be any damage to the court-house."

"It is good. Now you will eat."

Half an hour later, Tess sat back, stuffed. Maria had served dish after dish, each better than the last. Finally, the stately woman smoothed her red apron and nodded. "Enough. Too much and you do not sleep—or your dreams will be evil. It is time you both went to rest." She saw Tess hide a yawn. "Go now, before you both fall asleep over my food."

He pushed from the table. "I'll show you to your room."

The bedroom was all curves leading to two sets of windows. Dried lavender hung over the doorway and a collection of antique colored glass ran along the adobe niche above the bed. T.J. put Tess's bags in the corner. "I'm just down the hall. Call if you need anything."

"I'm sure I'll be fine." Tess took a step back, suddenly aware of his tall body only a foot away from hers. She turned down the bed, avoiding his eyes.

"You'll have to talk about what happened outside the jail sometime. We both know it was more than disorientation from the storm."

Tess looked away from his intense gaze. "Nothing happened, I already told you. I was just confused, but now I'm fine. Stop pushing, McCall."

"Oh, I'll push, Duchess. I'll keep pushing until I have answers. If you're feeling so wonderful, why are your hands shaking right now?"

"I don't know what you're talking about." But when Tess looked down, she saw that her fingers were locked around the colorful blanket.

And her hands were shaking.

His brow rose. "You can lie to me, but you can't lie to yourself." Then he turned and vanished down the hall without another word, his boots echoing over the tile.

Sleep pushed at her mind as she settled beneath the cool sheets. Twig shutters covered the broad windows and a kiva fireplace held embers of fragrant mesquite to keep out the night's chill. A row of stucco shelves filled one wall, every inch crammed tight with books. Tomorrow, Tess thought sleepily, she would think about what had happened. There had to be some sane, logical explanation.

But now the fragrant mesquite and the gurgle of water from the courtyard conspired to make her eyes droop.

She studied the huge mural on the far wall with pictographs representing hundreds of horses and fighting warriors. The figures seeming to twist and dance in the flickering glow of the embers, and Tess couldn't pull her gaze away.

She remembered Damien Passard's predictions. Hot skies. Red cliffs. A man who waited for her.

She might have heard an animal call in the distance.

She might have heard T.J.'s boots scrape softly outside her door.

And then she was swept down into a restless sleep.

■

A sharp burst of sound pulled Tess awake hours later. Moonlight drew patterns on the floor as she sat up tensely.

Once again the sound came, the scrambling of feet followed by unearthly howling. The shrill noises grew, a series of barks and howls that rose and broke in an eerie cacophony that made goose bumps rise on her arms.

She tugged a blanket around her shoulders and moved to the outer windows, but was unable to see anything. Shivering, she walked out to the living room and stopped.

T.J. was curled on a blanket in the middle of the floor, asleep before a fire that had burned down to embers in the huge kiva fireplace. He wasn't wearing a shirt. His jeans were unbuttoned and riding low on his hips.

Tess felt heat fill her face at the sight of him. She had a sudden thought that this might be some sort of bizarre dream until the unearthly howling began again.

"T.J., wake up."

He shot up with a curse, reaching for his pillow in the same swift movement. Tess blinked as she saw moonlight glint on the dull barrel of a gun.

"What's wrong?"

"There's something outside. Some kind of animal. Can't you hear it?"

"Hear what?"

Once again the wild cacophony filled the air. "*That.* What in heaven's name is it?"

T.J. ran a hand through his hair, then pushed to his feet. "Relax, Duchess." He strode to the window and pushed back the twig shutters. More discordant notes filled the room. "It's just coyotes. They tend to get social up here on moonlit nights."

"Coyotes?" Tess repeated. "But they sound so unearthly."

T.J. stood looking out. The rain had stopped and the

moon was high, its cold silver light tracing his hard features. "I guess the coyotes would say the same thing about the Three Tenors."

Tess tried not to watch the planes of muscle shift where his jeans rode low on his hips. With even less success, she tried to keep her gaze off the chiseled planes of his face, caught in a restless pattern of shadow and light by the fire.

She shivered.

Not because of the unearthly howling or the chill of the night. Here in this place she felt like a stranger to herself and all she had been. Instead of Tess O'Mara, she was a woman she barely knew, someone who stood on the brink of immeasurable discoveries. A voice whispered that the man before her would be part of those discoveries.

She remembered again what Richard's psychic friend had said about hot skies and burning red stone.

Not this place. Not this man, Tess told herself.

"I can't sleep, not with all that noise."

"Then come sit before the fire."

"I don't think—"

"Hell, I won't bite you." His face was unreadable. "In case that's what you're worried about."

After a moment's hesitation, Tess sat down on the pillow he'd tugged from the window seat. It, too, was handmade in bright tapestry squares. Tess wondered whose work it was.

She realized the blanket had fallen from her shoulders. Muttering, she yanked it higher and caught the scent of wood smoke and desert wind.

And there was something else, a male scent compounded of sweat and soap.

His scent, she realized with a shiver. There was something intensely earthy about being wrapped in his blanket and enfolded in the primal beauty of this amazing house he had created tile by tile and brick by adobe brick.

Tess closed her eyes. She wasn't going to think about T. J. McCall. She didn't need any more disturbing visions that left her yearning for things she couldn't name and wondering how his mouth would feel brushing hers, here in the moonlight.

"You must be chilled." Tess felt his light touch as he wrapped another blanket around her. She had been right about that smell. It *was* his—all wood smoke, desert wind, and man.

The coyotes' voices seemed to soften, to become more song than howl. She'd heard that before, too. . . .

Impossible. It had to be the heatstroke she'd suffered. She'd heard it could fool the mind into playing tricks on itself. She should shift away from him, put some distance between them but the bare brush of his shoulder against her seemed to ground her, to keep her from slipping away into visions of what couldn't possibly be.

"Talk to me," T.J. said softly. "Tell me what happened." He was studying her, seeing . . . what? "It's still happening, isn't it?"

She shrugged. "I'm tired, T.J. I'm still wobbly from the long drive and the heat." A deep sigh escaped her. "And this place is magic—the mountains and the sky and the desert . . . I can see why so many artists and writers come to the Southwest. It invites the imagination to run wild."

T.J. didn't move, didn't stop looking at her. "Imagination," he said thoughtfully. "So where did yours run to? What did it see?"

She forced a smile and lifted her hand, gesturing toward the windows. "The mountains, the sky, the desert . . . and ideas to help Mae."

He frowned and opened his mouth, then shut it again as if he wanted to challenge her answer and changed his mind. "Mae? How did she get into this conversation?"

"I spent some time with her this afternoon," Tess said quickly, relieved that she'd thought to bring Mae into a conversation that left her distinctly uncomfortable. She didn't want to bring him into it, to tell him that he'd been there in those odd moments spent in another time. She didn't want this man to be the one Damien Passard has spoken of. She didn't want to acknowledge aloud the strange bond she felt with him, growing with every minute they spent together.

"You spent some time with Mae . . ." he prompted.

She took a deep breath to banish the thoughts that lurked so close to the surface, focusing on the realities of the here and now of her life. "She wants to package and market some local foods and asked me for help." Tess took hold of the excitement she'd felt that afternoon as ideas had spilled from her mind. That kind of sudden inspiration was rare and always triggered restless energy in her. "Specialty foods are my newest area, and I've got some great ideas, starting with an Internet promotion and a four-alarm Web site with hot recipes using Mae's products."

"First a coffee klatch that involves the whole town and now Mae becomes an entrepreneur." T.J. shook his head. "I go away for a few hours and you've turned the whole town upside down."

She glanced at him, seeing the twist of his mouth in a

wry smile and the glint of approval in his eyes. He'd meant it as a compliment rather than censure.

"You're not here to work, Duchess."

"No, I'm here to hide," she said, the reminder of why she'd come here bringing a jolt of fear. "But I can't stop working, T.J. Ideas can't be turned on and off like the pump in your waterfall." She kept talking, driving thoughts of a million dollars and some unnamed threat from her mind. "I usually work with well-established companies whose presence is apparent in the market. But this will mean beginning from the ground up with a sole proprietor in a small town. Mae presented me with a challenge I can't refuse."

"According to Andrew, getting you to take a vacation is the real challenge," T.J. said, still studying her with a thoroughness that rattled her. "Why don't you work on that? See where inspiration leads you."

"Okay," she said brightly, "do you have horseback riding at this ranch you own?"

"That's not very creative, Duchess," he chided.

"It is when you're from Boston."

T.J. chuckled. "Ever been on a horse before?"

"A living horse?"

He shook his head and muttered something under his breath. "I figure living is important to get the full effect."

"I once put together a magazine layout for a Texas beer. We used felt-covered models of horses with silk cacti and sand trucked in from New Jersey."

"Silk cacti?" T.J. gave a strangled cough. "You don't say."

Tess turned to glare at him. "There's absolutely no reason to laugh. It was all perfectly beautiful and just as realistic as the actual thing, I can assure you. The only thing we didn't have was the flies and the smell.''

''There is that.''

''In the end, everything came off beautifully. The sponsor was thrilled. As I recall, the actor fell off only twice.''

T.J. ran his tongue along his teeth. ''Only twice, you say? That's mighty fine riding. And how much did you charge for this—er, magazine layout?''

Tess named a figure that had him swiveling around in shock. ''You mind saying that again?''

She repeated the amount.

''With that much money, Almost could build a new elementary school and add a wing to the library. And the fire department definitely needs a new backup generator.''

''I suppose it might seem wasteful to you,'' Tess said slowly, ''but businesses can die without proper print placement. That's a fact of life.''

All of that was true, of course. But his words still left Tess feeling a gnawing discomfort. She frowned at the fire, listening to the coyotes, amazed at how quickly the sound became a natural part of the background to her. ''Tell me about them. Why do they sing like that?''

''Depends on who you ask. The naturalists will tell you they use their cries to attract a mate, or as pack communication, or to keep their young located.'' He turned to adjust the blanket on her shoulders and paused as his hand brushed the side of her neck, then skimmed up to trace her jawline.

''Like whales and dolphins,'' she said, her voice ragged with a sudden yearning to be touched more.

Clearing his throat, he moved his hand away and

stared back at the fire. "The tribes say a coyote calls to hear his own voice because he likes the sound so much. Or maybe to trick his prey with his magic songs. His image is seen on ancient petroglyphs in the lands of the Hopi, where he is an animal spirit of the Coyote Clan." T.J. kept talking, kept staring at the fire as he sat stiffly, keeping his shoulder a good inch away from hers. "To Native Americans today, the coyote is trickster, savior, and fool—capable of heroics and utter savagery, an eternal survivor who is often tricked by his own vanities."

Tricked. Was that what had happened to her? Was it still happening as random thoughts strayed to visions that could not possibly be memories? "Like people," she mused aloud.

"Exactly," he said, sounding surprised by her assessment. "Miguel says that people and animals are not so far apart. Animals are just more honest in their motives. That's why the Native Americans have always believed their spirits were linked with animals."

"Do you believe it?" she asked around a yawn.

"The longer I live out here, the more I'm inclined to accept it as possible. And when Miguel tells me his stories of the beginning times, he makes it sound completely plausible. Even if he almost manages to frighten me with that chant voice of his."

"Tell me one of Miguel's stories," Tess whispered. Something compelled her to ask, to listen, to understand, as if it were important to her personally, necessary for some journey she was undertaking.

T.J. gave a faint smile. "Well, Duchess, it all started like this." He fixed his gaze on the fire, refusing to give in to the urge to kiss the top of her head, to tip her face up for another kind of kiss. "The Great Spirit made Coyote to bring fire and create the tribes in all parts of the earth. Coyote killed evil creatures and brought many languages to men. Finally his task was done, and the Great Spirit sent him away and told the tribes that he and Coyote would return when Earth Woman was very old. Coyote would come first, and by that the tribes would know that the Great Spirit was soon to return. With him would come all the dead spirits, and in that time all the peoples of earth would live together in peace.''

Tess leaned her head on his shoulder, wanting the night and the fire and the sound of his voice mingling with the calls of the coyotes to go on forever. In this moment, it seemed right and natural and she could even accept that it was preordained. She was too tired and too content to argue otherwise, even with herself. ''Tell me more.''

She sounded like a small child asking for a bedtime story with her sleepy voice and the trust she'd given him in the simple act of laying her head on his shoulder. The trouble was that she didn't look or feel like a child, and T.J. didn't think he could take much more of her trust. All day she'd infuriated and exasperated, fascinated and tempted him. Through everything, she'd handled herself well, with her independence a poignant counterpoint to the helplessness of her situation. Now he was having a hard time resisting the simple comfort she asked for so ingenuously.

T.J.'s chest rose and fell as he wrapped his arm around her, feeling the trust she gave him like a balm to his own torment over what he'd done that day. Tomorrow everything would be back to normal. Tess would be fighting his protection and stirring up the town into enterprising fervor. Crimes would be committed and he might be called to deal with them in ways that diminished his humanity.

But right now that world seemed very far away and he wasn't inclined to invite it back in.

Which was exactly why he had to do just that.

"Not tonight," he said gruffly as he rose to his feet and leaned down to scoop her up in his arms. Her eyes were closed and from the peaceful expression on her face, he knew she was more than halfway into a deep sleep. Focusing on that fact alone, he carried her back to her bedroom, painfully aware of the way her body curled into his, of her perfume and the warmth of her hair as it brushed his shoulder.

He muttered a curse for that awareness, knowing it was completely wrong. He and Tess came from different worlds and he'd been down that road before with disastrous results. Relationships conducted by commute never worked and he couldn't see Tess thriving in a place like Almost once the novelty wore off. Right now he wanted to believe that she was just as much a novelty to him.

If he really concentrated, he knew he could come up with another hundred reasons why he should keep his hands off her.

But all the reasons, formed and unformed, scattered as she opened her eyes.

"I don't want to go to bed," she murmured. "I like your stories."

He stared back at her, unsmiling, his good intentions feeling more like his downfall than his salvation. "Not a chance, Duchess." Not a chance in hell. Not when he liked the way she looked in his blanket. And in his house.

He liked it far too much.

His hands tightened their hold, feeling the source of his frustration in her softness. He couldn't get her back to her room and out of reach fast enough, even if he did hate himself in the morning. Kicking her door open with his foot, he laid her on her bed, adjusted the covers over her, and stalked out of the room, barely able to keep from slamming the door.

"Sleep well," he muttered grimly. "I sure as hell won't."

11

T.J. awoke to gunfire.

Thankfully, it was the hollow pop of territorial revolvers worn by steely-eyed lawmen from a different time. As a boy, he'd dreamed often about Almost's historic old jail. Usually his dreams focused on his great-grandfather and his violent death. But tonight his dreams had included a woman, though he couldn't seem to recall any details.

Wide awake now, T.J. rolled over and checked his watch: 5:12 AM.

Operating on the theory that the more closed doors between them the better, he had moved to his own bed last night once he was certain that Tess was finally asleep, freed from whatever strange disorientation had gripped her during the storm. She'd said it herself—she was a creative person and Almost's beautiful surroundings invited the imagination to run wild. His had been running pretty wild itself since he'd first seen her with her hair like fire in the sun and a tire track running down the back of her expensive suede jacket.

Muttering, he bunched the pillow over his head and closed his eyes, trying to go back to sleep. Ten minutes later he gave up, knowing the effort was wasted. With a sigh he swung the blanket over his shoulder and stood up to stretch. The sun was just peering over the horizon, where the Chiricahua Mountains cast tall shadows over the valley.

Barefoot, T.J. padded along the hall and took a quick glance into Tess's room. He had to grin at the sight of her body sprawled sideways on the bed with three different blankets tangled around her. The woman was definitely a hard sleeper.

And T.J. found that he enjoyed watching her sleep.

The plain truth was that T.J. liked women. He liked their laughter and their perfume, and he liked holding them in his arms while they slow danced cheek to cheek. It had been too damned long since he'd enjoyed a night out instead of tending to some kind of official business.

He hadn't expected Andrew's baby sister to be like this. He certainly hadn't expected to feel the gut-wrenching force of desire that he had experienced last night in the storm. T.J. sighed. What he needed now was an ice-cold shower followed by lots of caffeine.

Ten minutes later most of his sleepiness had cleared. T.J. put in a quick call to Tom Martinez, who assured him the night had been quiet except for a false alarm at the high school and one drunk-driving arrest. The storm had shorted out several backup generators, but emergency equipment was restored quickly. Reassured by the news, T.J. made himself a cup of coffee and headed off to his computer, hidden behind a bleached-pine armoire in his office.

He'd had a bad feeling about Tess's situation from the first moment Andrew O'Mara called him. He was isolated here in Almost, but crime had no boundaries, and in the last year there had been four cases of counterfeit currency at the local banks. T.J. stayed abreast of developments, including high-tech money laundering through the use of Smart Cards and Internet accounts. Just six months ago, he had attended a high-level conference in Denver on the subject, and the technical skills used by criminals had stunned him. Andrew O'Mara was right to be worried about Tess's safety. Crime was a growth industry, especially the kind of crime that involved high-tech electronic procedures.

Coffee in hand, T.J. stared at the newest state law enforcement reports. A quick scan showed no unusual activity in the area of counterfeiting or banking fraud. Next he logged in with three law enforcement contacts scattered around the country, asking if they had noticed any suspicious electronic wire transactions. While he waited for answers, he poured himself another cup of coffee and settled in for a more detailed search of the regional bulletins.

As he had expected, the banking community remained ultracautious about any mention of possible Y2K computer failures. No one wanted widespread public panic and a run on the U.S. banking system. But as T.J. accessed specialized networks that were closed to the average citizen, he picked up irregularities reported in a dozen cities. No criminal source had been identified.

His best contact for updated information would be Andrew O'Mara, who would divulge facts—in the interest of protecting his sister—that the government might be reluctant to release to the public.

McCall reached for the phone and punched in Andrew's number, then waited while a dignified secretary checked to see if he was taking calls.

''O'Mara here.'' Andrew answered tersely.

T.J. had a bad feeling that the strain in his friend's voice had something to do with Tess. O'Mara was usually a cool head in a crisis, but this time it was personal—

a situation that had chilling undertones for any law-en-forcement officer.

"It's T.J."

"Good. I was about to call you. There are some things you need to know."

T.J. definitely didn't like the sound of that.

■

Seven o'clock came and went.

T.J. couldn't remain patient any longer and headed for the kitchen to pour another cup of the coffee he'd made earlier. Mug in hand, he ambled to the door of Tess's room.

She was still asleep, her blankets tangled on the floor, the sheet twisted across her legs. He looked away fast before temptation could kick in. He hated to wake her but he needed to go into town in an hour and check on a few things, and he wasn't about to leave her there with only Maria for protection.

He knocked softly on the door. "Tess? Time to rise and shine."

Something that sounded like a pillow hit the door, followed by more muttering.

So the lady had a temper in the morning, did she? T.J. smiled at the idea as fantasies immediately took form about inventive ways that he could soothe that temper on top of those tangled blankets.

Even if he could never allow them to become more than fantasies.

T.J. walked into her room, eased back a corner of the pillow, and held a steaming cup of coffee a few inches from her nose, ready to move fast if she flung out her arm.

"Ummmm."

He blew coffee-scented steam toward her face and was rewarded with a little squirm of her body beneath the drifty bit of lace that passed for her nightshirt. One arm emerged, followed by the edge of her face.

"Where's that millennium cruise file, Annie?" she muttered. "And I need the caterer's bill."

T.J. watched, enjoying the sunlight on her creamy skin, liking the sight of her in that big white bed. "Right here, Ma'am," he said crisply.

"What about the new chocolate program?" she moaned. "Maybe a cooking seminar would work. Invitation only, of course."

"Of course," T.J. agreed gravely.

"Dessert for the press. Only chocolate dishes. Ummmm."

T.J. lifted one of the pillows. "Do you always plot out business projects in your sleep?"

Tess's face appeared, shadowed and sleepy. "T.J.? Is that you?"

"No other man in sight."

"Is it AM or PM?"

"AM."

Her eyes opened wide, then locked on the coffee in his hand. "If that's caffeine you're holding, you can name your price, cowboy."

"Now, that could be a dangerous offer."

Tess sat up sleepily, her hair a glorious cloud of color around her pale cheeks.

The sight of her slammed right into his solar plexus. The skinny straps of her silky top kept slipping off her shoulders, and T.J. decided it would be a good idea for him to look away before he did something stupid.

Like drop to his knees and howl.

"The coffee's right over here. I warn you, it's not that wimpy stuff with the pretty white froth. This is real cowboy coffee, the kind that will put hair on your chest."

"Just as long as it's hot and has caffeine," Tess muttered. "Where is it?" She shoved the strap back onto her shoulder and peered at him sleepily.

Grinning, T.J. backstepped toward the door. "It will be right beside me in the kitchen."

"There's one thing you'd better understand, Sheriff. It's dangerous to get between me and my morning coffee."

T.J. tossed her a robe and headed back into the hallway. If he stayed any longer to watch those long legs emerge from beneath the sheets, he might do something unforgivable, like pull her down and make certain that they didn't leave the bed for hours.

Dammit, what was wrong with him? He'd never had a problem controlling his fantasies before.

"Coffee," Tess rasped in the pleading voice of a desert traveler dying of thirst.

He smelled her before he turned and saw her standing in the doorway of her room, her perfume a complicated blend of citrus, cinnamon, and hyacinth.

T.J. took pity on her and handed over the cup, watching her gulp greedily. A heartbeat later, she made a strangled sound, squinting down at the cup. "What's in there, boiled shoe leather?"

"Equal parts fire and brimstone, to hear Grady tell it."

"That stuff should be classed as a lethal weapon." Tess took another swallow, shuddered, then tied her robe tighter and followed him to the kitchen. Once she was there, she shoved a shining tangle of hair off her face and immediately began to wrestle with her fancy silver coffee machine. As she did, her robe slid open to reveal those amazing legs of hers.

There was something painfully arousing about watching her pad around barefoot in his house, T.J. discovered. She was growing on him, he thought grimly. She was claiming his thoughts and stirring his body.

But he knew that the minute she was out of danger, Tess would jump in that fancy car of hers and head back to Boston and her high-powered career. Then T.J. would be standing here alone, trying to remember her perfume, trying to forget her radiant eyes and how her laughter had filled a room.

Which meant that he had to get a grip on his fantasies right *now*.

Tess thrust a cup into his hands and sat down at the table. "Try that for coffee," she challenged, her eyes glinting.

He took a gulp. Chocolate and cinnamon, he thought as the white froth on top teased his lips. "Not bad," he admitted.

"Liar. That's as close as anyone can expect to get to paradise in this life."

His eyes narrowed. "Oh, I can think of a few different ways." Flipping a chair around, he straddled it and rested his forearms on the back.

For a moment, just a moment, color filled her face. Then she swung around to fill her own cup.

There was something oddly intimate in sitting across from Tess at the table while sunlight streamed through the open windows, leaving sparks in her coppery hair. As her knee brushed his, T.J. swallowed hard and tried to control his short-circuiting nervous system.

"Do you always pay catering bills in your sleep?"

he asked, giving her time to wake fully before telling her about his conversation with Andrew.

"Sometimes." Tess toyed with her coffee. "Things get intense during a big project. Sometimes I can't turn my work off. My boss is very supportive, but he gives me lots of responsibility, and that makes for high pressure and stress. Lately we've branched out into the high-end cruise business, and on top of that I just received an international chocolate account. But a good PR campaign helps a client focus on their unique skills as well as their long-term planning. We have to help them see where they want to go and exactly how to get there." She sat back with a sigh. "Now, aren't you completely bored?"

"Don't apologize because you care about what you do." T.J. lingered over her smooth, rich coffee. "Or because you're good at your job."

"How do you know that?"

He saw her hands tighten. McCall realized his answer mattered deeply to her. "First, because you think fast on your feet. Second, because you seem to genuinely like people. Most of all because you love to ask questions—the more irritating, the better."

Tess colored slightly. "Hello? Have I just tuned into the Psychic Network?"

"Simple process of deduction, Duchess. You make people feel special when you listen to them." T.J.'s smile faded slowly.

"What's wrong?"

He had played and replayed this conversation, but somehow the preparation didn't help. He couldn't delay telling her the things she needed to know. "I talked to your brother this morning, Tess. He's had some news."

"Have they traced the money?" she asked stiffly.

T.J. shook his head. "Andrew says they've isolated

two similar account transactions. One was in Seattle, and one in Atlanta. They're digging for more details, but they don't want to tip their hand too soon, in case they send warning signals.''

T.J. rose to pace the room. ''One of the transfers went to a man in Atlanta. He got a surprise in his account, too—only his deposit was for ten million dollars.'' T.J. rubbed the back of his neck. ''The fool went on a spending spree and left a trail a mile wide when he did it.''

Tess's hands tightened on her coffee cup. ''Where is he now?''

''There's no use in jumping to conclusions.''

''Where *is* he?''

T.J. braced his palms on the table in front of her. ''The man vanished last night. No one has been able to contact him.''

But it was just a matter of time until he was found, T.J. thought grimly. More likely dead than alive.

Tess looked down, stirring the froth in her coffee. ''What happened to the person in Seattle?''

''Nothing so far. He's still under constant surveillance. Andrew didn't want to put you through that so he convinced the authorities to let you stay here—as long as you're under my protection.''

''And that means I'm safe?''

''Safe enough.''

Tess gave a shaky laugh. ''You seem to be going to a lot of trouble to convince me there's no real problem, but I'm not buying it. You're a poor liar, Sheriff. Your eyes go all flat when you say something you don't believe. That's how they look right now,'' she whispered.

T.J. hesitated, then covered her hand with his. ''It doesn't mean anything, Tess. The man in Atlanta could show up tomorrow, good as new.''

"He could also show up good as dead."

"There's no way to know that."

"Don't lie to me, T.J. Never lie to me."

"Okay, you're right. It's a bad sign." He drew a raw breath. "We won't know exactly how bad without more information."

Tess pushed back slowly from the table. "I want to talk to my brother right now."

T.J. started to protest, then realized she had every right to more information. "Be my guest," he said, pointing to the cordless phone on the counter.

But he didn't leave as she dialed, or even later while she bent over the pine table in the dining room, her eyes narrowed. T.J. saw the strain that filled her face and the small tapping movements she made with her hand on the polished wood. She asked Andrew a few questions and listened intently, then hung up.

"So, that's the long and short of it. Man reports finding millions of dollars. Man vanishes."

"You left out one major point. Man *spends* a big part of the money," T.J. said flatly.

"I spent a good deal of my money, too," Tess reminded him grimly. "In the wrong quarters that could be a cause for unpleasantness."

"No one is getting past me, Tess. Just remember that. You aren't alone in this."

"I feel alone," she said softly. "I keep wishing the whole problem would go away. But it won't, will it?"

"No."

Tess stared at him. "Tell me the rest."

"Chances are that things will get worse. But nothing will happen to you. I give you my word on that."

"I don't frighten easily, T.J. I'm an organized person and I'm usually disgustingly optimistic."

CHRISTINA SKYE   161

"You will be again," he said.

"Will I? This place has left me wondering who I am. Part of the problem is the strange dreams I've been having. They disrupt my sense of order and good sense."

"What kind of dreams?" T.J. asked carefully, remembering her odd behavior in the old jail.

"It's as if I were here, but in a different time." Her voice trailed off as she shook her head. "They don't really seem like dreams, yet what else could they be?"

"Any number of things," he said. He'd had his share of strange dreams, too, but he figured they were part of the general turmoil Tess had caused in him since the moment he'd first seen her. He decided it would be a good idea to change the subject. "And what's the other part of the problem?"

She shrugged. "You. You make me edgy. You also make me want things I've never wanted before."

"What kind of things?"

"Quiet dinners. Cooking." She swallowed. "Maybe more than that."

As she spoke, a wave of wanting hit him. So much for changing the subject.

McCall wondered why he'd ever thought she was stiff or aloof. There was nothing aloof about Tess. She was all soft skin and lingering perfume, and the sight of her mouth made him think of ripe raspberries. He wanted to skim his way down her neck, then explore lower—

He cursed softly, knowing that touching her would be the worst thing he could do.

No doubt about it. The sooner Andrew got this mess straightened out so Tess could go back to her warp-speed life in Boston, the better.

12

When T.J. walked down the hall, he found Maria standing in the kitchen with her hands on her hips.

"Señor McCall, you should not be awake so early on your day off. And why did you not call me to make your breakfast?" Maria tied her apron, giving T.J. a chiding look, followed by an accusing glare at Tess. "You were up worrying all night, I think. Always you worry, as you did over my son when he gets involved with those smugglers and goes to jail. You worried until you went down to Mexico and brought him here—I still do not know how you managed to take him from that terrible place." She shook her head as she pulled eggs, vegetables, and tortillas from the refrigerator. Then she fixed Tess with another glare, the story a warning.

"Maria," T.J. warned.

"No, do not tell me to stop. The *señorita* does not know how you stay awake for many nights when you worry. She does not know how far you go to do right."

So that was it. Maria thought he was up early because of this woman sleeping under his roof. She was in mother-hen mode, wanting to protect him from a conniving female. But then, Maria had been there when T.J. had been involved with a journalist and damn near ran himself into the ground traveling back and forth between Almost and L.A.

"Where is your son now, Maria?" Tess asked gently before T.J. could interrupt.

"The *señor* sent him to school. Now my son owns six grocery stores in New Mexico, and I have four beautiful grandchildren," Maria said proudly.

T.J. swiped the back of neck, avoiding Tess's raised brows. She didn't seem to be surprised by the news.

"Smooth your feathers, Maria," he muttered, annoyed at being cornered by two females in his own house. "Ms. O'Mara's brother is a friend of mine. He sent her down here because she might be in danger. No one you don't know personally is to be allowed in the house and Tess will be with either me or one of my deputies at all times. If you have any questions you should call me immediately."

"The *señorita* is trouble, I am thinking," Maria said, shaking her head.

"Aren't all women?" T.J. countered.

Maria threw up her hands and rushed out as the bell clanged in the outer courtyard.

T.J. scowled at his watch, wondering who could be downstairs at this hour. He had his answer even before Maria ushered in his guest. The low, off-key whistling could only be Grady's.

"If this isn't a certifiable emergency," T.J. drawled, "I just might have to shoot you."

Grady chuckled. "Nice words for a colleague and old friend." He grinned at T.J. "Maybe you're feeling poorly because you didn't sleep too well last night. On account of your visitor and all." He nodded in greeting to Tess.

"I slept just fine," T.J. lied. "Now, do you want some coffee or are you going to stand here jawing?"

"I'll take the coffee, but only if Tess or Maria made it. That brew of yours isn't fit to feed a cow."

In the kitchen, Maria frowned at Tess's cappuccino machine, studying it from every angle. "You are out of luck if you want coffee from this, Señor Grady. No one comes into my kitchen when I cook." Picking up her simple percolator, she filled it with water, added coffee to the basket, and plugged it in. "You will settle for my coffee, which will be finished in a few minutes."

"Good enough. Just so it doesn't get up and walk around, I'll be happy." Grady frowned at Tess. "You look worn out. He didn't do anything to you, I hope."

T.J. gave a disgusted sigh. "I didn't do a thing to her, Grady. She had a long drive and then she suffered heat-stroke, remember?"

"I'm fine," Tess said, sounding distracted.

"I guess you're right. There was also that excitement with your man friend who got himself arrested."

"You want to run that past me again?" T.J. said, sitting up straighter.

"She told me the fellow she was involved with turned out to be a criminal, and that's why she had to go on the run. Not that I'd dream of mentioning the truth to anyone else. She told me it was a strict secret until the investigation is finished."

Maria mumbled something under her breath and shook her head as she cracked eggs into a bowl.

"She told you all that, did she?" T.J. said, intrigued.

Tess regarded him with a level stare and a closed mouth.

Grady nodded, helping himself to a chocolate doughnut from a carton beneath his arm, then pushing the box across to T.J. and Tess.

What had made the woman concoct such a damned fool story? And if there was even a *grain* of truth to it, he'd find the man and tear him into tiny pieces.

He looked up to find Grady studying him intently. *"What?"*

"Just wondering, that's all."

T.J. took a gulp of his coffee and grimaced. "Wondering what?"

"Why you two were kissing inside the old jail last night."

"We weren't kissing." McCall and Tess spoke in unison.

"I've got six witnesses who say you were."

"Doc Felton being one, I suppose." T.J. ran a hand through his hair. "The man can't see across a room with his bifocals on. Mae isn't much better."

"That would explain two. Tom Martinez tells me you were snuggled up mighty close last night before you left the office."

"His shirt was caught on my dress," Tess said quickly.

"Must have been a trick of the shadows." T.J. said at exactly the same time.

Grady sat back, measuring the general uneasiness. "So what exactly is going on between the two of you?"

Maria slammed down two cups of coffee on the pine table. "Yes, you will please to tell *me* what is going on also."

T.J. gestured toward Tess. "I'm the sheriff; that little lady there might be a possible target of a crime. Other than that, nothing's going on, and I'd appreciate it if you'd stop digging for news where none exists." He eyed the brown paper bag Grady had set on the table with the box of doughnuts. "What's in there?"

Why was Tess so quiet, he wondered. He'd expected a sharp comeback—in fact, he'd wanted one.

But she simply gave him a tight smile.

"Mae's cheesecake," Grady said around a swallow of coffee. "It's chocolate pistachio swirl today. She put in some barbecue ribs left over from the café last night. She thought you two might be hungry."

T.J. rubbed his jaw, anticipating another glare from Maria if he so much as peeked inside the bag and sniffed. "Maybe for lunch. I'm primed and ready for Maria's *huevos*."

"Hmppph." Still sniffing, Maria carried in plates mounded with omelettes, biscuits, gravy, and sausages. Whisking the bag away, she muttered in Spanish about unhealthy breakfasts and how typical of a man to eat such things in the morning. "You will die young if you are not careful, and this would be a great pity," she added in English.

T.J. was too distracted by Tess's calm to comment. Why was she so damned quiet? And why hadn't she denied that she'd been involved with a criminal?

Personally involved.

T.J.'s fingers drummed on the table. She smiled at him and took a bite of omelette and chiles.

The whole story was a product of her imagination—it had to be. But suddenly T.J. seemed to have lost his appetite. He rubbed his jaw and pushed away from the table, ignoring Tess and Grady as he strode outside.

■

T.J. was still pacing the courtyard ten minutes later when Mae's bright red pickup truck rumbled over the wash. T.J. had visitors at the ranch once or twice a week, but now he was starting to feel suspicious. He went to the gate, his hands on his hips.

"If you're looking for Grady, you just missed him." He gestured to the dirt blowing over the narrow, curved road.

"I'm not looking for Grady." Mae shot a glance over T.J.'s shoulder toward the house. "Just thought I'd check to see how things were going. And I forgot to send you some potato salad with those ribs." She held up another brown paper bag.

"Things are fine," he muttered. "Any reason they shouldn't be?"

"None that I know." She studied T.J. keenly. "How does Tess like the ranch?"

T.J. noted that Mae, too, was on a first-name basis with Tess. "How about some coffee?"

Her eyes brightened. "You happen to have one of those cappuccino things that Ms. O'Mara makes?"

"Afraid not."

"Still asleep, huh?" Mae gave him a measuring glance. "Busy night, I guess."

"Not the way you're thinking." T.J. walked back through the courtyard and sat on a bent twig rocker. "And for your information, Tess is in the breakfast room right now, eating me out of house and home. Maria made enough for an army, as usual."

"And I'll bet you haven't eaten at all." Mae handed him a container of potato salad and a plastic fork. "I hear you two were standing awfully close inside the jail last night."

T.J. clamped down hard on his temper. "My blasted

badge got caught on her dress. I was trying to work it free. Nothing else was going on.'' He ripped the lid off the container and stabbed the fork into the salad.

"Is that a fact?"

"What's that's supposed to mean?"

"It means you're a damned poor liar, Jackson McCall.'' Mae paced through the courtyard, then turned to stare at him, long and hard. "I saw what I saw. So did a whole lot of other people."

T.J. crossed his arms in irritation. "Don't tell me you're a one-woman ethics committee sent here to find out my intentions toward our newest visitor. If you are, forget it. Maria beat you to it. But she was questioning Tess about her intentions toward *me*."

Mae smiled tightly. "So are you feeling guilty about something?"

"I might, if anything had happened, which it didn't."

"You're a moral man, Sheriff. That's a good thing. But that's a fine girl you've got sleeping beneath your roof. You might not want to be too moral."

T.J. stared at her in mute shock. "Too moral? Are you saying that Tess O'Mara and I should—"

"Damned right I am. Life's too short for regrets or apologies. Be sure to give my regards to the young lady. If she has some free time this afternoon, maybe she could drop by the café for a chat. I've got some ideas about those chile products, and I'd like her professional advice. After that the head of the 4-H club would like to talk to her about her lecture. She wants to know if Tess prefers to speak before or after the demonstration of cattle-castration equipment.'' Mae strode past him to the gate. "Give my regards to Maria, if you will. And you might want to close your mouth now, Sheriff, or stuff it with some of that salad. Otherwise you'll be catching flies.''

As Mae climbed back into her truck and drove off, T.J. slammed the lid on the potato salad and strode into the house.

Tess was dressed and sitting at the table, nursing another cup of her exotic coffee. ''Maria is doing laundry,'' she said absently.

He motioned toward the door. ''Let's go.''

''Go? Where?''

''I have business to take care of in town.'' Damn. Why couldn't she just stand up and follow him out to the car with no questions asked? He was in no mood for more talk. Being around Tess left him feeling too edgy.

''I'll stay here.''

''Dammit, you're coming with me.''

''It's not a good idea,'' she argued. ''I need to—''

''The point is not negotiable, Duchess.''

She snapped her head up and glared at him. ''You're not my keeper, McCall.''

''The hell I'm not,'' he countered, struggling to control his voice and his temper. ''No matter how you or I feel about it, it's my job to protect you. I can't do that if I'm in town and you're out here.''

She caught an angry breath. He saw anger fight with uneasiness. The sight stirred a painful wave of protectiveness in him.

''I'll bring the car around to the front.''

A tight smile curved her mouth. ''You sheriff; me possible victim?''

''That's right,'' he snapped. ''That's why you're here and we'd both better remember that.''

13

The instant Tess set foot in the sheriff's office, routine flew out the window. Heads seemed to turn in their direction more than usual. Cars slowed in passing.

Then the visitors started arriving. Grady showed up, papers in hand, asking for Tess's opinion on some layout changes he was considering for the *Almost Gazette*. She suggested more photos, more interviews, and a relationship column. Grady was planning to add all three by the time he left. After that, Doc Felton dropped in to check on his patient, and the two discussed the merits of French roast versus espresso roast coffee beans, while T.J. pretended not to listen.

Seated at his desk, he fielded four calls regarding his role in the hostage situation and tried to ignore the curious glances of half a dozen town residents who happened to be walking by the sheriff's office.

Tess seemed to be having the time of her life.

Dressed in her new red boots, a short, flirty skirt, and a brightly embroidered denim shirt, she sat in a wooden desk chair at the window, oblivious of the commotion outside or the fact that *she* was the cause. She answered every question with energy and enthusiasm. She listened, then made suggestions. Good suggestions, T.J. admitted. But she didn't understand that she was on display, being carefully measured as a candidate for a relationship with the town sheriff.

T.J.'s teeth ground at the thought. The last thing he needed was a dozen meddling residents trying to pair him off with a bed partner.

Even one with such amazing legs as Tess's.

"So what do you think?"

T.J. looked up with a frown. Doc Felton had gone, the high school principal had vanished, and Tess was staring at him expectantly. "About what?"

Tess shook her head. "You haven't heard anything I've said, McCall."

She was right about that, he thought guiltily. The night before had been bad enough, offering him damned little sleep and disturbing dreams that he couldn't quite remember. Now his frequent glimpses of her legs weren't helping his concentration, nor was the scent that drifted through the air every time she moved.

"I heard every word; it's a fine idea," he lied.

"In that case, I'll be sure to tell Grady that the paper needs a fire-engine-red headline and a weekly safety column written by you."

"I didn't say—" T.J. stabbed a hand through his hair. "Okay, I wasn't listening." He blew out a breath. Every time she moved, her denim shirt drifted open, giving him a painful glimpse of her simple white T-shirt. Up to this moment, he'd never found T-shirts arousing. He hadn't particularly enjoyed the sight of red hair before this either. All that had changed the moment he'd seen Tess fighting heat exhaustion while she tried to fold her map on Main Street.

She planted her hands on her hips. "If you want to get rid of me, just say so."

"I don't." T.J. rocked back in his chair with a sigh.

"Okay, maybe I do. I'm not used to having an audience while I work. Why don't you take a walk? You can go to the library and do some of that research you mentioned. I'll meet you at Mae's for lunch."

"First you drag me into town; then you tell me to get lost."

"I brought you into town so I could keep you in sight. That doesn't mean I have to keep you on a short leash," he shot back.

She paced along the far wall, where a picture of the governor hung beside a framed copy of the first *Almost Gazette* and a series of black and white photographs that were a gift from Doc Felton. Tess stood motionless before the last of the pictures, her fingers rising to trace the framed image.

"Tess?"

She pulled her hand away abruptly and murmured something T.J. couldn't make out. She turned, looking dazed and pale.

He'd seen that look before and chalking it up to imagination again would be a stretch.

"Doc Felton took those pictures right after he arrived in Almost," T.J. said carefully, hoping she was just preoccupied with the photo.

"This one," she said stiffly. "Where was it taken?"

T.J. studied the rugged landscape. "The ruins? They're about twenty miles north, up on the mesa. It's deserted country up there, even today."

"It's beautiful," she whispered. "Almost too beautiful. But the walls have crumbled and the roofs are gone." She said it as if she knew how the ruins had looked before and was surprised to find them changed.

Now *his* imagination was going into overdrive.

"Seven or eight hundred years of hard weather and neglect will do that."

She didn't move, didn't speak.

T.J. silently crossed the room to stand behind her, his shadow falling across the old photograph of the ruins.

Tess raised her hand as if to touch the grainy image again, then moved away stiffly. A shiver seemed to run through her as she bumped into T.J.

He caught her arm and steadied her. "Is something wrong?"

"No," she said sharply, playing restlessly with her collar. "I thought I recognized the place, but I was wrong."

"I'd be real surprised if you'd seen those ruins before. They're on private property, not state lands, and not many people know the way up there." He kept talking— anything to chase that vacant look from her eyes. "Not that these are the only ruins around here. Most of the canyons to the north have scattered signs of early habitation. In the thirteenth century this area must have been a regular melting pot."

"I don't understand."

"Anasazi, Salado, Mogollon—they were spread throughout the Four Corners region. Then the Athabaskan peoples moved in, possibly from the Great Plains. You'll know them better as Navajo and Apache." He nodded at the old photo. "When you see a place like this, there are half-a-dozen possibilities for who built it. Experts tend to argue about things like that for years," he added dryly. "Only Miguel might know, and he's not talking."

"Miguel," Tess repeated with a frown. "The man who was out in the storm with us last night?"

"You remember now?"

"Only bits and pieces. The rain, the wind, the drums . . ."

Light played over the row of old photos as T.J. stared at her. "There were no drums. You must have heard the thunder."

"Thunder. Of course." Her frown deepened as she turned away from the image of old ruins on a high mesa. "It's still rather a blur."

"Tess, are you—"

"I'm fine, McCall. My memory is just a little sketchy," she said. "I think I'll take your suggestion and head to the library. After that, I'll go see Mae at the café."

T.J. studied her face, relieved to see color washing back into her cheeks. "I'll meet you there in about two hours." T.J. eyed the paperwork on his desk with distaste. He had three theft investigations pending and he had to hire a new dispatcher. The last one quit after budget restraints had required a cut in pay. The truth was that he'd rather be anywhere but behind his desk today. "Have a nice walk," he said, knowing the buck stopped with him and as long as Tess was around he would have to catch up on paperwork when he could. "Just try not to cause too much trouble."

"Me?" she said with a grin. "In this sleepy little town?"

T.J. watched her walk toward the door, amazed that she really didn't know how she stirred people up. She didn't realize that her enthusiasm for new ideas was contagious. "Duchess," he muttered as she stepped into the sunlight, "you're a regular lightning rod for trouble."

As he watched her cross the street, he realized he already missed the sound of her low, husky laughter. He didn't want to consider why she bothered him so much or how he already knew every nuance of the complicated perfume she wore.

He was almost relieved when four drunken college students from Tucson began a raucous, off-key serenade in the holding cell they'd occupied since instigating a bar fight the night before. At least now he had something else to think about besides Tess.

When he returned from quieting the minibrawl, he found Miguel sitting in the chair beside his desk. His black clothes seemed to glow, backlit by the sun streaming through the doorway.

"There is trouble in the high desert," the old man said without preamble.

The nerves tightened at the back of T.J.'s neck. No one knew the canyons and wind-blown mesas better than this old man, and T.J. never questioned his observations. "You found something up there?"

"First I found prints made by men in cars and on motorbikes." His lip curved in disdain for the noisy, smoke-spewing vehicles that destroyed the delicate balance of the desert beneath their big, clumsy tires. "At first I could find only their tracks. Then I saw this." The old man tossed a photograph onto the desk. The photo captured the profile of a dead coyote, its body distended and rigid, its eyes blank.

This animal would never sing again, T.J. thought as he held up the photo for a closer look. "No bullet wounds. No knife marks. What do you think happened, Miguel? Rabies?"

The old man shook his head. "This coyote did not die a natural death. There were too many man-tracks nearby. It was poisoned with something that kills quickly."

"Any evidence of that?"

Miguel shrugged. "I think you should not doubt me."

"Where did you find it?"

"At the base of the Needle."

T.J. frowned. The Needle was a local landmark whose red sandstone columns rose above a tangle of box canyons long held in reverence by the Apaches. Now it was part of state trust land in a terrain rugged enough that few travelers knew of its existence, other than the occasional group of scientists who climbed the steep slopes in search of a new species of plant life, new evidence of ancient tribal migrations, or proof of whatever theory happened to be the current rage.

Some old-time residents avoided the place and whispered that a band of lost Apache warriors still survived in that desolate canyon-cut back country, hidden and undetected even to this day. T.J. bought into that possibility about as much as he did the legends about Sasquatch and the Loch Ness monster. But the Needle was a lonely and unforgiving place, and he supposed odd things might happen there.

"That's pretty barren country, Miguel. Any idea who would be hunting coyotes up there?"

The fine lines at Miguel's mouth deepened. "Perhaps men who hunt pots from the old ruins. I come across them now and again. When they ask me many questions about the old places, I shrug and say I have no English. If they lose their way and die of thirst, it is no worry of mine," he said, fingering the silver of his belt buckle.

T.J. sat motionless, staring at the image of the dead coyote. Was this animal the victim of an illegal pot hunter or a hiker in search of a few days of adventure in the desert? Tension knotted his shoulders at the evidence of more pointless violence against an animal that had been despised and hunted wholesale for decades.

As scavengers, coyotes were not protected by game laws and hatred ran high in ranchers convinced that the predator decimated their livestock population. Shooting was the knee-jerk response, followed closely by dropping poisoned bait. Most hunters considered the act to be a requisite part of manhood. But there were strict rules about what kind of poison could be used, and this looked like nothing T.J. had seen before.

He decided that a visit to the Needle was in order as soon as he could manage it. "I'll look into this, Miguel. I don't like what I'm seeing here."

Miguel nodded slowly. "Nor should you. Men who hunt the coyote hunt something in themselves. The shadows and trickery of the coyote howl in all of us, but we would do best to understand, not kill them."

T.J. felt the skin at his neck tighten at those words. As a boy, he'd stared into the eyes of a coyote and felt he was looking into darkness that had no end. Yet there had also been intelligence in those pale gold eyes and something almost familiar. Perhaps that sensation threatened some men far more than they liked to admit.

Miguel fingered the canvas bag on his shoulder. "Such an act comes from the hand of someone with fear and uncertainty, someone who doubts his own heart."

"I'll need something more concrete to go on than that."

"And I will find it. Whoever did this will pay, most certainly." The old man spoke in whispery tones that carried a strange strength. He opened his pack and pulled out a paper bag. "These are herbs for your woman with the red hair."

"She's not my woman," T.J. said firmly.

Miguel's face was as rough as the scoured granite walls that rose to form the Needle. T.J. had the odd feeling that the old man's gaze was probing deep into his heart.

"You both have much to learn and not a great deal of time to do it." His eyes narrowed. "But time is not always what it seems." He placed the bag next to the photo on T.J.'s desk. "She should take this three times each day. It will be bitter, of course, but good things often are at first." He turned, his eyes focused on the street. "Now I must go."

■

Tess pushed open the door to the deserted café, blinking as she stepped out of the streaming late morning sunlight into shadows. A frail woman with blue-gray hair looked up from a copy of the *Almost Gazette*. "If you're looking for lunch, I'm afraid we don't start serving for another hour."

"Actually, I'm looking for Mae."

"She's right through those doors. Last I saw, she was wrestling with a box of frozen turkey fillets." Her head tilted. "You must be that woman who was snuggling with the sheriff outside the jail last night."

Tess felt her face fill with heat. "Sheriff McCall and I were just talking. It was nothing personal." Tess delivered the lie with a big smile, hoping to make it slightly more believable.

The waitress's eyes crinkled at the corners. "Sure looked personal to me." Somewhere beyond the doorway to the kitchen came a bang of metal pots followed by indistinct muttering. "Lavinia, where's my Phillips head screwdriver? The fuses back here are acting up again."

"Right here, Mae." The woman shoved a tool into Tess's hands and gestured past the cash register. "Just head on back there." She studied Tess long and hard. "Sure do like your hair. Haven't hardly seen that color before."

Tess made her way back into the kitchen, where Mae was digging in a metal toolbox.

Tess held out the screwdriver. "I think you wanted this."

"You're a lifesaver. Glad you could drop by." Mae closed her toolbox. "Problem with the fuses again. The last electrician from Tucson said we'd have to rewire the whole blasted building. Needless to say, I had a different perspective on the problem. So we tinker along together, the wiring and me. Have a seat." She pointed to a hand-carved pine chair beside the narrow window. "How about you wash up and try your hand on that pie dough in front of you?"

She disappeared into the back room before Tess could protest. Pie dough? Tess didn't have a clue where to start. She could assess markets and develop new media campaigns, but making pastry had always terrified her.

"Don't worry, it won't bite you." Mae's voice drifted into the room. "The trick is not to work the dough too long. Otherwise it gets tough. Go on, give it a whirl."

Tess stared at the bowl. There was a mound of white flour and what appeared to be chunks of cold butter. "How do I—"

"Just dig in with a fork. Better yet, use two. Cut the butter twenty or thirty times until you have something that looks like cornmeal."

Tess made a swift, tentative movement. Nothing happened. Gritting her teeth, she tried again and this time she saw the butter and flour crumble together.

Five. Six. Seven. She was actually making dough. Amazing. Her mother would faint if she knew. And Andrew would tease her for at least a year.

"How are you doing out there? No blood in sight, I hope."

"It's working. It's actually working."

"Of course it is." Metal clanged. Mae reappeared with a layer of fine dust covering her head and shoulders. "One of these days I'll have that storeroom cleaned properly. At least my tinkering should hold off the electrician for a little while longer." She glanced down at Tess's bowl. "Not bad. We'll give it about a tablespoon of ice water, gather it into a ball, and then it goes into the refrigerator. Keeping it chilled makes all the difference." Tess watched her deftly add a small amount of water, stir the dough, and nod. "Just slip it over once, easy does it. When the butter melts in the oven, it leaves behind all those wonderful little holes and makes a perfect pastry." She covered the bowl, then whisked it away to a huge industrial refrigerator. "Nice work. Any time you need a new job, just let me know."

The idea was so fantastic that Tess almost laughed aloud. In her family, she was irrevocably classified as the kitchen klutz. She could just about manage to boil water on a good day.

Make pie dough? From scratch? No one would believe it.

"Have a seat. I'm going to finish this apple walnut filling." Mae peeled apples as she talked. "First off, I want something different here at the café. I'm tired of doing my chicken pot pie and black bean cornbread with chiles."

"Those sound pretty delicious to me."

Mae barked out a laugh. "Stop pulling my leg, girl."

"Why would I do that?"

After a moment Mae nodded. "No, I guess you wouldn't. You don't hardly look the type to mock a person. Nice, I call it." She cut a long apple peel and let it fall onto her cutting board. "So how do you like Almost?"

"Just fine. At least what I've seen so far, which isn't much."

"Not a great deal to see. Still, this town can suit a person fine, provided a person knows what he's looking for. Or what *she's* looking for." She cast a measuring glance at Tess. "Do you know what you're looking for?"

There was no malice in the question, only honest concern. It was clear that the answer mattered to Mae.

"I thought I did. Lately my life has been very confusing." That had to be the understatement of the new millennium.

Time to change the subject, Tess thought. "I need to know something about the history of Almost. That will help me develop the right theme for your Web site promotion."

"History? I guess that started with our illustrious founder. Some people swear he ran out of water on the way to California, which made him decide to stake a claim right here. Myself, I think that's just a nasty joke." Mae's eyes narrowed. "The fact is, people seem to come here for all the wrong reasons, then end up staying for all the right ones. Just like I did."

Tess pulled out her notebook. "What brought you to Almost?"

Mae chuckled. "Ever since I was a child, all I ever wanted to do was cook. To feed people and make them happy. Oh, I never had grand ideas. Just good, solid food—what you call comfort food these days. I lived in Atlanta then. I worked hard, put money by, and after a few years I found myself a small restaurant. Then I heard the Pope was coming to visit. All I could think of was cooking for the Pope. Stupid idea, wasn't it? A silly no-body like me cooking for the Pope.''

Tess propped her chin on her hands, smiling. "Not silly. If the man ever tasted your biscuits and gravy, he'd think he'd already gone to heaven. But what happened?''

"It didn't work out. Someone changed his itinerary at the last moment. That same day I decided it was time for me to try something different, so I sold the business and headed west. It seemed as good a direction as any.'' She shook her head. "When I saw the name on the map, I thought it had to be a joke. But it wasn't. The day I drove in, the old café was up for sale, and I decided to buy it, just like that. The funny thing is, I haven't had a regret in all those years. It might be quiet here, but people look out for each other. From all that I hear, that's pretty special today.'' She picked up another apple and peeled it care-fully. "And there's the mayor—Miss America runner-up, 1965. She was headed up to Vancouver to meet her fiancé when her car broke down. She waited for parts for two weeks, and just when she was ready to leave, her fiancé called saying he'd gotten cold feet and the wed-ding was off. At first she stayed here because she was too embarrassed to go back and tell her family what had hap-pened. Later on she stayed because she'd found a good man who appreciated her. That's her husband, Frank.''

"He came here from somewhere else, too?''

"Golly, yes. Frank was in the astronaut training pro-gram. He was fairly old to fly a mission—the ripe old age of twenty-seven, but he had a good shot of walking on the moon. Then after three solid years of preparation, the program was canceled. Given his age, that was the only chance he was going to get. He stopped in Almost on the way to do some hiking and then he came back after the hiking. Now he runs wilderness rock climbing treks in the rim country to the north. He also takes helicopter tours to some of the most beautiful country God ever made.''

Tess's pencil raced. She already had a dozen ideas for Mae's Web site, including a full-scale profile with photographs of the wilderness treks. It would be the perfect thing to appeal to jaded, stressed-out urban dwellers. ''What about Grady?''

''Now, there's a story.'' Mae shook her head. ''Grady's one of the few people I know who was actually born here. But he left the day he graduated from high school. Worked on a steamer, then did some construction work in Australia, and somewhere along the line became a journalist—and a darned good one. He sent some reports from Vietnam when the war was ending and almost got himself killed trying to save a family when a shell exploded on their junk. He never did find out which side dropped the shell. He said by then it didn't matter because he was tired of looking for excitement. So he came home to Almost. If you ask him real nice, you might get him to show you his desk full of journalism awards.''

Tess stared down at her notebook, drawing aimless circles. ''What about T.J.?''

''I figure if you want his story, you'll have to ask him. The man's mighty private about things like that.''

''I didn't mean to pry. I was just wondering about what happened yesterday with that hostage situation. Does he get called in like that often?''

''Often enough,'' Mae said grimly. ''T.J.'s marksmanship skills make him one of the first choices when a situation turns nasty."

Tess yearned to ask Mae how he'd gotten those skills and what secrets his past held.

But she didn't. His past wasn't any of her business.

Nor was his future.

She wasn't going to let this comfortable little town or its rugged, handsome sheriff get under her skin. The minute her case was solved, she'd be behind the wheel of her Mercedes with the wind whipping through her hair as she headed straight to Boston.

"So what about Sheriff McCall? How do you feel about him?"

"He's a nice man," she said tentatively.

Mae snorted. "T.J. wouldn't thank you for that particular description. Honorable, sexy, tough maybe, but not nice, though he's that, too." She diced a half-dozen apples with swift, practiced movements. "He was hurt before, you know."

Tess swallowed. "You mean in a shootout?"

"Not that kind of hurt," Mae muttered. "It happened about four years ago, not too long after he came back to Almost. He got himself involved with a hotshot television reporter from California. Any person with eyes could see it wouldn't work out, but no, they went at it like umpires with scorecards." Mae's lips pursed. "Two weekends here in Almost, two weekends over there in California—everything split nice and neat down the center. Any fool could have told them you can't take the square root of love or chop a relationship into nice, equal pieces. It doesn't work that way and it never has, never will." Mae scraped a mound of chopped apples into her bowl and sprinkled lemon juice over them.

"What happened?" Tess asked, consumed with curiosity.

"There were no fireworks or angry arguments, but one month he stopped going to California. Right after that, she stopped coming here. He never talks about it much. Men are like that. The big fools think it's a sign of weakness to talk about how they feel. At any rate, he heard three months later that she'd been reassigned to Paris. She didn't even call to say good-bye." Mae shook her head. "I think that's why reporters make him see red these days." Mae slid into the chair beside her and leaned forward. "So, Tess, that's why I want to know if you're planning to stay?"

Tess locked her hands. "I've only just gotten here. There are problems, complications."

"There are always problems. The question is what we do about them."

Tess peered down at her hands, shifting restlessly. "Things haven't gotten personal, if that's what you mean. I haven't been asked to stay."

"What does being *asked* have to do with it?" Mae gave a disgusted snort. "Life is short, and you don't always get an invitation to dance. If you see something you want, go after it."

"It's not like that." Tess shook her head. "T.J. and I are . . . well, we hardly know each other."

"Well, get to know the man! There's nothing stopping you. My advice is to decide what you want and go after it. Opportunity comes when it comes and you'd better not let it get away." The lights flickered as she banged on the counter for emphasis. "I guess I'll need that electrician after all."

"By the way, where is T.J.?" Mae asked.

"He had some work to finish." Tess smiled wryly.

"He told me to go take a hike." She looked out the window to the northeast, where rugged blue peaks rose against a cloudless sky. "Are there many ruins in the area?"

"All over the place."

Tess couldn't seem to pull her eyes from that particular jagged range. "What about the ones in the picture at the sheriff's office?"

Mae tapped at her jaw. "That's it there—right where you're staring. It's not so far, maybe about twenty miles. But it's rugged going. Why do you ask?"

"I was just . . . curious. I thought going there might help me to create a background for your products. You know: ancient spices, ancient cultures—that sort of thing."

"You'll never make it there in that car of yours. You're welcome to take my Explorer, if you want. I'll be here all afternoon and a good part of the evening."

"But I wouldn't want to—"

"No problem." Mae dug in her apron pocket and pulled out a set of keys. "The tank's full and there's a jug of water in the back. You got a hat?"

"No."

"Well, you'd better take mine." Mae tossed Tess a broad-brimmed panama that had seen a lot of miles. "Wear it. The sun out here can be deceptive. But I guess you know that by now."

"I'm not likely to forget." Not ever, Tess thought. Especially the part where she woke up and found T.J.'s hand under her skirt.

She flushed.

"You okay?"

"Absolutely. If you're certain you don't mind loaning me your car, I'll go now." Before T.J. could find her gone, Tess thought. "Maybe you could draw me a map."

"That's easy enough. The ruins are right up in those foothills." Mae pointed out the window to the rugged mountains in the northeast.

Somehow Tess had known that's where the ruins would be. The mountains seemed to call her, shimmering in the bright sun.

Mae quickly sketched a map and jotted down an estimate of the distance. Then she shook her head. "Maybe I should go with you after all. Or maybe T.J. should go. That's pretty deserted country up there."

"T.J. is busy. So are you," Tess said firmly. The last thing she wanted was company. How could she explain this compulsion she had to visit an isolated canyon that somehow seemed—familiar? "Don't worry, I'll be fine. I'll stick to the roads and I won't climb anything that looks unstable."

Feeling the hum of excitement, Tess glanced at her watch. It was almost noon. Everything would be fine. In fact, she would be back before T.J. even knew she was gone.

■

Blue foothills rose before Tess like a dream. There was something rich and intensely welcoming in the green chaparral and the waves of bright wildflowers. Above all rose one blue peak, calling her, claiming her.

She consulted Mae's map once. After that she had no need for it. She followed her peak and it guided her without error.

Where the valley floor rose into the foothills, she

slowed and rolled down a window. The pungent scent of juniper and piñon filled the air, while the sun beat warm upon her shoulders. Out of the corner of her eye she saw a brown shape running alongside the car. A coyote, she thought in awe.

Another brown form emerged from the opposite side of the car. In loose, loping strides they paced her up the winding road. There in the sunlight, when Tess should have felt uneasy, her fear vanished. The presence of these wild creatures seemed as natural as the rest of this day's magic.

By the time she wound along the twisting gravel road and passed a tangle of fallen boulders, the coyotes had vanished. She stopped the car where the road ended in a steep slope. With water and hat in hand, Tess set off along the path, as Mae had described it.

Then something stopped her.

The broad brown path seemed wrong somehow. She scanned the rugged landscape from horizon to horizon. Above her rose an ancient twisting piñon, and something whispered that this was the way. Once underneath those tangled branches Tess saw a smaller path, now over-grown with scrub. As she took her first step, an eagle cried high overhead, and for the space of a heartbeat, the air seemed to shimmer. Tess shivered at the sound of muffled drums, but she did not stop to question what pulled her along that steep, twisting path.

She simply followed its wild call.

At the top of the slope, she came to a dead end. Fallen rocks blocked the way where there should be none. But how did she know they did not belong?

Suddenly *how* did not seem to matter. Only the climb mattered. She fought her way forward, pulling herself up over the slope from rock to rock, scratching her hands and cutting her legs. At the top she came to a ledge— and beyond that a village of stone that slept in the shadow of the curving cliff, slept as if waiting for the laughter of returning families.

Or as if waiting for some lost magic to restore its life.

Tess looked up. Marks covered the weathered stone. Animals. A sun. A handprint, captured in deep red hues.

She hesitated, drawn to touch that handprint. Around her the air seemed to hum, to glow. Suddenly she couldn't breathe, and there was a blur of something like clouds before her eyes. Dazed, she walked through the whiteness and found her way to the other side.

But not to the village. Not to the cooking fires, the laughter, and the barking dogs. Up she went, where the path rose to the high cliffs. To the place where she knew her warrior would be waiting.

■

Into golden sunlight she climbed, following his marks. First a broken twig, then a feather left carefully on the ground. The air was still here, sweet with the scent of juniper, but she did not pause to enjoy it. Another sign, a circle of small stones. Beyond that a precious bead of carved jade.

She collected them all in her sack of leather. But where was he? What game did he play here, so close to her father's village? If she was discovered, if he was found here with her—

There was a movement at the corner of her eye. She was grabbed, spun, pressed back against the warm wall of the cliff. And his mouth closed hard upon hers, searching, better than all her dreams.

The scent of juniper faded. The weight of sunlight fled.

This was all.

"It is not safe," she whispered.

"No part of life is safe. But I have the trail watched. None will follow us without a warning." His eyes were hard when he shoved away her tunic. He gazed at her as if she were a stranger, then he drew her close to savor the soft fullness of her breast and hips. His fingers moved lower, lingering in the shadow of her thighs. He had thought of little but this, even in the dark pine forests where he stalked his kill. This, he had wanted, hungered for with burning blood. The first time after so many weeks he was not slow, not gentle. Nor were her own fingers gentle where they gripped his shoulders and dug hard, leaving white marks.

He felt heat churn within her, moving higher as her body tightened in need. Her hair was a black cascade around them as he brought his mouth to her hot sweetness, pleasing them both with his skill. He could not see her this way enough, could never have enough of her touch. While her broken cry still stirred the warm air, while her back was rigid with pleasure, he tossed away his hip cloth. His fingers locked with hers, pinning her against the cliff face, the only stability in a world of churning pleasure. He bit her mouth, then buried himself in her heat. They both trembled, thighs locked and hands tense.

Both cried out in their joining of the spirit.

Far below in the hot valley, the drums began.

■

When her eyes opened, the song star blazed in the darkening sky to the west.

"A visitor has come."

He stirred inside her, his fingers buried in her hair. "You can see so far, little witch?" He smiled, one hand drifting gently over her breasts.

She shivered at the instant return of desire, even now, after their bodies had joined with blinding completeness. "I know the sound of the drums. It is not an enemy or a stranger. It is someone who has come from a great distance, but he walks in peace."

Something stirred in the warrior's eyes. "Perhaps he comes to take you for a mate. You are a rich prize, after all. You are daughter of the chief and maker of great clay magic."

She pulled away with a gasp. "Do not tease about this." Pain filled her heart.

"I do not tease." The warrior rose, pulling her hands to his chest while his eyes measured her with painful intensity. "Go with me. Walk with my people and share our songs. Follow us when the snow comes to the high passes and share my furs before the fire."

This was not mocking, she realized. There was truth in his words and in his trembling touch.

It was what she had prayed to hear him ask— and also what she had feared, for this question meant the end of the life she had known since she was a child. It would mean many words, much arguing. In the end, it would mean leaving this valley she loved.

"My father would never allow it. We are field people, you are of the mountains. All around the fires I hear the grumbling that your tribe has used the river waters, which are lower this year. We cannot live without water." She drew a painful breath. *"He would never allow me to go, not to a man he considers his enemy."*

"I can give him many furs. Parrot feathers traded from the south and carved stone from the mountains to the north. Even your father does not have such things as this."

It might be possible, she thought. But it would take much time, much discussion and persuasion. She sensed that they did not have time, that already change stalked them in the gathering twilight. *"Perhaps. I cannot be certain."*

His lips curved, his face strong and beloved in the shadows. *"Then come here to me. I will show you what we can be certain of. Remember this now and as long as the sun shall rise."*

With the brush of his lips, she forgot about her father's power and all her uncertainty in the future.

■

The drums did not still. The sun burned beyond the mountains and stars came to light the darkness of the sky. The pounding throb of the skins continued, calling all of the tribe from the fields and canyons.

"I must go." She pulled away, feeling an ache in all her muscles, which had been well used in this peaceful glade.

He slid his fingers into hers. *"Stay. One more*

hand span of light. Just until the moon is mid-heaven.''

She was painfully tempted. But staying would bring greater danger—especially if she had been followed. She pushed away, slipped on her tunic, and found her deerskin bag. ''Do not ask this.''

''Then I will ask to come with you. I will speak to your father tonight and convince him that you honor us in joining our people.''

No.'' Her voice was strained with her panic. ''He is old, set as the rocks in his ways. I must talk to him first and soften his surprise. I am his only daughter,'' she explained.

''And you will be my only wife,'' her warrior said. ''Tomorrow I will come for you, bringing feathers and dressed skins.''

Her heart yearned, but she shook her head. ''Not tomorrow. Not the day after,'' she whispered.

She turned, moving gracefully over the rocks. ''Do not follow me. It is not safe for either of us.''

''Then I will watch you. Every step. Feel me as I stand here behind you, and know that I will protect you always.''

It was as he said. She felt the burn of his eyes upon her all the way down the path, through the forest of piñon back to the canyon floor. And leaving him brought clawing pain to her heart as she walked into the deep shadows of the cliffs.

■

Tess was alone. She was thirsty and hot and confused. She looked around her, seeing but not seeing, remembering things that were no longer there. As she moved from sunlight to shadow, her hat fell and was forgotten. Even the water bottle slid unnoticed to the dry rocks. She was lost in remembering, caught in sounds that were muffled, locked in a fragile past. Only the shadows saw, gathering around the red boulders.

Only the coyote watched, still on the highest rock.

14

Mae's café was nearly empty at the end of the lunch shift. Only a couple of booths and tables were occupied. T.J. looked around but didn't see Mae or Tess, so he headed for the backroom. He called out and received a muffled reply.

He found Mae at the refrigerator, wiping flour from her hands.

"Where's Tess?" he asked, a chill beginning to ripple upward from the base of his spine. He'd seen Tess walk from the library to the café earlier. She should have been here.

Mae continued to work her dough. "Tess took my car up to the ruins in the foothills."

T.J. hooked his hands on his belt as the chill spread. "When did she leave?" he asked tightly.

"About two hours ago."

Two hours. Tess alone in the hills, in isolated and completely unfamiliar country.

A muscle twitched at his jaw. "The damned fool. What has she done?"

"Relax, McCall. She's just doing a little sightseeing." A frown creased Mae's face. "She'll be fine. She's got water and a hat and I drew her a map."

"I told her not to leave here." T.J. stared stiffly at

the jagged peaks to the north. "She's in danger, Mae. That's why she came to Almost. I can't give you the details, but there are men who might be looking for her. There are about a thousand good reasons why she shouldn't go wandering off." He shoved his hat down hard on his head. "And I'm going to see that she learns those reasons right now, even if the irresponsible woman can't sit down for a week."

He heard the grating in his voice, the rage in his threat, yet all he felt was panic. He chose the rage instead. It would serve him better than panic.

He stalked from the café without another word, planning his next move, refusing to acknowledge the images of Tess hurt—Tess lost.

Dear God, Tess captive, at the mercy of criminals.

When he found her, he'd lock her in a damned cell if that's what it took to keep her out of trouble.

■

It was easy to follow her tire tracks over the deserted dirt road. T.J. was relieved to see there was no sound of any other cars as he roared up into the foothills. But there was no way of knowing if she had been followed from another direction—or even, God help them, if someone had been camped out up there, watching her every move. There were enough damned cults who'd gone to ground in these back-of-beyond canyons. With the right preparation and food and water, a man could hide here for weeks without being seen.

And a woman could be lost up here forever.

The thought sent fresh fear digging into his chest.

He pushed the Blazer hard, banging over boulders

and slamming over dry washes, following her trail with cold precision.

He stopped the Blazer as a form appeared high on a ledge to the left of the ruins. It was Tess's silhouette against the sky. Above her on a different ledge stood another form—a coyote, watchful and still.

How in heaven's name had she gotten up there? T.J. knew three trails up to the cliff, but none of them led that far up.

He felt a prickling at his neck, almost like a warning.

He gunned the motor and shrugged off this odd sense of premonition. He didn't have time for anything but finding a way to get her down. There was at least fifty feet of treacherous slip rock beneath her and no path to be seen anywhere. How was he going to talk her down to a place of safety?

He cupped his hands and called her name, the sound booming off the canyon walls. She tilted her head, standing rigid, her arms crossed over her chest.

She looked down at him—and then right through him.

Dear God, not now, T.J. thought. Not this odd disorientation of hers now, when a single misstep might send her tumbling down to the desert floor.

He jumped from the Blazer and sprinted over the rocky slope, already planning where he would climb up to join her. He dug his way over a wall of fallen boulders and hitched one arm across a gnarled piñon growing out of the cliff face.

He was only twenty feet below her now. He saw her face, pale and blank, as if she weren't really there, as if her body was simply holding her place as she stared down at the valley toward Almost. But her stance was too rigid, and she was making small, keening sounds that made the hair rise at the back of his neck.

The chill took him over completely. T.J. clamped down hard, driving away all emotion and letting instinct guide him upward with silent steps to keep from startling her.

Only ten feet to go. He could almost reach her, almost touch her.

Something skittered on the ledge above her. The sound of falling rocks split the silence, crashing down the cliff walls. She gave a startled cry at the same moment that he lunged for her.

But he found only air as she lost her balance, her body spinning sideways and tumbling down the treacherous slip rock slope.

■

Dimly, Tess heard the sound of gravel flying past her head.

She twisted, fighting branches that slapped and clawed at her as she tumbled down blindly. A shout rang through the air.

Tears ran down her cheeks and dirt blurred her vision. There was a ragged line of boulders before her. Then trees and sky bled together as she was thrown headlong down the cliff.

She awoke to splitting pain sometime later. One arm was crumpled beneath her side and her ankle was burning. She whimpered as something dug into her neck.

''Easy there.''

Opening her eyes, she saw a stranger beside her. Yet there was a gruff tenderness in his voice and something almost familiar in the glint of his startling blue eyes.

Dimly, she realized she was still on the ground. "Do I know you?" she rasped.

"You sure as hell do. You must have taken a real bang on your head." Frowning, he gently ran his hands along her legs and arms. "Tell me where it hurts."

"There." She winced as he brushed her ankle.

"Anywhere else?"

"My shoulder." She had to fight to understand his words. They almost seemed to come in a different tongue.

"You're not bleeding. Thank God, you missed landing headfirst. Can you raise your arm?"

Gritting her teeth, she did as he asked, though cold sweat formed at the effort.

He caught her hand and eased it down onto her chest. "Enough gymnastics for now. How many fingers am I holding up?"

"Fingers?"

He wiped her face with a bandanna soaked in water from his canteen. It felt delicious on her hot skin. He held up his hand. "It works well enough as a general indicator of trauma. Now give me an answer."

She closed her eyes. "Four." A very soft, very blurry four.

He ran his hand along her spine and under her neck. "Any pain there?"

"Just below my shoulder. A dull ache. Who *are* you?"

He made a flat sound of anger. "You'll remember soon enough. I don't think anything is broken, but I'm not inclined to take chances."

Bits and pieces of her memory began to return, more a mixture of sound and colors than lucid memories. And no matter how she concentrated, the picture pieces didn't match, as if they came from two different palettes.

The man with the metal badge pushed to his feet, and she saw him scan the slope to the south. "Did you hear anything before you fell?"

Had there been a cry of a bird or the sound of slipping rocks? Maybe something that moved in the brush? "I'm not sure. Everything happened all at once."

He stood for a moment, watching the clouds shadow the mountains. "I'm going to get my phone. Try not to move."

She blinked as his face seemed to come into focus. "I know you. You live here."

He gave a tight smile. "Glad to see your memory's coming back, Duchess." He fingered his hat, looking anxious. "Your leg looks pretty cut up. It hurts like hell, doesn't it?"

She blinked, tears rushing to her eyes at the tenderness in his voice. "You wouldn't happen to have some more water, would you?" She closed her eyes, fighting back a whimper as a fresh wave of pain shot up through her hip.

She heard the sound of his boots, then the creak of leather. Things were blurring again, and she decided all she wanted to do was sleep.

Water brushed her lips. "Drink some of this. And I want you to stay awake, so talk to me."

"About what?" she murmured.

"Anything. Start with why the hell you came up here alone," he said grimly.

"I didn't think I'd be long. And the mountains kept calling." She blinked at the sound of her own words. "That sounds crazy."

"How did you get up so high?"

Something kept her from explaining the strange vision that had begun the moment she'd set foot beneath the ancient piñon tree. "Just a guess."

"Duchess, I've walked these rocks about a thousand times and I never found a trail that runs up that side of the cliff. If that was a guess, then I'm the living, breathing backside of a mule."

She turned away, hesitant to say more. How could she explain the dream that drifted still, with the low throb of drums and the faint memory of a man's face. To distract him, she turned to her side, looking dizzily up at the shadowed ruins. "I fell from all the way up there?"

"You should have been in *Sports Illustrated*," T.J. said grimly. "A few more feet to the left and you'd have plunged straight to the bottom of the rocks."

"That bad," she whispered, shivering.

T.J. wanted to rail at her, but the sight of her white, drawn face cut off his words. He had to get her down to the Blazer, but he hesitated to move her yet.

Tess stared up the slope of slip rock beneath the shadow of high sandstone walls. She seemed mesmerized by the cave tucked into the cliff and the ruined stone walls that climbed in high, square towers. "Tell me about this place," she whispered. "Tell me everything."

T.J. didn't like the urgency in her voice or the way her hands worked back and forth over her arms.

"Please." She looked at him, as if driven to ask, to understand.

T.J. bit back a protest. "It's probably early Mogollon culture."

"I beg your pardon?"

He wasn't surprised at her ignorance. "Almost everyone has heard about the Anasazi, Hopi, and Navajo. But as early as AD 200, the people archaeologists term

Mogollon had flourished in half-buried pit houses in the mountains of Arizona, New Mexico, and Utah. Their ceremonial areas were imposing, but rectangular rather than the circular Anasazi type.''

T.J. offered her a drink from his canteen. ''By 1200 the Anasazi and the Mogollon were living nearby and sharing their techniques.''

''What happened to the people who lived here?''

''Everything changed around 1300. In Chaco Canyon, Mesa Verde, and the villages of Utah, the cliff dwellings were empty. No one knows why, even now.'' He stared off over the rows of smoke-blue mountains. ''Maybe it was overpopulation and degradation of resources. Maybe sickness and drought. We might never have the final answer.''

T.J. felt the loss personally. As a boy he had stood in the shadows of this cliff, yearning to know exactly what had happened to the mysterious civilization that had clung to the narrow cliff walls.

''Those holes are where the roof timbers used to be.'' He pointed up, all the time scanning the slopes for any sign of movement. ''Except for a few scraps here and there, the wood is long gone.''

Tess looked at the worn remains of steps carved into the rock face. ''How many people lived here?''

''Four or five families, probably. They knew about rudimentary irrigation and raised corn, beans, and squash. Possibly even native cotton.''

''Can people go into the ruins?''

He shook his head. ''Too dangerous. The walls are unstable. Until proper excavations can be completed, no one should go up there.''

Tess raised her eyes to the crown of the cliff and blinked dizzily.

"Take it easy," he muttered.

To Tess the words seemed to come from a great distance. Something had drawn her there, demanding answers. Even now it held her with relentless force.

She took a deep breath, trying to pull away from the beauty of its dark magic. But when Tess looked up, it was to the man beside her. Strong. Honorable. Infuriating but decent. She remembered all that now.

She wasn't sure what she wanted from T. J. McCall or from this mysterious, beautiful country she'd wandered into. Here it was easy to forget the outside world and her own problem with a million dollars that shouldn't be in her account.

Too easy to forget everything but the land . . . and the man beside her.

Layers of clouds sailed over the valley, touched with color. Far to the south she could see thunderheads rising, their bases purple and heavy with rain. For a moment Tess experienced the dizzying sensation that she was flying, soaring over the valley, so clear was the view. From this vantage point, the cliff dwellers could see strangers coming from miles away, an excellent tactical advantage.

Had there been danger here then, too?

Had strangers approached in stealth, avoiding signal fires?

Up the slope Tess saw that small, dried corncobs littered the rocks. Close by were two deeply indented stones, which might have been used for grinding the precious meal. She blinked, locked in a sense of past, remembering the handprint on the rock wall high above her.

She caught her breath, gripped by an ineffable connection to this ancient place and the lives that had passed here. Women had ground corn, woven their native cotton. They had laughed and worried and waited for their men to return from the fields or the high mountains to north and east, where game would be plentiful.

What had happened when the warriors returned? Was there singing and dancing before towering fires? Were there lingering glances, the brush of hands, and the hammering of hearts in the darkness?

At that moment, the mystery of the place became painfully personal, almost overwhelming. Tess could feel the hypnotic pull of the shadows slipping into her thoughts.

She turned to find T.J. staring at her. "Is it always like this? Is the sense of history always so close?"

"Always. Doc Felton owns this land all the way to the river. Someday he'll bring in a research team to investigate and document the site. But for the moment, we'll guard its secrets. After so many centuries, a few more years won't matter."

Wind sailed past the high canyon walls and Tess's hair fluttered over her cheeks.

T.J. looked away, scanning the slopes. Tess realized he was edgy, too alert. "You think someone's out there?"

"No, but I want to get you back to the Blazer. Can you move?"

T.J. saw her grit her teeth, watched her fingers tighten. He hated having to put her through more pain, but they couldn't stay there. He needed to get her back to town so Doc Felton could check her out.

"No choice?"

"Afraid not."

Her mouth set into a thin line. "In that case, let's go."

As gently as possible, he helped her stand. When he

saw how unsteady she was, he lifted her and carried her down the slope. Her body was rigid by the time he broke out of the shadow of the piñons, with the trucks just beyond. She had rare courage, he thought. He knew she hurt everywhere, but she hadn't uttered one complaint.

"How are you doing?"

"Let's just say I won't be performing *Swan Lake* anywhere tonight." Her hands were digging into his shoulders.

T.J. eased her higher, trying to rock with every motion to smooth his steps. That concentration was why he didn't notice that the Blazer was leaning at an angle.

He snapped out a curse.

"What?"

The tires were slashed through, and the car was resting flat on its rims. They wouldn't be going anywhere in his vehicle, he thought, scanning the slope below. Nothing moved. There was no sight of anyone slipping into the brush.

Damn and blast, who had done this?

He remembered Mae's truck, which was just past a low rim of junipers. T.J. strode past his Blazer, then saw that the red truck had suffered the same fate. His hands tightened on Tess's waist. He couldn't keep her exposed, in the event they were being watched.

"How are you feeling?"

"Kind of funny. Floating."

Not a good sign, he thought, sliding open the passenger door on the Blazer. Her eyes were closed, and she hadn't seen the damage to the tires. He decided that was probably a good thing. He pulled out his phone and punched in the number of the radio dispatcher, giving terse directions to send someone up as soon as possible.

"Why did you say that?" Tess was studying him curiously.

"Something's wrong with the Blazer."

"Mae's truck is just over the hill."

"Looks like that's not working so well either."

"You didn't try it."

He settled her against his arm. "The tires have been cut."

He felt her tense instantly. "Are they out there now?"

"Hard to say. You let me worry about that."

"I'm sorry," she whispered. "I never expected they would be here."

"We'll deal with that later," he said grimly. He was pulling a blanket over her, when a shell exploded down the ridge. T.J. sank down, covering Tess with his body while he scanned the trees below them.

"Was that a gun?"

"No doubt about it." T.J. sat up, turned the key, and shoved the Blazer into gear. Even with ruined tires, he could make his way up to the blind face of the cliff and turn around so that the passenger door pressed up against the rock face. Then Tess would be protected and he would have a clear shot at anyone foolish enough to try to rush him.

He pulled down his rifle and loaded it, then drew it onto his lap. After that he checked his holstered pistol.

She was staring at him in mute fear as he picked up the radio and was put through to his deputy, Tom Martinez, who was on his way up.

"Keep your eyes open," he said tightly. "A shot was just fired. If you see anyone on the road, I want a clear ID and plate numbers. And take precautions. This could be some cult or it could be vagrants. Don't get out of your car without checking the scene, understood?''

He put the radio away, then reached to take Tess's pulse. Sharp and jerky, just as he'd expected.

She swallowed. ''Going hunting for bear, Sheriff?'' There was a note of fear in voice.

''Just staying safe,'' he said. ''I noticed there's a truck on its way up here.''

''A friend of yours?''

''I can't say for sure.'' He cut off her questions, holding the canteen to her mouth and dribbling water over her lips, then soaked his bandanna and laid it over her face. The rumble was growing louder by the minute.

''You don't think it's one of *them*, do you?''

Both of them knew who she meant. T.J. didn't try to pretend otherwise. ''Hard to say, but I'm taking no chances.'' He stared down the hill at the dust rising in scattered plumes. ''I'll leave the canteen here with you.''

''Where are you going?''

''Just a few feet up into those rocks.'' To a place where he'd have perfect aim at anyone climbing the narrow path. ''No one can get into the car without getting past me,'' he grated.

The truck's rumble grew louder, blocking out the wind.

''Go on, McCall. I'll be waiting.''

He slid outside, then crouched low, making his way to a small fissure in the rocks that gave him a clear view—and a place to rest his rifle, should it be necessary. With his binoculars, he scanned the slope again and saw a truck halt at the edge of the wash near the road. He squinted as a man emerged, his features shadowed by a black Stetson.

The driver said a few words to someone in the truck,

then turned, one hand shielding his eyes as he looked up in the foothills.

Light reflected off metal. Field glasses possibly.

T.J. watched the man shove back his hat and scratch his head. There was something familiar in the gesture.

Suddenly, it struck him. The driver was Tom Stoner, who owned the Lazy C Ranch beyond the river. T.J. climbed up the rock, waving his arms broadly. Then he squeezed off one shot in the air for good measure.

Metal flashed again and T.J. saw the old rancher surveying the boulders where he stood. T.J. gave another broad wave of his hat, grinning as the old man climbed back into the truck and headed upward.

■

When the leathery-faced rancher jumped out of his truck, he stared at T.J. with concern. "I thought that was you, Sheriff. I picked up your conversation with Tom Martinez on the CB and thought you could use a hand. Something wrong with your Blazer?"

"Tires slashed. Same with Mae's Explorer."

The rancher scowled at the stark line of cliffs. "Slashed? Now, who would do a fool thing like that?"

T.J. chose his next words carefully. "It could have been a vagrant. Maybe someone is dug in up here and doesn't want visitors. I'll check it out later. Ms. O'Mara fell and she's in no state to walk to town. Can you give us a ride back in the truck?"

"No problem. I was on my way to town anyway. One of my workers went and cut himself with a saw and I need to get him to Doc Felton."

T.J. saw the man leaning sideways in the front seat. "Give me a minute to get Tess down here."

"Is it safe?" she asked with a bleak smile as he sprinted toward her.

"Better than safe. The truck belongs to Tom Stoner, a local rancher. He'll drive us back." He helped her slowly to her feet, noting the lines of strain at her mouth.

After a terse introduction, he settled Tess on the front seat and squatted behind it. Soon Tom was rambling on about grazing rights and stock prices. T.J. looked out the back window at the slope behind them. Nothing moved in the piñons. Only a hawk soared above the cliffs, gliding on the high currents. Only shadows dappled the worn, weathered rocks.

But as they slowly drove back down the pitted wash, light touched the roof of the cave, shimmering around the broken walls and roofless, slanting towers.

All wrong, he thought. There should have been movement and laughter and activity—anything but this bleak silence. Something pricked between his shoulder blades, almost like a memory.

But he forced his head to turn away and shoved that uncomfortable sense of awareness from his mind.

■

Doc Felton was waiting in his office when they reached town, thanks to a call on the rancher's cellular phone.

Tess was determined to hobble into the doctor's office, but T.J. scooped her up in his arms and carried her past a line of interested bystanders into the waiting room.

"I heard you have some nice bruises, young lady. Let's be certain there's nothing more," Doc Felton said as T.J. settled her in an examining room.

"Well, what do you think?" T.J. demanded.

"You just brought her in, boy. I don't think anything

yet." Doc Felton shined a light into Tess's eyes, checked her pulse, then asked her to raise each hand in turn.

"So?"

"Be quiet," the doctor snapped. "You want me to make him leave?" he asked Tess.

"No, it's all right." She flushed as T.J. gave her a narrowed look.

T.J. jammed his hands into his pockets. "For the record, neither of you are getting me to leave."

The doctor ran a hand along Tess's neck and shoulders, probing gently for signs of trauma, while T.J. watched in growing impatience. "Is anything broken?"

"I don't see any signs of concussion and Ms. O'Mara's vital signs appear to be normal. She has some superficial scrapes but nothing serious. That being the case, I'm going to have a look at Tom Stoner's man, who needs stitches." He frowned at T.J. "Why don't you go attend to some police business and let Ms. O'Mara get her bearings?"

"I'm not—"

"Yes, you are." Doc Felton crossed his arms. "In this room, I'm the law. You'd better remember that, Sheriff." He waved T.J. out, then nodded at Tess. "Now, you, my dear, are going to close your eyes and rest. Doc Felton's orders."

■

"So what do you think really happened?" Head bowed, Tom Stoner paced back and forth, frowning down at the oleander bushes outside Doc Felton's office.

T.J. hesitated to mention the gunshot he'd heard. "Have you seen anything odd in those foothills lately? Strange activity or people who don't belong?"

"We get vagrants now and again. Sometimes they come in from Mexico and move on north." The rancher's face reddened beneath his deep tan. "Lately I've seen only those damned survivalists. They tear around the desert in their dune buggies and campers, frightening my cattle. Last week I found a heifer down in a box canyon with her neck broken. Someone should run that whole outfit off, if you ask me."

"They've got a right to be on the land they purchased, just the same as we do," T.J. said dryly. "It's called the American way. Now, if they're on public land, that's something else."

"Reckon they were," the rancher said slowly. "I saw them out beyond the Needle yesterday. Looked like they might have been building some kind of temporary camp up there."

T.J. stored that away for future reference. "Anything else you've seen up there?"

"Couple of dead coyotes, I guess."

"When?"

The rancher squinted down the street and scratched his jaw. "Two—maybe three days ago."

"Any idea what killed them?"

The old man shrugged. "Didn't check. I figured it was a snake or some kind of disease. Why?"

Carefully T.J. toed a line in the dirt. "Miguel found two dead coyotes up there last week. He thinks it might be some new kind of poison."

"Sounds like nasty stuff."

"Maybe your foreman could bag up one of those carcasses and bring it in. I'd like to run a few tests."

"I can send someone up right now."

"No need to do it this second," T.J. said. "I'm going back up myself to take a look around."

"Don't blame you. Can't imagine anyone fool enough to tangle with you." He shook his head slowly. "Could be those survivalists. They must have ten or twenty children in that camp up there, and not a doctor or teacher in sight. Probably breaking a dozen laws, taking drugs and Lord knows what else."

T.J. shoved back his hat, his eyes narrowed. "Are you saying you've seen signs of drug use or sale up there?"

"Hell if I know. Just seems that someone's always coming or going." The rancher shook his head. "But that hasn't bothered you before, Sheriff. Makes me wonder if you haven't already taken sides."

"No one's taking sides here, Tom."

"No?" The old man sniffed. "Sure could have fooled me. Why not just hand them the keys to the courthouse while you're at it?"

T.J. tried to contain his irritation as the man walked stiffly back to his truck.

Tom Stoner was known to be wary of outsiders, but he was no kook, and two more dead coyotes couldn't be explained away as an accident. A visit to the survivalist camp would be his next priority.

But first he was going to recheck the wash. He hadn't imagined that gunshot.

He waited only long enough to hammer out instructions to Grady, who was going off duty in ten minutes. "Will you keep an eye on Tess for an hour or so while Doc finishes checking her out? I want to go back up into the hills. This time I'm borrowing a mount from the Bar W and going in from the west. No truck can cover those hills as well as a horse."

"No problem, Sheriff. You think you can find out who slashed your tires?"

"I mean to try."

Grady looked genuinely stunned. "You don't suspect someone from Almost?"

"I'm suspecting anyone and everyone until I know different. One more thing, Grady. No matter what she says, don't let Tess out of your sight, not for a minute. Don't leave anyone alone with her either."

Grady scratched his head. "I'm not exactly sure what you're saying here, Sheriff."

"Just what it sounds like. Either someone has followed Tess here, or it was someone from town. I'm not taking any chances one way or another."

"I don't like it." Grady rubbed his jaw. "These are people I've lived with for years. I don't like looking at them and wondering what they might be hiding."

"You think I like it?" T.J. jammed his hat down hard on his head. "But that's the way it is, understand?"

Grady suddenly straightened. "What about me? Why aren't you considering me a suspect? I was out on police business most of the morning. I had time to follow you up to the ruins."

McCall gave a crooked grin. "I'm not worried about you, Grady. In that broken-down truck of yours, the whole town would have heard you coming and going. Besides," he called over his shoulder, "you're such a bad shot that if you tried to aim east, the bullet would still end up somewhere in California."

∎

T.J. reined in his horse at the edge of the piñon forest an hour later.

He sat easily in the saddle, getting a sense of the terrain and all the places a man might hide without being seen. He took a slow swallow from his canteen, then replaced it carefully.

Late afternoon sunlight streamed over the canyons as he turned his horse in a wide loop. He meant to cover all the narrow side canyons and the foothills near the ruins. He was looking for anything and nothing, knowing that preconceived notions about what he might find would cloud his search.

At the edge of a dry wash, he dismounted, inspecting the ground carefully. He saw the marks made by Tess's boots beneath an ancient piñon. Now, why had she left the trail there, he wondered. How had Tess known about this path when even he and Doc Felton hadn't known it was there?

Farther up the wash he came across a narrow, heavily overgrown path that wound up the slope to the cliff. He followed the tracks and cursed as they vanished into a rocky ridge that led out of the wash to the north, disappearing behind boulders and piñon. Once again, he felt tension build in his neck.

A twig snapped not far away. T.J. spun around, gun level, scanning the area.

A deer turned and vanished into a thicket.

Cursing his rampant imagination, he holstered his gun and picked his way upward where the dry creek fanned out into a promontory that gave a perfect view of the valley. He covered the rocky slope on foot, studying the terrain. A flash of color caught his eyes. Bending down, he found a spent brass rifle shell: 30-06 caliber. He raised the shell to his nose and sniffed.

Fresh—fired within the last couple of hours.

Carefully, he wrapped up the casing and slid it into his pocket, hoping that the forensics team in Tucson could give him more information, though he knew it was unlikely. Virtually every hunter in America would have a 30-06. His only chance of identifying the person who fired at them earlier would be to find the gun itself and match the markings on the spent shells.

Muscles knotted along the back of his neck as he straightened and stared into the sunlight. Someone could have stood right here and surveyed the whole valley, unseen. With a good rifle and decent aim, there was no reason they should have missed either himself or Tess.

But they had.

Why?

One thing was certain. Tess wouldn't be leaving his side from now on.

McCall was about to make his way back down the talus slope when he saw a shape beneath a patch of sage and low trees. Pebbles scattered as he jumped down, pushing aside the greenery to scan the ground beneath.

His eyes glittered with anger at the sight of a mother and three coyote pups. All dead.

15

Questions left T.J. with a sour taste in his mouth and a bad temper as he strode into Doc Felton's office. He bypassed the curious receptionist and headed straight back to the exam room Tess occupied.

After one knock, he pulled the door open, his gaze homing straight in on Tess. He took one look at her drawn, pale face and decided to dispense with his questions—for now.

T.J. wanted to gather her close, wipe away her pain and uncertainty. Of course, he also wanted to give her a thorough tongue-lashing for putting herself in danger. "How are you feeling?"

"I'm fine," she said as she struggled to put on her boots. "Doc says I can go."

With a curse, T.J. swept up the red boots in one hand, then caught her as she swayed. "You sure Doc said you can leave?"

"I'm just tired and my leg hurts. Doc gave me pills and they're making me sleepy." She stared at him blindly, then swayed again.

"Hold on to me."

"I'm *not* going to faint," she whispered.

"Sure, you're not. You'll be just fine." His hands circled her waist, holding her steady.

She shuddered, her face losing even more color.

"That does it." T.J. caught her up in his arms, scowling.

"What are you doing?"

"Taking you home. That way I can be sure you rest when you're told to." He shouldered the door open. "It's about time I put you on a short leash," he said as he carried her into the waiting room and past a crowd of interested bystanders gathered at the door.

"I can walk perfectly well," Tess muttered.

"So can I. Next time you can carry me," he said dryly.

"Put me down, T.J. This is embarrassing."

"Get over it."

"Is she going to be okay?" the school principal asked anxiously.

"Fine," T.J. replied tersely without slowing down. The crowd parted in front of him as he kept moving, looking neither right nor left.

He yanked open the door to the Jeep Tom Martinez had brought back from T.J.'s ranch. By then he knew that the Blazer belonging to the Sheriff's Department would be hooked to a tow truck to be hauled back to town for new tires.

T.J. settled Tess carefully into the passenger seat, then reached across to snap her seat belt, fighting an urge to kiss some pink back into her cheeks. He wondered if she had any idea that her face was the color of putty and her hands were shaking.

Probably not. The crazy female truly did have the temperament of a Gila monster. "Stop fighting me," he growled as her hands wrapped around his arm.

Her eyes darkened. "I'm—not fighting. Actually, I don't feel so well. I think I'm going to—"

T.J. whipped off her seat belt and angled her head outside. "Take it easy, Duchess. Just let it go."

He heard her breathless gasp. It was several moments before he realized he was hearing ragged laughter. "What's wrong now?"

"Not that kind of sick. Dizzy."

T.J. brought her back up slowly. "Easy. Take deep breaths and think about something else." He felt her muscles tense, her whole body going rigid. Cursing, he worked the knots in her shoulders.

"I'm better now."

He raised her gently. Her face was still too pale, her pupils dilated—all to be expected after the experience she'd just been through. He offered her a drink from the water bottle he kept in the car, wishing it were brandy.

She stared at him, just stared, as if she were trying to read all his secrets.

T.J. fastened her seat belt again, slid behind his seat, buckled in, and started the car.

"Where are we going?" she asked wearily.

"Home—where I can keep an eye on you without getting the whole town involved."

"That's not necessary—"

"The hell it isn't." He brushed her cheek gently, giving lie to the roughness of his voice. "You're going to rest." He cupped her chin, interrupting her as she started to say something. "My house, my rules."

"That's blunt."

His finger fanned out over her cheek. "No, that's honest." He saw color filter through her face and indecision fill her eyes.

"Bully."

"Damned straight." His fingers fanned out over her

cheek. Then he put the Jeep into gear and backed out onto the street.

"Did you find anything when you went back to the ruins?"

"A spent rifle shell and what looked like a set of tracks leading down into the wash."

"Someone was there. Do you think he shot at me?"

"It's possible. I won't know much until I have that shell analyzed."

"They can tell you when it was fired?"

He nodded. And berated himself for being too slow. She could have been badly hurt, maybe even killed. He should have been prepared, not letting her out of his sight or his reach.

He wouldn't make the same mistake again.

T.J. touched her hair. "If it gets too bumpy, tell me and I'll pull over."

"I'll be fine," she said flatly.

T.J. drove slowly, choosing the smoothest stretch of road, which wasn't saying very much.

"I can't believe they found me here so soon." She stared out at the dusty road before them, her expression set. "But I'm not going to be paranoid about this."

She didn't have to be, T.J. thought grimly. He would be paranoid enough for both of them.

"So what happens next?" she asked. "Why don't we just run a full-page ad in all the Boston papers: 'If you've lost a million dollars, call this number.' "

"Your brother is working on this, Tess." T.J. frowned. "I'm sure a lot of people are putting in long hours."

Her mouth thinned in a mixture of pain and groggy irritation. "I still don't see how a million dollars can slip through banking records without a trace."

"Andrew will have news any day now."

Tess drew a shaky breath and stared at the mountains. "What's taking him so long? Why haven't he and his powerful friends in Washington figured out what's going on?"

T.J. wondered the same thing, but said nothing more until they reached the ranch. He rounded the Jeep to open her door, then slid his arms beneath her and lifted her to his chest. For a moment, just a moment, her head touched his shoulder and he heard her small, broken sigh of pain.

"That does it. You're taking another pill the second we get inside."

When he reached the front door, with Tess in his arms, he swore silently. Maria was off for a couple of days. He could have used her help in tending to Tess. He pushed open the door and headed straight for Tess's bedroom. After he settled her on the bed, he poured a glass of water and shook another pill from the bottle Doc had given him for her.

"Take this."

"I don't want it."

T.J.'s jaw clenched. "Take it or I'll hold your nose and make you swallow it."

She raised the glass, swallowed, shuddered. "Cold." She gazed up into his face, her eyes darkening. "I want a shower." Tess looked up at him, swaying slightly, her face still too pale.

Muscles tensed throughout his body. Doc Felton had said that a hot shower would be a good idea, but T.J. wasn't sure he could manage it and keep his sanity, too.

Frowning, she gripped the bottom of her T-shirt and tried valiantly to tug it upward. "Pathetic," she whispered. "Can't even strip properly."

As she struggled with the shirt, T.J. pulled her against him.

Somehow he kept his touch cool and impersonal as he tugged off her shirt and tried not to stare at the wispy lace that captured her breasts.

"Are you going to try anything, Sheriff?"

"Like what?"

She sank against him. "Like maybe take advantage of the situation."

Hell, it was just like her to bring up the one thing he'd been dreaming about for two days straight. Unfortunately, she did it at a time when no responsible male could think of acting on the offer.

"Well, what's wrong?" Her eyes narrowed. "You don't like the way I look?"

T.J. closed his eyes, fighting back the image of full, pale breasts and crimson tips that teased delicate white lace. There wasn't a single thing he didn't like, but he wasn't going to think about it. Savagely clamping down on his desire, he unbuttoned her skirt and shoved it down to the floor. A quick glimpse of her bright pink underwear left him dry-mouthed.

He swallowed hard and gave a silent prayer of relief that there were no stockings to deal with today. "Into the shower. You're freezing."

But Tess didn't move. Her nose nuzzled his chest.

T.J. tried to forget just how much he wanted to slide his hands into her wild copper hair and kiss her senseless. But she needed calm and strength from him now, not blistering desire.

Suppressing a groan, he carried her to the bathroom and stood her up in the stall shower. Gripping her with one hand, he managed to whip the spray to full force, then center her beneath it. The jetting water drowned her angry protests. It also left a good part of T.J.'s shirt soaked through.

Worst of all, one part of his mind screamed for him to strip and join her beneath that steaming water. The sane part of his mind swore at him for even thinking about it.

She twisted in his arms as she shoved wet hair out of her face. Her breast nudged his arm and sent a jolt of electricity right up his chest. To distract himself, he found the soap and swept it down her arms.

Touching her body, wet and slippery with soap, was a whole new kind of sensual experience. He couldn't help but enjoy it, even though it knotted his muscles painfully.

"So you're *not* going to take advantage of me?" Her voice was wistful.

"Damned right, I'm not."

"You're not going to strip off the rest of my clothes, pin me against the wall, and do what's on both our minds right now?"

T.J. turned her face and framed her cheeks gently with his callused fingers. "You're living dangerously, Duchess."

She ran her tongue across her full, wet lips. "It appears so," she whispered. "Maybe because of what I saw up at those ruins." She blinked hard. "Or what I felt."

T.J. bit back an inventive string of curses. Didn't the little fool realize she was playing with fire?

Angrily he swept up a bottle of shampoo. In his haste, he squirted half the bottle onto her hair. She yelled as his fingers ground down, scrubbing up a thick lather.

"Watch it. I'm dying here."

"That makes two of us," T.J. said grimly.

"What did you say?"

He didn't answer, concentrating on shoving her back under the shower and rinsing the foam free. Then he made the mistake of looking down.

The water had turned her lingerie nearly transparent. Her breasts were full and high, perfectly crowned with crimson nipples. At the juncture of her thighs lay a triangle of lush, dark curls.

The damned woman might as well have been wearing cellophane.

And damn him for staring at her like a drowning swimmer staring at a life preserver.

He turned off the shower, yanked a towel from its bar, then wrapped her up tightly. If he couldn't see her body, it had to make the pain better, he reasoned.

"Are you hoping to frighten me or simply smother me?"

"Neither. I'm trying to get you warm," he said harshly.

She brushed at her face. Even with her hair slicked back like a wet seal and her skin stripped free of makeup, she was radiant, her beauty jolting through him like electricity.

T.J. pulled his heavy cotton robe around her. Forcing his hands not to shake, he gripped her shoulders. "You'll have to take off the rest yourself."

She leaned against him, her back to his chest. "Maybe I'd rather that you do it," she said in a shaky voice. "Unless that's a problem."

"Why should it be?" he snapped. He pulled the robe from her shoulders, then flicked the front opening of her bra free. His teeth locked tight as he swept the lacy straps down. She didn't protest, didn't move, her body warm against him. And that silence more than anything else made T.J. pause, turn slowly, and stare down at her.

It was his worst mistake.

Her naked body could have been pulled right out of his most erotic fantasies. Except for the scrapes and bruises that marred her creamy skin and made him want to treat her with the utmost tenderness. She was pale, her eyes huge, a pulse leaping at her throat. And below that, except for her hot pink bikini briefs, she was all curves that left him aching.

"Dammit, Tess, stop looking at me that way."

She stared at him, two spots of color high on her cheeks. "What way?" she whispered.

"As if you want what I could give you."

"Maybe I do." Her hand rose, tentatively sliding over his jaw.

T.J. closed his eyes, blocking out her words. She was feeling the influence of Doc Felton's pills and probably didn't know what she was saying. "No, Tess."

"No what?"

"No, to all of it. It's not going to happen," he said tightly.

"So Mae was right; you are an honorable man," she murmured. "Well, since you're against taking advantage of me, at least answer a question."

T.J. didn't want to answer questions. He wanted to touch her, savor her, bury himself inside her. "What question?"

"What's your never-never thing, Sheriff McCall? What's the one wish you've always had but never hoped to achieve? Everyone in Almost seems to have something they regret not doing."

The wish that I was happy, T.J. thought grimly. But

the words that came out were very different. "I wanted to be on the team."

"What team?"

"The one that guards the president." His hands tightened.

He hadn't meant to tell her. Then again, he hadn't meant to hold her, to look at her, to want her desperately. Somehow whenever Tess O'Mara was around, sparks flew and things happened in a way no one expected.

"So what happened?" She raised her hands slowly to his face.

So damned warm. In a second there would be nothing between them, and he would feel all that lovely sweetness while they both pounded to a wrenching release.

He cleared his throat. "There's nothing to tell."

"Are you afraid to remember or just afraid to talk about it with me?"

Damned perceptive female. "Neither," he growled. *Both,* he thought.

He pulled away from her hands, which were combing through his hair. Had it ever been like this before? Had his whole body ever been twisted in knots while he watched as if from a distance, aware of another person's needs more deeply than his own?

"What happened?"

"It didn't work out. They only wanted the best and the brightest, and I didn't make the cut."

He felt her stiffen. "I don't believe it. There's something more you're not telling me."

There was more, all right. But T.J. had told her enough already. "Let it go, Tess."

"I might." She turned her head slowly. "Under certain conditions." Her lips opened on his damp skin.

He closed his eyes, cursing when he felt her tongue feather across his neck. "You're playing with fire, Tess."

"You're still angry with me, aren't you?"

A few hours ago he'd been angry enough to want to leave his handprint on her backside. But now he was only angry with himself.

For wanting things he shouldn't even be considering.

"No, I'm not angry now. You're safe and that's all I care about."

"Maybe being safe isn't enough."

It wasn't the husky catch in her voice that clawed at T.J.'s control, but the wistful, uncertain note of honesty that smashed through all his defenses. "Tess, stop. Listen—"

"I'm tired of listening. I'm tired of waiting for something special to happen, when I can just as easily make it happen." She drew a quick, shaky breath. "And *this* is special. You are special. You make me catch my breath, wanting things I've never wanted before."

T.J. tried not to listen. "You don't know what you're saying right now. This will all seem like a dream tomorrow." He stared at her, his hands opening and closing as desire lashed out at him.

"You're wrong," she said gravely. "Tomorrow *this* will be real and everything else will be the dream, like those coyotes and the drums. So here's what I think, Sheriff. If you want the last damp piece of clothing taken off me, I figure you're just going to have to take it off yourself."

He didn't want to hear her. He couldn't bear to look at her. He gripped her shoulders and tried to put her away from him, only to feel her turn back into his arms.

Desire flared hotter, fueled by a kind of primal madness T.J. had never known before.

Too late, he thought blindly, pulling her back against him, his hands gripping her arms as he slid down to find the tight, aroused buds of her nipples. "You'll regret this, Duchess," he said hoarsely. "We both will."

16

If she hadn't gone to the ruins, none of this would have happened. If she'd been her normal self, things never would have gone so far and she would never have admitted to these reckless feelings for T.J. But Tess wasn't thinking, wasn't sane and normal.

And she liked it just fine.

She was glad she'd gone to the ruins. A lingering sense of danger brushed her skin and left her heart pounding as he touched her. Even that made no difference.

Every time he moved, the maddening friction of his hands on her wet body turned her inside out. She forgot names, reasons, all the normal, tidy conventions of her well-organized life as time shifted, stopped. All that mattered to her was the small, heated space where their bodies met. She stopped trying to understand why or explain it away.

She closed her eyes, afraid that the lancing pleasure would wane. Death had come so close that afternoon that all she could think of was life.

Heat.

Skin.

"Tess, we can't."

"Why? I'm not afraid."

He didn't move, didn't even seem to breathe. Then he put his hands on her breasts, his callused fingertips stroking with exquisite friction. "Maybe you should be," he said hoarsely. "If you knew the things I'm thinking, you'd be running as fast as you can."

With a curse he turned her in his arms, then froze. Looking, just looking. At her face. At her chest.

Lower.

Over the taut stomach and down to the line of silk at her thighs.

Her heart pounded. He was quiet suddenly, staring at the skimpy bit of fabric she wore. Then his fingers jerked downward, stripping away the last barrier.

Her breath came in a harsh rush only seconds before Tess felt his mouth.

"You can't—"

"I warned you," he growled. "You pushed until you got answers. Yes, dammit, I've wanted you and it won't be nice or tidy or convenient now."

Dimly, dimly, she heard his warning, but the meaning was lost, drowned out by the slam of her heart and the exquisite shock of his hands moving in places no man had ever touched so intimately before.

"God, you're soft." He eased lower, teasing her to some trembling edge she'd never approached before. "I'm going to have you, Tess," he whispered. "Now."

She stared at him through a haze of desire, unable to speak as his rough hands moved, feathering down into the nest of curls at her thighs. "Do you understand?"

His chest was an anchor, his hands a lifeline. She couldn't breathe, couldn't think. "Yes," she whispered.

It was the only answer. She didn't stop to worry

about what would happen later. She wouldn't let herself wonder what kind of future a hardscrabble, tight-mouthed cowboy from Arizona could find with a high-tempo, micromanaging worrier from Boston. . . .

Because there was no future.

No future at all.

It didn't matter. Now was all the world that counted—this raging, edgy now of trembling muscles and driving nerves.

"Look at me, Duchess."

She looked. Savored. Wanted. He was as wild as the summer wind, as hard as the brushed sandstone walls of the high desert canyons. He was a man that no woman could turn away from.

And by some impossible trick of fate, he was touching her, wanting her.

Tess drew a ragged breath, suddenly needing to question, to analyze. He didn't give her time. His fingers flexed. Dewy skin parted and sheathed his intimate caress.

Tess almost buckled at the shock of that deep stroke. Why hadn't she realized? Why had no one told her that skin could sear, that a heart could sing?

"Show me what you want, Duchess."

All of it.

Everywhere.

Now.

His mouth closed over her breast. She whimpered as he nipped her skin with his teeth. "Like that?" he said hoarsely.

Just like that.

Againagainagain. Now.

The words were silent, speech beyond her capability

as his fingers stripped away the last reasoning part of her brain. She wanted control and safety, but he didn't give it to her. This was all racing energy, all vicious pleasure.

And she wanted nothing less.

She ground out his name, her mouth pressed to his hot, salty skin as her body strained against his. "Please—"

"Easy, love."

Madness gripped her, left her shaking.

Then he moved, and a wave of need was inside her, rising, racing. It was close, so close, and she didn't have a clue what to do.

His fingers were relentless, spearing her, enflaming her. Skin to her skin, he was so much a part of her, so deep in the wave that all Tess could do was cry out blindly as she climbed, shattered.

Too fast.

Too dangerous.

Even before her blood stopped burning, it came again, nerves jangling, muscles shuddering. Dimly, she heard someone scream. But not her. Impossible for such a thing to happen in her ordered, reasonable world.

Her fingers tightened. The scream came again, torn from her own raw throat as she swayed and almost fell beneath the shocking pleasure.

Her knees collapsed. With a curse, T.J. wrapped his hands around her and carried her to the bed. She lay beyond words, stunned by the pleasure he'd given her.

She started to speak, to tell him all he'd made her feel.

But Tess saw his face, lined and set. He was regretting what he'd done, angry at her for goading him. She turned her head, averting her gaze from his regret. . . .

And then she saw what lay on the table beside the bed.

Gun.

Holster.

Handcuffs.

Her whole body froze.

Dear God, what was she doing? Who was this hard-eyed stranger she'd allowed to invade her body and probe all her secrets?

"I—I have to go."

She tried to sit up, only to be sent rolling back onto the bed.

"Not until this is finished between us." His eyes were bottomless and hard. His hand slid to his belt and whipped it free.

"No." Tess pushed to one elbow, torn and uncertain, devastated by how deeply he'd laid all her defenses bare. Part of her mind knew that he'd warned her in unequivocal terms.

It made no difference. She couldn't stay, couldn't bear to want so much. No woman like her could ever hold a man like this.

"Stop."

He pinned her arms with relentless fingers. "Not yet, Duchess."

Through the open windows came the hiss of distant thunder, followed by the slam of a car door and sharp footsteps. Grady's voice echoed from the courtyard.

T.J. cursed long and well. "It's not over. Not nearly."

He tossed a blanket over her, then pinned her back with a savage slide of lips and tongue and teeth that lanced right into her heart.

And then he tore away from her and strode from the

room, leaving her with nothing but a shattering memory and cold answers. . . .

Devastating answers that she didn't want to hear.

■

It took T.J. three agonizing minutes to scan the fax that Grady had brought for his signature. Two minutes more to learn that his Blazer and Mae's truck were both back in town with new tires installed. Meanwhile, Tom Stoner's foreman had brought in a coyote carcass for analysis and there had been a report made about a health hazard at the survivalist camp in the foothills.

T.J. forced his mind to concentrate on business, issued terse orders, then strode back inside the house. Still stunned by what had just happened between him and Tess, he halted outside his door, paced the hall, then pushed the door open and walked inside.

Her head was turned away from him.

"We can't stay like this, with questions left hanging." He forced himself to say the words that had to be said. "We have to get some things straight."

The pillow stirred.

"Are you listening?"

He heard her low, breathy murmur.

Agreement? Invitation?

Hell if he knew.

But they were going to talk whether she liked it or not.

"Look at me, Tess. We've got to talk." T.J. stared down at her grimly.

And cursed.

The impossible woman was curled up on the bed, hands gripping the pillow.

Sound asleep.

■

For an hour McCall paced the courtyard, berating himself.

How had he let things get so out of control? Tess was supposed to be under his protection. So far his batting record was dirt poor.

He heard his cell phone ringing. "This is McCall," he said impatiently.

"I've got bad news," Andrew O'Mara said.

T.J. sat on the porch glider and leaned back, watching a dust devil whip across the valley, spinning a funnel of dirt and debris. Tess was sleeping for the moment, but T.J. was close enough to hear her if she called. "Let's have it."

"First I want to talk to Tess."

T.J.'s jaw tensed. "Not available."

"Why not?"

"She's resting."

"Rest? My sister?" Andrew snorted. "What kind of miracle did you work to make her do a thing like that?"

"I gave her some pain medicine." T.J. closed his eyes, trying not to remember the wrenching fear he'd felt when he'd seen her on the cliff. He was still reeling at how easy it would have been for her to break her neck in the fall down the slip rock. "She fell near some old ruins. No broken bones, but she's going to be black and blue for a week."

Silence stretched out, then tightened. "Don't tell me

this has some connection with Boston.'' Andrew's voice was harsh.

''My instinct tells me no, but I can't be sure. Our tires were slashed at the scene and I found a spent rifle shell in the dirt. I'm running a check with forensics to see when it was fired.''

''I hope Tess isn't stepping into the middle of an old-fashioned range war down there.''

''Whatever it is, I'll handle it,'' T.J. said firmly.

''I'm convinced of that. Otherwise I'd pull her out of there today.''

''So what's your bad news?''

''Someone's broken into Tess's apartment. They were damned sharp, so we didn't find out until we tracked a bogus floral delivery to the building. There was no information in the apartment about her whereabouts, but this means they are definitely on to her. I thought you should know.''

''What about you? Have you traced the source of that money?''

T.J. heard papers rustling. ''There are fifteen branches to investigate, and that deposit could have been routed through any one of them. The bank's internal records have probably been altered, but I'm going to have to prove it. That means sifting through thousands of deposit records, both written and electronic. Meanwhile, we're going on the assumption that these people have someone with excellent electronic skills.''

T.J. made the connection instantly. ''That means they could have access to all her credit records and credit cards.''

''Bingo. I'm sending her a new card by express delivery. It's registered under my name, so no one can trace her through it. Meanwhile, be sure that she doesn't use any of her own cards.''

"Not a problem. There's not a whole lot to buy here anyway." McCall watched the dust devil whip over the valley. He could imagine the churning gravel, the blinding cloud of dirt and twigs. "One more thing."

"Give me a break. Tell me you don't have more bad news."

T.J.'s fingers tightened on the phone. "That's for you to decide. About Tess—things between us might be turning personal." T.J. didn't say more. He didn't have to.

Andrew let out a slow breath. "*How* personal?"

"If you mean have I taken her to bed, the answer is no." T.J. stood up slowly and braced one shoulder against the bleached wood beam on the porch. "That doesn't mean I won't. If it happens, it will be because we both want it, Andrew."

"Shit."

"That sums it all up nicely."

"Just take care of her." Andrew cleared his throat. "Tess doesn't have a whole lot of experience with men. She's always been too busy working."

The knowledge of Tess's limited experience didn't come as a complete shock to McCall, but he was surprised how it punched through him immediately, unleashing a wave of protectiveness.

"I'll take good care of her; you can count on it. Now, why don't you get off the phone and get me some answers. A big, tough T-man like you ought to be able to pull a few strings around the Beltway."

"If I pull any more strings, I'm going to be thrown out of Washington. And in this administration, that's saying something," Andrew O'Mara said dryly. "Give my love to Tess."

"It will be a pleasure."

"And, T.J.?"

"What?"

"Tess could do a lot worse than you. I don't think I'm too unhappy about this."

"Now, that's a comfort," T.J. muttered.

Andrew O'Mara chuckled dryly as he rang off.

The dust devil was halfway up the mountain now, its restless winds cast onto solid walls of rock. Thin plumes of dust furled up like smoke and scattered in the air.

T.J. was thinking about dead coyotes and stolen money when he heard a light step behind him. He whirled around, frowning at the sight of Tess standing white-faced in the doorway. Her hands were crossed over a lacy, silky garment that stopped midthigh. For a robe, it left little to the imagination.

"Dammit, woman, you should be in bed."

Her eyes were shadowed and uncertain. "I was in bed, but I was restless. Couldn't sleep—" Her hands twisted sharply. "Who am I kidding?"

"What is it?"

She drew a shaky breath. "You wanted the truth, and here it is. I'm frightened, T.J. I keep thinking, and every thought is a bad one." Her voice fell. "Would you—could you hold me? Just for a few minutes?"

17

She was wearing a skimpy piece of silk.

Searching green eyes. Tousled red hair with streaks of gold and a proud, generous mouth.

And plain black glasses.

The combination short-circuited something inside him. All McCall could think about was inventive ways to take off those glasses.

Then he thought of reckless, uncivilized ways to take off everything but those glasses.

He cleared his throat. "We can both fit here."

"You don't mind?"

There were faint lines under her eyes. A bruise darkened her right wrist. Every instinct screamed for T.J. to sweep her close and use the heat of their linked bodies to drive away the fear in her face.

But he didn't move. She was probably still in pain and definitely under the influence of Doc Felton's pills. He wasn't about to take advantage of either circumstance.

He had pushed her earlier, and now he regretted it keenly. This time T.J. was determined to be sane and reasonable.

"It's fine. Come and have a seat."

It pained him to see that she was awkward and uneasy as she sank down beside him on the glider.

Briefly, T.J. considered telling her about his conversation with Andrew. She was entitled to the facts, but not just then. Fair or not, he couldn't bring himself to cause more shadows under her eyes. Andrew's news would have to wait.

Her hands twisted again. "You *really* don't mind?"

He answered by wrapping his arm around her shoulders and pulling her closer. "There's no place better for watching the stars come out. It's also a perfect spot to talk."

"Wait. Just wait. There's something I need to say." Her hands twisted again. "What just happened—well, it was wrong of me to push you." She raised a hand as T.J. started to speak. "No, let me finish. Andrew shouldn't have sent me here. You can protest all you want, but my presence here endangers you and everyone else in Almost." Her gaze met his. "What if someone is hurt? How could I live with that?"

T.J. didn't insult her intelligence by laughing off the question. Her concerns were real, and the danger could affect others. "We'll do everything possible to avoid that. But if it happens, we'll handle it."

She stiffened slightly. "That's all? You pick up your life and go on as if nothing had happened?"

"Your apologies are duly noted and recorded. And no, I won't ignore anything. Neither will you. But I'm the one who's paid to worry about the risks and how to control them."

Something flared in her eyes. "Paid? My brother's paying you to protect me?"

"Andrew's not paying me a penny, Tess. I meant

that it's my job as a law-enforcement officer to assess threats and provide security.''

She latched on to the subject with fervent determination. ''If Andrew's not paying you, then I will. I know how busy you are and I want to make some reasonable compensation.'' She frowned at him behind the black glasses. ''Is one hundred dollars per day enough? No, I suppose not. A professional like you can probably get five times that much in the private sector.'' She gnawed at her lip. ''Well then, let's make it three hundred dollars per day. I'd go higher but I can't touch my bank account for reasons that you already understand. Money might be a little tight for me until I—''

Fury boiled over at her offer. Pay him? She wanted to pay him, as if he were an employee?

He threaded his fingers through her hair and anchored her head, locking his mouth in a way that was almost as rough as the curse that exploded from his throat. He didn't give her time to move, protest, or question as he nipped her mouth, savored thoroughly.

As anger flared hotter, he let her feel his tongue, let her feel the need fisted at his gut. Then he prowled, tormented, stroked—to please himself. He hadn't meant to feel anything, but he was doing it again. Dimly he sensed that this time he would have no strength to walk away.

Gone was the subtlety and the wooing. He took and took again, bending her back in his arms while he devoured the wet satin of her mouth. She tasted like mocha cappuccino and one of the raspberries he'd left on the kitchen counter. The combination hit him like a kidney punch.

When her pulse was slamming and her breath came jerkily, he pulled free. Locked his hands on her hair. Scowled at her. ''No money.''

Even behind the glasses, he saw her eyes were dazed. Her lips were reddened from his kiss. T.J. wanted to kiss them for a few lifetimes more.

"You don't want money? But I owe you for—"

His fingers tightened, just at the edge of ruthless. "I said *no* money." T.J. didn't like the vicious kick at his chest, the hammer of his pulse, and he hated the way his control was unraveling. "Andrew asked, and I agreed. That makes this a favor, something personal." His jaw clenched. "Very personal, Tess. So don't mention money again, or I just might get nasty."

"Fine." She stared, just stared, color streaking her cheeks. Then she touched the tip of her tongue to her lip.

Just once.

T.J. felt the effect slash all the way to his knees.

To his credit, he didn't move as she traced his jaw with her finger or even when she rested both palms flat against his chest. "I might be able to compensate you some other way, Sheriff."

T.J. lost the ability to think for a moment as anger climbed to new heights. "Compensate?" he asked carefully, keeping a leash on the shreds of his control.

Her tongue moved again, this time dipping over her full lower lip. Her fingers skimmed across his chest. "For your protection efforts."

With a snarl, he gripped her wrists. "This isn't about compensation, dammit. It has nothing to do with official business."

Her chin rose. "No?"

"No."

"Fine. I just wanted us both to be certain of that."

The words left him cursing. "What kind of man do you think I am?"

"A decent man. A man with a streak of honor a mile

wide. A man who's being pushed to the limit, and in the process he's turned my world upside down," she whispered. Her fingers feathered lower. "A very hard man."

He closed his eyes at that slight, skimming touch. Unbearable if she continued. Even more unbearable if she stopped.

Twilight draped the peaks in flawless electric blue. One cloud topped the horizon, pink and purple in the fading sunlight.

"Look. There's the first star."

He managed to relax enough to chuckle. "That's Venus, not a star."

"It looks like a star to me."

"No," T.J. whispered, "you look like the star." His throat was dry. He knew he was about to do something irreversible and reckless, but he couldn't seem to care. "You're beautiful enough to make a wish on."

"So make one."

"I did. I think it's already happening."

She smiled with aching beauty, fitting her body to his. "I doubt anything could be better than this."

"You're wrong about that." His voice was husky. "I'll show you just how wrong, Duchess."

Her eyes shimmered like the planet gleaming above the far horizon. She wasn't his type, T.J. knew. She didn't know the first thing about relaxing, and public relations was only a phrase to him. There wasn't a single compatible thing between them.

And it made no difference. There was only one way this amazing awareness between them could end, and he didn't want to take any bets on who would be hurt the most.

Tess brushed a strand of hair from her cheek. "Venus. That's the lovers' star, isn't it?"

There was a pounding in his ears as her perfume drifted around him. "Could be."

Abruptly Miguel's words whispered through his mind. *This woman could be many things to you, I think. Sometimes a path must lead far away before it brings one home.*

Her head moved to the curve of his shoulder. Her hand stole around his waist. "Sorry I brought up money." She looked up, her gaze searching in the velvet twilight. "I had to be sure that this—" She brought her hand to his chest, where his blood hammered. "That this *was* personal. Not business. Especially if things went further."

"Oh, things *are* going further," he said, realizing he'd made his decision the second he'd seen her so worried and uncertain behind those crazy black glasses. "And it's damned well going to be personal when I touch you, Tess." He brought her palm to his lips, surprising them both with the gesture. He enjoyed the way pleasure skittered over her face as he found the warm center of her hand and nipped softly.

Her eyes closed on a sigh. Her body flowed against him, all curves to his hard angles. "In that case, there's something you should know." Her head tilted, giving access to her neck as he covered her with slow, measuring kisses. "Just so you're sure—so you understand."

He skimmed her shoulder and eased her robe lower, greedy for more of her. "Understand what?"

"Things." She swallowed as he opened the robe, inch by slow inch, his eyes hot with intent.

"What kind of things?" he muttered hoarsely.

The robe trailed lower, then settled on the upper swell of her breasts. "It's important." Her breath caught.

"To you, especially." She held the robe in place, her fingers trembling.

"Is there someone else?" His whole body went tense.

"No. Not in a long time."

"Fine." Past tense he could live with. He didn't want a list of the other men she'd known. Andrew had said there weren't many and one or a dozen made no difference. T.J. knew her body and her moods. What she felt with him would be different from what she'd tasted with any other man; he'd damned well see to that.

The dark, feral part of him growled that he would be her last, her best, the one who'd strip her bare and make her scream in pleasure. They'd spend the rest of their lives learning how to please each other.

But it was a dream.

Forever wasn't possible. Boston and Arizona were at two ends of the continent, and two poles apart in state of mind. So he'd settle for tonight, for making a now that felt like forever and a joy that would be an enduring gift for both of them.

He traced the corner of her mouth and frowned. "I hope you're not going to tell me you were behind that bank job in Flagstaff last month."

"Of course I wasn't."

He nodded gravely. "What about that counterfeiting ring in Nogales?"

She shook her head.

He brushed her breast beneath the fine lace and silk and watched the crown stiffen and swell at his touch. He followed with his mouth.

Her eyes darkened. He enjoyed how her breath caught.

"Not part of that car-jacking operation over in

Yuma, were you? If so, I'd have to get my cuffs." He held her captive beneath his palms, her skin hot and tight with arousal.

"N-no. Of course not. But I—"

"Good." The robe fell. Only her skin met his callused fingers. He closed his eyes, wanting her everywhere, in every way a man could possess. When he looked at her again, desire hazed her eyes, and color skimmed her cheeks.

Then T.J. froze at the sight of the dark streaks at her rib and elbow.

His hands gently skimmed the bruises from her fall. He didn't want to hurt her, but there were ways to manage that. In fact, he was planning to be infinitely inventive about what he did next.

He swept her up before she could question or protest, the robe clinging to her waist. Five steps brought him across the porch, beneath a tangle of crimson bougainvillea. Five more brought him to the waterfall that raced down into a pool of churning water.

"T.J.?"

He worked off her robe and let it fall to the hand-cut flagstones, savoring the sight of her until color swirled through her face. Then he stepped over the rocks into the pool with Tess locked in his arms and let warm water lap around them.

"You—you're still dressed."

He was devoutly thankful he'd already kicked off his boots. Wet jeans might even be an asset, holding back the savage fantasies that had to stay just that until her bruises healed.

"It's lovely," she whispered as the water frothed and swirled around them. "But aren't you uncomfortable?"

With wet denim hugging his rigidly aroused anatomy, uncomfortable wasn't even close. He managed a casual shrug. "Forget about me."

It wasn't hard to stare as water streaked her skin, rendering the narrow strips of lace translucent, but the sight of her all-too-fresh bruises left T.J. clamping down viciously on his desire. He was congratulating himself on his success, when her hip brushed his thigh.

She gave a startled sound, her gaze on his face. "You're so—that is, you feel as if—" Her face went crimson. "Of course you are. It's the heat, the water. It's perfectly normal."

Cursing, he pulled her astride his thighs as the water jetted around them. "News flash, Duchess. The heat and the water have *nothing* to do with it." He tried to ignore the wet action of her thighs, covered by a mere wedge of lace. "Now, what was so important before?"

"Important?"

"Something that you had to tell me."

She drew a breath. "It's not easy to say. To remember."

Another man? Jealousy swiped at him with vicious claws, but he kept his expression calm. "Whatever it is, you can tell me. I'm a police officer, remember? You can't say anything I haven't heard before."

She moved restlessly and sent fresh pain slashing through his groin. "You have a right to know. People should be honest, don't you think?" She frowned, chewing her lip. "No matter the consequences."

He was starting to worry. "Generally, yes. But sometimes honesty can be overrated." Water lifted her up and down, skimming over the wet silk covering her breasts.

T.J. wanted desperately to rip the silk free and bury himself in the sweeter silk of her body.

She frowned. "You're saying sometimes people should lie to each other?"

"I don't know *what* I'm saying right now." He closed his eyes as she anchored herself by gripping his shoulders while their bodies gently drifted up and down.

Wet jeans *didn't* help, he discovered.

"I don't want to lie. Not to you," she whispered, brushing the wet hair at his shoulders. "It's about me." She looked up, her eyes full of shadows.

He couldn't stand the weight of her anxiety. He steeled himself for painful revelations. "What about you?"

She lost her hold and the current pumped her against him ruthlessly. She grabbed for something solid. Missing his chest, her hand struck his waist and slid over his straining zipper. "Sorry," she hissed, jerking her fingers away.

"Tell me the rest."

"It's me. How I feel. How I *don't* feel. Usually." Their bodies brushed, bumped. He gave up trying to understand as she wrapped her knees around his waist to keep from floating off again. Muscles screamed. Heat seared.

His hand opened, sliding over the scrap of fine lace. "How do your bruises feel?"

"Bruises? Oh, much better. It's the water." She gave a crooked smile. "Or maybe it's the company."

"Definitely the company." His hands moved over her thigh. He studied her face as his thumbs hitched under the elastic barrier.

Her breath puffed free. "T.J., I want to tell you about—"

"Later." His voice was hoarse as he skimmed beneath the barrier of silk and lace. She clutched his shoulders, closing her eyes with a gasp at his slow exploration. She was tight and sleek and he took a keen pleasure in watching her surprise shoot into desire.

"But you aren't—you haven't—"

He bit gently at her shoulder, feeling her back arch when the first tremors hit. Each rhythmic stroke made her moan and press against him. She was beautiful in her passion, beautiful as she gasped out his name.

Night was a curtain of velvet as she collapsed against his chest. The pounding of his heart was oddly distant, as was the unrelieved torment centered in his straining lower anatomy. Neither mattered. All focus was reduced to the woman now softly cradled against his chest.

When she tried to pull away, he tilted her face up to his. Even in the darkness, he saw her distress. "What now?"

"You. Me. It wasn't—"

"Wonderful?" His eyebrow rose. "Maybe I missed something amid the shivering and those soft, broken sounds you made."

Color flooded her face. "It was wonderful. But—"

"Good." He pulled her back against him, loath to give up the pleasure of her warm body. "So what was that other thing you had to tell me?"

She ran a hand through her hair, frowning. "It doesn't matter. Not anymore. That's just it, don't you see?"

He didn't, not for a second. But he was enjoying the sight of her too much to be irritated. McCall was a patient man, and his thoroughness always resulted in answers. "Move your leg. Just there."

Frowning, she complied.

"Now the other. That's right."

"Why?" The wisp of lace drifted over her ankles and floated off into the steaming currents. Then the front clasp at her chest snapped free, and her last scrap of clothing bobbed in the water.

"You're very efficient."

"I try to be." A weight settled over his chest as he stared at her, pale and beautiful in the light of the rising moon. "I've never seen anything I've wanted more." With one slow movement he cradled her against his arm while his mouth savored the lush curve of her breast. He saw her eyes glaze over, heard her soft, broken sound of pleasure as his hand slid low to close over her again.

She shuddered beneath his callused fingers, then twisted free and jammed her hands against his chest. "No. Not again."

"It's pleasure, Tess. I have no problem giving you this." His voice was rough, testament to the battle he waged with his control.

She closed her eyes, shivering as he eased higher into the sleek heat and found the exquisitely hidden nexus of her desire.

"Or this," he murmured.

Her body snapped back. Passion slammed through her. After her broken cry faded, she studied him through the steam. "That wasn't supposed to happen."

Her heart was pounding. He felt every jolt against his palm.

"I don't—" She broke off with a muttered oath. "That's what I tried to tell you before."

He brushed a curl from her cheek, savoring the energy in her vibrant face, the intensity of her eyes. "I'm listening."

"Stop distracting me," she ordered. She caught his

wrist and pushed him away, hissing in surprise when he palmed her breast instead. "It's this—whatever you do. I've never—" She gave a soft whimper as his teeth closed exquisitely over her nipple. Her head sank back as he sent desire spilling in a new wave of heat.

Her eyes opened as he anchored her cheeks in his palms. "Don't tell me that you've never been with a man before."

Her smile was a pale curve of moonlight. "Only two. Eminently forgettable, I'm afraid."

"Colleagues?"

"Do we really have to talk about this?" She sank against him, her cheek to his chest. Her hand eased beneath his collar. "We're going to have to get you out of this wet shirt."

"Later," he grated. "Talk to me."

She slid open a button and combed through the damp hair beneath. "It was a few years ago. He was a geologist who traveled a lot. In fact, we managed to spend only one weekend together. It wasn't exactly . . . memorable."

T.J. wished he had the geologist within reach at that moment. "No?" he probed.

She moved closer, her hand drifting over his chest. "It was all very organized."

Organized? What the hell did *that* mean? "He was methodical?"

She nodded. "Everything was timed down to the minute. He said if he wasn't organized in his line of work, he could miss a gusher."

It was all T.J. could do to choke back laughter.

She looked up at the strangled sound he couldn't quite suppress. "It was over in a few moments. After that, he fell asleep and snored."

"Tell me about the other one."

She shook her head ruefully. "Remember the wooden horse in the photo shoot I arranged?"

T.J. nodded.

"The other one was the actor for that campaign."

T.J. felt a grin forming. "The one who fell off only twice?"

"That's him. It was probably a minor error in judgment. Actually, a major error in judgment." Her voice tightened. "It turned out that he didn't—that I couldn't—" She looked away.

T.J. pressed her head against his chest, fighting the urge to take her beneath him now and show her exactly how different it could be. "They were fools," he said hoarsely.

"I figured it was my problem, something that was wrong with me." Her fingers drifted low and his shirt opened.

Irritably, T.J. stripped the garment free and let it float away to join hers. "Anything else you want to tell me?"

She smiled into his chest, her fingers raking him lightly. "That I'm not good at this. That I haven't ever been able to—let go."

"I guess you were wrong." His voice went smoky. "About four times wrong, by my count." He turned gently. "And that's just for starters."

She leaned forward, gripping his shoulders for a kiss that left him dizzy. "That's for correcting my mistaken impressions."

"So you had a thing for cowboys even then."

"He wasn't really a cowboy. I found out that he'd learned his Texas twang from watching old reruns of *Rawhide*. He bought his boots on East Forty-second Street in New York."

"Not many horses there," T.J. drawled. "Except for the mounted police units."

Her husky laughter spilled into a breathless sigh as she found his belt and tugged slowly.

"You might not want to tackle that right now, Tess."

"No?" She slid the prong free. "Why is that?"

Pain jolted, hot and swift as she brushed the straining outline of his erection. "Because it might take you places you don't want to go."

Her lips curved in determination as she straddled him, tugging his belt free loop by loop. "Are you telling me what I do and don't want to do, Sheriff?"

"No, Ma'am," he said through gritted teeth. "But—"

"Good." Her fingers eased the single button free, then found his zipper. "Because I wouldn't be listening very hard." The metal tab eased downward. "I want to see you. Feel you," she whispered. "And I can't wait any longer. If what you did felt good, then I can't even imagine what the real thing will be like. Actually, I'm tired of imagining."

"Tess." His fingers locked over her wrist, holding her still. "You're sore and bruised. It's probably been a while for you."

Her smile came, fast and crooked. "It's been forever, McCall, in every way that counts. Now, stop giving me excuses I don't want or need and take off those damned jeans before we both scream."

18

Water frothed over her high, full breasts. T.J. closed his eyes, aware that he was about to do something stupid. Irresponsible.

Wonderful.

"Let me handle the belt." He stood up, then yanked against the wet, clinging denim. He felt her gaze burning on him every second.

It took him too long to kick free of the denim and dispose of the white cotton beneath. He didn't know whether to be pleased or self-conscious when her eyes widened.

"Very impressive, McCall." She caught his hand and pulled him back into the water.

He fought for finesse, for care and control.

It appeared that Tess wanted neither. Her hands speared into his hair and her mouth moved hungrily against his. "I don't know how or why, but all I can think of is you. This." She scraped her nails lightly along the length of him, her eyes dazed.

Patience shattered.

He found her hips first, lifting her to meet his rigid heat. "Now," he muttered, lost in her. Lost in heat and magic.

Skin to skin, he felt the night close around them, a

drifting warmth that left them cut off from noise, bustle, or the reality beyond the adobe walls.

He whispered her name and felt her nails dig into his shoulders.

Offering.

Offering.

The rush of hunger nearly overwhelmed him, but the way he touched her was gentle, questioning, open to the wonder of the night's magic.

Man to woman. Skin to wet skin.

At his first stroke, she shivered, her eyes darkening with pleasure. Her legs straddled him as he built the pressure slowly. Again he moved, pleasure spilling like a dream.

T.J. closed his eyes, caught in the churning sensations of warm desert wind, clinging water, the hot, sweet dance of her skin on his. Too long denied, his body screamed for a savage release, yet finishing was the last thing he wanted.

So he played out the pleasure for both of them, his lips at her jaw while he slowly, exquisitely, brought them together as one. At the moment of full joining, a shudder worked through her, then ripped into him. Linked, bound, they felt every sensation as one.

He smiled grimly as a new tremor rocked her where she held him. Even then he didn't move, bending his head to plant a kiss in her hair, then framing her face with his hands, meeting her gaze.

He saw trails of moonlight in her eyes, hints of promises as she moved against him, gripping his shoulders, and sliding along his heated length, while the water rippled with magic.

Because he wanted to take, he gave. Because he craved speed, he chose delay instead. Slow, hot, and probing, he moved within her until she rocked backward, a broken sound of pleasure spilling into the air.

T.J. knew he wanted nothing more than this, feeling her pulse where she sheathed him so tightly. He closed his eyes. "I need you, Tess. I've needed this forever."

Her answer was a broken laugh, a brush of hands, and the urgent movement of her body on his. Together they strained, yearned, matching stroke to stroke. She threw back her head, her soft moan drifting.

Entranced, T.J. watched moonlight gild her body in the water. Then heat burst through him, and reason fled. All was hot pleasure, screaming need. Her fingers slipped and he gripped her hips fiercely. When her deep tremors began again, he drove blindly, pouring the heat of himself deep within her, grating out her name with a dark madness that knew no end until she wrapped her legs around him and joined him in the spinning silence.

■

The water drifted.

Wind played over their slick bodies.

Tess drew a shuddering breath. "Was that normal?"

There was nothing normal about what had just happened, T.J. knew. He had never come so close to seizing rather than sharing. "There's nothing usual about anything we do."

He felt her move, felt the delighted laugh she pressed against his shoulder.

"I wondered. It seemed—good."

His brow rose. "Good?"

"All right, amazing. Stupendous."

His grin was slow and dark. Their bodies were still joined, drifting on the water, wreathed in steam. It felt as if they'd been this way forever, lovers keenly familiar with every nerve and mood.

She eased up his body, smiling in dazed satisfaction. "So I suppose we should call it a night and try to get some rest." She raised her arm, started to turn.

T.J. moved first, catching her wrist and pulling her back against him. "That's another thing you'll have to learn. There's no time clock or play book here. There's only us, Tess, and I'm in no particular rush." As he spoke, he moved deep within her.

Her eyes widened. "Again? You mean you can—"

Her words fell away in a shiver of pleasure as he showed her, hands to her hands, heart to her heart.

High overhead, a single star tumbled from the darkness, then cut a bright silver curve across the velvet sky.

■

Thunder rumbled.

The sound of rain skittering over the tile roof above the bedroom roused T.J. He grinned at the feel of Tess's hands draped over his chest, her breath soft at his ear as they nestled on soft sheets that carried a hint of Maria's prized sage.

When the phone rang, he answered quickly, not wanting to wake her.

Grady sounded tired and just a little rattled. There was another dead coyote up by the Needle, according to Miguel. T.J. had also received a call from his old friend, the sheriff in Brinkley.

"Probably calling about that hostage situation and the paperwork it generated."

"Most likely." T.J. tried to shove the memory from

his mind as he shifted the phone closer to his mouth. "Any report back on that rifle shell yet?"

"Nope. But there are storm warnings. Possibly a big blow coming in from Mexico. And I almost forgot that one of those survivalists was in town, drunk as a skunk. Got into a shoving match with Tom Stoner from the Lazy C. I separated them and called someone to take that fellow back to their camp. He seemed nice enough, but Stoner sure was blowing fire."

T.J. muttered a curse. The last thing he wanted was for hostilities to flare into a volatile showdown between lifestyles and ideologies.

"You think those folks could be behind the coyote killings? Stoner sure thinks so."

"Anyone could have done it, Grady. The question is why."

"Beats me."

Lightning crackled, and Tess muttered in her sleep, rolling closer to T.J.

"You still there, Sheriff?"

"I'm here."

"I heard something. You got coyotes up there tonight?"

T.J. grinned. "Only one small one."

"What?"

"Never mind. I'll check in early. Let me know if anything else comes up."

"Will do." Silence played out. "Never heard of one small pup howling before. Especially in a rainstorm."

"It appears there's a first time for everything, my friend."

Tess stuck her head from beneath the pillow as he replaced the receiver. "What's wrong?"

T.J. pulled her onto his chest. "Not a thing. Sorry to wake you."

"I wasn't asleep," she said, yawning hugely. "Just drifting. I like the sound of the rain. Somehow you appreciate every drop when you're in a desert." Her fingers skimmed his chest. "Did you sleep well?"

"Best in my life. Of course, I had an unbelievable dream. Something to do with a woman in black glasses and a hot tub."

"That makes two of us." She combed her fingers through the hair at his chest. "Probably there was something illegal about what we did. Anything that feels that good has to violate one ordinance or another."

T.J. grinned again. "No, Ma'am. I checked, just to be sure."

"I think I saw shooting stars." She leaned back on one elbow. "Then again, maybe that was an amazing hallucination. Do you know a lot about stars, McCall?"

"I met a few in Hollywood." He almost laughed at the way her brows flew up.

"Hollywood?"

"I did a little security work, a little stunt work. Some stand-ins." He shrugged. "Pretty boring. Hurry up and wait, most of the time."

The dimple in her cheek was irresistible. "But it had its moments?"

"I suppose."

She leaned away, eyes narrowed. "As in moments when you had to kiss beautiful half-clad women?"

His lips twitched. "There might have been one or two. My recollection's a bit hazy."

"I'll just bet it is."

He caught her chin and brought her face back to his.

"Am I dreaming or is that a major streak of green I see in your eyes?"

"Jealous? *Me?*" She laughed tightly. "Not on your life."

"Is that a fact?" he drawled. "Then, why are your shoulders stiff and your hands clenched around that pillow?"

"As usual, you've managed to misinterpret a perfectly normal set of events."

He ran his tongue over his teeth, not quite hiding a smile. "Such as?"

"It doesn't matter," she snapped. "Who did you stand in for?"

He toyed with a strand of hair at her neck. "A few people."

She swatted away his hand. "Names, McCall."

He named a star who'd banked ten million in a thriller that had packed theaters with crazed fans for weeks.

"Him?" He could almost feel the shock snap through her. "You're kidding."

"Actually, no."

"How can you be so calm about a thing like that?"

"It was a job, Tess. Just a carefully orchestrated illusion. The glamour comes in the cutting room, when the gunfire and special effects and music are layered in."

She opened her mouth, then closed it again. "Okay, I'm not impressed. Not a bit." She sank back, then plunged her hands into her hair. "You really did? But your hair's darker than his."

"Dye."

"And longer."

"I cut it."

She drew a breath. "Okay, I admit it. I'm so impressed I can barely breathe. What was it like?"

"Sometimes boring. Sometimes maddening. On a few occasions downright dangerous. But the show always goes on. They're people like everyone else, Tess. Highly paid, highly creative, and highly stressed people. It just so happens they have the ability to light up whenever the camera rolls, so that they make you forget it's all a huge illusion."

"I bet you were good." She stared at him beneath lowered lashes. "Now, why don't you tell me about all those half-naked women you had to rescue."

He turned swiftly, pinning her beneath him. "Right after you tell me all about that client in Boston who taught you how to pick locks."

"Purely business, I assure you." She didn't quite manage to sound prim.

"Yeah, right."

"Are you always this suspicious, Sheriff?"

He answered by catching her bottom lip with his teeth, then skimming her tongue with his. Suddenly the teasing snapped into something desperately serious. He gripped her wrists. "How do you do this to me, dammit? All I can think of is having you again." He moved so that she felt the heat of his erection at the junction of her thighs.

"No complaints here," she whispered, drawing his mouth down to hers.

But he took a slow, hot detour. Taut nipples, trembling stomach, and dewy curls met his tongue as he tasted, goaded, enjoying the sounds of pleasure she made.

Her hands fisted in his hair. "Now. God, make it now or I'll—"

"Now," he grated.

He clutched her hips, held her fiercely. His eyes burned as he pinned her beneath him and slammed home inside her, while her moan of pleasure joined with his own guttural cry of release.

■

"Tess, I've got to go."

The pillows stirred. The sheets rustled.

"Work?" She peered out, sleepy and disoriented, her hands rising to his shoulders. "You're already dressed."

"You'd make a sharp detective, Ms. O'Mara." As he slanted a kiss at her forehead, she made a soft sound and dragged him down for something far more substantial.

Heat flared through her, stirring memories of the amazing hours they had just shared. Then Tess's hand struck something cold, something metal.

His gun.

She froze. "Has something happened?"

"There are some reports I have to take a look at. It's the normal flotsam and jetsam—a few hell-raisers in from Tucson and a stolen vehicle sighted." He slid his hands through her hair and took his time in a searching kiss.

Then he bit off an oath and rose, his eyes hot as he looked down at her. "Grady's outside. He'll keep an eye on things here until I get back." His lips curved. "Put the poor man out of his misery, will you? Make some of that cappuccino for him. He won't ask, but he's dying for a cup."

Tess sat up and stretched slowly. She made no effort

to grab the sheet as it drifted slowly down her naked body.

His eyes narrowed. "If I were a paranoid man, I'd think you were trying to cause me real pain."

Her smile was slow. "Excellent detective work, Sheriff."

He raised his eyes skyward. But the fact was, he simply couldn't stay. Work had piled up since he'd left, and several important reports were waiting on his desk. "I'll be back in three hours."

The sheet drifted lower. Her smile grew. "Make that two hours, and I'll put a huge smile on your face, cowboy."

T.J. cleared his throat. "I've always like smiles. You've got yourself a deal, Ma'am."

19

The fax machine across the room grumbled and T.J. stared down at the tall stacks of papers on his desk. An hour had passed and he had barely finished one-quarter of the paperwork that was pending. At least he had been more fortunate in his employee interview and had found a good candidate to replace their dispatcher.

He stared at a dozen pink sheets containing names of radio and television stations, several of them national. Somehow word of his participation in the Brinkley hostage crisis had been leaked. Ever alert to a story involving blood, violence, and death, the media were now tracking him for interviews.

Muttering, T.J. crumpled the papers into a ball. He'd talk to the press when hell froze over.

Meanwhile, he had enough work to do, and to his disgust, progress was slowed by his sudden tendency to watch the clock.

■

Meat loaf and potatoes.

What could be hard about a simple little meal like that?

Tess stared at the kitchen with absolutely no idea

where to start. Oh, she knew about potatoes—as a botanical specimen at least. She knew they'd been grown in the Andes and brought to the Virginia colonies, from there to England. She knew they were good mashed, fried, or baked.

But she didn't have a clue how to do any of that.

She turned to Grady, who was smiling his way through his third mocha latte. "Does T.J. have any cookbooks here?"

"I reckon he's got a few packed in boxes. His sister always liked to cook. He's not half bad himself when Maria lets him near a pan, which isn't often."

"I guess I should be glad that Maria has two days off," Tess said. "She'd probably have my skin if she found me in her kitchen."

"Oh, she's more bark than bite, though she's pretty protective of the sheriff after the way he fished her son out of that scrape in Mexico."

"Protective," Tess muttered. "She could give a mother lion lessons."

Grady rubbed his jaw. "She's real particular where T.J. is concerned, that's a fact. Now, let me see, I think he put some cookbooks in his spare room in a box."

Tess followed Grady to the other side of the house. Sunlight streamed through the high windows, outlining fragile pieces of white pottery carefully wrapped in acid-free paper. "It looks like the sheriff is starting his own art gallery," Tess said.

"He wanted to get these checked out by an expert in Santa Fe," Grady explained. "He took them from a smuggler who was trying to truck them over the border to Mexico. T.J. figures they're probably authentic Mimbres pottery from over in New Mexico. If so, they'll go to a museum."

Tess knew that these pieces could be worth a fortune if they were authentic. A man with less honor might be tempted to claim them for his own and pocket the proceeds.

But not T.J.

"The man researched adobe styles for months before he designed this place. He's got more pottery and rugs than he can display at one time. Even Doc Felton's impressed, and that's saying something." Grady pulled another box across the floor and opened it. "Maybe he put those cookbooks in here. I could have sworn he—" Suddenly the deputy bent forward, trying to close the cardboard flaps.

"What was in there?" Tess demanded. "It looked like photographs."

"It's nothing important. I reckon I'll just close it up and put it back," Grady muttered.

But Tess reached past him, digging away wrapping paper to reveal a dozen framed photographs. She blinked as she recognized the smiling faces of two senators, a dozen movie stars, and one presidential hopeful. T.J. was in every photo, dressed in a dark suit with his Stetson nowhere in sight.

"I don't understand."

"Hell, McCall's going to have my hide now," Grady muttered. "He never wants to show those to anyone. That was all a long time ago."

"Only six or seven years, I'd say. What was he doing?"

"Secret Service. He was working up to the presidential protection unit when he left."

Tess stared at the photos, seeing a younger Jackson McCall, who hid his tension well, in spite of the lines of strain at his forehead. "I should have guessed. He always has an air of watchfulness, as if he's ready for something to happen. Now I know why."

Tess turned at a sound from the doorway. Maria stood glaring at them, hands on her ample hips.

"Why do you come here? This room is private for the *señor*."

"We were looking for cookbooks," Grady said quickly.

"I come back because I hear about the *señorita*'s accident and I find you where you should not be." Maria rolled her eyes, then fixed Tess with a suspicious stare. "You wish to cook for Señor McCall?"

Tess barely heard, still studying the pictures of a confident, assertive man who could have gone to the top of his profession. What had made him give it all up?

"*Señorita?*"

"Yes?" Tess swiped at the tears blurring her eyes. Now she realized why Andrew had sent her to Almost— not because of a laid-back, slow-talking sheriff but because of a man who'd been good enough to guard the country's most important people.

"*Señorita* Tess." Maria was touching her arm, Tess realized, and the housekeeper's eyes were also blurred with tears. "You care about him very much, I think."

"Very much," Tess whispered. "I just want him to be happy, Maria."

"Then you will have your cookbooks, even if it pains me very deeply to allow another in my kitchen." She looked Tess up and down, then nodded. "You will cook something simple, yes?"

"Meat loaf and mashed potatoes."

"This is not so simple."

"But I'll bet he likes them."

"Yes, he does, but—"

"Then I'm going to cook that for him," Tess said firmly. "I *want* to do this for him, Maria. And I hope you'll help me, because I'm not exactly stellar in the kitchen."

"This is bad, no?"

"Very, very bad."

Maria gave a little chuckle. "Yes, I will help. And then I think I will disappear, because you and Señor McCall will wish to be alone."

Tess flushed, and the housekeeper patted her hand. "He is a good man, the *señor*. He will take very good care of you. Now come. We will work."

Tess frowned as she followed Maria into the kitchen.

Not that her sudden interest in cooking was a sign of anything serious. It wasn't a *commitment* or anything close to that. She was just showing her appreciation by cooking a few dishes for a nice, decent man, for heaven's sake.

Common sense called for her to keep things light. No matter what happened, she had to be flexible, to stop remembering how he made her laugh. To forget how his mouth felt on all the soft, hidden places of her body.

Tess cleared her throat, aware that Grady was studying her curiously.

"Anything wrong, Miss Tess?"

"I'm just making a grocery list," she lied, pretending to scan the refrigerator.

She and T.J. were two calm, mature adults. It was merely because of certain circumstances that they'd been thrown in each other's way. He could be regretting his breakdown of control at that very moment, regretting the temporary insanity that had gripped them both in the hot tub.

She forced down a pang at that thought and decided it would be best if she kept her mind on food.

■

An hour later, Tess pushed open the door of the sheriff's office with her hip, balancing a heavy grocery bag in her arms. Grady followed, struggling with two more.

"You planning another cappuccino party?" T.J. asked from his desk.

"Only for two. And it's dinner." Tess studied his face. "Something is wrong, isn't it?"

"Give us a minute, will you, Grady?"

Grady cleared his throat, then left quietly.

"Tell me." Tess's palms were clammy, and she couldn't seem to breathe as T.J. put a rectangular piece of plastic on the desk.

"Have you ever seen one of these?"

"A credit card?"

"Close, but not quite. It's a Smart Card. These little beauties can be used like phone cards. They can also be programmed to store medical records or personal identification for security purposes."

Tess studied the card curiously. "How does it work?"

"Just slide one through a vendor's access and you're set." T.J. turned the card slowly. "These will entirely change the way people do business. In five years, they could replace our traditional banking systems, bypassing them in favor of local retailers who provide all transactions via cards like these. You'll be able to load your card via the Internet and then head straight to the store."

Tess felt a tiny wave of uneasiness. "Do you think

these cards have something to do with the deposit in my account?''

"Possibly. Andrew tells me that there have been a number of suspicious activity reports from banks in Boston and Atlanta, where retailers have significantly increased their Smart Card transactions.'' He laughed grimly. "Not many mom-and-pop grocery stores do eighty thousand dollars worth of business in toilet paper and chewing gum in a week. There's a possibility that Smart Cards are being used to process criminal transactions, avoiding normal banking procedures, then transferring the money into a dummy company that appears above reproach. But the millennium might have been their undoing, courtesy of a Y2K computer glitch in the banking system.''

"You mean that's how their money got into my account?''

"It's possible. Andrew and his team are checking other cities for suspicious account activity right now. Unfortunately, your brother is only one of the players, and that's driving him crazy.'' T.J. touched her hair. "He wants to be sure you stay safe.''

"I don't understand. How does that affect my safety?''

"With others involved, he can't call the shots anymore.''

Tess swallowed. "I guess that's why I need you, isn't it?'' She fingered the Smart Card. "How come I haven't seen any of these before?''

"They're bigger in Europe and the Far East. The first are just beginning to be launched here in selected markets. When you mix Smart Card technology with Internet-accessible electronic wallets, you've got major headaches for law enforcement.''

Tess's eyes narrowed as she realized that beneath his cowboy drawl, T.J. had a razor-sharp technical mind that was tracking every detail of this investigation. Though that knowledge comforted her, the silver plastic rectangle on the table still looked ominous as it gleamed in the sunlight.

■

Tess had dried potatoes on her elbows.

An hour's work had left her sweating and muttering tensely. The kitchen was a ruin of dirty pans, discarded utensils, and damp towels. Boiled potatoes ran in a streak down the nearby wall, the result of a little mishap with Maria's pressure cooker.

Tess scowled at the scene of devastation.

Who knew that cooking could be so exasperating? In spite of all her work, her meat loaf tasted dry and over-cooked, not at all like the delectable item pictured in T.J.'s cookbook.

Tess stared at the exotic bottles lined up on the work-table. Tamari, seasoned vinegar, and chile sauce gleamed in the sunlight. Maybe it wasn't too late to spice up the finished product.

She added a liberal dose of the red bottle she'd found at the back of T.J.'s refrigerator, then mixed in a little ketchup and hoisin sauce for variety. But the potatoes were going to need more than sauce to improve them. What was it with those little lumps? The more Tess beat, the more they noticeable they became.

Finally she gave up trying for improvement and arranged everything in a pan in the oven as an attack of nerves set in with a vengeance.

■

T.J. watched her pacing in the kitchen, her hair glowing like fire in the afternoon sunlight.

"She's been pretty busy in there," Grady murmured. "Cooking something special for you, I figure."

T.J. felt a little kick near his heart. He tried to tell himself it was nothing earthshaking, nothing that spoke of permanence and commitment, but the words seemed to fall short.

"You can go now, Grady. I appreciate everything. I'll see you get an extra week off next month."

"No problem. I sure do enjoy that coffee she makes. Well, I'll be heading off." He hesitated, scratching his head as he watched Tess pace the room yet again. "I think she drank about ten cups herself. The woman has to be pretty jumpy by now. You might want to do something about that, Sheriff."

T.J. plowed a hand through his hair. He had quite a few ideas of how he'd relax her. The problem was that it would probably be a mistake. Honor demanded that he try to put some distance between them until they sorted out where this relationship was headed. And of course there was the matter of her safety. Too often when things became personal, security became lax.

No matter how he looked at things, it was time to back off.

Sunlight slanted through the high windows as T.J. strolled toward the kitchen, stopping to watch Tess in silence from the doorway. There was an odd pain in his chest, and as he watched her pad barefoot in his kitchen, he almost forgot his good intentions.

"Am I interrupting something?"

She spun in a rush and T.J.'s breath caught at the

sight of her long, slim dress of purple linen. A simple silver chain decorated her wrist, and he thought he had never seen a woman half so beautiful.

Not that her radiance was going to influence him to change his mind.

"These are for you." He held out a bunch of wild-flowers.

"They're lovely." Tess looked around her, smiling crookedly. "But your kitchen isn't. I appear to have used every dish and glass in the house. Cooking hasn't ever been my strong point, you understand."

T.J. pulled down a crystal flute from a high shelf. "Problem solved." He avoided looking at her eyes. "Mae will be dropping by later. She wants to discuss plans for the Founders Day celebration." He cleared his throat and studied the table. "Looks like you went to a lot of trouble."

"This is my best effort; I warn you, cowboy."

T.J. pointed to her hand. "Unless I'm mistaken, you've got mashed potatoes on your wrist."

"I had a tangle with your pressure cooker, and I lost. Give me a minute to wash off."

T.J. had a sudden urge to pull her down to his lap and stroke her skin clean with his tongue. After that there were a couple of hundred other spots he'd enjoy stroking . . . and tasting.

He frowned at the realization that keeping his distance was going to be a whole lot harder than he'd thought.

Instead of kissing her senseless, he focused on the food she'd made.

"I had a problem or two with the meat loaf."

T.J. kept a straight face as he eyed the full plate, valiantly ignoring the lumps in the potatoes. "It looks just fine.'' He managed to keep his expression from changing as he bit into the potatoes. ''Great texture,'' he murmured between careful bites.

Next was the meat loaf. His first swallow created an explosive wave of five-alarm heat in his mouth. Fortunately, he was used to the heat, but Tess wouldn't be so lucky. ''You might want to hold off on the meat. It's going to be a mite too hot for you. Which bottle did you use for the sauce?''

She gnawed at her lip. ''The one in the back of your refrigerator. The one with no label.''

''The little red one?''

''I think so.''

Wild chiles, a gift from Miguel. Enough heat to send a grown man to his knees, weeping. Even Maria steered clear of its punch.

T.J. had to struggle to maintain a bland expression. ''In that case, you'll definitely want to pass on the meat loaf. Try some potatoes instead.''

Tess locked her fingers together anxiously. ''Potatoes. Now, that's a subject. Did you know there are over two hundred varieties in existence?''

All that caffeine was definitely making her edgy, but there was something else. Was she having regrets? Second thoughts?

''Actually, the first potatoes originated in South America,'' she said, talking fast. ''They go back eleven thousand years.'' She gave an uncertain laugh. ''Even the cultivated varieties go back ten thousand years in the Andes. Potatoes are one of the few edible plants that can thrive above eleven thousand feet. The Incas actually froze them for their armies to use as rations on the march.''

She was definitely on edge, but that didn't explain why she wouldn't meet his gaze.

She took a breath and charged on. "Of course, there were problems."

"Aren't there always?" he said dryly.

"History says that either Sir Francis Drake or Sir Walter Raleigh presented potatoes to the court cook of Queen Elizabeth I. Unfortunately, the whole plants were boiled, including the stems and leaves. Since that's where most of the toxic alkaloids are contained, everyone became terribly sick after the meal. Potatoes got a bad rap for years. No one realized they were supposed to peel off the skin either." She looked down, toying with the silver chain around her wrist.

"Tess."

She went on nervously. "And then there's vodka. Did you know it was made from mashed potatoes? Schnapps, too. And some Scandinavian aquavit comes from fermented potatoes. Amazing diversity." She studied her hands, scrubbing at a streak of potatoes she had missed. "One of my clients had a chain of fish and chips stores. That's how I got to know so much. I had to write press releases and radio spots. . . ." She paused to take a sharp breath. "Oh hell, I'm no cook. Who am I trying to kid?"

T.J. felt his control begin to crumble. Maybe he could work on instituting some distance between them tomorrow. Right now all he wanted to do was kiss her.

"I realize that a few ruined potatoes aren't going to wreck the world. That's not the point," she said jerkily.

"Then, what is the point?"

"There's a reason it's called comfort food. I know you have things on your mind, so I thought a nice, comfortable meal might help. Meat loaf and mashed potatoes are a snap, right? But look around you. I streak your walls and leave your kitchen looking like the aftermath of an air strike. I tried to do something for you and failed miserably."

"Forget about the food," T.J. muttered, feeling the first vicious stab of desire.

To hell with distance.

He pulled a wildflower from the vase and held it out. "About this fellow with the fish and chips—is he another client I'll have to track down and torture?"

She didn't smile. "Henry was eighty-five years old. He had twelve grandchildren."

"You have to watch out for these old guys," T.J. whispered, bending closer. "They figure they don't have much time so they work fast." He gently tucked another wildflower behind her ear, then pulled her to her feet. "Would you care to . . ." He closed in for a long, hot kiss.

"To talk?" she whispered once she could breathe again.

"Try again, Duchess."

Her head tilted. "To clean up those mashed potatoes streaking your walls? I tried, but I'm not much better at housecleaning than I am at cooking."

He shook his head, pulling her closer, even though his conscience screamed that he was a fool and worse for pursuing a relationship that could never be more than temporary.

She tilted her head. "To discuss Y2K hazards and the potential vulnerabilities of cybermoney in the private sector?"

He slid his hands into her hair. "Not a chance."

"I guess that shoots all the possibilities."

"We haven't even *started* on the possibilities." His

voice was gravelly. "I want to feel you again, Tess. Right now."

Even if they both regretted it later.

"This is never going to work." But her fingers were already sliding over his chest.

"Tell me about it."

She freed his top button. "We don't read the same books. We don't like the same music. We don't even talk the same."

"Probably not." He tugged blindly at the zipper on her dress. "You don't know anything about vigas and I don't know beans about rollovers."

"Rollouts," she said breathlessly. "And about those potatoes." She worked at the buckle of his belt. "In some cultures they were believed to bring fertility."

"Sounds intriguing." His shirt fell.

Her dress landed right on top of it.

"Sweet God, you're beautiful," he whispered in awe, drinking in the sight of her.

"No, it's you. This . . ." She ran her palm over the hard, muscled lines of his chest. "You make me forget everything, including the fact that we have nothing in common."

"We have this," he said.

"Whatever *this* is."

Whatever. That's what he wanted: whatever she'd give him. Whatever he could take. He speared his fingers deeper into her hair, desire a drumbeat in his blood. "Now, Tess."

"What are you—" Sunlight streamed through the window, glinting in her hair.

"Here. I can't wait. Not when it feels as if I've been waiting for you forever." T.J. caught her in his arms and lowered her to the floor, working her last lacy garments free. Then he simply looked at her while his heart pounded painfully. The rug was thick and soft beneath them as he pulled her onto his thighs.

Tess gave a broken sound of pleasure at his intimate touch. "We aren't being reasonable," she said, closing her eyes at the nip of his teeth on her breast.

"To hell with being reasonable," he said harshly, caressing her with rhythmic strokes that left her trembling.

Tess caught a racing breath. This *wasn't* like her. She never yearned, never sighed. And yet here she was— pulse surging, skin fevered.

If it was madness, she didn't care. If there were regrets, she'd deal with them later.

He reached to the floor, protecting her even then, taking care of her with hands that weren't quite steady. And Tess felt her heart turn over, loved him for that care.

He entered her with a deep, hot friction.

Too slow, it intensified.

Enflamed.

He knew her too well already—where to skim, where to linger. He brought her hand to his mouth, biting her palm lightly as their bodies reached, joined. It was a dark sweetness to hear his harsh groan as she moved against him. It was sweeter still to know that the man beside her was just as confused and blinded as she was. By need. By desire.

Tess refused to call it love.

Love was untrustworthy, a changeable emotion suited to poets with short memories and a fickle sense of fidelity. No, she wanted stability and the kind of deep, wordless connection that stretched over good times and bad, through boredom and strife.

Not love.

She told herself so as waves of pleasure slammed home, pulling her inside out and shaking her very world. *Not love,* she swore again, whispering his name as he found his own shuddering release, locked in her arms.

■

Lifetimes later, the sound of a car roused them from their breathless satiation. Gravel crunched, and then footsteps tapped to the courtyard.

"Someone's coming," Tess said drowsily.

"So I hear. They can just go away again." T.J. smoothed the angle of her jaw.

"They might not want to." Tess sighed as his hand moved over her breast.

"Nothing is as important as this," he said darkly, palming her hip.

The doorbell chimed.

Once and then again.

T.J. scowled and turned Tess against his chest.

"Aren't you going to—"

"*No.*"

Gravel crunched again. "McCall, are you in there?"

T.J. went still.

The bell chimed again. "It's Drake," a deep voice called out. "I have to talk to you right now."

20

With a sigh, Tess rolled away, rose to her feet, and gathered her clothing. "Who is it?"

"An old friend who happens to be the sheriff over in Brinkley." T.J. drew a ragged breath. "He said he was coming in tomorrow. I guess I'll have to see him." He turned, searching for his shirt through the clothes scattered around them.

"Tobias, are you in there?"

Tess mouthed the name, trying to hide a smile. "Is that what the *T* stands for?"

"One word and you're history, little lady." He scowled at the mound of clothes. "Where are my—"

Tess dangled a piece of white cotton. "Are you looking for these?"

He snatched the item from her fingers, cutting off an oath. "Now, where are my—"

Tess tossed him his socks.

"No, my jeans."

Those followed a second later. T.J. yanked them on and jammed his arms into his shirt. "It might be personal, Tess."

"I know. Scram." She smoothed an unruly strand of his hair. "Love me and leave me."

He pulled her to his chest, his gaze searing. "Don't joke."

"All right, I won't." She brushed his jaw, then gave him a push. "Go do your work, Sheriff. I'll leave some coffee in the kitchen, and then I'll vanish like the fog."

■

Drake looked tired and edgy, a state T.J. was beginning to know well. "Sorry to track you down here at the ranch." He pulled off his battered gray Stetson and rubbed his forehead. "I hear you and your visitor had some problems yesterday." His keen eyes were troubled. "A shot was fired."

"No one was hurt, and that's what counts. Ms. O'Hara took a tumble from the cliff, but Doc Felton says she'll be fine."

"How is the doc? Still as ornery as ever?"

"Hasn't changed a bit. Still gives orders to everybody." T.J. crossed his arms over his chest, measuring his oldest friend. "Care for some coffee?" T.J. asked as he headed for the kitchen.

"Not if you made it—no offense intended," Drake called.

"No, you'll like this coffee." T.J. emerged with a steaming cup of coffee topped by white froth. "Ms. O'Mara has a way with caffeine."

"So I hear." One brow rose as Drake took a sip. "Mighty fine. I hear she's got a way with a certain sheriff, too."

"You ought to know not to listen to gossip, Drake."

"There's gossip . . . and then there's gossip. Folks tell me the lady is a real looker. From Boston, isn't she?"

T.J. rocked back on his heels. "Any problem with that?"

"I guess that depends on you. A woman like that can ruin a fine career before a man knows what hit him."

T.J. and Drake had enough history between them for T.J. not to bridle at the warning. "I appreciate your concern, Drake, but I don't figure you came all the way to Almost to coach me on my love life."

The tanned officer studied his dusty boot. "I'd be about the last person to give advice on how to handle a woman." He fingered his holster, his eyes unreadable. "I came to warn you that some hotshot journalist from DC has been sniffing around Brinkley, trying to put together a story about that hostage situation. He got your name from the mayor and now he's pulling in some details about your stint of protection duty in Washington. My sense is that he wants to paint a picture of a flawed man whose judgment was off."

Drake made an angry motion with his hand. "If he'd listened to what I told him, he'd know that was a load of horse manure, but the man has a mission and he isn't about to let a little thing like the truth get in his way."

T.J. shook his head. "So what else is new?"

"Only that he is headed for Almost. You've got a nice sociable town here, but you might tell folks to watch what they say around this hothead. I hear he's already talked to the kidnapper's family and is taking the position that the man was just bluffing."

"Tell that to the people he was holding hostage inside the bank," T.J. said harshly.

The last thing he wanted was to see his prior career and personal life emblazoned on the front page of a national newspaper, especially considering the danger of Tess's current situation.

"I know you did everything by the book," Drake said. "So does this reporter, but you're a former security man for high government officials and that makes you fair game. Next thing he'll want to do is give you a break in his story if you'll give him some juicy secrets about the powers that be. Just thought you should know." Drake turned with a frown, staring out into the courtyard. "That looks like quite a woman pacing out in your garden. Is she going to be staying long?"

"No. She's—just passing through." He met his friend's gaze head-on. "You have a problem with that?"

"Not a bit. I'm just remembering a few nights we spent getting good and drunk after that lady friend of yours went back to California."

"This is different."

"Sure it is." Drake finished his coffee and set the cup on the table. "You know I always wanted to ask why you left the service. It wasn't because of what happened in Atlanta, was it? That wasn't your fault, McCall. No one expected that boy to break out of the police barriers. He was damned lucky that you were there to stop him."

T.J. felt a sudden wrenching at his chest, and it was all there, as if it had been yesterday. The crowds. The noise. The sour taste of adrenaline in his mouth. The security teams on full alert after a death threat against a member of the Cabinet.

The boy, gangly but no more than fifteen, broke from behind a police barrier and fell to the ground in what could have been a simple misstep.

Or what could have been a sniper stance.

It had happened on Agent McCall's watch and in his line of fire. There had been only a split second for him to analyze thousands of disparate bits of data and then make a decision—whether to fire or not to fire.

McCall always wondered what had kept his finger from the trigger. At the time it was raw instinct that made him leap over a low stone fence, sprint across an alley, and throw himself on the boy, blocking his weapon.

It had taken only seconds to discover that the boy's weapon was a toy made out of plastic. He'd been convinced he was visiting a movie set, where he could pretend to be a government agent.

All of it made sense, given that the "assailant" had the mental capacities of a child of six.

After his shift ended, T.J. had turned in his weapon and walked away. He'd decided that playing God, meting out life or death, was not to his liking. He still did not care to explain his decision, even to an old friend like Drake. "I made the call. It was fortunate for everyone that I was right and that boy was no threat. But it was time for me to leave. Atlanta only made it happen a little sooner."

"From what I hear, you were missed. But their loss was Arizona's gain, and I'm damned glad you're back." Drake twisted his Stetson between his fingers. "If there's anything I can do, you let me know. I owe you for protecting my sister."

"You don't owe me a thing," T.J. said flatly. "I did my job and I'm glad I was able to help." He rubbed his neck. "I do have one question for you. Have you had any unusual types over your way? Like drifters or those millennium cultists?"

"Unusual? Hell, we've got people who claim to have been abducted and others who claim to be representatives from the constellation Orion. We've got back-to-nature fanatics who say that electricity and running water are the work of evil. How unusual do you want?"

T.J. cracked a smile. "I'm not looking to the stars,

Drake. I've got my eye on a group of survivalists backed by a young millionaire from California who's bought about sixty acres up north. Seems they wanted a self-contained community since they were dead certain the world was going to crash and burn January first."

"I guess they were wrong." Drake laughed dryly. "Some people are determined to see the worst, no matter how much good is right in front of them." Drake held out his hand. "Like I said, I owe you. If there's something you need, I want to know about it."

They shook hands in silence, each remembering his own world of shadows as T.J. followed Drake out into the twilight and watched his friend drive down the gravel road back toward town.

T.J. was planning how best to thwart the interfering journalist, when he sensed a stirring of air behind him, carrying a hint of Tess's perfume. Even that was enough to make every muscle clench, every nerve hum. He didn't turn, one hand tensed on the peeled wood beam. "I guess you heard that?"

She stepped up to him, her chest to his back, her arms circling his waist. "I heard enough to know he was worried about something. And to know that you had good reason to leave your security position in Washington."

He turned slowly, studying her face. The moonlight haloed her cheeks as she stared back at him, her eyes wide.

Dear God, he wanted her again. Beneath him. Against him. Legs entwined and bodies moving in reckless desire. Insanity, he thought.

But an inner voice whispered a different explanation. A single word that he refused to consider. The implications were too immense.

And there were things he had to explain. "It happened in Atlanta. I had to make a choice. Playing God was part of the job, and I found I didn't like it."

She brushed his jaw and his muscles tightened in response. "It wasn't so simple. I heard what your friend said. You saved that boy's life, and I'd say that makes you a hero."

"It makes me a fool. I put people I was supposed to protect in danger. In the end I was right, but things might have gone differently. I don't regret what I did, but I don't intend to throw myself into that kind of situation again. I'll leave the life-and-death decisions to God. He's had a lot more experience than I have."

Tess took his hands, threaded her fingers through his. Without a word she pulled him to the glider on the porch, then tugged him down beside her.

Together they watched, silent, hand-in-hand as the stars flickered into sight overhead—Sirius, Orion, Vega, and the moon like a pale curve of hammered silver against the velvet darkness. They heard the distant bark of a dog and the lazy whisper of the wind through the mesquite trees, and then the wild magic of the coyotes serenading the night from a distant ridge.

Somehow in that silent vigil of spirit, they found themselves linked. No questions were important and no explanations were necessary.

■

One more to kill.

He stared at the fresh new map with its red circled heart, then measured the dark road ahead.

Almost. How many towns had a name like that? It had made his job almost too easy.

And when the woman was dead, he would be a billionaire sipping daiquiris from his yacht docked in the Seychelles—or anywhere else with soft breezes and docile females who knew their way around every inch of a man's body.

He laughed softly as he fingered the grainy photograph stolen from the apartment in Boston. It was the woman's eyes that held his attention—wide and full of curiosity.

But not for long.

Carefully, he slid the photo back into his wallet with all the others.

One more to kill.

21

Tess awoke to the whisper of the desert wind in the pink glow of dawn.

She gave a slow sigh of contentment, then turned to find that the bed was empty. She had a tiny bruise from his teeth at her shoulder, and her muscles ached delightfully. She flushed as she tried to sit up, feeling cramps in places that didn't even have names.

An antique gold pocket watch lay on the pillow beside her, probably a century old. Tess lifted the polished gold carefully, feeling the weight of long tradition. Had this belonged to T.J.'s grandfather, the lawman?

Watching the timepiece gleam in the sunlight, Tess read the worn inscription.

For honor.

The gold blurred beneath a haze of tears. Everyone had a different idea of honor, but she realized that T.J.'s was here in this wonderful little town. He was a deep part of life in Almost, bound with the town in a dozen ways. He could no more leave here than he could stop breathing.

But life went on and so would they. They'd make a few phone calls, maybe send cards at Christmas. He might even come to visit her in Boston once. She could show him the harbor. They could take in a Celtics game, then head for Chinatown and—

She stopped, the gold watch clenched in her fingers. Who was she kidding? It was a dream and nothing more. As soon as the case was closed, there would be no more reason for her to stay. They had lives on opposite ends of the continent. Sensual fireworks just didn't make the basis for a lasting commitment.

Regret lingered, burning in Tess's throat. But she put on a smile and went in search of T.J., determined to make the most of every minute they had. He stood in the courtyard, shaving beneath a mesquite tree with his shirt off. The sight made Tess's heart jackknife, stirring her with sharp memories of how his skin had felt beneath her fingers in the long, sleepless night.

Business, she reminded herself. She had a project to complete for Mae.

Summoning all her willpower, she looked away from his bare chest and pulled out a notebook and pen. "I have some questions for you."

"What, no kiss?" He slanted a slow look at her bare legs beneath her flirty skirt.

Tess gave him a quick peck, avoiding a layer of shaving cream. When his hands rose to hold her, she squirmed free. "Be serious. I have things I need to ask you." She smoothed her jacket, trying to remain focused.

"No, I am not, nor ever have been a member of a subversive political party."

"Not that kind of question. I need to know about food."

"I like my eggs over easy, my steaks rare, and my whiskey neat."

"Whiskey, steak, and eggs. I suppose those would constitute your three major food groups."

"Well, I can take or leave the eggs," he said with a devilish smile.

"This is serious."

He put a hand on his heart. "You think good whiskey and a prime aged steak aren't?"

"I need to know about chiles. Mae wants me to promote a line of mail-order products, remember?" Tess tapped her pencil against her jaw. "First, I need to know where the best wild chiles grow, and how hot they are. I want to investigate authentic old recipes and how early pioneers—"

With a curse, T.J. tossed down his razor and pulled her into his arms. Tess's notebook dropped forgotten to the flagstones, followed seconds later by his razor.

From the west came a thrum of distant thunder. "Could be rain," T.J. muttered. He managed a crooked grin. "Then again, it could just be my heart."

"You probably ate too much of my meat loaf."

His lips skimmed the curve of her jaw. "Where's your romantic side, woman?"

"I think I left it back in Albuquerque along with my last spare tire." Tess slid her pen into her pocket. "I guess I won't be getting any work done this morning." She stopped as her hand closed around a small object with sharp edges. She slipped it from her pocket, frowning. "I don't remember this. I must have picked it up at the ruins yesterday."

She turned the shard over in her hand, studying its delicate white surfaces touched with fine black lines. There was something compelling about the small, uneven piece of clay, which seemed to take on warmth at her touch. "Does it look familiar to you?" she asked T.J.

He stepped closer, bending over her shoulder. "It could be Mogollon. The design is careful and the color is good, but it's hard to say without more to go on. Where did you find it?''

Tess continued to turn the piece over slowly. "I don't remember. It might have been when I was climbing the path along the cliff. So much of that is still a blur.'' Feeling oddly shaken, she closed her fingers around the ancient piece of clay. "Do you recognize the design?''

"An animal, probably—a lizard or maybe a bear. That's not too clear, either. I can take it to Miguel for his opinion.''

"No.'' Her hands tightened around the shard and heat grew against her palm. Over the adobe wall she heard a muffled sound that might have been drums.

Calling her.

Warning her . . . before it was too late.

"Tess, can you hear me?''

Wind tugged at her hair and she felt different hands, a different voice.

Equally beloved.

"Dammit, Tess, snap out of it.''

The bell at the front gate clanged, and Tess shuddered at the sound, gripped by an unreasoning fear that made her drop the piece of pottery.

T.J. circled her shoulders and pulled her against him while she drew great, gasping breaths.

"It's okay. Everything's fine.''

There was a light step on the gravel walk. Tess looked up to see a slender man with a tanned, weathered face. He bent down and picked up her piece of pottery.

"You dropped this.'' Carefully, he placed it on her palm.

T.J. pulled away with soft oath. "Miguel, I didn't hear you come in. Not that I ever do. Tess, I'd like you to meet Miguel Trujillo.''

Tess stared at the man, then at the piece of clay in her hands. "We've met before."

The pale light of dawn seemed to cling to his silver belt buckle. "Yes, in the storm."

"May I?" Miguel asked as he stared at her hand.

Without question or protest she opened her fingers, revealing the pottery fragment.

"It is very old, this piece. You found it in the hills?"

"At the old ruins. At least I think that's where it came from." She gave a shaky laugh. "I can't seem to remember that either."

The old man turned the shard over, studying it intently and watching the light touch the design. "Whoever made this had a light hand. They worked with brushes made of yucca fibers split many times. Even artists today find it hard to match such details." He pressed the clay piece back into Tess's hand, watching her face. "If you carry it, it will become yours, sharing your heat, hearing all your unspoken thoughts. Perhaps it may even protect you."

He made a small movement with his hand, and for an instant, sunlight seemed to gather over the fine white surface.

Then he coughed and stepped back. "We were to visit the camp in the mountains today, but I have come too early."

"What? Oh, the survivalists." T.J. jabbed a hand through his hair. "I got a little caught up."

"It is easy for a man to forget when he is in the arms of a beautiful woman." He bowed with grace to Tess. "I am glad you have recovered from the sun sickness. Your face now carries the glow of many dawns."

"Thank you." Tess tucked the pottery shard back in her pocket and turned to T.J. "So you have to go?"

   T.J. sighed. "I'm afraid so. Tom Martinez should be here any minute." As he spoke, the bell in the outer courtyard chimed.

   "I will greet your guest," Miguel said. "You may wish to say your good-byes with privacy." He made no sound as he crossed the gravel.

   "How does he do that?"

   "Don't ask me. I've been trying to figure that out for years." Again, he sighed. "I have to go, Tess."

   "I know," she said softly. "Whatever it is you're doing, promise me you'll be careful."

   "Always." T.J. traced her mouth. "I'd appreciate it if you stayed here with Tom until I get back. Not an order, but a request."

   Tess knew it cost him something to frame the words that way in spite of his concern for her safety.

   "I'll be here. I want to work up some ideas for Mae's new project. Just you hurry back, because I've got a thousand questions to ask you." She smiled. "About chiles. And about other things."

   "I'll be back," T.J. said huskily. "To answer your questions about chiles . . . and other things."

◾

Leaving Tess was the last thing T.J. wanted to do.

   He glared at the road, wishing this visit would keep and knowing it would not. He slanted a look at Miguel. "I appreciate your coming along. I'd like your help."

   Miguel's eyes flickered to T.J.'s face. "What is it that we look for?"

   T.J. made a flat sound of irritation. "I don't actually know yet. Maybe for signs of drugs. You're the most observant man I know. You'll see things that I won't, and any one of those things may be useful."

T.J. turned off the main road, heading north. "If they're involved in killing coyotes, I want to know that, too."

The old man nodded. "Why do they camp up here?"

T.J. smiled thinly. "Because they believe civilization is toppling. Jeffrey Graystone, their leader, has gathered his tribe to wait out the end of the world. It wasn't just on December thirty-first, you see. They believe the effects of the computer errors are only beginning. Markets will topple. Electricity will fail. You get the general idea."

The old man nodded slowly. "It has been said before. Many of our old ones spoke of the world that ended in darkness because of the evil of man. Of course they are right." His eyes glinted like polished obsidian. "This world will end."

"Are you telling me to get my food bags ready and head up into the hills because the skies are about to split open?"

"Many will choose this way. Many burn with the fear of change. This is why the problem you call Y2K still brings such discord. It exists and yet it does not exist."

"Run that one by me again," T.J. muttered.

Miguel gestured slowly to the landscape before them. "All this will change. Among the old ones of Yucatan, the year of turning is given. The Mayan stones record that mankind will awaken from a long, bleak dream, and as our eyes change, the world around us changes and from our pain will come great joy." He fingered his herb bag. "This is their prophecy."

"Do you believe it?"

The old man stared into the desert sunlight and inhaled slowly. "Each will believe in his way and time. Those who choose darkness will see darkness." He smiled, holding out his hand. "Will you have one?"

"Cactus candy?" T.J. felt as if he'd been wrenched back sharply to earth. First the end of all human life, and now cactus candy. "I haven't eaten one of these since I was six."

"Sometimes it is good to see things as a child of six. Perhaps our eyes were clearer then."

T.J. took the bright red candy. As its sweetness filled his mouth, he sensed that Miguel spoke on many levels—most of which T.J. missed.

The old man rubbed his jaw. "Your woman will prefer the green ones. The ones that taste bitter."

"How do you know she—" T.J. stopped, sighing. He didn't bother to question how Miguel knew such things. He simply did. "She's still not my woman."

"A matter of opinion." Gravely, Miguel reshouldered his worn cotton bag. "Only the heart can speak, yet we live in such noise that we do not listen. You must be careful, for your time of choosing comes soon." He nodded. "We are at our destination, I see."

As usual, he was right.

Four children were playing on a rough wooden bench as T.J. drove into the compound through a gate cut in a mud-brick wall. A dozen homes of adobe were completed and more stood waiting for roofs. Horses stood in a corral beside barking dogs. There was noise and activity, but the camp appeared to be well maintained.

Every inch was self-contained, T.J. had been told. There was no external electricity, no outside water lines. Everything began and ended here, stemming from Jeffrey Graystone's fanatical certainty that all civilization was on the verge of crumbling and isolation was the only protection.

T.J. stopped his car in front of an unpainted building that appeared to be a social center. A woman with long braids and a baby on her back was sweeping the porch. She looked up warily as T.J. and Miguel emerged from the car.

"Sorry to bother you, Ma'am, but we're looking for Jeffrey Graystone."

She shielded her eyes, glancing at the official insignia on the side of T.J.'s Blazer. "Are you police?"

"Sheriff McCall. Could you tell me where to find Mr. Graystone, please?"

She put down her broom in a resigned gesture and pointed up the slope. "That's his house, but I don't know if he's there. We've had a lot of visitors here lately. They take up a lot of his time. His name is Adam now."

"Adam?"

"Ask him; he'll tell you."

It wasn't exactly a warm greeting. T.J. hadn't expected one.

The adobe up the slope was slightly larger than the rest. A dog lay sleeping on the front porch and a metal chime clanged in the wind. When no one answered their knock, T.J. moved around the side of the house, where a dusty Jeep stood with engine idling and hood raised. A man was bent under the hood, muttering as he worked on the engine. An interesting contradiction, T.J. thought. The survivalist who wouldn't depend on city water or the trappings of a dying civilization still ran a car and used gasoline.

"Excuse me. I'm looking for Jeffrey Graystone."

The man straightened slowly. T.J.'s first impression was of rigid determination. His next impression was of a man whose eyes flickered because he had something to hide. "Who is asking for him?"

"Sheriff McCall." T.J. showed his badge. "I'd like to ask him a few questions."

The sun cast deep shadows over the man's face as he leaned back against the fender of the car. "Who's your friend?"

"Miguel Trujillo. He's a naturalist."

The man wiped his hand on the rag in his pocket. "I used to be called Graystone."

"And now you're Adam?"

"A new name for a new social order. All the old must be swept away, Sheriff." His eyes narrowed. "Even the law will be useless when the storms come upon the land."

"I guess I missed that particular weather report," T.J. murmured.

The dog trotted around the corner and gave a low growl.

"He doesn't like strangers." Graystone's eyes narrowed. "He gets that from me. What kind of questions do you want to ask? If you're looking for our building permits and property deeds, they're all in order. Our children have been vaccinated and our plumbing works." His face hardened. "If you plan to search, you'll need a warrant."

"Things look orderly." T.J. turned, running a hand along the smooth wall of painted adobe. "Nice work. Is it straw bale construction?"

"You know about that?"

"I used it in my own house. There's no better form of insulation for the money. Recycles resources, too."

Graystone nodded. "Soon the resources will be gone. People will have only what they grow or make with their own hands. We're prepared, Sheriff. Are you?'' he demanded.

Before T.J. could answer, Graystone gestured toward the steps. "Come with me."

The interior of the house was hung with bright textiles of desert landscapes and abstract patterns. There was order and careful design, but too much rigidity to suit T.J. He touched a bronze figure of a Kachina.

"That's my wife's work. She's off in Santa Fe teaching a class right now." Graystone stared out the window. "I didn't want her to go but she insisted."

T.J. touched the fine detail of the figure's mask. "I have some of her work."

Graystone's brow rose. "You do?"

"*Storm Dancer*. It's one of my favorite pieces. I had no idea she was here."

"We live simply here, and Marina doesn't care for visitors."

T.J. suspected that Graystone didn't either, especially when they came to see his wife and not him. There was a large ego at work beneath those shifting eyes. It took more than luck for a man to make his first million by the age of twenty-two the way Graystone had.

T.J. swept a glance over the rest of the room. "Do you get a lot of visitors up here?"

"A dozen or so every week. Mostly kids out to stare at the weirdos. But they'll soon see that we are right."

T.J. fingered a bright tapestry of masked figures holding stalks of corn. "I don't suppose you have any drugs here."

Graystone's shoulders tensed. "Old tools for an old world. We have no need of your numbing pills up here, Sheriff. Now, is that all of the interrogation?"

"Not quite. Have you seen any dead coyotes in the area?"

T.J. watched the man's face for any change in expression.

The survivalist shrugged. "Several. They were pretty badly eaten by the vultures when we found them."

If he was a liar, he was a good one, T.J. decided. "Have you seen anyone up near the Needle?"

"We've seen what could be lights. Or it might be the sun's reflection off metal. Nothing that stays in one place. Why?"

T.J. ignored the question. "Has anyone been up here asking questions in the last week?"

"Someone was here yesterday. Two men. They wanted to know if there had been a woman here in the last few days."

T.J. felt his muscles tense. "Did they give her name?"

Graystone shrugged. "They said she was from back east and driving some expensive car that she'd stolen from them." He moved to the door and called out.

A young man with fluorescent Oakley sunglasses trotted into the room and brightened as Graystone rapped out a question. "Car? Yeah, I saw it, Adam—a baby-blue Mercedes CLK300. I saw her about five days ago over near the interstate."

T.J. managed to keep his voice steady. "Did you tell them that?"

"Sure."

Graystone looked at T.J. "Is something wrong?"

"Could be." T.J. stood up to leave. "If anyone else comes around asking questions, I'd appreciate it if you let me know. You might want to get their license plate, too. Here's the number where you can reach me." He handed over a card.

Graystone fingered the card, frowning. "That woman you mentioned. Is she in some kind of trouble?"

T.J. looked to the south. The sun was a ball of white over the mountains, and the wind blowing in off the wash carried the scent of sand and dead sage. "I'm afraid so."

"We're all in trouble," Graystone said flatly. "There will be more deaths like those coyotes, only soon it will be people. Then the time of madness will be upon us all."

There wasn't much he could say to that, so T.J. didn't try. With a tip of his hat, he left, Miguel beside him.

They were walking along the porch, when T.J. saw a truck being unloaded.

"Delivery day?"

Graystone nodded. "We have our supplies trucked in. It's cheaper that way. We buy in bulk with a group order." Just beyond the courtyard, four people were busy lifting boxes and metal drums.

T.J. studied the boxes marked with names of standard brands of canned goods. Then he noticed a small metal drum standing at one side of the truck. It was covered with wire, but the red letters were visible. So was the universal symbol for danger.

"You keep poison on your grocery list?"

Graystone made an irritated sound. "That was delivered by mistake. We found it this morning."

"That poison is rare. You could kill a lot of prairie dogs with a can that size." He watched Graystone's face. "Or coyotes."

The man's expression didn't change. "It's not ours. Do you think we need that up here? More poison in a world that's already half dead?'' He turned away without another word.

In the car, with Miguel silent beside him, T.J. mentally reviewed the visit, but nothing became clearer. He glanced at Miguel. ''Did you pick up anything unusual?''

''There were tracks of a truck near the delivery area. There were prints of many boots. But there were also the tracks of a horse. One single horse, separate from those in the corral.''

''You think someone carried the poison in by horse and left it there without being seen?''

''It is for you to judge the law.'' Miguel's mouth tightened as he fingered the heavy buckle at his waist. ''I can tell you only what I have seen.''

■

Andrew O'Mara scowled as he stared at the phone.

He had just skirted insubordination for the third time, and the result had been exactly the same.

From the start it had been agreed: allow the criminals to complete one transaction on the Atlanta account. Then, when they tried to remove the funds, field agents would close in and apprehend them.

Unfortunately, another department had taken control of the operation. As a result, the plan had just changed. Now the Atlanta account was sealed tight. There were to be no chances that the money could slip through their fingers.

With the Atlanta account sealed, Andrew O'Mara knew who would be next on the target list.

Tess.

He kicked his garbage can across the room, watching paper explode over the floor. January sleet streaked down the office windows overlooking Connecticut Avenue. Pedestrians bent beneath dark umbrellas, moving in a silent stream.

Maybe it was time he took a vacation in the desert. Just in case.

22

While T.J. was tied up with his official duties, Tess paced the courtyard. She'd read the *Almost Gazette* twice. Then she'd tried Andrew, only to reach his voice mail. She'd skimmed and reskimmed her one copy of *The Wall Street Journal*.

After that, she stared at the phone, valiantly fighting an urge to call Annie and find out how things were going in Boston. At twenty minutes to twelve, she gave up the fight and dialed.

"Tess, thank heavens you called! Where in the world are you?"

"Somewhere quiet," Tess said evasively. "I decided I needed a rest after all that cruise work. How are things there?"

"Wholesale mutiny, that's how. You'd better grab a seat on the next airplane from wherever you are, because two of your high-profile passengers have left the cruise and five more are threatening to leave when the boat docks in New Orleans tomorrow. The berths have been mixed up, the captain has juggled the ports of call, and the champagne appears to have been lost."

"Impossible." Tess gasped at the thought of all her months of careful planning gone awry. "What does Richard say?"

"We haven't been able to reach Richard. But the cruise director swears that we'll have a shipload of furious passengers if you don't get down to New Orleans fast and pour oil on those troubled waters."

T.J.'s warnings filled Tess's head. "But—"

"But *what*? This is your baby, Tess, and the baby's in trouble. This could be our first and last cruise venture." Her assistant's voice fell. "There's even talk of litigation."

"Litigation?" Her hands locked on the telephone. "Can't you go?"

"Out of the question. Now I'm due in Chicago to placate the chocolate people in six hours. You're the one with the cruise contacts and the people skills. It will take you a day, Tess, no more. Just stroke them a little in that special way of yours."

New Orleans wasn't that far, Tess thought. She could be in and out the same day. "Well, I suppose I could—"

"So you'll go?" Annie asked breathlessly. "Where are you, by the way?"

"Somewhere you've never heard of," Tess murmured. "Annie, I don't think this is such a good idea."

"Are you in some kind of trouble?"

Tess swallowed. "Not really." She grimaced at the lie. "It's just not convenient for me to travel right now."

"Have you met a man?" Annie asked.

"No. That is, it's not what you think."

"My advice is for you to get on the first plane to New Orleans. Those passengers were out for blood, Tess. You'd better take a bulletproof vest in case things get worse before you reach the boat."

"I'll keep it in mind."

Tess hung up, then sat stiffly. To the east a bank of

clouds spilled over a jagged blue peak and rain darkened the horizon. She couldn't close her eyes and walk away from this problem. The cruise was her project from start to finish. The more she thought about it, the more she realized that Annie was right. A few hours of soothing and stroking would do the trick. And she'd be very careful. She'd pay cash and she wouldn't even stay overnight.

She was reaching for the phone when it rang. She answered, expecting it to be T.J.

"Tess, it's Andrew. Where is T.J.?"

"He's at work." Her body tightened. "Why?"

"I need to talk to him now. I think we've got a line on whoever broke into your apartment."

"Wait." The room seemed to sway. "Someone . . . broke into my apartment?" She swallowed hard. "T. J didn't tell me that."

"He probably forgot."

"Forgot?" Her hands opened and closed. "He forgot to tell me that my apartment was burglarized?" Fear was fast sliding into irritation. "When did it happen?"

"Probably two days ago, but we can't be sure. Whoever did it knew all the moves. We found out only because Mrs. Spinelli on the third floor wasn't expecting any flowers."

"Mrs. Spinelli?" Fear closed in. "She wasn't hurt, was she?"

"She's fine, Tess. She said to say hello and that her cats miss you."

Some of the panic slid away, but anger boiled up in its place. "How long has T.J. known about this?"

"Since yesterday. I called while you were sleeping after the hiking accident. How are you feeling, by the way? Still bruised?"

"I'm doing fine. At least I *was*," she said grimly.

"Don't make a case out of this, Tess. I'm sure Mc-Call meant to fill you in. He probably got caught up in something else that demanded his attention first."

"Right." *Like take me to bed and turn me inside out until I forget my own first name.*

Tess drew a shaky breath. "He should have told me. You should have told me. I won't be left out in the cold, Andrew. I'm the one these people are after, remember?"

"I remember. That's why you're in Arizona right now—because T.J. and I are trying to keep you alive." His voice hardened and Tess heard the snap of command that had brought him to the top of his profession in a little under ten years. He'd always had the cold stare, Tess realized. Now he had the voice to match.

"It was still wrong."

"Forget the ethics. That's not part of the equation."

"For me it is. How can I trust him if he lies to me?"

God help me, how can I share his bed and sigh his name until he makes me love him?

Tess stared blindly as the words echoed through her mind.

Love him.

Was it true? Had T. J. McCall stolen beneath her defenses, bypassed her professional tunnel vision, and locked down hard on her heart?

Her face felt cold, dangerously cold. She wasn't ready for that kind of intimacy and commitment. They were worlds apart. They were too volatile, too different. Too—

"Tess, are you there?"

She stared at the distant blue curtain of rain creeping up the valley. "I'm here, but I have to go. You can reach

T.J. at the sheriff's office. I'll tell him that you called."
There was a note of finality in her voice.

"Tess, I—"

"Good-bye, Andrew."

She didn't pause to regret or consider. She was stabbing in numbers before her anger could cool, running on a mix of panic, determination, and raw anger as she reserved a seat on the next morning's earliest flight from Tucson to New Orleans. Oh, she'd be careful.

Cash only. No hotel and no stops except at the cruise ship.

She glanced at her watch, waiting for the agent to complete the reservation. She'd have to leave very early to make the flight. Three hours should be enough to—

The phone was yanked from her fingers, and Tess was spun around hard.

His eyes were churning. His shoulders could have been carved from stone.

"Take a seat, Duchess," he ordered. "Then tell me what in the hell you were doing." Grimly, he twisted the receiver away from her fingers.

Sputtering, Tess grabbed it back. "Give me that."

"Not a chance." He slammed the phone down.

"Just who do you think you *are*?"

"The man who is supposed to keep you safe," he growled. "But you seem hell-bent on giving these people a clear target. Are you always this reckless, or have you got the idea that you're immortal?"

"Immortal? That's a big word for a cowboy," Tess snapped.

"Oh, I know a few. Stick around and you might hear them."

Tess's fingers locked into fists. "Use a few, in that case. Tell me about my apartment. Andrew told you that someone broke in, but neither of you saw fit to pass the news along to me. I want to know why."

"You were already upset. I didn't see how it could help matters to tell you."

"Who gave *you* that choice?"

"I did. As someone who cares about you."

"Then, don't care about me, not if it means censoring my news and controlling where I go."

"It's called protecting you," T.J. said savagely. "At least I'm trying to. The first place these people will look is for flight records. Any hacker with a friendly travel agent can check tickets reserved anywhere around the globe. You'd better pray that reservation didn't go through," he said flatly.

Tess shoved angrily at his hand, which had locked around her wrist. "Forget trying to scare me. It won't work."

"I'm not trying to scare you. I'm trying to talk some sense into that head of yours. Do you think the burglary at your apartment was an accident?"

Tess swallowed. "Of course not. But one day won't matter. I'm leaving first thing in the morning and I'll be back by evening. There's no way they can—"

He gripped her shoulders hard. "Are you deaf? You're not going anywhere. Not to New Orleans or Tucson or Tombstone. Forget about it."

Furious, Tess wrenched at his hands. "Don't give me orders."

"It would be easier to hold a conversation with a rabid steer." He pinned her to the wall, his face unreadable. "Someone fired a shot at you by those ruins. I was too slow, too unprepared. They might have taken you, Tess. Right now you might be shoved in the back of a car or locked in a room while they—'' He swallowed a curse.

"So this is about you, because you believe you failed in your duty?''

"I did fail. But it won't happen twice,'' he said grimly.

Tess watched something flicker in his eyes. "There's something else, isn't there?''

He didn't answer.

"Tell me,'' she whispered.

"It's the man in Atlanta.'' He drew a hard breath. "He's not missing anymore.''

Tess felt something twist at her chest. "What do you mean?''

"I mean that they found him. He was facedown in a half-filled irrigation pipe. There was a bullet through his left temple.''

He didn't tell her the rest: that the man had been badly beaten before he was killed, most likely in an effort to extract every detail of his account information. "And here you are, calmly booking a flight that would make you a walking target for men with no scruples about torture or murder.'' He gripped her shoulders. "You're staying, and that's that. Don't try to sneak out, or I'll tie you to the bed. I might even decide to join you there.''

Tess started to lash out, only to feel the reality of the danger she was in. T.J. was right. If she wasn't very careful, she could end up in an irrigation ditch with a bullet in her temple, too.

She drew a slow breath, then put a hand awkwardly on his shoulder.

He didn't move. His shoulder was corded, taut beneath her hand.

"T.J.?''

He turned swiftly, his eyes burning. "Dammit, these men aren't playing games, Tess. They could be up in the wash right now, watching us, waiting for a chance to close in. I can't guard every foot of terrain and I can't keep you safe if you try to run from me. And I don't want to fail. Not with you," he added harshly.

She stared at him, watching emotions race across his face.

"I won't let them get to you," he whispered.

Her breath came swift and unsteady. She caught a breath as his fingers locked around her.

Then he peeled off her sweater and shoved her against the wall.

His thigh nudged her hips and his hands were tangled in her hair. A muscle pumped at his jaw as he drew a slow, angry breath. "You were wrong to make that call."

"I can see that now."

He took another breath, his thighs moving restlessly, his body rock hard against hers. "I'm sorry about what I said. All I could think of was what might happen to you."

"So am I."

Tess jerked at his shirt, shearing off all the buttons, then sighed as her fingers rode down his chest. Her skirt was bunched around her waist and T.J. had one thigh between her legs when some shred of sanity returned.

He bit off a graphic curse, then let his head sink down against her forehead. "I have a whip here somewhere," he muttered. "You might want to use it on me."

"Why would I do that?"

"Because of this." He shook his head as he found a tiny bruise on her arm and two others at her shoulder. "You still have bruises. In a few more minutes, I might have added my own, dammit."

He kissed them slowly, one by one, then eased his hands under her skirt and whispered in her ear.

"What parade?" she muttered.

"For Founders Day. In twenty minutes. Everyone will be there," he said hoarsely. "Including us."

"But I don't—"

He slipped inside her while her heart pounded, his body hard and demanding. Tess felt the instant slam of desire as he drove deeper. She raked his back with her nails, shocked at how easily he swept her into this blindness again.

She heard the sound of distant fireworks as pleasure burst through her.

Or maybe it was simply the sound of all her careful defenses finally shattering.

■

He was sweating beneath his light jacket.

He thought of the money and all the incredible things he could do as he fingered the roll of electrical tape in his pocket and stared down at the motionless body on the ground. Taping the mouth was a nice touch.

Time to go. He checked the ground, making certain he'd left no clues. He'd have to be fast now.

He wouldn't think about the money or all those lazy, beautiful days on the beach that it would buy. He wouldn't think about anything else until he was almost done.

He laughed mirthlessly.

Almost.

23

It was three o'clock, the temperature still hadn't reached eighty-five, and a brisk breeze was blowing in from the eastern mountains.

Ms. Eliza Jenkins' fourth-grade class was handing out small plastic flags and the rotary club was dispensing free sodas in front of the courthouse. Mae was selling steaming cups of cappuccino as fast as she could brew them in the shiny new machine that had arrived via express mail that morning. Meanwhile, the high school band was tuning up for a musical reception to formally open the Almost Founders Day Celebration.

It was sweet and honest and yet Tess could not escape how out of place she felt here. She kept her gaze on T.J., who was shaking hands with a rancher whose face was the color of burned leather.

Grady saw her staring. "Glad to see you looking so good, Ms. Tess." He studied T.J.'s back. "Glad to see Sheriff McCall looking so good, too. It's been a while."

Tess wanted to ask him why, but she didn't. T.J.'s past would make no difference to her future. She had an odd feeling that events were pushing them forward, driving them to the moment when they would be forced to make choices that would sweep them apart.

Tess sighed. Almost was a place for protection and

escape, but she could never make her home there. When her problem was solved, they both knew she would head back to Boston. There would be no challenge for her here, and she needed challenge the way she needed air.

Like it or not, their future was clear. T.J. couldn't leave, and she couldn't stay. Oh, maybe for a month. Even for two.

Then what? Cards at Christmas? A short and entirely awkward visit to Boston, which they both would regret after an hour?

Better the break should be clean and complete. No regrets and no dragging out the proceedings. She owed T.J. that much.

Sunlight gleamed on his badge. He raised a little girl onto his shoulders, then turned to wave at Tess before moving through the crowd gathered beneath the large red streamers.

As she watched him smile, her heart hurt.

■

She was beautiful, T.J. thought.

Her hair was like sunlight, and her smile reached all the way to his toes.

Already she had changed the town. Mae was doing a land-office business in cappuccino and mocha lattes, right beside a rough sketch of the new clinic that was being planned, thanks to Tess's fund-raising ideas.

T.J. had to laugh as he saw Mae's niece pass by wearing bright red boots and sporting highlighted hair almost as bright as Tess's.

Yes, Tess had already left her mark on Almost. He wondered how he would bear all these reminders if she left.

Not if, but *when* she left. Because they both knew she had to. That was the kind of woman she was. That sassy wit and edgy drive were part of why she fascinated him.

He wanted to argue with her—to argue with himself. Even when he knew that words would make no difference.

A shadow fell in front of him. "I need to talk to you, Sheriff."

T.J. tried to hide his irritation, flicking a glance at the man beneath the broad, battered Stetson. "I'm kind of busy now, Tom."

The rancher moved, blocking his way. "This can't wait." T.J. lowered the little girl from his shoulders, then passed her to her waiting father with a smile. Then he rounded on Stoner.

"What's happened?"

"It's about those dead animals. Those coyotes." The graying rancher picked at his frayed cuff. "I reckon I lied when I talked to you." He swallowed hard. "You see, it wasn't those folks up in the foothills. I killed those coyotes."

T.J.'s first instinct was that the man was lying. Then he saw the hard lines at Stoner's mouth. "Why in the hell would you pull a crazy stunt like that?"

"To get out. My land's worth less every year. Between taxes and irrigation costs, I'm losing more and more, and my Mariah's too old for this kind of life." He turned his hat back and forth in his fingers. "She wants a nice little place over near Tucson, but who's going to buy one thousand dusty acres in the middle of a mountain range?"

"You did this to sell the Lazy C?" No matter how T.J. looked at it, it just didn't make sense.

"I figured those survival people changed everything. If I could pin it on them, it would make the news. Then that Graystone fellow would fight the arrest and Almost would be knee deep in TV crews, so people would see how beautiful it is up here. Maybe a developer would pay to put up some houses or a resort and I'd be ready to sell." He gave a bitter laugh. "I guess I didn't plan it out very well. Mariah says I never was much for thinking things through."

"What did you use as poison?"

"My brother found something down in Nogales. It's an anticoagulant."

"And I'll just bet it hasn't been approved for import either." T.J.'s eyes were icy. "I should run you in for this, you know."

The older man nodded. "Figure you should. I'm ready to go when you are."

"Did you cut those tires?"

"Yep."

"What about that shot fired?"

Stoner's shoulders slumped, but he didn't avoid T.J.'s eyes. "It was mine. Hell, I didn't come anywhere close to her, Sheriff. I just wanted to scare her off, so that you'd pin that on those survival people, too. I was damned sorry that she fell; you have to believe it."

T.J.'s hands curled into fists. "*Sorry*? You think that makes it all fine?"

"No. I reckon not. It was a bad thing to do. You better run me in."

T.J. looked around at the crowd. These were friends and family and neighbors, people Tom had known for fifty years. "What made you do such a damned fool thing?"

"I'm getting tired, I guess. Or maybe I'm just old.

I'm afraid I'll lose Mariah, and loneliness can be a terrible thing, Sheriff. I think I'd put a gun to my head if she left me.''

''Not if I know about it, you won't.'' T.J. fixed him with an angry scowl. ''That damned poison probably doesn't degrade. You remember where you left those animals?''

Stoner nodded.

''How many?''

''Twelve.''

T.J. rolled his eyes, muttering angrily. ''You give me your word there will be no more of this?''

The rancher looked confused. ''You aren't going to arrest me?''

''I haven't decided yet.'' He thumped Stoner's chest. ''I expect you in my office tomorrow morning at the stroke of eight. We're going to talk about exactly what you did and where you did it. Every hint of that poison has to be removed, and every dead animal will have to be recovered. After that I'll decide whether to arrest you or not. I can't say that the EPA people might not like a piece of your hide, too.'' T.J. gave a tight smile to the mayor, who was motioning him toward the stage.

Time for his speech. T.J. hated speeches.

He glared at Stoner. ''Go on before I change my mind.'' T.J. turned away, rubbing his jaw. He'd deal with Stoner in the morning. The man wasn't going anywhere until then.

Meanwhile, he had to say something stirring. Elections were coming up, and these people were voters. He liked being sheriff. More important, he was good at the job and he knew he was making a difference.

Hell.

The high school band built to an off-key crescendo,

then fell into silence. As T.J. moved forward, papers rustled and people coughed in the restless silence.

He climbed the steps to the stage, thinking about how different his work was today. In the past, he had guarded senators and celebrities while they did the talking. Now he was the one at the mike.

He saw Ms. Eliza Jenkins' fourth-grade class. He saw their parents and their friends holding white cups filled with Mae's coffee. All of them were good people. All were entitled to promises made and kept.

He intended to do just that.

After the mayor finished his introduction, T.J. cleared his throat and pulled the mike closer. "My grandfather always told me there were three things a person had to know to live in Arizona. Never stalk a bobcat from the front, a jackass from behind, or a politician from any direction."

He rubbed his jaw as laughter rippled through the audience, followed by loud applause. Tess and Grady were grinning as he continued. "The problem for me is that I'm standing here as your sheriff, and that means I get elected just like your other politicians. We've done good work here in Almost over the last few years. We've upgraded the 911 service, and so far there have been no problems with Y2K. We're fully connected with the state crime database, and we have acquired two automated accident assessment computers. In short, the millennium has passed us by almost painlessly." Applause broke, interrupting him for a moment. "But that doesn't mean we don't have challenges before us. We need higher qualification in firearms for all officers. We need better staffing for our search-and-rescue team. Our holding facilities could do with a major renovation, too. Of course, we all know that those things take money, something we don't have a lot of right now."

T.J. stared out at the crowd, feeling a glow of pride for these people he'd been elected to protect. "Meanwhile, we're catching up with the rest of the world, and we will continue to improve our record." He linked his fingers at the podium. "Today is the day Almost was founded one hundred and twelve years ago. If legend holds true, the first mayor had the disposition of a mule and the determination of an Apache scout. Those are traits we can all cultivate if we hope to survive here for another century or two." He pushed back his hat and studied the crowd, then looked up at the drone of motors over the hillside, where a sleek helicopter churned into view. He picked out the bright red call letters of a television station in Tucson.

"One last thing and I'll stop talking. All of you know where to find me if you have complaints or suggestions. Meanwhile, enjoy the celebration and thank you for making Almost the best place in the world to live— for me and everyone else I know."

As the applause rippled, T.J. watched Tess turn and move through the crowd toward the drinking fountains just across the square near the library. He relaxed as he saw Grady right beside her.

The helicopter landed, the din of its motor drowned beneath applause from the crowd.

T.J. saw Grady pacing awkwardly outside the women's room. He was heading across the square when two town council members cornered him, eager to talk about a fund-raiser for the new clinic.

■

Tess washed her hands carefully, then splashed some water on her face. She was pleased to see that her cheeks had taken on a healthy glow.

Her friends in Boston would be full of envy when she returned.

When she retuned.

Tess swallowed hard. Did she really want to go back?

She tossed the crumpled paper towel into the garbage, avoiding her reflection in the single mirror.

She was barely outside the door, when a bank of lights flipped on, blinding her. A man with perfectly even white teeth shoved a microphone into her face. "Ms. O'Mara? Morning News Arizona. We'd like to ask you a few questions, please."

"Questions?" Tess blinked into camera lights that were blinding, even in the afternoon sunlight. "About what?"

"We want to talk about your experiences here in Almost. What does someone from the East think about a small town like this? You're from Boston, aren't you?"

She stared at the bright red logo on the microphone. "Boston?" she repeated flatly.

How did they know that?

"Sorry, I have to go."

Distracted by the lights, she didn't feel the pinprick on her arm until it was too late. By then the sky was tilting, going dark above her.

■

It took T.J. three minutes to escape the council members. He crossed the square at a trot, searching for Grady, but only a mother with two toddlers stood outside the library.

There was no sign of Tess anywhere.

His trot turned to a sprint.

He was running now, pushing through the crowd as he fought down a premonition of danger. He was almost to the other side of the square when he saw the news helicopter lift off from flat ground behind the courthouse. The blades droned, shining in the late afternoon sunlight.

He looked up, shading his eyes against the sun. Something about the call letters on the side of the helicopter seemed wrong.

A moan drifted from the far side of a little garden outside the library, where Grady lay crumpled on the ground beneath a mesquite tree.

T.J. cursed as he crouched and performed a quick check for broken bones. "Grady, wake up," he ordered. "Where's Tess?"

The deputy rubbed his head, wincing. "Last thing I knew, she was in the bathroom."

T.J. tapped on the door and drew his gun. "Anyone in there?" A mother came out with a baby in her arms. "No one else is in there, Sheriff." She frowned at T.J.'s gun, held in a tight line down the side of his body. She moved out of range fast, and T.J. edged inside.

He searched each stall and found them all empty.

Grady was standing unsteadily when he emerged. "No one in there. Where is she?"

"They hit me from behind. I didn't see anything until it was too damned late."

T.J. felt the shock hit him in the chest. Tess was gone, in the hands of men who would squeeze whatever information they wanted from her. When they had that, they would kill her.

Fury blurred his vision.

But T.J. shoved down his anger and his fear. Emotions weren't going to get her back safely. He reached for his cellular phone, dialing the television station, only to be told what he already suspected. They had posted no news team to Almost.

"They must have taken her in the helicopter," he said flatly, trying to stay calm while his stomach twisted in knots.

"The news crew?" Grady looked confused.

"That was no news crew."

T.J.'s mind was already scanning possible locations, every thought focused on Tess, as if he might somehow pick up her subtle mental signals if he tried hard enough. The kidnappers would need a place that was secluded, where they would not be easily seen. Most canyons in the area were visible from the air. That left only two places.

The back country near the Needle would be perfect, but there weren't many places to land a helicopter there. That left only one.

T.J. ran to his Blazer, shouting orders to Grady on the way. He considered borrowing a helicopter from a rancher to the north, but discarded the idea almost immediately. The noise would give them away as clearly as a police siren.

The only answer was to go by car and track the chopper.

He needed Miguel to do that.

Grady directed him to the library, where Miguel was hunched over a computer terminal. He looked up, his eyes questioning.

"Someone has taken Tess," T.J. explained tersely. "I need help to track them, and it might be dangerous," he added. "But no one can read the landscape like you."

Miguel's only answer was to rise and shoulder his canvas bag.

∎

Ten minutes later, T.J. had assembled a backup crew by phone. Thirty hand-picked men were waiting in town, ready to follow at his order. Grady had notified the state authorities. That left one more call to make.

T.J. tracked down Andrew O'Mara, his voice terse.

"Dammit, how did they get past you, McCall?"

"They did. That's all that matters. We're going after them now."

"What's your plan?"

"Wait till dark. Stay close but not too close." T.J. stared at the line of mountains to the north. "We know the desert, and they don't."

"That's an assumption. They could be working with someone local."

"No one from Almost, I promise you that." T.J. thought about Tom Stoner, unable to believe he could be involved in kidnapping.

Not that T.J. was taking any chances. He had already told Grady to run the rancher in and hold him until their return, just in case.

"I'm taking the next flight out. I'll give you a number to reach me en route." O'Mara muttered an oath. "Hold on, McCall. My assistant is waving at me like it's World War III."

The silence stretched out. T.J. waited impatiently, staring into the shining red ball of the setting sun.

"Andrew?"

The line was dead.

24

Pressure throbbed inside Tess's head. She opened her eyes, and nearly gasped at the pain as light burned past her eyelids. She rubbed her neck, trying to focus her tangled thoughts through the drone of motors and a tilting sensation.

She twisted, only to feel her hands bound tight. Panic engulfed her as the motors abruptly died.

From the silence came drifting bits of conversation. She was certain that one voice belonged to the man who had claimed to be from the television news crew.

She remembered the prick at her arm.

Drugged.

Kidnapped.

The money . . .

She lay still, giving every appearance of being asleep.

Another voice came, lower and more nasal. "Shouldn't she be coming out from under by now?"

The first man answered. "Anytime now. And we definitely need her conscious."

"You want me to slap her around?" The man sounded pleased at the thought.

"Just use water. I don't want her to be any more difficult to deal with than necessary."

Tess forced herself not to move, groaning and refusing to open her eyes when they shook her. Instinct told her to feign unconsciousness as long as possible.

"What about that sheriff? He'll be coming after her."

"Only if he has some kind of superdog that can track a helicopter over the mountains," the other man snapped.

"Still, he'll be coming. He or one of the deputies has been with her every day. By now he will have found that officer outside the library."

"Let them come. None of them will know where to look. By the time they get trucks out to these canyons we'll have what we want and be long gone. Most people in the area don't even know about this place, so you can stop worrying. You'll get your money."

The nasal voice cut him off. "So you keep telling me. I haven't seen any of it yet."

"You will. We all will. Now, stop whining—I have to make a call."

Tess heard the sound of rustling. Then the man cleared his throat.

"Give me Andrew O'Mara. Tell him it's an emergency."

There was a pause, broken only by the sound of the wind.

"No, you listen to *me*. It's time to make a deal, O'Mara. You want your sister back, you're gonna have to give us our money. That's right, all of it. A million dollars. You have two hours."

"Time? That's *your* problem." There was a bark of laughter, but to Tess it sounded strained. "Talk to her? Sure you can, the very next time I call. Right now you'd better work on getting that cash together. Small bills. I'll give you the drop location when I call back."

Footsteps crunched over gravel. Hands tightened, pulling her upright and slapping her face. "Wake up, dammit."

She gave a low groan.

"Still asleep." It was the nasal voice again.

"The next time I call, he'll demand to speak with her, and I want her conscious."

She lay unmoving, her palms sweaty, praying they would go away.

"Wake her up."

A hand clamped down on her neck.

■

T.J. was fighting impatience as the silence stretched out. What was happening? Had O'Mara turned up some news already?

Finally Andrew cut back onto the line. "Bad news." His voice was clipped and tight with anger. "These people are well connected, McCall. They had my name and my office number. Here it is: they want their million or they'll kill Tess, and I can't negotiate after a ransom threat. It's against all government policy." Metal clattered as if a can had been thrown against the floor. "I told them not to freeze the damned account. I told them it would push these people into a corner, and it has."

T.J. fought for calm despite a surge of rage. "Get someone on the call. It's probably a cell phone, but it could still be tracked."

"Already done. It's going to take time."

"Keep them dangling. Tell them the money will be brought in tonight."

"I know the drill," Andrew snapped. "And you can

be sure I'll make them let me talk to Tess when they call back.''

"Good. Stay on them." T.J. swept the valley before him. "We're on our way."

■

Miguel stopped above a deep wash shaded by cotton-wood trees. The leaves shook like tiny coins in the wind as the wiry man moved slowly, crisscrossing the rocky ground. T.J. paced restlessly, seeing nothing be-yond the double tracks of a jackrabbit, but he bit back his impatience, knowing Miguel had good reasons for stopping.

He had thirty men waiting to head out from Almost. At his call they would move instantly.

But T.J. had to wait. The last thing he wanted was Tess caught in the middle of a firefight.

Miguel squatted, scanning the ground. Finally he stood up and pointed. ''They came this way, flying low. They were headed northeast.''

"How can you tell?" It seemed like pure imagina-tion to T.J. Miguel was good, but no one was *this* good.

"The tracks tell me that the animals fled. All the prints move in the opposite direction and they are made at the run. Only three things can do that. Floods, fire, or something that terrifies with deafening noise, like a heli-copter.'' He swept his hand to the right. ''The bobcat moved here, and a rabbit ran beside it, unharmed. Only great fear would cause such a thing.'' He moved higher up the slope and beckoned to T.J., who saw running sets of double oval tracks.

"Javelina. Three or four of them.''

Miguel nodded. "Running. Very frightened." He crouched, fingering the willowy bough of a young mesquite. "See how the branch is broken in many places? A great wind can do this, or blades that cut fast. They would also send the sand in shifting patterns like water."

T.J. looked down and saw just such a pattern on the sand before them. His admiration for Miguel's skills grew tenfold.

Back in the Blazer, T.J. gunned up the slope, sand spinning angrily beneath his wheels. At the top, he slowed, feeling his first hint of optimism since he'd discovered Tess was missing.

He knew the place before them. He recognized the dark walls across the distant cliffs, even in the gathering twilight. Near the base of a granite outcropping he saw the glint of metal. He looked at Miguel, who nodded.

"We will find her, my friend. Soon it will be twilight, and I know a dozen ways in. No one will hear us."

◼

"There."

T.J. and Miguel were crouched behind a gravel ridge banked by dense scrub. Below them stretched the undulating waves of the foothills with the ancient ruins like a dark scar in the gathering shadows. They could make out activity near the base of the canyon.

T.J. pulled out his rifle, focusing through the night vision sight. "There are two men by the canyon wall beside the helicopter." He scanned the scene twice and cursed. "I still don't see Tess."

Miguel stared for a long time in silence. "She is

there. I sense her." He pointed carefully. "There is a small path from the left. It follows the old ruined walls."

T.J. studied the slope with the night vision sight. "I see it."

"You will take that path. In the darkness, you will not be noticed."

T.J. turned his head to study his companion. "What about you?"

"I will come from the opposite side. It is better that we go separately. If one of us is caught, the other will find her."

After a long time T.J. nodded. He didn't want to think about Tess huddled in the darkness, alone and frightened. She must know that he would follow her, no matter what.

He prayed he was in time.

Ruthlessly, he forced his thoughts to the task before them, knowing it was the only way he could help her. The shadows were already shifting into darkness as he slid his rifle, phone, and canteen into a black pack. Over his shoulder he heard a soft sound, almost like the whisper of sand in the wind.

He turned sharply. "Miguel?"

There was no answer. Only the mesquite fronds moved, ghostlike in the night. The spot where Miguel had been standing was empty.

Through the trailing greenery of the mesquite, T.J. thought he saw a brown shape lope up the wash toward the cliff.

■

They pulled her upright and shook her hard. Tess groaned and made a weak twisting movement.

"Untie her feet and put her on the ground. Then douse her with water." The words were hard and clipped. "I want her awake and vocal when I call her brother. What happens after that is a different matter," he added roughly.

After that they would kill her.

Tess fought back panic, knowing she had to stay calm. She felt them work at the ropes on her ankles. Then she was toppled to the ground in a blur of pain that was followed by the slap of freezing water. This time she didn't have to feign a moan.

Somewhere nearby she heard the flare of a match. "Use more water. Then shake her."

She steeled herself to another onslaught, listening to something rustle up the slope. She prayed it wasn't a snake.

"Sanchez, is that you?"

There was no reply to the clipped question.

"Dammit, if he's drinking again, I'll slit his throat myself." Footsteps crunched loudly and Tess caught the scent of cigarette smoke. "I'll deal with the woman. You go see what's keeping Sanchez."

"Sure thing."

Tess waited, braced for another burst of cold water and a sharp slap.

Neither came.

Instead, she heard a muffled thump, followed by a rain of skittering pebbles. Smoke wafted close by her head.

"Sanchez?"

No answer.

"Dammit, Hammond, is that you?"

The silence stretched out, heavy and unnatural.

Boots crunched away up the slope. Above the fierce slam of her heart, Tess heard the sigh of the wind and the lonely yowl of a single coyote.

Her feet were free now. With luck she could work the blindfold off. Instinct screamed for her to move before they came back. Twisting hard, she strained at the blindfold with her bound hands, careful to make no noise. She finally managed to shove the dusty cloth high enough to make out a thin line of darkness.

Overhead she saw the glitter of a million stars, like a beacon of hope arching through the sky. T.J. would come for her. But until he did, she wouldn't be waiting around. She had to save herself.

"Sanchez, where are you?" The angry question drifted over the slope.

Tess braced one arm carefully. When the silence held, she pushed to a crouch and slipped past a barrel cactus into the darkness.

■

T.J. stared at the body.

Miguel must have gotten here already and handled this kidnapper. It was the pilot, judging by his flight suit with the bogus TV logo. He was bound with heavy black tape, legs to hands and an extra piece across his mouth. He was out cold, but Miguel was clearly taking no chances.

T.J. pulled the battery from the chopper and clipped two sets of wires, just in case they had any plan of heading for Mexico.

Three more to go. And it had to be done fast, before the kidnappers realized they had company.

He heard a noise up the hill. Swinging the night

scope, he saw a man with a metal can running toward the helicopter.

"Sanchez?"

T.J. flattened against the wall of the chopper.

Liquid sloshed in the metal can. "Dammit, Sanchez, if you're drinking again, you're dead."

T.J. dropped behind the curve of the chopper, then went flat under its belly, waiting.

"Sanchez, answer me."

T.J. figured that Sanchez didn't answer because he was out cold and bound with tape, thanks to Miguel. In ten more steps his body would be visible. T.J. cupped a hand over his mouth. "Over here."

"Sanchez, if this is some new trick, you're going to be eating dirt for a week."

The boots crunched closer. The metal can rocked, then slammed down onto the ground inches from T.J.'s face.

He drew a length of steel wire from a coil over his shoulder and reached closer, circling the dusty boots. In one sharp movement he jerked the coil, bringing the man down while he rolled free of the chopper and smashed down on his target's throat, cutting off his cry mid-breath.

He needn't have bothered. In the man's plunge to the ground, he had struck his head on the strut of the chopper. Now he lay prone, eyes closed. T.J. gagged and cuffed the motionless figure, then stood slowly.

Two more to go.

He swung his head, listening to the restless sounds of the night. A small animal skittered up the other side of the cottonwood trees. Probably a rabbit. A javelina would have a characteristically unpleasant odor at this distance, and no coyote would come so close to men.

T.J. swung the rifle to his shoulder and swept the hillside, picking up the green phosphorescent flare of a cigarette bobbing up the hill. He was inching closer when something broke hard through the scrub near the cliff base.

Then he heard Tess's broken scream.

25

R*un.*

Ignore the pain and run.

She stumbled, hitting rocks and sand and bushes, her heart pumping in terror. A shout came from behind her, and she dodged beneath the thorny arms of a palo verde tree. A branch snapped at her face, clawing at her cheeks as she plunged furiously up the slope.

The ruins were somewhere before her. All she had to do was dodge her pursuers until she got there.

Frantic, Tess tried to remember where the path came in. Had it been beside the boulders at the wash or in front of the broken walls on the east? The memory was a blur.

She stopped, panting, bent double in pain as she tried to find the dark outline of the stone steps.

A bullet exploded beside her, burning through her shoulder and tearing a scream from her throat. Instantly, she heard the slam of running feet and knew she had only a second to make a choice.

Which way?

She summoned up the memory of that strange afternoon when she had stood in the shadow of the cliff walls, transported by images of an eerie past.

Remember.

The shout came again. Tess stood shaking, certain if

she made the wrong choice, she would die there in the restless night.

Some instinct made her work one trembling hand into the front pocket of her jacket to grip the ancient piece of pottery.

She closed her eyes, concentrating, letting its heat fill her fingers.

Suddenly light flared, outlining the broken edge of the ancient stone walls. She raced forward, oblivious to the wild poppies, oblivious to the sharp thorns of a saguaro cactus that dug into her ankle. Ahead of her the light grew, flickering higher. She followed, half in a daze, her attention locked on the dancing glow as if it were a lifeline. Somehow Tess knew the steps were just before her, and driven by an instinct she could not name, she plunged through the darkness, tripping over debris and fallen bricks that seemed to be out of place. Another bullet flashed, ricocheting off the walls and shattering the stone in sharp fragments that burned against her skin.

She stumbled and fell to her knees on a flow of slip rock and gravel, gasping as she struck the hard outline of the lowest step. Without hesitating, she lurched forward in the darkness. Somewhere she heard the low drone of voices—and what almost sounded like drums.

An illusion. It was only her heart, slamming in terror.

Or perhaps it was the helicopter, motors whining as it prepared to take off.

She didn't stop to question the strange images. At the top of the uneven steps, she pressed her fingers to the ancient wall, following it higher. A few feet farther there would be a doorway. Somehow she knew this, just as she knew that beyond the door were three storerooms.

Though she couldn't see them, somehow Tess knew they were there.

She gripped the clay shard tightly, feeling its heat against her palm.

A bullet cracked off the cliff wall, its angry ricochet bouncing among the towering stones. Boots clambered behind her as she found her way to the last room and huddled down in the darkness, curling her body into a tight, frozen ball.

Waiting.

■

He made no effort to be quiet. He had lost one man and possibly two. The helicopter had plenty of fuel and he had a man to fly it, which meant he could always go to his backup plan.

But first he was going to find the woman. He had come too far to leave loose ends. He was actually looking forward to dealing with Tess O'Mara after all the trouble she had caused him.

She was right ahead of him now. He heard her feet on the narrow stairs that led to the ruin and raised his halogen light, outlining the ragged walls. Not many places to hide there. He would take his time, follow silently.

And then he would kill her.

Something drifted through the shadows behind him. He turned sharply and saw a shadow form near the underbrush. Probably another coyote. He'd seen too many since he'd come to this damned desert waste.

A howl rose from a boulder up the trail. A moment later the cry was echoed by another and then three more. The coyotes didn't frighten him. When a shape rose, silhouetted before him, he snapped off three bullets from his high-power pistol, then smiled as the creature gave a sharp yelp and tumbled from the rock.

That would teach the damned things to get in his way.

While the pleasure of the kill still throbbed warmly, he made his way upward in the darkness.

■

He was coming.

Tess shrank back, crouching behind a low wall. It would hide her from a brief glance, but if he had a light, he would find her.

She cast a wild look around her, searching for a handhold or an opening she might have overlooked. Her mind seemed to hold a shadowy image, almost like a memory of an opening near the top of the rear wall, but in the darkness it was impossible to see.

Something brushed the wall behind her. Tess heard the whisper of an indrawn breath and flattened herself, holding her breath.

A form dropped into the darkness and plummeted against her chest. She was struggling blindly when callused fingers closed around her throat and clamped over her mouth. She heard nothing beyond the roar of her pulse, struggling, telling herself over and over that she had to hold out because T.J. would come.

"Tess, it's me." His voice was a hiss, his mouth at her ear. "Stop fighting."

Tess took two gulping breaths. "T.J."

"Right here."

She sank against him, shaky and trembling. There were a thousand questions she wanted to ask, but for the moment only one mattered. "What about the man coming up the steps?"

"First thing to do is get you somewhere safe." He pulled her down as a bullet whined across the walls overhead. "There's a second path that leads down the cliff face. It will be hell in the darkness, but we'll have to try it."

Rocks spilled over the nearby steps and vanished into the darkness. There was no time left. "Come on," T.J. rasped, guiding her up through the opening in the wall and out onto the narrow stone walkway at the front of the ruins.

More stones clattered into space, and a beam of light cut across the front of the cliffs. T.J. jerked her back out of sight as the light swung past again.

"We can't go that way." Tess turned, inching along the base. Images were forming in her mind in a way she couldn't explain. "There's some sort of tower at the end of this corridor. I think there's a ledge above it."

"What kind of ledge?"

"Just trust me." Tess wasn't sure herself about the source of her knowledge. All she knew was that they would lose precious time talking.

T.J. moved in front of her, one hand to the wall. He trotted into the last room, then cursed softly. "Nothing here," he whispered.

Tess drew a shaky breath. Was she crazy to trust a vision that had neither basis nor explanation? "It has to be there." She stretched onto her toes and traced the wall, trying to ignore the flashlight beam playing back and forth over their heads. "There was some sort of stone bench. You could hear the drumming from there." As she spoke, memories welled up like churning water.

"From the bench, you could just touch the wooden beams, and the ledge was right there beneath the roof."

"Tess." T.J. spoke low and tightly. "The roof is gone, and those beams have been rotted for centuries. We have to go back."

"No." She stood tensely. Light flared, as if from a small fire. She heard the muffled beat of great skin drums.

The vision of the ledge came again, more clearly than before. "Through here." She tugged him past a huge slab of fallen stone. Beyond it stretched a wall of mortared clay bricks.

The remnant of a bench was just behind the fallen slab, half concealed by the debris of centuries. Tess climbed up, searching the top of the wall while the drums pounded furiously in her blood.

The room was entirely familiar to her now.

Here her blood had burned. Here she had met her warrior when the drums sobbed. He had waited for her beneath the ledge, stroked her long hair and whispered where he would meet her in the rocks above. She remembered that his skin bore the marks of many battles and a necklace of ocelot teeth that was the envy of her brothers.

She moved blindly, caught in flickering memories. As she reached up, a rock cut her fingers, making her sway. Then she felt the ledge. "Here."

"You found it?" T.J.'s voice was tight with surprise as he touched the high inset, then braced his hands and caught her foot. "Go on, climb up. I'll hold you."

"But how will you—"

"I'll use the bench."

Tess clutched at the tiny ridges in the wall and struggled up, slipping back onto the ledge. She turned, reaching a hand down for T.J.

But he was already moving away. "I've got to go, Tess. Trust me."

"But—"

He faded into the darkness.

The drums sobbed as she pressed close to the wall. The world seemed to shudder like a picture tossed between positive and negative images, leaving her chilled by a sense of unspeakable tragedy and betrayal.

In the faint light of the rising moon, Tess froze as a second figure slid past the edge of the wall. It was too late to warn T.J. Her voice would echo, alerting anyone else who waited in the darkness. She searched the ledge until she felt the heavy outline of a rock, then peered down across the broken masonry.

The shadow crept forward, nearly beneath her. Moonlight glittered on the barrel of a gun.

The drums coaxed, warned, boomed, part of her blood, like a too-vivid dream. She prayed he would not look up where she crouched.

One more step. One more drumbeat.

He was directly beneath her as she held her breath, heart pumping, danger screaming in her chest.

She threw the stone at his head with all her strength.

■

T.J. heard a low crack, followed by a curse. He flattened himself against the rough wall, watching a shape sway on the walkway.

He realized the falling rock had been no accident. Tess must have seen the man following him and had taken matters into her own hands.

He smiled grimly as the figure slid to one knee, mouthing a string of curses. Then T.J.'s smile fled as bullets cracked against stone. The man stumbled back onto his feet, firing wildly. Over the slam of gunfire came an odd yelping that rose and fell in eerie cacophony.

Something rustled behind T.J. He could have sworn he saw a dark shape shoot past, headed toward the man on the cliff face.

A bullet whined near his feet. Metal clattered as the gun hit the stone walk, followed by another high-pitched howl that echoed through the ruin. T.J. shot forward and grappled with the man, toppling him to the cliff floor. They struggled, panting, then T.J. landed a solid punch that sent his opponent's head snapping back against the mortar wall. This time the man did not get up.

T.J. stood slowly, wondering at the presence of the coyotes. Normally, they were wary of humans, ever careful. Yet there had to be at least four or five animals here, he realized. Maybe they had a den somewhere in the back of the ruin.

Straining, he made out the dark shape where Tess was still stretched on the ledge. It would take a direct beam of light to pick her out, and he wasn't going to give her kidnappers that opportunity.

Rocks clattered below him. T.J. heard something like the muffled slosh of liquid. Crouching, he inched forward, glad to feel the weight of his holstered pistol. He had counted three men down so far, and if his initial assessment was right, this should be the last of them.

But he was taking no chances.

He swung back to the narrow doorway as a flashlight beam shot over his head. Gravel skittered, raked by stealthy steps.

T.J. eased his weapon from his holster and slid the safety free. Outside the wall he heard a panting breath.

With luck, his own presence had been unnoticed, and the kidnapper would only be looking for Tess.

On the other hand, they had to be wondering why at least three of their party weren't answering.

Boots scuffed against stone.

A flashlight beam cut through the doorway, stopping only inches from where T.J. crouched. He waited tensely, watching the light move closer. A hand emerged through the near doorway, light scattering off the outline of a gun.

The figure swung left, searching the small room, and T.J. lunged, knocking the gun and flashlight to the floor. He wanted to bring the kidnappers back for questioning, and that meant using his own weapon as a last resort. He took a step back, circling in the shadows while the intruder panted and groped at the shaft of his boot.

T.J. didn't give him a chance to find a second weapon. He drove forward, ramming him with one shoulder. They tumbled to the debris-covered floor while the unearthly howling rose around them, rippling and dancing off the cliff walls, amplified by the empty rooms of stone.

T.J. almost had his target pinned when he slipped on a rock and swung sideways. The man was on his feet in an instant, driving forward as a blade glinted in the faint moonlight. The slashing blow burned across T.J.'s chest, and he spun backward with a grunt, slamming at his attacker's hand.

Too late.

The man was on his feet, dodging out through the doorway. As T.J. followed, a bullet cracked inches from his head. Even then he didn't slow down, coming in low and crouched, thinking only of bringing down this man for once and for all.

Another bullet screamed past, spraying sharp fragments of clay and stone against his cheek. The eerie howling grew around them, a macabre counterpoint to the man's half delirious laughter as he sent another bullet into the shadows, then turned to clamber down the narrow steps.

Liquid sloshed, echoing against the walls. T.J. heard the scrape of metal. A veil of liquid sprayed out in the darkness, soaking his head and chest, and he caught the sharp odor of kerosene a second later.

Tess's kidnapper tore at his pockets. His ragged laughter echoed as he pulled out a flat square of metal.

One click sent flame dancing from the cigarette lighter.

T.J. leveled his gun. He didn't dare go closer, not soaked and ready to become a human torch. He'd have to risk a shot at the man's knee.

The kidnapper was spinning and twisting, denying T.J. a clear aim as he scrambled to a boulder above the stairs. With a wall behind him, T.J. could only edge sideways, gaze locked on the small silver lighter and its dancing wedge of flame.

But as the kidnapper's hand moved, a dark figure blocked him, yellow eyes pale in the moonlight. The pointed head lifted with a short bark that climbed to a keening howl. Whether a simple warning or a primal statement of superiority, it set all the hair rising on T.J.'s neck.

As the howl stretched on, the animal jumped high, slamming against the kidnapper. Each movement was a blur of shadow and speed, the unreality compounded by the wild song cast up around them.

Rocks skittered.

The kidnapper's lighter clattered over the steps, down forty feet or more to the valley floor. Then T.J. saw the man sway, arms flailing, realizing too late how close he was to the edge.

Cursing, T.J. lunged, trying to grab him. But his out-stretched hand met only restless wind and a scattering of cold pebbles.

■

T.J. pulled Tess from the ledge and caught her tightly, the night's horror a tunnel he could not escape. Through the slam of his heart he heard her gasp.

"Tess, were you hit?" He searched her face and neck, terrified he would find blood.

"I'm fine. J-just a scratched knee and something that brushed my shoulder. But that man—"

"He's gone." T.J. took a deep breath. He still couldn't believe what he'd seen.

"I heard the coyotes. They were calling all around the ruins. Did you see them?"

T.J. frowned. The biggest animal had been right at the top of the stairs, forty feet up from the ground, but who was going to believe that? "In the shadows it's hard to say."

Tess gripped his shoulders. "What's that smell?" She sniffed at his chest. "Is it kerosene?"

"I got caught when the can spilled."

Her body stiffened. "He was going to burn every-thing, wasn't he? You, me. Even the ruins."

T.J. drew her head against his chest, his hands tight-ening. "Forget about him."

Motors droned up the hill.

Car lights cut through the darkness.

"Police. Put down your weapons!"

T.J. grinned at the sound of Grady's tense order booming from a bullhorn. "Stop shouting, Grady," he called. "Everything's calm up here."

"McCall?"

"Right here. We're coming out now, so don't fire." He guided Tess into the light at the top of the stairs. The howling had abated, and the coyotes appeared to have made a strategic retreat. "You'll find two kidnappers down by the helicopter and one up in the ruins." T.J. guided Tess slowly down the steps, his arm tight at her waist. "Another one fell from the cliff."

A man jumped down from the front truck and sprinted toward them. "We got tired of waiting for news."

Tess's eyes widened. "Andrew? When did *you* get here?"

"I phoned him as soon as I realized you were gone," T.J. said, shaking hands with his old friend. "He had a call from the kidnappers about the same time that I did. They wanted an exchange."

Tess shivered. "Me for the money?"

"Forget about it." Andrew O'Mara gripped his sister's shoulder and tilted her head back in the truck lights. "Your cheek is a mess, and your shoulder is bleeding."

"Just a scratch. It's good to see you too, big brother."

Muttering, Andrew caught her in a fierce hug. When he stepped away, he fixed a measuring stare on T.J. "You don't look so good either, McCall."

"Didn't know I'd be getting points for appearance," T.J. drawled, Stetson shoved back on his head. "Next time I'll wear the tux."

"There was a time when you wore a tux well." Andrew stared at T.J., then nodded. "You saved Tess's life. I owe you for that, cowboy."

T.J.'s lips curved. "Actually, she saved *my* life. I guess that means I owe you."

The tall Treasury officer slanted a surprised glance at his sister. "She did? But how—"

"Later." T.J. gathered Tess into the curve of his arm. "Right now her shoulder needs attention."

"It's fine." She gave him a crooked grin. "I saw it, T.J. The ledge was right there where I imagined it was," she said wonderingly.

"What ledge?" Andrew poked his head over T.J.'s shoulder. "What does she mean?"

"Never mind, O'Mara." T.J. didn't look up, his gaze locked on Tess's dusty, scratched, and very beautiful face. "Why don't you and Grady go find that can of kerosene at the top of the steps before something unpleasant happens to it."

Andrew O'Mara gave a flat sound of confusion. "What kerosene? Will one of you *please* tell me what happened here?"

A figure moved out of the shadows at the far side of the ruins. Grady crouched instantly, his rifle leveled. "Hold it right there, mister."

The man came to a halt and raised his arms slowly.

"That's Miguel." Grady lowered his rifle. "What's he been doing out there in the wash?"

T.J. watched the old man trot down the slope, his bag over his shoulder. "Keeping an eye on me, most likely. He took the first man down. Are you okay?" he called.

The old man nodded, and somewhere in the darkness beyond the gathered vehicles, a low howl split the night, echoed on three sides by answering calls.

"What the hell was *that*?" Andrew demanded.

Ignoring Grady's curious stare, T.J. turned, sliding his hands into Tess's hair. He smiled as he locked his mouth against hers while Andrew sputtered behind them and the song of the coyotes rose to the high dark canopy of the sky.

26

Midnight.

The road stretched before them, unbroken in its darkness, and T.J. felt as if they were the last two people left on earth.

He didn't look at her. He didn't dare.

Had to keep his eyes on the road. Had to focus on the darkness or they'd never make it home. What he really wanted was to turn off the road, pull her astride him, and claim her in the most primitive way a man could claim a woman.

They'd both been dazed, caught in the downswing of adrenaline, when they'd reached town. T.J. had kept his arms around her through an hour of questions from Andrew and two other government investigators who'd just flown in from DC. As they'd talked, Doc Felton had insisted on checking them both out, then tending to the shallow wounds on Tess's shoulder and cheek.

When Andrew's questions had turned personal, T.J. had pulled Tess away, still bundled in his battered leather jacket, ignoring her brother's sputters of protest.

Now he felt her turn, her fingers searching.

Don't think about touching her.

Don't think about having her.

"I've got one question. Well, more than one." Her voice was husky. "What brought all those coyotes?"

"I think we were lucky. Maybe more than lucky." T.J. watched a rabbit dart over the road, captured in the headlights. "I shouldn't have left you today," he said grimly. "Not for anything."

"Grady was with me. You couldn't know what those men had planned."

He forced himself to take a deep breath, fighting down the thought of what might have happened to her. "I should have been prepared." He felt her hand tighten on his thigh.

Desire exploded through him in a savage burst. He wanted her against him, wanted her hands urgent and hot on his back there in the darkness.

She slid closer, flowing into the hard line of his body. "You're still tense."

"I'll survive. Why don't you get some sleep?"

"Can't. I'm too edgy." Her fingers shifted, drawing his hand onto her thigh.

He felt her tremble, felt the warm yielding of her skin. "Dammit, Tess—"

She rose against him, nipping at his neck.

He muttered a curse.

They were at the main road now. Through the churning clouds he saw the luminous bow of the moon.

He envisioned bringing her home this way every night of his life. He imagined the husky laughter and the warm silences while their hands brushed in slow, aching seduction. The thought was almost more pleasure than he could bear.

He forced his gaze to the road ahead. "Funny how things worked out. It looks as if you'll be able to ride herd on that cruise outfit in New Orleans after all."

"I'm sure Richard's desperate for me to put things to right."

He felt her breath at his neck, her hair on his shoulder.

Torment, he thought.

And the only thing worse would be *not* feeling them.

They were at the end of the gravel drive. The moon darted between the clouds. He swung the Blazer around in front of the gate, got out, and then pulled open her door, wishing the moonlight wasn't his enemy, wishing her face wasn't so beautiful dusted with silver.

"You should sleep," he said harshly.

"Sleep's not what I want." She raised her hands to his shoulders, her eyes glinting.

"Duchess, I can't swear I'll be gentle. Not wanting you the way I do."

"Then don't be gentle. Not tonight."

He made an angry sound. "I'll take, Tess. I'll take and take." With a low oath he gathered her up into his arms and strode through the courtyard.

He didn't look at her.

Couldn't look at her as he pounded up the darkened steps where bougainvillea trailed low, leaving restless shadows in the moonlight.

"Look at me, T.J.," she whispered, unbuttoning her blouse, baring silvered skin.

Something raw and restless growled to life inside him. His hands clenched as he slid her along his body and brought her down onto the top step, his hands gripping her hips.

Somewhere a bird cried.

And all he could see was the perfect curve of her cheeks, the tight, aroused outline of her breasts. All he knew was the blinding urge to claim and possess. "Dammit, Tess, I warned you. I told you how much I wanted you. If I have you now, I'll have you a dozen times before morning. There will be no end to it.''

"Then . . . have me.'' Her words made desire knife through him.

Heat.

The jagged edge of anger.

Restraint, he thought dimly.

Logic.

Both were simply memories with the restless heat of her mouth claimed beneath his.

He swept her into his arms and strode into the quiet house, at the edge of control. She was the only woman who'd ever touched him this way, shredding through all his restraint. Tonight he meant to return the favor.

As he moved inside, he saw Maria in the foyer, white-faced and uncertain. "Señor Grady called me. He said you—''

"We're fine, Maria. Just tired,'' T.J. muttered, tugging Tess's blouse closed.

"But the *señorita* is hurt. I see the bandage at her arm. I will make her something hot to drink.''

T.J.'s hands tightened. "I'll give her everything she needs tonight, Maria. Go back to sleep.''

The woman's eyes narrowed, and then she nodded slowly.

In silence T.J. carried Tess to his bedroom, where moonlight spilled through the open windows, pooling over the crisp white sheets. "It starts here, Tess.''

"What?''

"All the things I want to do to you. All the ways I mean to leave my mark on you tonight.'' His voice was hoarse. "Do you trust me?''

She lifted her hand to his rigid jaw. "Always. From

that first day when I saw you in the shimmering heat and thought you were some amazing mirage.''

He set her down. "I wanted you like this then. You made me ache with all the ways I wanted to have you.''

Standing before him, she smiled tremulously, then brought her hand to her blouse.

"No,'' T.J. said hoarsely, catching her fingers. "I'll do that.'' His voice was very rough. "Tonight I'll do everything.''

Her breath caught at the hunger in his eyes. Her heart pitched at the pressure of his mouth sliding along her neck. "T.J., you don't have to—''

"Yes. This way. Every way. Until I've left a mark you can't forget.''

He pulled off her blouse and let it fall to the floor. Deftly he stripped away the rest of her clothing except for the white lace briefs. Then he lifted her hands to his shoulders as he worshipped her in the moonlight with callused fingers. Tess moaned with pleasure.

"T.J., your clothes,'' she murmured.

"First I want to look at you. To touch you,'' he said hoarsely. Something moved in his eyes, an emotion she couldn't find a word for.

"But—''

Tess felt her heart pound as he feathered her lips with his mouth and then skimmed a path along her neck.

She shuddered when he gripped her hips, sensing the desire that he fought to hold in check. "T.J., you don't need to—''

She felt his hot breath before the hard, stroking pull of his mouth at her breast. Already swollen, already needy, her nipples rose to dark buds, which he claimed with his hand and his tongue as pleasure drove her trembling against him.

"But I want you," she said raggedly. "I need to feel you."

"First like this." He ran his fingers along the lace edge of her briefs, wringing a soft cry from her lips as he slid beneath the silk to explore her heat.

"Why don't you hurry?" she said huskily.

His laugh was low and dark. "Hurry something as sweet as this?" He stroked her slowly, making her breath come more heavily. When she thought she couldn't bear another second, he slowly found her tight, slick center.

And entered her.

She whimpered as he pushed his finger deeper, arousing her with unbearably slow circles that left her knees shaking and her whole body seared.

"I want you, Tess. I want to feel you just like this. Why should I hurry?"

He made a low, hard sound of triumph as she tightened against him, breathless in a wave of pleasure. He watched her face as he moved his hand, unleashing another jagged bolt of need. This time her back arched and she dug at his shoulders, his name a husky plea.

His eyes were narrowed and predatory as she stared up at him. Dimly she felt the ridge of his belt and the brush of his clothes. Even the slightest touch was unbearably arousing on her flushed, sensitized skin.

The wind danced through the open window, touching her face. Her heart raced and her mind didn't seem to work. All she knew was his touch and how much she wanted him.

Loved him.

Her breath caught as the full force of that truth struck her. "No more," she ordered.

"Yes."

He moved again, finding her in a deep stroke that left her body twisting blindly against him.

The wedge of lace fell to the floor, lost in the white pool of moonlight. "Beautiful," he whispered, his hands closing possessively over her hips.

She moved before he could claim her again.

Reckless, she pulled his shirt free and jerked the buttons aside, sighing when she touched his chest.

He plunged his hands into her hair and seized the lush curve of her mouth. Not gentle. Not careful now, but with the anger and desperation of a man who'd come close to losing all he held dear.

He trapped her, molded her to meet the rigid line of his erection, and there might have been a hint of tears on her cheeks as she flowed against him.

Yielding.

Offering.

Driven by a desperation that was as great as his.

His belt whipped free. His pants hit the floor.

"Don't wait," she whispered. "Let me feel you inside me."

"How, Tess?" He was huge and hard against her. "Slow until you scream?" He gripped her soft hips, fitting her against his thighs.

"Hot," she whispered. "Because I was so cold. Because I thought I'd lost you forever. And I think I'd die if—"

She didn't finish, the words lost in a cry of joy and shock as he tumbled her backward and pinned her to the bed for a swift, hard slide of friction that trapped her completely and brought him as deep as he could be.

And then he waited, his eyes unblinking, his hands circling her wrists where their pulses raced.

Her back arched. "Now," she said wildly.

"Wait."

"I can't. I won't." She tightened around him, muscles clenched, pulling and claiming until he made a ragged sound and closed his eyes. Every dark tremor smashed at his control. Every touch of her hands made him curse silently.

He took her then, hot and fast against the cool white sheets while the wind played over their fevered skin. With a curse he wrapped her legs around his waist and sank into her heat, then slowly pulled free.

He wanted all of her.

He wanted forever.

He meant to have both.

She twisted beneath him, raking his back, all control shredded as he claimed and withdrew, then claimed again with a need brought just to the edge of violence, trapping her.

Trapping them both.

Thunder rumbled, drowning out the beat of the rain, and somewhere in the night came the long, wild cry of the coyotes.

Only now the sound held an air of desperation.

He felt her shudder, heard her ragged moan as pleasure tore through her again. In the madness of his possession, he had a sudden sense that he'd taken her this way before, with stars blazing overhead and hot stone against their backs while drums beat in rhythm with their bodies.

Heat poured through his blood, and he angled his mouth over hers to drink in her husky moans, sliding deep and deeper again.

Then her eyes opened.

She studied his mouth as if she had never wanted a man before and never would again. Her hand was wedged against his chest, trembling in the moonlight that haloed her beauty in a way almost too painful to bear.

Through a haze of desire he palmed the tantalizing triangle between her thighs, where she cradled him and rose restlessly against him.

His fingers moved. He watched her cry out, watched her fall, lost and panting, then closed his eyes and let the magic grip him.

At that moment, taking spilled into giving and capture merged with surrender. His body was hard with demand, harder with love as he drove home, claiming all the last, hidden places of her heart.

He felt her shudder, felt her open to him when the silver rush of desire leapt up to grip them tight.

Then he locked her against him and followed her over that jagged edge of madness and need, down into a shining oblivion that somehow felt as familiar and ancient as the rocks that brushed a turquoise sky.

27

Tess awoke in dim gray light before dawn.

She stared at the silent room, remembering the heat and frenzy of the night before. They had tumbled and fought their way across his big bed, giddy from need and too little sleep. He had worshipped her, claimed her, turned her inside out and touched her soul until their desperation had finally been banked in sheer exhaustion.

The way he'd touched her had been like nothing she'd ever imagined.

Which made what she had to do now even more painful.

She watched him sleep, a lock of his dark hair against his forehead. She felt a sharp urge to brush it gently with her fingers.

But she didn't.

Reason and common sense had returned, and in the painful clarity of dawn Tess knew this was a time for endings, not beginnings. Suddenly she remembered Mae's words in the café. Almost was a place that people came for all the wrong reasons and stayed for all the right ones. But for Tess the situation was reversed. Her brother's sending her there had been the wisest course of action, but now leaving was the only thing that made sense. Even one more night spent in the sensual haze that

T.J. had evoked so perfectly would make it impossible for her to leave.

No, it had to be today. That morning. Before she had a chance for second thoughts or before he could persuade her otherwise.

After one lingering, wistful look, she carefully rose from the bed so as not to disturb him, swept up her clothes, and tiptoed from the room.

Fifteen minutes later, fully dressed, she sat on the front porch, waiting for Andrew to bring the Mercedes from town. After that they would go directly to the airport, where their flight left in a little over two hours. She stared at the gray clouds over the foothills, reminding herself this was the best choice.

The only choice.

It would be a disaster for her stay.

She stiffened at the sound of bare feet behind her. She had hoped to escape without having to brave this last encounter with T.J.

She didn't turn as he strode down the steps and braced one arm on the wooden porch beam. "It's a little early for you to be enjoying the sunrise."

Her hands clenched on her lap. "I'm leaving."

"Look at me, Tess."

She did. It was the worst thing she could have done. His hair was unruly from sleep, and his eyes were tense and smoky. He wore only a pair of well-worn jeans that rode low on his hips, unbuttoned.

She looked away, angry at the naked desire that streaked through her at that one glance.

"You want to run that by me again?"

"You heard me. I'm leaving. We've come to the end of the line, T.J." She tilted her chin and forced her voice to stay calm. "Last night was wonderful. I can't thank you enough for the memories you gave me."

His hand opened, gripping the wood beam. *"Thank me?"* There was a snap of anger in his voice.

"You should go inside. It's cold out here."

"We won't be cold for long," he said hoarsely, sitting down beside her and pulling her onto his lap.

She twisted blindly, shoving at his chest. "Stop, T.J."

"Like hell I will."

She was wound up tight, but the worst part was that some part of her wanted him to rage, wanted him to hold her and tell her that she couldn't leave today or any other day because he loved her.

But he hadn't said the words or anything close. Not once.

And she hated herself for caring so much.

"We both know what was happening between us had to come to this, T.J."

"What?"

"The part where I say good-bye. The part where you shrug stoically and let me go."

"To hell with being stoic." He pulled her back against his chest. She closed her eyes, remembering all the fierce pleasure he had brought her through the long, sleepless hours of night.

But memories or not, she was leaving.

She moved off his lap and turned her face away from him to the east, where the first tendrils of dawn curled over the mountains. "Why are you doing this?"

"Because you moaned my name about a dozen times last night, Tess. Because two hours ago you went to sleep with your chin tucked at my chest and your hand nestled right between my thighs. That particular position might have kept me from sleeping if you hadn't already exhausted every muscle in my body." His eyes burned. "I guess that entitles me to ask a few questions."

She flinched. "We both knew this would happen. I don't fit in here, T.J."

"Fit in? Hell, you already *own* this town. Grady wants to give you your own column in the newspaper, and Mae is already talking about running your campaign for mayor next year."

She closed her eyes, swallowing hard. "I can't stay. I've got my work, my friends. All the life I know is back in Boston." She took a tense breath. "Besides, there will be weeks of depositions and legal proceedings—things I can't possibly do from here."

"Is this about depositions or is it about us?"

"Both. And there's no reason to shout."

"I'll shout all I want to. After last night, I'm entitled. Look at me," he said, forcing her face up to meet his gaze. "I want to see you when you lie to me."

"I'm not lying. But it would be a lie for me to stay, can't you see that? Life goes on. We can't just—"

"Do you love me?" The words seemed wrenched from deep in his chest.

She dug her fingers into her skirt. How could he ask such a question, when he'd been so careful to keep his own emotions hidden? "No," she whispered, but there was a broken note in the word. "Now let me go."

"Not today, tomorrow, or the next thousand years, Tess."

"Don't do this, T.J. I'm not up for arguments. I didn't get too much sleep last night."

"Neither did I," he said tightly. "We were both too busy tearing off each other's clothes and causing grave bodily harm."

"*After* that, I meant."

He laughed grimly. "As I recall, that part went on most of the night."

She angled her face, glaring at him in the filtered gray light. "I'm going, T.J. I have to." Softening a bit, she added, "You can keep the cappuccino machine."

A note of violence dug at his tight control. "To hell with the cappuccino machine. Don't you like Almost?"

"I like Almost. I just don't belong here, not long-term." She closed her eyes and shook her head angrily. "This isn't a fairy tale, and I'm no damsel pining away in a tower. I have a good life back in Boston and you have a good life here. We just aren't meant to have them to-gether."

"So that's your sage parting advice? I should stay here and forget you."

"Precisely." She ignored the stab of pain at her chest. "I want you to be happy, T.J. I want you to meet a wonderful, amazing woman and have wonderful, amaz-ing children who—"

She didn't finish. He grabbed her in an angry move-ment and anchored her head between callused fingers. "Then tell me again that you don't love me, dammit. Tell me that you don't think about having my hands on you all night long. Tell me that, Tess. Then I'll let you go," he said fiercely.

Their eyes held. Tess raised her chin, angry and de-termined. "We hit all the high notes last night, T.J. It can't get any better than that. Things will start sliding down from here, and one day—in a week or a month—you'll wake up bored, resentful, and trying to hide it, because you're the decent man you are." She took a jerky breath. "There's nowhere to go after an experience like last night, can't you see?"

"We've got a lot of high notes left, Tess."

Car tires spun over gravel, headed toward the house.

"If that's Grady, I'll have to shoot out his tires."

"It's Andrew," Tess said tightly. "I called him to pick me up since I'm ready to leave."

T.J. muttered a curse. "Just *when* were you going to say good-bye?"

"At the airport. I was going to call you." Her face was pale but entirely resolute.

"How many cups of cappuccino have you had?" he growled.

"Not enough."

The Mercedes came to a hissing halt. Andrew appeared at the wooden gate and took in the two of them side by side on the steps. "If I'm interrupting something, I can always come back later."

"No," Tess snapped.

"Yes," T.J. said. "Come back next week. We're not done talking here."

"Yes, we are," Tess said. "You're not going to change my mind." She pushed away from him and crossed the courtyard in tight, controlled steps, two suitcases in hand. Andrew started loading the rest of her belongings.

"If I stay, I'll end up hating Almost, and you'll end up hating *me*. That would hurt more than anything."

He jammed a hand through his hair. "Dammit, Tess—"

"No. That's the only answer there is."

He stared at her in the gray light, his shoulders stiff and angry. "I never took you for a quitter, Duchess."

Andrew cleared his throat. "Tess, maybe you should—"

"We need to go, Andrew. We'll miss our flight," she said.

Very stiff, very grave.

She didn't look back as she slid behind the wheel.

In the passenger seat beside her, Andrew crossed his arms. "McCall looks pretty upset."

"He'll get over it," she said as she drove away from Rancho Encantador.

"You look pretty upset, too."

"I'll get over it, too." *Maybe in another millennium or two.*

"Hear him out, Tess. The depositions can wait. We'll be handling most of the proceedings."

"Andrew, I—"

He plowed right ahead. "By the way, we finally managed to track down Richard. Your bonus wasn't an even million, but I'm pleased to say it was half, and Richard swears you were worth every penny." His eyes narrowed. "So what will you do with all that money? Retire?" He sniffed. "No, not you. You'll work till you drop. Work and work and more work."

For some reason, the huge size of her bonus didn't excite her anymore. "What's *wrong* with working?" she asked, irritated.

"Nothing. Not a single thing. After all, I understand if you can't wait to leave this wretched little town behind you."

"It's a *lovely* town," she snapped.

"And I can certainly see how you can't wait to see the last of McCall."

"McCall isn't the problem."

"Yeah, he's way too small-time for you. What kind of future does he have in a jerkwater town like Almost?"

Her hands gripped the wheel. "T. J. McCall is the

best thing that's ever happened to me," she whispered. "We both know that."

Her brother's hand closed over hers. "So go back. Argue, complain, rant. Then work things out. Don't let this chance get away."

The road blurred for a moment, and Tess brushed at her eyes. "I can't, Andrew. He deserves someone who can be wholehearted. The last woman in his life wasn't, and I won't see him hurt that way again. And I can't just walk away from Boston and my career." She blinked hard. "He's honest, stubborn, and absolutely wonderful. That's why I won't make him choose between me and Almost. Now shut up and stop trying to make me change my mind."

"Who's arguing?" Andrew muttered. "I can't get a word in."

They were on the main highway, racing toward the airport. Giant saguaros towered beside them in the canyons, silent and majestic.

A motor gunned behind them, and they both turned as an approaching siren gave two sharp bursts.

"I couldn't have been speeding," Tess protested, slowing the Mercedes.

"Nudging ninety," Andrew muttered. "But who's counting."

Tess shook her head as she pulled the car over to the shoulder. "I wasn't. I couldn't—"

A red Blazer with tinted windows cut in front of her, lights flashing. Tess stared at the tall, uniformed figure who emerged, a gray Stetson tilted low over his forehead.

"No," she whispered. "He wouldn't. Not like this." She drew a breath and rolled down her window, fighting for calm.

"Afraid you were speeding, Ma'am." T.J.'s eyes

were unreadable behind his mirrored sunglasses. "Eight-nine in a fifty-mile-per-hour zone."

"I—I didn't notice."

He fingered his belt. "Appears that you were swerving, too."

"Don't do this," she whispered. "Please. Just let me go."

He rubbed his jaw slowly. "No left brake light. Looks as if you're also missing a side reflector." He shook his head. "Could be serious, Ma'am."

Why was he doing this? Hadn't she made all her reasons clear? "T.J., stop this ridiculous behavior. There's not a single thing wrong with this car. You know very well that I—"

He tossed a red piece of plastic up and down on his palm. "Yes, that makes at least three solid violations. Ma'am. I'm afraid I'll have to ask you to step out of the car." There was an edge of command beneath the low drawl.

"No, I won't. This is ridiculous."

T.J. rocked back on his heels and glanced at Andrew. "I'll have to take your sister back to town, O'Mara. There are a lot of citations to deal with here."

Andrew rolled his eyes. "Fine. You two can sort this out without me. I've got a plane to catch." He was already yanking Tess's suitcases from the car and piling them beside the road.

"Andrew, you can't just—"

T.J. opened Tess's door, his expression unreadable. "Step out of the car."

Muttering angrily, Tess got out, her heart pounding. "Why? What's the meaning of this, T.J.?"

"Highway safety is one of our priorities. I need to see your license, Ma'am."

"Fine." Tess grabbed her purse and dug out her license, waving it in his face. "There, are you satisfied?"

"This license is out of state. We've had notices about counterfeits being circulated in New York and Massachusetts." He shook his head. "I'm going to have to run you in for some questions."

Tess put her hands on her hips, her whole body quivering. "T.J., this is absolutely ludicrous. You're embarrassing me and—" She turned with a gasp as Andrew gave a two-finger wave, gunned the motor, and sped away, grinning broadly.

"Now I'll ask you to walk up to the Blazer and put your hands on the window."

Her face filled with heat. So he was going to be insufferable and arrogant, was he? She straightened her shoulders into a line and stalked to the Blazer, resting her hands against the window. "Search me, by all means. Don't miss the knife in my belt and the gun in my left boot."

"Oh, I'll be thorough." He moved behind her, caught her wrist.

Then he turned her very slowly, trapping her between the Blazer and his broad chest. His eyes were hidden beneath his mirrored sunglasses.

"I'm going to miss my plane," she hissed.

"That's a distinct possibility, Ma'am." He reached in his pocket, drew out his handcuffs, then snapped one carefully around her wrist.

"You wouldn't *dare*."

The other cuff slid around his wrist, pulling their bodies even closer. "Now, about those questions."

"I won't say a word."

"I don't suggest noncompliance with a police officer, Ma'am."

"I refuse to stand here and—"

A muscle moved at his jaw. "Will you marry me, Tess?"

Time stood still. She heard the thud of her heart as she stared at her reflection in his glasses. She had long ago given up expecting to hear those particular words. Now that they'd come, they didn't seem quite real.

She blinked at him. "Marry you?"

"The truth is, I never expected this, Tess. You represented everything I'd walked away from—stress, fast-track career, and nose-to-the-grindstone work ethic." His jaw clenched. "I certainly never expected to want you. I damn well never meant to fall in love with you. But I did."

There was a strange, unraveling sensation in the pit of her stomach. "Could you repeat that?" she said breathlessly.

"I love you. As in will you marry me? As in will you share my life and have about a dozen children with me?" He jerked off his sunglasses and Tess saw all the desperate tension that had been hidden in his eyes. "Tell me you love me, Tess. Give me an answer," he said raggedly. "Before I die here."

Heat shimmered, raced. Around them dawn spread halos of light across the valley. Tess leaned against the Blazer, praying that the ground would stop swaying. "I may have to sit down."

He shook his head. "Not until I have your answer."

As Tess began to speak, she was interrupted by the low rumble of a pickup truck. T.J.'s head shot up, and he glared at Grady, who was grinning at the open window. "What'd she say, Sheriff? Is she staying or is she leaving?"

"I'm definitely going to have to shoot that man,"

T.J. muttered as a camera flashed and the pickup thundered past. He looked down at Tess. "Well, are you staying?" he demanded gruffly, catching her hand. "Since you don't seem to like wearing my cuffs, maybe you'll wear this instead."

A heavy silver band with a cabochon star sapphire picked up the gleam of dawn as he slid it onto her finger. "This was my mother's."

"It's beautiful," she whispered.

"I'm offering you everything I am, Tess. I'm offering every dream you ever had and everything we can make together."

She wanted that, too. Here in this place of beauty and solitude, it seemed perfectly natural to throw caution to the wind and let herself dream big.

About six-foot-four big.

"Yes," she whispered.

"Yes to what?" He was going to have all of it, every word.

Her eyes rose to his rugged face. "Yes to everything. Yes to you and me and yes to this wonderful little town."

"Thank God. Now I can breathe again."

"Not so fast, Sheriff." She hid a smile as she traced his top button slowly. "Now I have a question for you. Is it or is it not an officer's job to serve and protect?"

"Always." His eyes filled with heat. "Did you have something particular in mind?"

"You could say that." She rose onto her toes and whispered in his ear. "So what do you think?"

He looked like speech was beyond him for a moment. Then his hands tightened on her hips. "Is that possible in the backseat of a Blazer?"

Tess realized that the wedge of fabric at his belt was straining tighter by the second. Her glaze flickered downward and she smiled slowly. "I'm willing to find out if you are."

Something came into his eyes, a mixture of tenderness and determination. "You won't give up your work here, Tess. We'll set up home everything—teleconferencing, fax, scanners. We'll both do some traveling. This isn't going to be one way."

"We'll discuss it later," she whispered. "Meanwhile, you might want to unlock this cuff, Sheriff. It's going to make what I have in mind very difficult."

There was a slight tremor in his hands as he slid off the cuff. "I don't need it anyway," he muttered. "I've been entirely defenseless since the moment you tossed that garter belt in my face. All I could think of was putting it back on you." He smiled slowly. "And then taking it off again."

A jackrabbit peeked from behind a prickly pear cactus, and a family of quail darted up the wash.

From the road behind them came the screech of a horn. T.J. turned as a dusty pickup slowed, its driver waving wildly. Mae called through her open window. "If that's an engagement ring, I expect to get a close-up view of it later today at the café." She gave another long burst on her horn, then vanished over the hill.

T.J. shook his head. "If I'm not careful, I'm going to have to run *myself* in for disturbing the peace." He stared down at Tess's radiant face. "On the other hand, it might be worth it."

A brisk breeze worked through the canyons. Back on the highway, a dozen more cars appeared, lights flashing, horns honking and arms waving.

Tess's eyes widened. "How—"

"Grady." T.J. rolled his eyes. "He must have reached them on their CBs. The man's probably raised half the town by now and has the wedding announcement for the paper, complete with photographs.''

Tess eased closer. ''I suppose I can't refuse a duly elected sheriff and distinguished law officer of the great state of Arizona?''

''Don't even try,'' he said huskily.

Their hands met as a school bus approached, carrying the fourth-grade class to a statewide singing competition. At the front of the bus, Ms. Jenkins stood up, clapping. ''Show us the ring,'' she called out the window.

''Does *everybody* know?'' T.J. muttered.

Tess raised her hand high so that the sapphire gleamed in the early light. As she did, the bus stopped. All thirty-two children leaned against their windows, cheering while they waved their thirty-two tiny flags.

''I guess that makes it official,'' T.J. whispered, gathering Tess tightly in his arms. ''The people of Almost have spoken.''

The warm heat of the Blazer was behind her and the warmer heat of his body in front of her.

''Kiss me, Duchess. I don't think I can wait another second.''

Tess flushed. ''But the children. T.J., we shouldn't—''

He grinned wickedly. ''Let's make their day.''

She tilted her head back, looking up at his chiseled face, seeing the joy and naked exhilaration in his eyes. ''Well, maybe just this once . . .''

The children were giggling and squealing with glee when their lips met. The bus driver gave a long, noisy blast on his horn, and then went on his way.

Tess laughed through the kiss, laughed through the tears of happiness shimmering at her eyes. T.J. opened the passenger door of the Blazer, settled Tess, then slid behind the wheel. Above them the air glowed as the rising sun climbed free of the mountains. For a moment, just a moment, the whole valley flashed, caught in a perfect flare of blinding pink light.

Neither of them noticed the two coyotes loping behind them as they headed home to the ranch.

Epilogue

"Once upon a time," Tess said to the smiling baby on her lap, "there was a town. A beautiful, friendly, and very small town."

She sat on the twig rocker on the adobe porch overlooking fifty miles of mountains, clouds, and rolling desert foothills. On her lap was her daughter of two months, red-cheeked and powdered, fresh from her bath.

Katie McCall had dark hair like her father and bright green eyes like her mother. She did a lot of laughing, probably because her parents did, too. Just then she was watching her mother intently.

"Everyone in this town came from different places and for different reasons. Some were down on their luck, some were lost, and others were simply drifting. But that's the funny thing," Tess said quietly. "This town didn't have many streets, and there were no giant skyscrapers or fancy condominiums. It was just what it was: home. A place for them to take a long breath and find out what made them happy. It did that a lot, sneaking up on people and making them happy before they even knew it."

Tess stroked her daughter's cheek. "And that's why everyone who came to this town stayed for just one reason: because they loved this place. And aren't you lucky, Katie, because the place I told you about is right here, a little town called Almost.''

Wind drifted through the mesquite trees, rustling the long green fronds. Tess looked down at the town she had come to love, surrounded by mountains, canyons, and a sky so blue, it stole her breath away.

In two hours most of the town would be descending on T.J.'s ranch, anticipating music, dancing, an outdoor barbecue, and fireworks. They were welcoming back Mae and Doc Felton, who were returning from a month's honeymoon in Venice.

Tess had flown down to New Orleans and soothed the unhappy cruise passengers. With the problems settled, she and T.J. had vanished for a two-week vacation exploring the side streets and culinary delights of the lovely old port city.

The criminal investigation had finally ended. A network of money launderers had been tracked into five American cities. None of them would be making ATM withdrawals for the next thirty years or so.

When she'd resumed her work, she didn't lack for clients. A surprising number were glad for an excuse to visit the Southwest to discuss product rollouts or media campaigns. T.J. had been true to his word, setting up home everything.

But he'd been especially involved in setting up the brightly painted nursery that overlooked the mountains to the east.

Tess brushed a curl from Katie's cheek. ''And even here in Almost you can learn about market campaigns—like what we did for Mae. Remember, when you plan a campaign, know the areas where you work best. You could jump in line and try to do everything, but do we do that?'' She tickled Katie, who trilled with laughter. ''No, never. We specialize.''

Tess smiled down at Katie, but her eyes were serious. ''And never compromise your integrity or your quality. It will show in your work—and in your life.''

On her lap Katherine Matilda McCall cooed and her bright eyes blinked. She seemed to tilt her head, listening seriously.

''Most important of all, plan well but dream big. Your father taught me that.'' Tess smoothed a silky strand of hair from her daughter's forehead. ''That was the most wonderful gift he gave me.'' Her lips curved. ''Well, almost the most wonderful gift. I have to say that you win the grand prize there, my love.''

Behind her, Tobias Jackson McCall stood motionless in the doorway, watching the two females he loved most rock quietly in the afternoon sun. There was a fullness at his chest as he thought how Tess had made his house a home and had won the trust and admiration of a whole town.

The new clinic was half built and the high school now boasted a brand-new computer department, thanks to Tess's expertise and unflagging enthusiasm. There was even a weekly lecture program at the historic jail.

Shouts drifted from the courtyard, where Maria's grandchildren were playing astronauts with the mayor's husband. A bus lurched over the gravel drive, laughter spilling from its windows.

T.J. watch the excited faces of the children, who had been documenting desert ecology on the other side of his ranch. Back at school, their photographs and finished reports would be transferred to computers for an exchange with their sister school in Boston. Through her contacts, Tess had arranged for computers for both schools and an

Internet link that would allow both sets of children to glimpse a way of life that was different from all that they held familiar. The exchange program was being studied as a possible model for other schools in rural areas.

Yes, T.J. thought, Tess was dragging them all kicking and screaming into the twenty-first century, and she didn't even seem to realize it.

He crossed the slope toward his wife, who was speaking softly to her daughter.

"And always, always give the client more than they expected."

T.J. bent and tickled his daughter's cheek. "You'll have her a tycoon before she can walk," he murmured.

Tess tilted her head back and received a very satisfactory kiss. "And you'll have her riding bareback before she can talk, cowboy."

"I walked her around the corral only a few minutes. She was safe in my arms the whole time," he protested.

"I knew she was safe." Tess had loved the sight of the two of them, gently moving on a docile mare handpicked by T.J. A photograph of that day now graced the big refrigerator in the kitchen, surrounded by congratulatory notes about Katie's birth sent by Annie, Mrs. Spinelli, and her other friends in Boston.

"The chairs are all arranged. Grady and I put out the tables and tablecloths, and the musicians just arrived."

"I'd better go help Maria."

"Maria told me to keep you right here so that you rest. You've been running yourself ragged for a week, and she said she can handle everything." As he spoke, the first strains of music drifted over the hill.

"But she needs—"

"She needs nothing. There are already twenty people

in the kitchen helping her." His eyes filled with warmth. "So why don't you dance with me instead, Ma'am?"

Her brow arched. "Well, Sheriff, is that an official request or a personal invitation?"

"Personal." His eyes darkened. "Very personal."

He cradled Katie in one arm and caught Tess in the other, moving carefully to the drifting music of guitars.

T.J. pulled his two girls closer. "I like to feel you both in my arms."

"The feeling is mutual, Sheriff." With a sigh of pleasure, Tess settled against him, more happy than she could ever have imagined. The new millennium had turned her life upside down.

But she had no regrets.

She'd walked away from her hectic life in Boston without a backward glance, knowing everything she needed and wanted was right here.

She had had no more dreams about the city in the sky and the pair of lovers who had met high amid the canyons. Their story seemed finished, their journey completed in peace.

If they were ghosts, they were benign ghosts now.

Some instinct made Tess touch her bright piece of pottery, now set in a bezel of silver and hung from a fine chain at her neck. It brushed her skin, as warm as the glow she saw in her husband's dark eyes.

His fingers moved, tracing patterns along her back. "Ready to go inside?"

She tilted up her face and received a slow, lingering kiss. "Almost," she answered as the gentle wind played through her hair. Then the music rose, filling her heart just as the man beside her had filled her life.

And she could have sworn that somewhere she heard the high, restless cry of a coyote.

Author's Note

Edward Abbey said it best—nature has a grandeur and beauty surpassing anything man can create. Tess and T.J. would certainly agree.

I hope you have enjoyed this look at their corner of the beautiful high desert. If you would like to read more about the Southwest, Edward Abbey is one of the best authors to start with. *Desert Solitaire* remains one of the finest books of its kind, offering an unflinching look at the "old true world of the deserts." If you develop an interest in vigas, latillas, and adobe homes, you'll find detailed descriptions and lavish photographs in *Behind Adobe Walls* by Landt and Lisl Dennis. T.J., of course, could write his own book on the subject.

With Tess's help, perhaps he will.

Arizona is home to hundreds of archaeological ruins that continue to perplex experts today. For a wonderful introduction to a complex subject, try *The Archaeology of Ancient Arizona* by Jefferson Reid and Stephanie Whittlesey. Another excellent source is *Ancient Ruins of the Southwest* by David Grant Noble. A different perspective comes from the memories of a contemporary resident in *A Pima Remembers* by George Brown.

History continues, if only we know where to look for it.

And now for chile—a truly hot topic these days. (I can't resist the pun.) This resilient plant has both medicinal and culinary uses. For authentic southwestern recipes, stop by my Web site at www.christinaskye.com. Mae has promised to post the best of her four-alarm dishes, specially created for Grady and T.J. While you're there, you'll also find excerpts of past and future books, reader contests, and the latest updates on life in Almost. You can send me e-mail at talk to christina@ christinaskye.com.

You can also write to me at:

> 15730 North Pima Road
> #D4
> Suite 313
> Scottsdale, Arizona 85260

It has been an absolute delight to write about this luminous corner of the Southwest and some of its eccentric, resilient inhabitants. I have a sneaking suspicion that I will be paying a return visit to Almost sometime in the near future. Until then, I hope that you dream of hot turquoise skies and double rainbows. Most of all, to paraphrase Edward Abbey, may the coyotes always serenade your campfire.

Happy reading,
Christina